BEHINDHISEYES

The Consequences series companion box set

The tragic or the humorous

is a matter of perspective.

— ARNOLD REISSER

New York Times and *USA Today* Bestselling Author

Aleatha Romig

Editing by Lisa Aurello
Interior design and formatting by JT Formatting

First Edition as a box set: July 2016
Library of Congress Cataloging-in-Publication Data
Behind His Eyes (The Consequences Series Companion Box Set) – 1ˢᵗ ed
ISBN-13: 978-09968394-3-3

– DISCLAIMER –
*

The CONSEQUENCES series contains dark adult content. Although there is not excessive use of description and detail, the content contains innuendos of kidnapping, rape, and abuse—both physical and mental. If you're unable to read this material, please do not purchase. If you are ready, welcome aboard and enjoy the ride!
- Aleatha Romig

http://aleatharomig.com

For exclusive releases and giveaways signup for Aleatha's newsletter at
https://goo.gl/tZMw9x

Dear Readers,

Before purchasing, please understand that this is *not* a standalone book. These two companions are not meant to be read independently of THE CONSEQUENCES SERIES. They are meant as a *companions,* to be read following the experience of the ENTIRE CONSEQUENCES SERIES, after all five books.

This first companion, BEHIND HIS EYES CONSEQUENCES was not designed as a *retell* of the entire novel CONSEQUENCES from Anthony Rawlings' perspective, and as such, will not make sense on its own. It was meant to share significant scenes and behind-the-scenes information.

Therefore, *after* you have completed CONSEQUENCES, TRUTH, CONVICTED, REVEALED, and BEYOND THE CONSEQUENCES please join me for a dark journey into the mind of a man who believes that he controls everything but in reality, controls nothing.

Join me for an insight into the man who …

Once upon a time, signed a napkin that he knew was a contract. As an esteemed businessman, he forgot one very important rule—he forgot to read the fine print. It wasn't an acquisition to own another person as he'd previously assumed. It was an agreement to acquire a soul.
– Aleatha Romig, CONVICTED

This first companion centers on CONSEQUENCES and includes chapter references to that novel. The end of this box set also contains a glossary of characters and a timeline of significant events in CONSEQUENCES. and TRUTH.

Thank you again for your support!

~Aleatha

Table of Contents

BEHIND HIS EYES

Reading Companion to the bestselling Consequences series

CONSEQUENCES

New York Times and *USA Today* Bestselling Author

Aleatha Romig

Before the beginning – fall 2004

Men may know many things by seeing;
but no prophet can see before the event, nor what end waits for him.
– Sophocles

Anthony Rawlings' private jet soared east toward Indiana. Looking around the cabin, he took in the empty seats. It wasn't often that he flew alone. Most of his travels were business-related, and he had assistants, negotiators, and legal counsel who usually accompanied him. This trip was different—sudden, unexpected, and confidential. The only person who knew of this trip was his pilot and trusted employee, Eric. He wouldn't discuss the business of this trip with anyone; of that, Anthony was confident. There were other aspects of the journey that didn't leave him as secure.

Throughout the years, Anthony had become a public figure and had a reputation that needed to be upheld. To that end, he surrounded himself with the best—the best people, business decisions, and belongings. Rarely did Anthony Rawlings act impulsively. Every move was considered, debated, and evaluated—yet this trip could qualify as impetuous. He never considered flying to Indiana until he received the phone call informing him of the automobile accident claiming the lives of Jordon and Shirley Nichols. Truthfully, even now, the trip wasn't necessary. He'd told the private investigator who'd called to attend the funeral and take pictures; nonetheless, as he hung up the telephone, Anthony knew that wouldn't be enough.

He'd been observing Claire Nichols from afar for over a year. Enjoying the freedom that comes with seclusion, Anthony leafed through the most recent report from the PI for the umpteenth time. It contained pictures of Claire—lots of pictures. He couldn't pinpoint his curiosity regarding this girl; after all, she was just a child—merely a sophomore in college! Catherine called it an obsession, and more than once, she claimed that it was unhealthy. She reminded him that the names on their list needed to remain just that—names, not people. That sounded good in principle, and for most on their list, it was possible. Claire Nichols was different. He found himself drawn to her, wanting to know more; however, Anthony wouldn't classify his interest as an *obsession*—it was more of a *diversion*.

In real life, he had a lot on his plate. Rawlings Industries was doing well, very well. He had more than enough to keep him busy. Claire Nichols was something of a fantasy, his *distraction,* like an exhibit at the zoo. Perhaps that was a bad analogy. Animals at the zoo can only be watched. At first, that was what he did with the Nichols girls: he watched. Then, with time, he experimented. *What good is having money if you can't use it to your enjoyment?* He wanted to know if he could influence the lives on their list. Emily Nichols didn't hold the draw that, somehow, her younger sister possessed; therefore, he made a few calls and learned some information. With his connections, it wasn't difficult to take that information and change the course of history. A call here, another there, and suddenly, Claire's suitor had an amazing intern opportunity across the country. It was exhilarating and proved that Anthony could manipulate Claire's world. She was young, vivacious, and attractive; he doubted that his impact thus far would prove significant, but it proved that without a doubt, he could influence the course of her life. That knowledge was intoxicating and addicting. He continually wondered how far he could go.

As the saying went, knowledge was power, and Anthony Rawlings thrived on power. In everyday life, he had the power to change lives— those of employees and the futures of companies. Claire Nichols was unlike those decisions made from behind the desk as a CEO. Altering her life was done covertly, without Claire's knowledge. The risk of discovery added to his elation.

Placing the most recent photos of Claire into a file folder and securing them in his briefcase, Anthony closed his eyes. The ever-present voice that worked day and night pushing his inner drive for success began to fill his thoughts. There were times that Anthony yearned for the real live, breathing mentor who'd influenced his life in such a dramatic way, but that wasn't possible. His grandfather, Nathaniel Rawls, had been taken from him and from the rest of his family by the workings of seemingly inconsequential people—people who had changed the Rawls family forever. Not only did they change it—they eliminated it. The name Rawls ceased to exist.

It was a favor Anthony Rawlings intended to return.

Nathaniel's voice echoed in his thoughts ... words that Anthony would never forget, words that were aimed toward both Sherman Nichols and Jonathon Burke. *Not just them—hell, no. They took away my world. They took my family. Their damn kids, their kids, and their kids' kids ... they'll all face the consequences of their actions!*

That promise was spoken by the once powerful entrepreneurial giant who'd been reduced to nothing more than a common prisoner. Nathaniel's threat repeated as a constant cadence in Anthony's life, often accompanied by the shame now associated with his birth name. Public shame—failure for the world to see, all of it brought on by those individuals. Anthony had been born a Rawls—Anton Rawls. He longed for his current success to honor the name his grandfather wore proudly as a soldier and a businessman; however, that homage would never be. Each time he penned the name *Anthony Rawlings* on a contract, a completed business deal, or a monumental acquisition, he'd recall his grandfather's words, and the roots of Nathaniel's final desire would plunge deeper into his being. Those roots were now so ingrained and intertwined that they completed one another. He didn't know when it had become so consuming, yet it filled so much of him—had pushed away other desires and feelings—until Anthony couldn't imagine his life without the vendetta. It wasn't debatable; Nathaniel's wish would be fulfilled. Without fulfilling Nathaniel's wish, Anthony Rawlings would be incomplete.

Anthony didn't ask for the rewind reel of Nathaniel's voice, which continually ran through his subconscious, and he didn't need it. No, he had an everyday living, breathing reminder of his obligation—his grandfather's second wife. Perhaps, without Anthony realizing, she was wise with her words. She never told Anthony that he *failed* his grandfather; instead, she'd subtly remind him that he had *yet* to succeed. Although her impatience grated on him, she was one of the few people Anthony allowed to fully voice her thoughts—especially when it involved his decisions. He overlooked her redundancy, because she too had lost everything. Anthony knew that if it weren't for him, she'd have lost more, but the truth stared at him with steel-gray eyes almost every day. It was his failure in controlling his father's vengeance that cost Nathaniel's wife dearly.

Overlooking her reminders was Anthony's penitence. He'd promised Nathaniel that he would look after Marie. If he'd succeeded in stopping his father's retaliation, things could have been different. When Marie lost her last name, Anthony failed Nathaniel. He also failed his parents the night they died. He wouldn't fail Nathaniel again.

The way Anthony reasoned, his planning, or procrastination as Marie called it, regarding the vendetta had paid off. Although he allowed her prompts for retaliation, he also reminded her that Anthony Rawlings worked on his own schedule and towards his own goals. Their list of *children* had grown shorter by the day through natural attrition. Jonathon Burke and his wife, Sherman Nichols and his wife, and now Jordon Nichols and his wife were gone. The original two and their wives passed away of natural causes. He had provided the funds to watch their health fail from afar, but his true interest lay in observing their children and their children. The PI explained that wet leaves were believed to be involved in Jordon and Shirley Nichols' automobile crash. Anthony didn't care about the cause, as long as he could cross them off their list. Now, his concern centered on the next generation.

As the plane touched down, his anticipation built ... instead of pictures and reports, he would, for the first time, see Emily and Claire Nichols in person.

In an effort to minimize his visibility, Anthony dressed down and walked to the back of the church's sanctuary. It didn't take long for him to realize he could easily be lost in the crowd. The Nichols had been well-respected members of their community, and the church was overflowing with mourners. He'd never been to a funeral with so many people willing to speak. Apparently, Jordon had been a first-rate policeman; the church was wall-to-wall with uniformed officers. Shirley had also been a well-loved teacher. As the afternoon wore on, Anthony couldn't help but watch Claire. She was seated next to her sister, and often, the two held onto one another's hands. That wasn't what captivated him. What caught his attention was how Emily had the man to her left. Anthony knew he was John Vandersol, Emily's longtime boyfriend. Occasionally, Emily would break down and John would console her. Claire, on the other hand, remained steadfast. The pain was visible in her expression, yet only occasionally did she bow her head or wipe her eyes. Her stoic veneer fascinated him. *Was she truly that strong? What were her limits? Could she be broken?*

Anthony assumed that if he hadn't lured Simon Johnson away to California, the young man would be present to offer Claire his shoulder. That had been Anthony's first attempt to manipulate her life, and it had been too easy. He would continue to look for more opportunities.

The preacher spoke, countless people gave their condolences, but Anthony's mind was on Claire's future. As he watched her, he thought about all he knew. He didn't know how long her future would last; however, he did know that it was now at his discretion, and in some way, he would be a part of it.

The first step would be the scholarship at Valparaiso; it would be necessary for her to complete her degree. He'd already started the groundwork. After all, he'd originally assumed that he'd be at the Nichols' funeral due to more manipulation. The fact that the vengeance gods looked down and blessed his plans reinforced his determination.

After the service concluded, the caskets were wheeled down the center aisle followed by the family. The church was a murmur of whispers as organ music played from somewhere above. Anthony couldn't suppress his curiosity as Emily, John, and Claire headed his direction. Soon, they would pass mere feet away. If he reached past the older gentleman on his left, he could seize Claire's hand; however, he knew that couldn't happen, even though, as she moved toward him, she had already paused a few times to hold a mourner's hand and accept his or her condolences. It wouldn't look right; Anthony didn't look sad. He wasn't heartbroken over the loss—no, he was intrigued.

Then, just as the family neared, the man on Anthony's left reached forward and spoke. "Emily and Claire, please know how sorry I am for your loss."

They stopped and each young lady reached out and hugged the older gentleman. It was Claire who responded, "Thank you for coming. I know Dad and Mom would have loved to have seen you." Her voice was strong despite the burden of her loss.

"You know that I wouldn't have missed ..."

Anthony didn't listen to the man's words. He was mesmerized by the green eyes he saw before him. He'd seen them in photographs—he had a whole file. They were different in person, more vivid, alive, and so full of emotion. Sadness prevailed, yet there was something else, Drive? Ambition? Determination? He wanted to gaze longer into their depths, but before he could speak and offer his condolences, Emily smiled sadly at the gentleman and the three were gone.

It was there, in that church, in Indianapolis, Indiana, that Anthony resolved that his and Claire's paths would cross again. Someday he'd learn just how strong she could be in the face of greater adversity.

One

Tardiness has Consequences – April 2010
(Consequences – Chapter 5)

To know the rules of the game, you have to be educated.
— L.L. Cool J.

Mindlessly, the pad of Anthony's thumb ran laps around the smooth rim of the crystal tumbler. He wasn't thinking about the glass in his hand or even the Evan Williams bourbon swirling near the bottom. No, Anthony's thoughts were centered on the monitors above his grand desk. From multiple, well-placed cameras, he could watch Claire move about the S.E suite.

During his time in Europe, the appeal of the woman held captive in his home had begun to fade. In all honesty, having acquired his goal, his return home seemed somewhat anticlimactic. After all, the hunt had taken years, and with each bit of new information, and each time he manipulated fate, Anthony felt invigorated. For a long time, Anthony had known that one day his target would be his.

The capture was all that he'd imagined and more—the true climax! From the moment he stepped into the Red Wing, Anthony knew he'd succeed. He was, first and foremost, a businessman with an impeccable record of success, especially when an endeavor had his full commitment. Whether in business or in pleasure, Anthony understood that planning and patience were essential elements for success. Before embarking on any deal, Anthony Rawlings thoroughly assessed the situation, eliminated the risks, and accentuated the assets.

This acquisition was different. Unlike the average acquisition, such as one of a company, *this* acquisition had risks that he couldn't avoid. Sometimes that happened in the game of chance. The first risk was his public interaction with Claire; sitting with her in the Red Wing and taking her out to dinner were undoubtedly perilous. After all, he's well-known, and the possibility of being associated, even coincidentally, with a missing person wouldn't fit his perfect persona.

In all reality, he could have paid for Claire Nichols' disappearance— only to have her reappear in his home—but that would've increased the number of people privy to his plan. With her ultimate future unsure, Anthony felt the fewer number of people on that list, the better. Most importantly, if he'd paid someone to bring her to Iowa, he would've missed out on the euphoria that came with finalizing the *big deal*. Anthony had experienced that feeling over and over in business, but that was nothing like the sensation of slipping the GHB into Claire's wine glass. At that moment, he knew that there was no turning back—he didn't want to.

Being a professional businessman with an image to maintain, Anthony worked out every possible scenario and created believable contingency plans. The time and energy he'd put into Claire Nichols' acquisition could have been billed in millions—literally. Anthony Rawlings' time was incredibly valuable. Suddenly, his lips twitched upward. *Perhaps he should add his billable hours in planning and executing Claire's acquisition to Claire's bill? But, wouldn't that be like a jail sentence of 'life' plus 1000 years? Her first debt was practically insurmountable; adding more to it was truly adding insult to injury.*

Movement on the screen caused him to refocus. He watched as Claire unsuccessfully tried to open a bottle of water. After a few attempts she wiped her hands on the arms of the chair and finally removed the cap. If he'd have zoomed closer, he would've seen her complexion pale as she forced herself to swallow the refreshing liquid. Satisfaction filled his chest; his delay was working—Claire knew he was coming to her, and her anxiety was obviously growing with each passing minute.

Maybe—just maybe—he'd been wrong to think the fun was over. Perhaps there'd be more opportunities to enjoy the woman in the black dress and heels he was watching. He reminded himself, it wasn't all about enjoyment, well at least not hers. No, Claire Nichols had a bill to pay and lessons to learn.

Anthony was in a place he'd never been. Metaphorically, he was entering virgin territory. After all, he'd never before held a woman captive. There'd never been a need—or a desire. Women were a nice accessory and a necessary complement for many occasions, and through the years, more women than he could remember were willing to fulfill that role, as well as be attentive to his physical needs. Of course, he treated each one with respect. Anthony Rawlings couldn't have disgruntled women running around talking about him in a negative way. Each separation was his fault—*his* plate was too full, *he* had too many responsibilities. The fact that he usually dated high-profile women helped. They, too, had lives, responsibilities, and reputations that required discretion. If he tried to remember half of the gorgeous women he'd dated, Anthony believed that all of his separations had ended amicably.

Thankfully, he had people like Shelly, his publicist, and Patricia, his private assistant, to remind him when he'd be encountering an old flame. It even seemed that at times, Patricia found his lack of sincerity regarding these women amusing. After all, many of them, at one time or another, considered him a boyfriend. The reality couldn't be farther from the truth. Never in forty-five years had Anthony Rawlings considered himself someone's *boyfriend*. The concept was laughable.

It wasn't that he didn't enjoy the company of women; it was that, in the game of life, women were a liability, a risk that he wasn't willing to take. He was a master at appearances. Accepting a woman as anything more than an accessory for an evening or as an outlet for physical needs would be to allow that woman to be part of his persona—part of his life. That had never happened, nor did Anthony Rawlings foresee it happening in the future. He had too much at stake.

Bringing his thoughts back to Claire, he felt a renewed sense of anticipation. New experiences were rare for him. Viewing the monitors as Claire pretended to read—since she hadn't turned the page in over ten minutes, he knew she wasn't concentrating—he conceded that undoubtedly this would be a brand-new experience. He just had to figure out exactly what he would do with it—and with her. His grin reemerged.

Oh, he knew what he would do with her—whatever he wanted. The question that loomed in his mind was how she would respond. Although she'd willingly engaged in vanilla sex in Atlanta, since coming to Iowa, she'd been considerably less compliant; however, Anthony reminded himself, that was before—before her nearly two week *time-out*. After watching the short interaction between Catherine and Claire on the video recording, when Catherine informed her of his impending arrival, Anthony believed Claire had experienced an attitude adjustment.

Truly, he didn't know how he wanted her to react when he entered the suite. The fact she was dressed appropriately held potential. Perhaps she could be trained to work off not only her bill, but the un-payable invoice that included the life of his grandfather—*and* perhaps some of his own billable time.

Briefly, Anthony changed a section of the screen to the Atlanta news. He'd been watching and scanning it daily during his travels in Europe. After over two weeks in his possession, he was happy to see that there hadn't been any news reports or voiced concerns about the disappearance of Claire Nichols. It appeared as though Anthony's efforts had paid off—emails, text messages, and Facebook messages all accomplished their goal. Claire's friends and family believed she'd left town to pursue a new job opportunity—Anthony grinned as he switched the screen back to the S.E. suite—and their beliefs were in essence true. *This* was and would be her new job. Momentarily, he closed his eyes, as mental images of Claire's growing list of *job* responsibilities filled his thoughts. *Perhaps he should compile a written list?*

A knock at his office door pulled Anthony from his sinister thoughts.

With a click of his mouse, the screens turned from the monitors in the S.E. suite to the closing stock market results for Rawlings Industries and its plethora of subsidiaries. Without inquiring, Anthony hit the button to allow access to his domain. It was after 9:00 PM and this was *his* home. He didn't need to inquire as to who was about to enter his inner sanctuary; there were few possibilities.

"Mr. Rawlings, did you want to see me?" Catherine's voice echoed as she stepped into Anthony's office. Once the door was shut, she lifted a brow. "I would've thought you'd have investigated yourself, Anton."

"I plan to. First, I want to know a few things."

Catherine perched herself on the edge of a chair near his desk. "You weren't watching from your trip?"

"I was, but there are some things you can't decipher from a video feed—such as attitude. Tell me about the last two weeks; how have they been?"

Catherine smiled. "Educational. I happened to look inside the suite a few minutes ago. Did you see what she's wearing?"

"I did. Did you tell her what to wear?"

"No, I told her that it was up to her."

Anthony nodded as he sat back against his leather chair. "So, she seems to understand the importance of appearance—that's good. What about interaction?"

"Until today, since you left, she's only had access to Carlos. He delivered all her meals and returned for the dishes. The rest of the staff entered only when she was occupied with her showers."

Anthony grinned. "Carlos—Carlos doesn't speak English, at least not well."

"I know."

"Very good, Catherine, I applaud your resourcefulness."

"Thank you, Anton. I may not agree with your plan; however, I told you I'd do my part. Now, what do you expect when you enter the suite?"

"What do I expect? I expect respect for the authority I obviously hold over every aspect of her life. At this moment, I expect her to have the good sense to recognize the magnitude of her current situation."

Catherine leaned forward, her voice held the tone of a warning. "Caged animals fight. I saw the scratches on your arms when she first arrived."

"That won't happen again."

"And you're sure of this?"

Anthony nodded confidently. "I am." He wondered if Catherine would ask for more clarification. If she had, he wasn't sure he'd share his plans. After all, those plans were why his excitement at their reunion was once again growing. Anthony glanced at his watch. "Did you tell her I'd be there at 10:00 PM?"

"I told her between 9:00 PM and 10:00 PM. She seemed desperate for me to stay and talk. I believe she's lonely."

"I saw that on the video." The woman he'd observed in Atlanta was both social in her work and her private life. Perhaps this time away from others *was* beneficial. He planned to emphasize how he controlled her interactions. His grin broke through his facade with the realization—*there wouldn't be anything he didn't control.*

"Thank you, Catherine. I think I can handle this from here."

She stood. "This was very risky for a man of your—"

"Thank you, Catherine," he interrupted. "It's a roll of the dice. High risks yield the best results. It's about time I learn if your manipulation has added to my yields."

Before stepping from the room, Catherine smiled. "I'm sure you'll capitalize on your investment ... Mr. Rawlings."

Anthony looked at his watch again, 9:51 PM. One last click of his mouse and he saw Claire, up on the screen, pacing near the fireplace in her suite. There wasn't anything he didn't know about her, from her family to her medical history. He knew that she and her sister were all that remained of the Sherman Nichols line. He also knew that she liked her coffee with cream, and that about six months ago, Claire had had the birth control device inserted. During his observations, he didn't find her to be promiscuous; the doctor's notations stated something about *convenience*. Grinning toward the screen, Anthony agreed: the insert was convenient.

Standing, Anthony put on and buttoned his double-breasted suit jacket. *No, he'd been wrong when he thought the actual acquisition had been the climax—there would definitely be many more to come!*

Anthony depressed the button on the side of the doorframe while simultaneously hearing the *beep* and opening the door. Claire's eyes opened wide while she remained seated in the chair near the fireplace. The last time he'd seen her—in person—she'd looked like hell, wearing a robe, her hair a mess, and her face discolored. Tonight was definitely an improvement. It wasn't just her appearance, although Anthony approved; it was her demeanor. That morning, nearly two weeks ago, Claire had been out of control—demanding, yelling, and crying. It wasn't that she was in control now; Anthony saw the fear in her eyes. It was that she was ... composed.

"Good evening, Claire."

She stood and replied, "Good evening, Anthony. Shall we sit?"

When he stepped toward her, he noticed her quick intake of air. Confidently, he sat on the sofa, leaned back, and unbuttoned his jacket. He watched intently as she sat on the edge of the chair with her back straight. The *hum* of the fireplace fan filled the room as he considered the woman before him. Without a doubt, she was an improvement over the one he'd left on the floor of the same suite.

He waited to see if she would ramble. When only the fireplace blower prevailed, Anthony spoke, "Do you think you're ready to continue with our agreement? Or do you need some more time alone to consider the situation?"

"After consulting my attorney, I feel I have no choice but to continue with our agreement."

Anthony felt the hairs on the back of his neck stand to attention. *What the hell?* He glared toward the woman who had the audacity to sound trite. "Claire, I know you're joking, but do you really think it's a good idea? Considering your circumstances?"

"I've had a lot of time to think; joviality has sustained me."

He tilted his head. *The woman had nerve—he'd give her that.* "I must say your demeanor impresses me. I'll need to deliberate on this new personality."

He sat silently and contemplated this petite woman who had the fortitude to maintain eye contact, and answer his questions with a hint of bravado, all while knowing she was at his mercy. *Or did she know? Did she think this was some kind of sick reality TV show and any minute it would be over?* He stared. "Tell me what you've learned during your reflection time."

She rambled about clothes and food, truly inconsequential things. Anthony interrupted, "That's all very nice, but what have you discovered about your situation?" He couldn't contain his condescending tone, perhaps he didn't want to. After all, she needed to know who held the answers. "Do you even know where you are?"

After only a moment's hesitation, she said, "I'm in Iowa, or at least somewhere near Iowa City."

How the hell? He'd scanned hours of video—did someone pass her a note of some kind? Anthony couldn't imagine that they'd disrespect him like that. "And ... you learned this ... from whom?"

"I learned it from the *Weather Channel—Local on the Eights*. The local weather for this area comes from Iowa City, Iowa."

Anthony exhaled. *Damn, he was on edge. Her flippant attitude needed readjustment.* "Very well, that will spare me telling you. For the sake of clarity, since that seemed to be a problem in the past, you're aware that your indebtedness *to me* can only be determined paid *by me*?"

Her smile appeared pained, yet she managed to keep it in place as she nodded. Anthony waited for an answer. When she didn't speak, he proclaimed, "I prefer verbal confirmation."

"I am aware that you are the only one who can decide when my debt is paid in full." Though her words sounded too calm, her hands remained clenched. She'd never know how that unconscious act helped to calm her captor. He wanted—no needed—to know that she understood his authority.

He continued, "You are also aware that your duties require you to be available to me whenever, wherever, and however I demand?" His eyes never left hers.

"I am aware."

He reiterated for clarification. "You're aware that you must at all times obey my rules?"

"I'm aware that I must do as I'm told."

She was good. He didn't believe a damn word she said, but he had to admit, she was good. Oh, he considered demonstrating more of his authority, but perhaps Catherine had been right. Claire Nichols was lonely, and she was grasping at the straws of *any* interaction. Perhaps no interaction would prove to be the most educational tool. Besides, he had plenty of time—as much as he wanted—for interaction. Finally, he spoke, "Very well." He stood and walked toward the door.

Before he reached his destination, Claire's determined tone rang throughout the suite. "Wait."

Anthony turned, unable to hide the shock at her demand, his eyes locked onto hers.

Apparently, she had the good sense to realize her breach of station. Immediately, her tone softened, "I'm sorry ... but may I leave this suite?"

Apologetic and requesting permission—yes, Anthony could deal with that. "As long as we are certain on the terms of our agreement, and you follow the rules and orders given, I see no problem with your roaming the house." He reached for the door handle. "It's rather large. I'll be working from home tomorrow. Your services will be utilized then, so be prepared for my call. When I have a chance, I'll give you a tour of the house and define your limitations. I think it's best that you don't roam tonight. I don't want you getting lost." Within his pocket, he depressed the sensor, causing the *beep* to sound once again. Anthony reached for the handle.

"Anthony?" The earlier strength he'd heard in her tone was gone. "I don't have any ... *duties* tonight?"

"I've recently arrived from a series of meetings in Europe and am quite tired. I'm glad to know we have a mutual understanding. Goodnight, Claire."

As he shut her door, he heard her say goodnight.

Walking toward his office, he thought about the bourbon he'd left sitting on his desk—there were about fifty emails that needed reading and probably responses to be written—and he had at least two web conferences tomorrow. He'd need to check to see if Patricia had sent him his schedule.

Oh, yes, and apparently his *acquisition* was adapting to her new reality—that was good. Anthony Rawlings had too many things to think about other than to be concerned with the woman upstairs. Hell, Catherine had been spot-on with the isolation. Perhaps he should allow her to deal with the day-to-day maintenance; he'd utilize Claire when it fit his schedule. Besides, a little alone time seemed to be just what the doctor ordered.

Damn, in a week and a half the proposal from Arkansas was coming in. Did he have that preliminary report? There were too many other things to think about besides Claire Nichols; however, it was comforting to know she'd adapted. Tomorrow, Anthony decided he'd take that theory to the next level. *Would her actions be as accommodating as her words?*

The morning light had yet to penetrate the heavy drapes of his suite when Anthony turned toward the red numbers. It was only 4 42 AM, yet he was wide awake. The woman—about whom, he reminded himself, he didn't give a damn—was inside his house. She was undoubtedly sleeping soundly under *his* roof. *How many nights had he imagined what it would be like to have her where he could watch her, train her, and control her?* Now she was here and he was a floor away. If he went upstairs and took what his body obviously wanted, what difference would it make? This wasn't a normal dating scenario. Claire wasn't going to go to the press and proclaim his actions. She wasn't going anywhere. Besides, this wasn't about sex, although he was painfully erect. It was about power. Everything about her existence was his to determine. If he wanted her to sleep, she would sleep. If he wanted to use her, he would use her.

Though the thought of entering her suite—no, not *her* suite, the *S.E.* suite—and asserting his dominance while assessing her reaction appealed to him, Anthony reconsidered: the more accommodating he made her, the better. He didn't relish the idea of continued daily battles. Yes, he liked things his way; however, his energies could be better utilized if she were more compliant.

Catherine was right. Showing up to the office with scratches on his face or arms would instigate questions. Making his way out of bed, Anthony walked to his bureau, opened the top drawer, and found what he'd purchased in Europe. Running the long lengths of black satin across his palm, his mind considered the possibilities of their use. It wasn't that he was into the kinky shit; this was more about self-preservation. He could even consider it a favor. Claire's fighting hadn't worked well for her in the past, and he wouldn't allow it in the future. With the use of satin restraints, he would assure that when he exited the S.E. suite, he'd be scathe-free, and with her cooperation, albeit forced, Claire would be able to boast the same.

In his mind, he was giving her a choice. She would accommodate him; how much independence she had while doing that would be up to her.

A little after 7:00 AM, Anthony scaled the grand staircase. He hadn't acted upon his earlier thoughts of Claire; instead, he'd gone to the pool, swam laps, and lifted weights for an hour. After a shower and breakfast, he decided to spend some time preparing for his web conferences. As he read, each sentence disappeared into the memories of the innocent emerald-green gaze from last night, the one that asked, *I'm sorry ... but may I leave this suite?*

He wasn't concerned about fulfilling her desires. It was basic psychology: operant conditioning—positive consequences for positive behavior, negative consequences for negative behavior. Her respectful tone, her demeanor, and her appearance—they all deserved a positive consequence. *After all, wasn't that what he wanted to do—to promote the positive and rebuke the negative?*

He also remembered telling her to be ready in the morning. *Would she be? Did she truly deserve a positive consequence?*

The *beep* sounded as he moved silently into the S.E suite. Scanning the room, Claire was nowhere to be found. His first thought was the bathroom, but the door was ajar and no one was there. Before he could look further, he heard movement from the closet/dressing room. Staring in that direction, he waited for her to emerge. When she did, the startled *yelp,* accompanied by the dropping of her shoes, made his cheeks rise. "Good morning, Claire." She was ready—*another reason for a positive consequence.*

"Good morning, Anthony; I didn't hear you come in."

Amused, he watched as she picked up her shoes and feigned calmness. It was then he noticed her uneaten breakfast on the table. "Are you ready for your tour? Did you plan to eat first? I have a web conference in forty-five minutes."

She asked him about a web conference. As he answered, he had difficulty suppressing his amusement at her behavior. It was as if carrying on a mundane conversation with the man who held her future in his hands was an everyday occurrence. Snickering to himself, he reasoned, *it will be from now on.* Maybe she was working from her years as a bartender. Whatever the cause, her ability to converse effortlessly was a welcome surprise. Before long, Anthony found himself leading her down corridors and describing the estate. As he discussed pieces of furniture and fine works of art, he knew that there was no way Claire could know the items he pointed out were originally owned by his grandfather. She didn't know that it had taken Anthony years to track down significant pieces of his history, after they'd been auctioned off to undeserving bidders. She also couldn't know how the mention of each item fortified his resolve for restitution; instead, Claire walked beside him, blissfully unaware. A saying about a spider and a fly came to mind.

They were in the library when she asked something about computers. He didn't know if she were joking about the size of the library and the magnitude of books, yet her comment hit him wrong. Suddenly, Anthony felt the need to remind her of her status. She may be receiving a tour that few others had experienced, but she wasn't a guest, and he wanted to make that clear. "I think it would be best for you to not have access to computers, the Internet, or telephones." Oh, he wanted a verbal response; however, the unspoken acknowledgement of his authority that flooded her eyes momentarily satisfied that need. He silently vowed that they would discuss the need for verbal responses in the future.

She didn't speak again until they entered the indoor pool. Anthony never gave the room much thought—it was a pool. There were windows, tile, and water. Yet as they entered, Claire gasped. He responded before he had a chance to think. "Do you like to swim?"

"Oh, yes. This is amazing."

"You shall have bathing suits tomorrow." As soon as the words left his lips, Anthony wondered why he'd been so forthcoming. She hadn't asked and that was his rule—requests must be made before they can be granted; nevertheless, he'd approved an unspoken request. He would follow through, because he was a man of his word, but he didn't intend to offer more. The tour *and* bathing suits—her positive rewards were outnumbering her behaviors.

At the entrance to his office, Anthony realized the time and proclaimed, "I have business I must do. It's 7:25 AM. I want you back at my office at 10:30 AM. You have some debt to pay." He watched for her reaction. It wasn't overt, but her eyes momentarily drifted toward the wall. To her credit she recovered quickly. He asked, "Do you think you can find your way back to your suite?"

It was then that she did it again. Her voice softened as she asked permission to go to the library. *As long as she stayed in the library and returned to his office at 10:30 AM, what harm was there in allowing her request?* Besides, it was a *request*—well worded. While reiterating the importance of her returning at the appropriate time, he apprehensively acquiesced; however, before he dismissed her, he reminded her of his control. "We have not discussed all of the rules pertaining to the house. At this point, do not go outside. Permission for going out on the grounds will be contingent upon your ability to follow rules within the house."

Anthony liked how she bristled at the mention of her restrictions. Yes, he had thousands of jobs and people's livelihoods in his hands, but never had he had one person's life completely in his grasp. He had to admit, the power was intense and even erotic.

Anthony watched the clock as the web conference dragged on. When he finally disconnected, he looked at the time. Claire was due in his office in six minutes. Anthony clicked a few times with his mouse and entered a code. His screen filled with a view of the library. It didn't take long to find Claire wandering about, pulling out books, and reading the backs. He waited and watched as she opened a book and leaned against a bookcase. The numbers on the clock changed. *Didn't she realize the size of his house?* There was no possible way, unless she ran, that she would make it to his office in time. *Did she think he was joking about returning on time?* She didn't even have the good sense to turn toward the library clock.

At 10:37 AM he entered the library. This time, Anthony found no humor in the fact he'd again startled her. She was stupid to even think that she could blatantly disobey him. He'd provided positive consequences—obviously it wasn't enough to mold the appropriate behavior. When her eyes met his, he saw the remorse.

"Oh, Anthony, I'm so sorry. I was just engrossed in all you have—"

Excuses! He didn't make them and he didn't listen to them. His hand struck her cheek. Before she could look away, Anthony seized the back of her neck and pulled her eyes toward his. "Simple instructions, which are what I gave you—perhaps you're not ready to leave your suite quite yet."

He heard her plea—telling him that she *could* follow instructions. Her words didn't match her actions, and he didn't have the time or the patience for coddling.

"Follow me to my office—now." Not waiting for her to respond, he took off through the library and down the corridor. With each step he contemplated his next move, reminding himself that this was a critical time in Claire's training. *If he didn't demonstrate his dominance now, he couldn't guarantee her compliance later. Didn't she understand that this was for her own good? This arrangement would never last if she didn't cooperate, and then what would his options be? She needed to recognize his authority!*

By the time they reached the grand doors to his office, red infiltrated his vision. It wasn't intense, but the world had a crimson hue. Catherine had told him that he was wrong to take Claire. Nathaniel's plan had been clear, yet there was something about Claire that fascinated him. He wouldn't fail and prove Catherine right. He *would* make Claire behave appropriately—this *would* work.

Shoving her inside his office, Anthony reeled in the red and spoke in his most even tone. "So, you say you *can* follow instructions. We'll see." He watched as she stood before him trembling. He wondered how she could be trembling—his anger warmed him to an uncomfortable heat. Then he realized, it wasn't cold: it was fear. That was good. Fear was an excellent motivator. He continued, "Let's start with you taking off your clothes."

Though her hands shook as she unfastened the clasps, she didn't argue. Whenever she looked away, he reached for her chin and redirected her eyes. There was so much he could see in her eyes; he refused to allow her to hide that emotion. After he redirected her the second time, she maintained eye contact. Once she was nude, he assessed. There was nothing wrong with her body. She'd even seemed to have lost some weight since she first arrived. Her earlier markings were gone, and her skin tone was lighter—probably due to staying inside. After all, she wasn't in the warm Georgia sun any longer.

"Lie down on the floor," he directed.

She didn't speak, yet he saw her indecision. Anthony Rawlings wouldn't make the same request twice. Just as he was about to assist, Claire knelt on the carpet.

"Lie on your stomach and keep your face and eyes down."

He didn't know if it was his imagination or if time was indeed moving slowly; nevertheless, each of her movements seemed to occur painfully slow. *At least they were occurring.* Despite the fact that she was still trembling, she eventually lay down, totally nude, and prone on the carpet.

Anthony had had his fair share of experiences in life; however, this was once again entering the world of new and untested territory. He'd accepted the responsibility to train this woman, to make her into a compliant soul. Catherine said it couldn't be done. She said that women today were too independent. Watching Claire lie as still as possible, Anthony almost laughed—*independent indeed.* Claire Nichols would learn to behave.

Perhaps it was a childhood memory, or maybe something he'd read; regardless of the source, physical negative reinforcement was often very effective in molding behavior. Even Pavlov's dog learned to *stop* responding to the bell once the reinforcement turned from food to an electrical shock. Claire Nichols would learn to listen to Anthony. When she replied appropriately, she earned house tours and time in the library. When she disappointed him, she earned negative reinforcement.

Slowly, Anthony unbuckled his belt. It wasn't the fulfillment of the punishment he sought. No, it was Claire's reaction. He needed to hear her response. When his belt contacted her back for the first blow, she let out a satisfying scream. It was his reinforcement, confirming her understanding of his control. That scream told Anthony that she understood her behavior was unacceptable. He wanted more.

He listened as the belt contacted her skin—again and again—however, his reinforcement was gone. Claire remained silent. Moving his eyes from the growing welts, Anthony noticed Claire's fist at her lips. He felt the red return with the realization that she was refusing to give him his satisfaction.

Crimson flooded the room. *Damn her!* She *would* learn that he was in control. She *would* learn to behave. She said she could follow directions—then by God, he had directions for her to follow. Reaching for her shoulder, he turned her over. Maintaining eye contact, Anthony began to undress. He didn't give instructions—at first. His intent was obvious.

With time, he began to direct her movements. His desired positions required her compliance and manipulation. Sometimes he told her what to do, other times he moved her as he saw fit. There were times he heard her ragged breaths or tasted her salty tears; nevertheless, Claire never argued nor told him to stop. *At least she seemed to comprehend their arrangement—this was consensual.*

By the time he finished, Claire seemed incapable of complete sentences. Her eyes no longer revealed her emotions; they were momentarily void and puffy and her cheeks were wet. Anthony refused to be affected by her demeanor. It reminded him of the woman he'd left two weeks ago in the suite and he didn't like it.

When he returned from the bathroom, Claire was still sitting on the floor holding her clothes. He walked toward her. Her disheveled appearance and vacant look disgusted him. More than anything, he wanted her out of his office. "You may go to your suite, clean yourself up, and get ready to demonstrate to me again your ability to follow directions." It was as if his words unlocked the invisible bonds that held her in place and allowed her to move. While she mechanically dressed, he did his best to ignore her occasional ragged breaths. Before she left, he callously added, "Do not leave your suite until I decide. Your pass to roam has been revoked."

When she reached for the door handle, Claire turned back toward Anthony. Her lips incapable of words, her eyes questioned. Only after he nodded did she open the door and walk away. He listened to her shoes on the marble corridor. Out of mere curiosity, he went to his computer and found the camera's view of the foyer. When Claire started to walk past the stairs toward the outside doors, Anthony shook his head and began walking toward the front of the house. He didn't need to hurry. There was no way that she could escape the grounds; nevertheless, he'd just told her to stay in her suite. Going outside was definitely forbidden. By the time he made it to the foyer, she was halfway up the stairs. Though he stood near the banister and watched, she never turned toward him.

Satisfied, he went back to his office and resumed his work. Although he had a lot to accomplish, every now and then he would utilize the cameras and look into her suite. He had difficulty hiding the anticipation as he saw her on the sofa, freshly showered and redressed. A grin emerged from time to time as she sat and obediently waited for him.

Anthony Rawlings did not fail. Catherine was wrong. He would teach Claire that there were consequences.

Later that night, Anthony tested Claire's reflexes as he rolled her hard nipple between his fingers. Their perspiration, combined with his recent oral assault, left the dark red nub slippery under his grasp. Though it appeared that she tried to anticipate his next move, her bristling and flinching indicated that she was unable. It wasn't as though she could see what he was doing; her eyes were completely covered by the satin material. He imagined the green that lay beneath. Brushing away long, damp strands of hair from her blindfolded face, his thumb traced her swollen lips. Anthony was mesmerized by their color. It was almost as if she were still wearing lipstick, though he knew that hours earlier it had been worn away. Nearing his mouth to her ear, his warm breath bathed her skin, as goose bumps proclaimed their presence over her arms and legs. Though she had spoken earlier in their training, more recently only sounds had been offered. Anthony whispered in his most seductive voice, "I'll be right back."

She nodded and turned away from his voice.

Pulling her chin toward him, he asked, "Claire, what have I said about verbal responses?"

"Yes," her words choked, "you'll be back."

Stroking her hair, his cheeks rose. "That's a good girl. You're learning."

He lifted himself from the side of her bed and walked toward the bookcase. With each step, his muscles pulled, tight and defined by their recent exertion. The constant vibration of his phone suggested that something of the utmost importance required his attention. As he reached for his phone, he contemplated the woman before him. Truthfully, he didn't mind the break. After what had transpired earlier in the day in his office, he was prepared for this night to go on for a long time; besides, he was beginning to enjoy the role of teacher. With Claire's recent attitude adjustment, he must be doing well. Grinning ruthlessly toward his student, he watched as her legs twisted in a way as to try to conceal her exposed body. He could help her—lift a sheet and cover her; after all, with her hands bound to the headboard, she wasn't going to succeed alone—but he didn't. He liked the view. She had an attractive body. As his gaze reluctantly moved from the bed, he tapped the screen of his phone and words and icons appeared.

Instead of the urgent business on the screen, he recalled the beginning of this lesson. He wasn't sure if the satin scarves were necessary or purely an exhibition of his control. Either way, Anthony knew he wasn't going to tolerate her ridiculous fighting any longer. She would learn her place.

The afternoon must have been educational, because as he secured the satin around her wrists, she didn't argue or beg. He asked her, "Do you know why I'm doing this?"

At first, due to her tears, her response was difficult to understand.

He continued, "A few weeks ago, I had scratches on my arms. That's not going to happen again."

Her eyes, yet to be covered by the satin, opened wide. "I'm sorry, Anthony; I won't scratch, I promise."

"You won't, but you did. Behaviors have consequences. Can you remember that?"

"Yes."

"Repeat what I just said."

"Behaviors have consequences."

"So, whose fault is it that your hands are bound?"

Again, the waterworks. "Mine—it's my fault."

He stroked her hair. "That's right."

"This morning, I told you to be in my office by 10:30 AM. Did you do as you were told?"

Her shoulders shuddered with her response. "No."

"Say it ... what is my number-one rule?"

Claire's words were separated by exaggerated gasps of air. With each deep breath, her exposed breasts trembled. "Your rule ... is to ... do as you say."

"Did you do that?"

"No, I didn't do as I was told. I'm so sorry—i-it won't happen again."

He looked deeply into her eyes just before covering them with the satin. "No, Claire, it will not." Securing the knot, careful to avoid her hair, he asked, "I'm going to tell you what to do right now. Will you follow my number-one rule?'

Her hands were now secured and her eyes were covered. He considered her ankles, but liked the possibilities available if he left them unbound.

"Y-yes," she replied.

"Yes, what?"

"Yes, Anthony, I'll do as you say."

The screen of his phone brought him back to present and told him that he had two voice mails and three text messages. He looked past Claire to the clock. It was almost 7:00 PM and they hadn't eaten. He checked the text messages first. One from his assistant, informing him of an important email she'd sent regarding an upcoming meeting. The next was a text message from Brent Simmons, head of Rawlings Industries' legal department and Anthony's closest friend. It, too, discussed the email.

Anthony could access the email in question from his phone, but perhaps both he and Claire could use a break. Besides, he may need to make a call or two if this truly was a big issue. Whatever was happening apparently had more than a few feathers ruffled. Looking toward the bed, he knew that calling from this room was too risky. *What if Claire decided to make a noise?* He walked over to the bed and leaned over her. As he neared, he watched her body grow still. Running his fingers slowly over her breasts and down her stomach, he said, "I have to make a few calls. I'm going to untie you."

First, he untied the scarf, exposing her green eyes. Her makeup from earlier had smeared, and large black streaks covered her cheeks; nevertheless, from the moment he'd removed the blindfold, her eyes were fixed on his. She was learning the importance of eye contact. That was the first step of Anthony's *one step at a time* training. He thought of the process as somewhat similar to what it must be like to break a wild horse. It took time and the correct balance of negative and positive reinforcement. Smiling, he continued, "When I untie your hands, are you going to behave?"

Her response was barely a whisper. "Yes."

"As much as I appreciate verbal responses, I like them better if I could actually hear them, and I'd like them if they had more elaboration. Yes, what?"

Her lips trembled as she replied, "Yes, Anthony, I'll behave."

While he untied her wrists, he spoke, "I want you to take another shower and dress in a negligee—something black and long. I assume you remember my rules regarding attire? There'll be nothing under that negligee." Not waiting for an answer, he ran his thumb under her eye to smear more of the mascara. "You'll also need to fix your makeup. Don't take too long. I'll be back soon." Though she was no longer bound to the headboard, her hands were together over her chest as Anthony continued to release her wrists from the length of material. "You need to drink some water. I don't want you to dehydrate, but do not go to sleep—I have plans. We have a long evening ahead."

Claire didn't speak. Once her hands were free, she rubbed her wrists, and her gaze searched for the robe she'd left lying near the bed. When she started to reach for it, Anthony corrected her. "No. I want to see you."

He watched as she struggled with the decision to leave the robe and obey his command. Finally, she started to step away from the bed. As she did, Anthony noticed the ever so slight shake of her head and grasped her arm. She stilled where he held her. "What?" he asked. "Tell me why you shook your head."

Claire stuttered. "I-I didn't, or at least I don't think I did."

His grasp tightened. "Claire, you'll be honest with me at all times. I saw you shake your head. What were you thinking?"

She closed her eyes and more tears cascaded down her cheeks. When she opened them, she said, "I was thinking."

"Don't make me ask you to elaborate—again."

"I-I was thinking that this can't be real. It's some kind of nightmare. It can't really be happening to *me*."

Anthony let go of her arm and noticed the redness from his grasp. Claire's hand immediately went to the spot and massaged. Standing, he looked down at her. "Oh, my dear, it's real, and don't pretend that you hate it. I can tell when someone enjoys herself and you," he inclined his head and broadened his grin, taunting, "have enjoyed yourself more than once this evening." When her eyes started to look away, he lifted her chin. "Haven't you?"

"Please—I don't want any of this."

"That wasn't what I asked." He intensified his grasp. "I like my questions answered the first time. Do you understand?"

Her neck straightened. The sudden determination he saw in her expression surprised him as she replied, "I understand, and despite what you think you may have sensed, NO! I have not enjoyed myself."

Oh, there was fire yet to tame.

When he didn't release her chin, Claire's tone softened, "Now, may I please go take another shower?"

Amused by her candor, he replied, "First, my dear, I don't believe you; however, I believe that you believe you. Therefore, I'll allow this little bit of dishonesty to go unpunished. I recommend that you remember for future reference, I will not tolerate lying or deception. When it is discovered, you will be sorry. Second, expressing gratitude for positive consequences is not only appreciated, it's expected. So, Claire, what do you say when someone does something nice for you, like for example, untying your hands?"

He savored the moment as she comprehended his words. With her neck still straight, her words issued forth, saturated with a combination of rebellion and sarcasm. "Thank you, Anthony."

He released her chin. "Very good—do you remember my instructions?"

"Yes, I remember." She stayed still. When he didn't speak, she added, "I'll be waiting for you."

"Then you may go."

He watched appreciatively as she walked unclothed to the bathroom and closed the door. Yes, she would come around. It may be a slow and agonizing process, but he had all the time he wanted. After the bathroom door shut, he walked around the bed and pulled on his trousers. He, too, could use a shower. Momentarily, he considered joining Claire. The smile that emerged had more to do with her reaction than his actions. There would be plenty of time for that. He'd told her that he would leave and return, and he was curious to see if she'd follow his directions. If she didn't, there would be consequences.

As he exited the suite, he called the kitchen. "Have dinner sent to Claire's suite in an hour."

The symphony – Late May 2010
(Consequences – Chapter 8)

In nature there are neither rewards nor punishments; there are consequences.
— Robert Green Ingersoll

From the speaker on Anthony's desk, he listened to his assistant's voice, "Shelly is on line three."

Anthony's thoughts went from the spreadsheet on his screen to his publicist. "Patricia, put her through."

Immediately, he heard Shelly's concern. "Mr. Rawlings, Jennifer McAdams is in Italy on a photo shoot, and it's lasted longer than she planned."

"And you're telling me this because—"

"Because, sir, she's supposed to accompany you *this* evening to the Quad City Symphony at the Adler Theater."

Anthony ran his fingers through his hair. *Damn—he'd forgotten all about that, and he actually enjoyed Jenny's company, unlike many of the women he's been seen with over the years.* "Well, then I'll cancel."

"With all due respect, you can't. The theater will remain open because of your donation. They're planning on your attending, and there's a long list of guests coming to see you ..."

Shelly rambled about the importance of his presence, as Anthony thought more about the outing. *Could this be an unplanned opportunity to test Claire outside the estate?* His grin emerged—*outside*. She'd just recently earned her way outside of the house. Truthfully, she'd been doing much better than he imagined, and *outside* would've happened much sooner, if only she'd *asked*. He shifted slightly in his large leather chair. Even the slightest thought of his complete control over her life had an effect on his body.

Shelly's voice brought him back to the subject at hand. The idea of a new test intrigued him. This would push her outside of her newly established comfort level. Besides, if she accompanied him and succeeded, she could earn more privileges. If she failed—well, they both knew what that could bring.

Shelly's voice quieted. Anthony waited for her to continue. When she didn't, he asked, "What was that?"

"Do you want me to call Julia?"

"No." Although, like Jenny, Julia too was a model, she was too high-maintenance for Anthony's liking.

"Do you plan to attend alone?"

Anthony wrestled with his thoughts. *If he took Claire out in public and she failed, wouldn't Davenport, Iowa, be a better testing ground, than say Chicago or New York?* He could manage damage control much better in his own backyard, and taking her out into the world would accomplish another goal. Anthony truly wasn't convinced Claire contemplated the magnitude of his power. Oh, she saw his wealth regarding the estate, and her behavior had steadily improved over the last two months; however, *did she really comprehend his reach? Did she truly understand that any attempts at escape could be quickly thwarted?* Taking her to an event where he's the man of honor would show her firsthand the depth and breadth of his power. Anthony made his decision: it was time. "I won't be attending alone."

"You realize if your assistant accompanies you to any more events the papers will start to speculate."

What? He hadn't even thought about taking Patricia. Yes, she'd accompanied him to a few events, but it was totally platonic and, at the time, an outing of convenience. "I can assure you that *speculating* would be all they could do. She's only accompanied me a few times, and they were all business-related. There's nothing to speculate about. I'll be taking someone else."

"Would you like to ask this lady, or would you like me to call her?"

He had to stifle the chuckle that rumbled in the back of his throat. *Ask?* He had no intentions of *asking* this person. This person didn't have a choice in the matter—or any matter. After the first few *glitches*, she seemed to have come to terms with this reality. This outing would be another duty she could fulfill. Anthony was growing tired of the parade of women on his arm. He had a lot of deals in the works, and listening to some woman prattle small talk didn't sound appealing. If he took Claire, he could avoid the whole wine-and-dine thing. They would simply attend the symphony and come home. It was much simpler.

"No, I don't need you to call."

"Mr. Rawlings, I'll need a name."

Of course she would. "Her name is Claire Nichols. She's from Atlanta."

Shelly didn't speak.

"Did you get that?"

"I did, sir. Is there more?"

"No. That's all that needs to be released."

"Perhaps you'd like me to do some research and verify that there isn't a history that could negatively affect you?"

"No." He sat taller. "There's no history. If that's all, I have work to do."

"Mr. Rawlings, can you please spell Nichols for me?"

Anthony gripped the receiver. "N-I-C-H-O-L-S." He tried to soften his tone. After all, Shelly was paid very well to maintain his reputation. He'd never before turned down her help in assuring its untarnished veneer. He explained, "I've already had her investigated." Sighing. "You know me, Shelly. I wouldn't take that risk; however, she's not the type of woman I normally see. The whole public thing is new to her. I don't want her getting unwanted publicity."

Shelly exhaled. "Yes, I can imagine that would be difficult. Very well, her name and hometown will be all the information that I release. Thank you, Mr. Rawlings. That's all I have at the moment."

"Very well." He hung up the receiver. *Shit! Was that the right call?* Rolling his mouse over the mouse pad, Anthony Rawlings' spreadsheets came back to life. A committee had worked days—perhaps weeks—compiling all the data; yet he wasn't seeing the numbers. No, he was seeing the woman back at the estate.

In the beginning, Anthony worked to make her a faceless person—perhaps like an employee at a business he was about to close. He told himself that she was nothing to him. Allowing Claire to pay her family's debt was not Nathaniel's original plan; however, Anthony reasoned, that some fates were worse than death. Catherine disagreed—at first—but she came around, and although he valued her opinion, Anthony's money propelled their plan. He'd do whatever he damn well wanted. He saw by the way Catherine pursed her lips and stared, that she wasn't pleased with his decision, but when it came to this matter Anthony wouldn't budge—Claire was different.

Truly, it was ironic that he'd made his case—*his* basis for *his* decision—based on the fact that she was *unique*, when he continually told himself she wasn't special. That was why he wanted to take her to the symphony—because she *wasn't* special. He wouldn't need to listen to her small talk, although he knew for a fact that Claire liked to talk! He wouldn't need to do anything that was expected on a *date*. Anthony could do whatever *he* wanted—this wasn't a date!

This outing would be a test. He squared his shoulders and dialed Catherine's cell number on his private cell phone. She answered after only a few rings. "Yes, Anton?" *Obviously, she was alone.* In the company of others, she maintained a more formal appearance.

"Have Claire ready by 6:00 PM. She's accompanying me to the symphony in Davenport."

"Excuse me?"

Anthony slowed his words. "Did I stutter?"

"I just think I misunderstood you. I'm not sure she's ready for this. Do you realize what could happen if—"

"Then make sure she's ready and that nothing happens. I'm not in this alone."

"I was not in favor—"

"But," he paused, "you've supported my decision. I believe the word is *accomplice*."

Catherine's tone hardened. "I'll have her ready."

"Six PM, there's a cocktail reception at 7:00 PM, and the symphony begins at 8:00 PM. Eric will be driving us in the limousine."

"Anton, I'll prepare her, but you must be sure she—"

"Do you doubt my control?"

"No, that's not what I mean." Her tone changed. "Mr. Rawlings, she'll be ready."

He placed his cell phone back in his pocket and once again concentrated on the report before him.

Anthony looked at his watch—5:52 PM—as he stood near the front door and replied to the text message that had just come across the screen of his iPhone. Eric was in front of the house with the limousine. Just as Anthony was about to hit *SEND*, he heard a cough from the top of the stairs. Looking up, he saw Catherine whisper something into Claire's ear, just before Claire began to descend. He scanned her figure from head to toe. Anthony liked her hair style. It was up, with curls hanging down, accentuating her slender neck. The dress she wore looked like it had been made especially for her petite frame. He also saw her heels peeking out from the bottom of her skirt with each step. She definitely looked the part—a far cry from the woman in jeans and tennis shoes at the Red Wing, the one he'd seen a few months ago.

He had a fleeting thought about Claire's public behavior; however, as he watched his acquisition gracefully approach, his concern evaporated into an aura that had enveloped the foyer. It felt nothing like the women who usually accompanied him. They had a confidence—no, arrogance—that surrounded them like a cloud of perfume. Claire's semblance was different. She had to know how beautiful she looked, yet he saw the question in her eyes. He'd seen it before. Claire wasn't contemplating her escape; she was seeking his approval.

A split second before his words of approval left his lips, he saw Catherine. After their discussion earlier, he questioned whether she would do her part to make this happen. Anthony turned from Claire and with a satisfied grin, bowed toward Catherine. "My dear Catherine, you've outdone yourself. You're an artist."

He saw the smirk in her eyes. Oh, if they were alone, he was sure Catherine would let him know exactly what she'd done to prepare Claire, not to mention what she thought of this outing; instead, she replied, "Mr. Rawlings, an artist is only as good as her canvas. You're accompanying a beautiful canvas."

"Or, should we say," he smirked, "she's accompanying me?" Turning back to Claire, he said, "We must go; Eric's waiting."

Claire didn't respond other than to nod. When Anthony offered his arm, she dutifully placed her small hand appropriately and walked with him to the limousine. Eric stood ready and opened their door. As they neared, Claire hesitated. *What was she thinking?* Many times her feelings were transparent; however, when he looked down at her, dressed, styled, and painted to perfection, he found it intriguing that he couldn't read her thoughts. Anthony motioned toward the open door, and once again, Claire nodded and eased herself inside.

After the car began moving, Anthony asked, "Have you ever ridden in a limousine before?" He knew the truth; she'd been in a limousine in Atlanta, as well as in Iowa. Anthony doubted she remembered either of those times—just as well.

"No, I haven't." She turned back toward him. "Anthony?"

Before she could continue, his phone vibrated. He held up a finger and she pressed her lips together. The call was from Tom, a friend as well as one of his legal staff. Before long, Anthony was in a full-out discussion about a company in Rhode Island. Thankfully, he could access some of the documents from his iPad. It wasn't until he sensed the car slow and turn, that he even realized how close they were or how much time had passed. If this had been a date, he never would have gotten so much accomplished. Smiling at his productivity, Anthony turned off his iPad, put his phone away, and turned toward Claire. "Has Catherine prepared your behavior for this evening as well as she has your appearance?"

Her eyes widened as she turned from the window to face him. "She's given me her advice," Claire answered. "But I'd feel better if I heard yours."

He liked her respectful tone. "Very well, when we arrive there'll probably be photographers. Don't act surprised or shocked by the attention. Just flash a beautiful smile and radiate confidence. Stay next to me at all times. There'll be reporters who'll try to learn your identity. I have a publicist who'll know the time to release any necessary information. That is *not* you. I'll do most of the talking; however, common sense will need to be with you. If spoken to, you will respond, but do *not* share information that is privileged. Do you understand?"

"I do."

"I've been asked to attend this event because of a donation I made to the Quad City Symphony and the Support the Arts Foundation. Have you ever been to a symphony before?"

"No."

"The symphony is a delightful evening. I believe you'll enjoy the music. This conductor is incredibly talented."

"Thank you, Anthony, for allowing me to join you this evening."

"I admit you've learned your lessons well. Now it's time to see if you can continue to follow the rules outside the boundaries of my estate."

"I'll do my best."

Anthony reached for Claire's chin, turned it toward him, and slowed his words. "You *will* succeed. Failure in a public setting is not an option."

He locked his eyes on hers and waited for an appropriate response. It didn't take long. "Yes, Anthony. I will continue to follow your rules."

"I assume you're currently following *all* of my rules?" He lifted a brow.

Claire nodded as her cheeks flushed.

"We can investigate that later," Anthony taunted as he placed his hand on her thigh.

When he moved his hand upward, she whispered, "I am."

He already knew the answer. First, she didn't own any panties, and as he helped her into the car, he'd allowed his hand to graze her firm behind. If there'd been anything under the beaded fabric, he would've known. He only mentioned his rule as a reminder of his authority. Anthony knew from Catherine that his forbiddance of undergarments continued to make Claire uncomfortable. He wanted Claire to remember as she interacted with strangers that he controlled everything. There was nothing he couldn't do to her, or make her do. Exposing her in public with absolutely nothing under her expensive dress reinforced his stance.

When the car slowed and stopped, Anthony whispered, "Wait for Eric. He'll open the door and assist you in getting out. I'll be right behind you, and we'll enter the theater together."

As he glanced out the limousine's window, Anthony realized that he'd underestimated the importance of this event. It may be only Davenport, Iowa, but the sidewalk was roped off and cluttered with reporters. If Claire chose to stand before them and make a public announcement about kidnapping, even he might not be able to manage damage control.

Although he was glad that he'd just reminded Claire of his rules, he worried if it had been enough. He didn't have time to discuss the consequences of failure. As soon as they were out of the car, Anthony put his hand in the small of her back and directed her away from the reporters. The contact served as her reminder—her warning. By the time they reached the second level and cocktails, people were coming from every direction.

It was as he handed Claire a glass of champagne that his anxiety began to wane. He saw in her eyes—those green eyes—her unfulfilled need for his approval. This time, he smiled and whispered in her ear, "You are truly lovely tonight." Instantaneously, he knew that Claire wouldn't disappoint him. She wouldn't escape or make a public announcement. It wasn't her words; she hadn't spoken. It was her countenance—he just knew. Each time he introduced her or she spoke, she impressed him with her performance. When the lights flashed, he guided her to their private box. It was a place where he'd sat many times—just a box; nonetheless, Claire scanned the auditorium like a child surveying the tree on Christmas morning.

He reminded himself that she hadn't seen anything, other than his estate, in over two months.

Before he could process her behavior and allow the relief of her compliance to truly settle in, the auditorium darkened, and the curator began to speak—it was about him. Suddenly, the spotlight hit their box, and Anthony did what he'd always done—appeared the perfect gentleman. The entire time he smiled and waved, he imagined the possibility of Claire jumping up and running for the hills. As he sat back down, her expression was unexpectedly pleasant. He leaned over and gently took her hand. Quite honestly, there wasn't anything he couldn't or hadn't taken from her. She belonged to him—all of her. They had a contract. He reached for her hand for one reason. It was an unspoken warning, just as when he touched the small of her back. The contact was his silent reminder to follow his rules.

When the last song ended and the conductor faced the crowd, Anthony looked toward his acquisition. The evening had gone even better than he imagined. His mind swirled with the possibilities of future events. It would be a relief to not have to deal with other women and their baggage. With this arrangement, he could do anything he wanted and, apparently, still be accompanied by the perfect companion. When Claire whispered her gratitude in his ear, Anthony knew she deserved something for her behavior—a positive consequence.

In the limousine, he watched as she fidgeted near the window. The confidence from the theater seemed to dissipate into the cool evening air. Before he could give it much more thought, she turned toward him. Her voice filled the quiet cabin. "That was a magnificent evening. Thank you, again."

Her sudden surge of straightforwardness caught him by surprise. "Do you really think so?"

"I do. The music was performed beautifully, and you were right about the conductor." After a pause, she asked, "Did I do all right?"

"What do you think?" he taunted.

After a moment, she replied, "I think I did well. I listened to Catherine, and to you, and d-did well."

It wasn't that he didn't enjoy the trepidation in her voice; however, if she were to accompany him on future outings, positive reinforcement was in order. He was prepared. Anthony reached into his briefcase and found the black velvet box. He didn't know that Claire would be accompanying him until this afternoon and didn't have time to buy anything; then he remembered the old necklace he'd found in her apartment. While he was home, he put it in his briefcase in anticipation of just such an occasion.

Extending the box toward her, he softened his tone. "I believe you did well. I've told you that every action has a consequence. That can be negative—as we've seen—or positive. I believe that tonight you earned a positive consequence."

"Anthony, I don't need a gift. I wanted to make you proud. If I did that, then I'm happy and that's enough."

"It's a gift, or at least I believe it was; however, it's not new." He continued to hold the box in her direction. Her tentative response caused his cheeks to rise. She was so unlike the other women he'd dated. Curiously, he asked, "Will it always be this difficult to get you to open gifts?"

She took the box. "You have my curiosity piqued. What are you giving me that's old?"

Before he could answer, she lifted the lid. When she looked up, tears silently glided down her cheeks. He'd seen her cry before—this was different. He listened as she choked back her emotion. "H-how did you ... where did you get this? It was my grandmother's."

"It was in your apartment in Atlanta when it was cleaned out. I thought you might want to have it. Do you?" He watched as Claire internalized his words. In essence, he'd just told her that her old life was now cleaned out, disposed of—gone. She hadn't asked, and he hadn't informed her, but now it was confirmed. Anthony waited for her to respond.

"Oh, yes, I do!"

Her concentration on the necklace and acceptance of her apartment's fate satisfied him more than he'd expected. It confirmed that the *old* Claire Nichols was ceasing to exist, and with each passing day, the woman before him was new and created solely for his liking. His cheeks rose with the unexpected wave of relief. Eagerly, he asked, "Would you like me to help you put it on?"

Claire nodded and turned away as he draped the delicate chain around her neck. Past experience confirmed that the woman he initially acquired from Atlanta would've dwelled on her loss and become emotionally distraught. Claire's steadily improving behavior filled Anthony with pride. He'd done this! There wasn't a challenge that Anthony Rawlings couldn't overcome. Perhaps some of the credit should go to Catherine. Either way, he was enjoying the benefits of *their* dedication to their project.

As he fastened the clasp and the tips of his fingers touched her warm skin, Anthony remembered why he liked Claire's hair styled up. He leaned nearer to taste her exposed neck, but before his lips contacted her skin, she bent forward and pulled a small compact from her purse. A reprimand was on the tip of his tongue, when he realized that she hadn't moved away from him. She was still too wrapped up in the necklace to sense his intentions.

Her gaze flitted from the small mirror to him, as she said, "Anthony, there isn't a necklace you could've bought that would mean more to me than this one."

He'd seen many emotions in her emerald eyes, but what he saw at that moment gave him an unexplained sense of contentment. Anthony's thumb gently brushed her cheek, confirming that her tears from earlier were dry, unexpectedly her lids fluttered, and she moved toward his touch. Anthony knew that many times her words were false. He didn't consider it deception, but rather obedience. She said what she was expected to say and did what she was expected to do. There were also times when her expression failed to hide her trepidation, and he saw her true exposed reaction. This moment was different—real, not contrived—but honestly pleasant. He'd planned to give her the necklace as a reward, if she performed well; however, what he said next hadn't been planned. "People who know me well, and they're numbered, call me Tony. You may call me *Tony*."

"Thank you, *Tony*," she replied. "This has been an amazing night. How can I ever thank you?"

He pulled her close, feeling the pressure of her breasts against his chest. Turning off the riding lights, he smiled a devilish grin. "I have a few ideas."

Claire's glance darted toward the dark glass partition separating the back from the front of the car.

Tony laughed. "I promise we're alone; Eric can't see or hear us." He leaned toward her. She instinctively reached for his neck and settled onto the long leather seat. As he hovered mere inches above, he watched her cheeks flush, and his erection came to life. Over the past few months, Claire had learned to respond to Tony's commands—both verbal and otherwise. There'd been times when she'd hesitated. It was on those occasions that she earned the punishment she deserved. Turning his tone more serious, he raised a brow and demanded, "Now, show me that you've followed my rules. I want to see."

Claire's immediate response fortified the pride of his accomplishment. She maintained their gaze as her small hand fumbled for the hem of her dress. "I can't reach—"

Tony wouldn't let her finish—he couldn't. He needed to taste her. Entwining his fingers in her loose ringlets of hair, he tilted her lips upward and heard a small moan before his mouth seized hers. Unable to soften his approach, he took what was his. It wasn't enough—he wanted more. When his tongue probed, her lips parted, allowing him to enter her warmth. Tony savored her sweetness as her arms once again encircled his neck. With his other hand, he reached for the hem of her dress and the cabin filled with her whimpers of anticipation.

He slowly lifted the beaded material and teasingly brushed her inner thigh. "Open your legs for me," he commanded.

She obeyed and he continued to caress her soft skin. When her breathing labored and he neared his destination, Tony stopped. Releasing her hair, he sat up and gazed down at her blushed cheeks, smudged lipstick, and nearly exposed body. Grinning, he murmured, "You were amazing tonight."

Softly, she replied, "Thank you."

Taking her in, he reminded her. "But the night isn't over." His playful tone vanished. "Now, lift your dress and let me see if you have truly behaved."

Slowly reaching for the length of material, Claire kept her eyes fixed on his. As the material rose, she replied, "I promise, Tony. I've followed your rules."

He couldn't help but think how beautiful she looked—offering herself to him. That, combined with the sound of her calling him by his personal name, was enough to release the painful tightness in his slacks. It seemed unreal that he could be on the verge of exploding, and she'd yet to touch him. Surprisingly, at that moment, that wasn't what he wanted. He yearned for something else, and they both knew his desires came first.

Taking off his jacket and then his tie, Tony continued to devour Claire with his intensifying gaze. He couldn't look away as she silently watched his every move. When he slowly and deliberately moved to his knees and grinned, he sensed her relief. It intoxicated him that something as insignificant as a change in his facial expression could influence her world. Beckoned by her scent, his sultry tone returned. "Yes, I would say you have been a very good girl."

He lifted each one of her soft, smooth calves, savoring their shape while in the high heels, and rested them on his broad shoulders. With his intentions clear, Claire tipped her head back against the leather seat. Soon, her moans from earlier returned and grew louder. When her fingers gripped the leather seat, and he knew that she was about there, he stopped. It was his private game, but she was learning the rules.

"Tell me," he commanded.

"Anth—Tony, please."

"Tell me who you belong to."

"You, I belong to you." She fidgeted against the leather.

"Because," he prompted.

"You own me."

"Until?" He taunted her, teasing, kissing, and suckling her inner thigh.

"Please!" She took in a deep breath. "Until you decide."

"Say it."

"You own me until you decide."

"Good girl. Perhaps—" he reached for her skirt, bunched around her waist.

"Please," she begged, holding tightly to the material. "Please, don't stop."

Grinning and satisfied, Tony resumed his quest. Oh, there were times he'd leave her like this—unsatisfied—and make her switch places. It would be then that she would fulfill her duty. Of course, she didn't have the option to stop or taunt. Other times, he'd take the conversation further, making her tell him the amount of money he'd spent to secure her financial freedom.

Not tonight. Tonight Tony wanted to experience the benefits of her positive consequence. It didn't take long before he did.

Three

Passing and failing, both have Consequences – July 2010
(Consequences – Chapter 9)

Failure is no more a permanent condition than success!
For even if you succeed, there's still another test.
– Gene Bedley

As Eric approached the house, Tony took in the dark windows and glanced at the corner of his iPhone—after 10:00 PM. Since Claire's windows faced toward the backyard and woods, he couldn't see them or her balcony. He could imagine them and her suite ... and her in her suite, with no other purpose than to wait for him. It was a thought that seemed to be recurring more and more often, slipping unexpectedly into his consciousness. *Why not?* She was in his house solely for his pleasure and enjoyment, and after the day and evening he'd just had, he deserved some *him* time.

After three months, he admitted—at least to himself—that this arrangement was working better than he ever predicted. Each test he presented, or that presented itself, solidified his control and power over Claire's life. He controlled everything about her—almost. Tony had allowed Catherine to share in his power, to a point. He set boundaries and Catherine adhered to them. She couldn't overturn any of his decisions. Tony didn't want Claire to think she could pit one of them against the other. Besides, Catherine's reign dealt with mundane day-to-day issues—clothing and schedules. Tony controlled the more important matters, and of course, if he decided to trump Catherine's plans for a day, he did.

That would happen on days that Tony decided to work from home. He'd made it clear that when he was home, Claire was to be available to him at all times. On those days, he'd not only trump Catherine's plans, but Claire's too.

From the first time he'd allowed Claire access to the grounds of the estate, Tony saw how much she enjoyed that little liberty. Without saying it, she savored those outings as her own personal escape. The fact that she willingly and of her own accord returned to the house at her appointed time, appeased his sense of control, enticing him to allow that privilege to continue.

Each morning Claire followed a routine that included swimming and weights. Tony enjoyed the benefits of her workout and had no desire to stop that activity; however, by 10:00 AM on the days that he worked from home, her plans no longer mattered. She was expected to be in his office. Sometimes he'd acknowledge her presence; other times he'd be preoccupied. It didn't matter. On those days, her time, her schedule, and her body were at his disposal. He found it as intoxicating to make her sit and waste her day as it was to use her services. One of the best aphrodisiacs he knew was looking up from his computer or watching during a telephone call as Claire looked longingly out the window. Hell—he'd even find himself imagining that scene while in his corporate office.

As he walked through the dimly lit hallway toward his office, his anticipation grew. The day had been long. There was no better word. It wasn't bad or upsetting; it wasn't good or rewarding—it was *long*. Not only were there multiple big deals and negotiations in the works, Tony had to spend the evening at a dinner meeting that turned into a few drinks and more negotiations. Public outings weren't his thing.

Fundraisers and social functions that could double as tests were increasingly more fun. Being a multi-tasker extraordinaire, Tony could shake hands, carry on a conversation, and monitor Claire's every move. That said, his preferred evening destination was more intimate, and lately had become even more inviting. At the end of a long day, he wanted to be behind the iron gates of his estate.

Inside the top side drawer of his desk, Tony found Claire's driver's license. For a long time it had been stashed away with other items from her apartment, but just like her grandmother's necklace, it was time to present Claire with a new gift. A grin came to his lips as he considered the small card; it would have a companion, or should he say, a tool for a test. The companion card arrived to his office earlier in the week. It was an *American Express* platinum card with Claire's name embossed upon the front. He planned to tell her that it was her reward for her recent public behavior—that wouldn't be a total fabrication. The way she handled the reporter recently was stellar; she'd been presented with an opportunity to reveal her true status and chose instead to abide by his rules. Nonetheless, providing her limited access to a credit card and her driver's license had other benefits. Over the last two months, she'd been seen with him on multiple occasions; he needed a cover story. If she ever attempted to reveal the truth, he needed something to make her accusations seem implausible. *What better cover than his money?* He'd taken away her debt—he could prove that. With her new credit card, she wouldn't only be seen as his *companion*, but as a woman spending *his* money. No one would believe that she wasn't enjoying his fortune of her own free will.

When he first brought Claire to Iowa, he wasn't sure how involved the plan would become. Each day presented additional choices and decisions. Thus far, in his opinion, Tony had developed the perfect plan—one that continued to weave fresh possibilities. As each new thread was revealed and sewn into place, Tony's omnipotence grew. There wasn't an angle he hadn't considered.

He placed her driver's license and the credit card into a small, feminine leather wallet, flung his jacket on the desk chair, and headed toward Claire's suite. The summer heat was sweltering, and the loss of one layer of clothing felt liberating as he briskly walked up the backstairs. Mindlessly, he imagined that in a very short time he'd be losing more layers. It was a scenario that had been playing in his head over and over throughout the god-awful dinner meeting. Grinning, he wondered if that was what had kept him from going off and telling his dinner guests what he really thought of their ideas.

Often, when he first got home, Tony would go to his suite or office and relax before joining Claire. On those days, he turned on the feed to her suite and watched as she prepared for his arrival. Tonight, it was too late for him to check the video feed, and honestly, he was too anxious to use her and forget his long day. It didn't matter. Her behavior had become re-assuringly predictable.

In stunned disbelief, Tony opened Claire's door to an empty suite. He walked to the closet/dressing room and then to the bathroom. With each unoccupied space, his sense of gratitude for her recent obedience swiftly morphed into a combination of alert and anger. *Where the hell was she? Why wasn't she where she was supposed to be?*

Throwing the wallet—the reward he'd meant to present to her—onto her table, he stormed out of her suite. When he reached the bottom of the stairs, he called out for Catherine. She'd better damn well know Claire's whereabouts. As he turned the corner, the glow of the pool's colored lights illuminated the windows at the back of the sunporch. The movement of the water caught his attention. He'd found Claire.

He stood unseen within the darkened room and watched her every move. It was like his hidden cameras, but somehow more intimate. Claire moved slowly, floating on her back and staring up to the sky. It wasn't that he gave his acquisition much thought; however, there were times that it amazed him that Claire could find pleasure in the most mundane of activities.

As he watched, his thoughts of anger and betrayal returned. She was outside enjoying a swim, when she was supposed to be available to him! She had the whole damn day to do whatever she wanted. Disappointment and fury overcame him. Perhaps he was wrong to present her with a new freedom. After all, he'd thought they were past reinforcing the most basic of his rules.

Cloaked in the shadow of the night, he stepped from the house and approached the pool. Within seconds his linen shirt dampened and clung to his back. Each step away from the air conditioning reminded him of the oppressive summer heat. Even in the darkness, he felt the heat of the day's intense sun roll off the concrete deck. His voice boomed over the hum of the pool's filter and the distant call of country crickets. "Claire, what in the hell are you doing?"

She didn't move as she blissfully floated, staring upward. Momentarily, Tony followed her gaze. It was a sky and there were stars. He saw no reason for her to give it her full attention. "Claire, get out of the damn water!"

Each insubordination added fuel to his nearly combustible disposition. Walking out of the shadows to the edge of the pool, he saw how the brightly illuminated water ebbed and flowed over Claire's flat stomach and her bathing-suit-clad breasts moved with her steady breathing. Her hair floated in a halo around her face, and the streaks of blonde that infiltrated her chestnut hair reflected the fountain's colorful display. She wasn't watching the stars: her eyes were closed. His volume decreased, but his tone remained determined. "Claire, you know better. You know my rules. You're supposed to be in your suite."

It was then her eyes sprang wide and she righted herself, beginning to tread water and twist her head from side to side. "Tony, you startled me. Catherine said you wouldn't be home until late."

He stared at her for a moment, waiting—he wasn't sure for what, perhaps an apology, perhaps an explanation. She continued to tread water as she looked up at him with her damn green eyes. It wasn't his plan for the evening, but as the perspiration dripped from his shoulder blades to the middle of his back, Tony knew what he wanted.

Without speaking, he stepped back into the darkness and ridded himself of his encumbering clothing. With each article removed, he felt the weight of the day lift, as oppression transformed into a newfound source of energy. His goal for the night—his chosen activity—hadn't changed. Tony knew what he wanted, and without question, it would be his. The destination of his conquest was truly insignificant, and besides, the water looked increasingly inviting. Moments later he dove into the colorful liquid and seized the object of his quest.

He didn't need to ask permission or engage in customary expected conversation. She was his for the taking. When he surfaced mere inches away, he wrapped his arms around her body, and Claire gasped. Her soft, cool skin did nothing to cool his desire. Turning her to face him, his mouth emphasized his claim while his skillful fingers removed the top of her bathing suit. A simple pull of two strings and her round supple breasts were his for the taking.

The pressures of the day and the disappointment of her empty suite erupted in a force of energy he had no wish to control. As her hard nipples pressed against his chest and their tongues united, his anger waned. The fury that had been building found a new outlet. Walking toward the deep end of the pool, he tugged at the strings on the side of her bathing suit bottom and it too floated to the depths.

Lifting Claire momentarily away, his eyes scanned up and down her newly exposed flesh. Dutifully, her gaze met his. Releasing his hold, her small hands reached for his shoulders. It may have been due to the depth of the water, but that was not what Tony chose to believe. In his mind, it was her silent way of accepting what he had to offer. As she wrapped her legs around his torso, he fought the urge to take her right then. He could do whatever he desired, but rushing was not his plan.

When his mouth once again found her breasts, his teeth nipped at the hard nubs, and his fingers explored and caressed. Her wordless moans encouraged, and despite the coolness of the water, when Claire's back arched, allowing him better access, his body responded.

No longer was he thinking about his day at work or his dinner meeting. Even memories of Claire's empty suite were lost to their new world. No one else existed within their colorful abyss. He nipped and taunted, cheered on by Claire's wordless sounds. He watched as her beautiful body stiffened and convulsed within his hold. By the time she fell slack against his shoulder, tried to steady her breathing, and held tightly to his neck, Tony knew what he wanted next. Carrying her to the steps, he helped her from the pool. She took his hand and followed him on wobbly legs to one of the large cushioned lounge chairs hidden in the shadows. Even in the darkness, he watched as her eyes fluttered and her body accepted him without question. He didn't need to verbally direct her movements. A simple touch and she responded to his desire.

With their bodies damp and their breath resuming normal inhales and exhales, Tony grinned. He watched the clouds of uncertainty dissipate from her emerald eyes as they glistened with the reflection of the pool's fountains. "Good evening, Claire." Her responding smile quickly faded when he added, "I wasn't happy when you weren't in your suite." He touched her lips, stopping whatever it was that she was about to say, and continued, "But your idea of a swim on this hot evening was much better than what I had planned." As the words left his lips, Tony felt her body relax and watched her smile return.

Allowing his own grin to emerge, Tony asked, "Maybe we should go back into the water to cool off again?"

"That sounds nice," she agreed, as she willingly placed her small hand in his, and followed him back into the pool.

By the time they'd returned to Claire's suite and showered, Tony remembered his gift. The sight of her walking toward her side of the bed, wrapped in only a black silk robe almost pushed the conversation from his thoughts; however, he was interested in her reaction. He recognized that the best weapon in his arsenal that had worked to keep her compliant was her seclusion. Even with the vast expanse of his estate, she had limited personal interaction. Tony wasn't sure if she had truly accepted her fate, or if she were just so lonely that she would settle for his presence. Either way, it was obvious that Claire craved interaction. Whenever he presented the opportunity, she could talk for hours. Sometimes she spoke about her family or her previous life, but mostly it was about books or movies or nothing at all. During those times, it was as if a day's or a week's worth of conversation had been backlogged and suddenly released. He didn't mind. Actually, Tony learned a lot about Claire Nichols during those times.

As Claire was about to untie her robe, Tony pulled back the covers and patted the bed at his side. On most nights, Claire would lie down and silently wait for him to come to her. Her eyes darted to his, searching for the reason for his invitation. He smiled in response.

When she secured the silk, sat on the bed, and turned toward him, he purposely lowered his brow and shook his head. "No, Claire, the robe needs to go." With as many times as he'd seen her nude, it amazed him that she still held an air of modesty. He liked to push her to the edge of her comfort zone. Oh, who was he kidding? He liked to take her *out* of that zone. Watching her silent battle of wills, as she fought with what he told her to do and what she wanted or felt was proper, was addicting. He could do it all day.

After removing the robe, she worked her way across the expanse of the large mattress. He reached out and brushed a damp lock of hair from her face. Even without makeup, her eyes were stunning. They spoke to him in ways her lips would not. He knew her question before she asked; nevertheless, he waited for her to speak. "Why do you want me over here?" He enjoyed her directness. God knew, his request could be anything.

"I wanted to talk."

Her eyes lit as if someone had hit a switch. "Really?"

He smiled as he motioned for her to sit next to him. With her tucked against his shoulder, he allowed his fingertips to caress the softness of her shoulder.

Finally, she asked, "What do you want to talk about?"

"Your behavior." Her muscles went rigid. Tony lowered his tenor and commanded, "Claire, look at me." Her eyes slowly moved to his. Grinning at her obvious trepidation, he reassured. "Your behavior has been very good, and I believe you deserve a reward."

"Tony, I—"

"I'm specifically referencing the University of Iowa's Children's Hospital event."

Claire exhaled, her tension dissipated, and her body molded against the pillow. Tony marveled at how her warm, small frame fit perfectly under the crook of his arm. As she spoke, the sound of relief filled her voice. It seemed that as of late, she'd learned to control her words, especially when she was apprehensive or concerned; however, when she was comfortable, she spoke more freely. Surprisingly, he found that equally as rewarding. After all, with whom else did she have to talk? It was another of her needs that only he could fill. She rambled on. "I was so afraid. I was afraid that he'd get me to say something or misinterpret something that I said. I didn't want to interrupt you, but I didn't know what else to do. I—"

Shifting, she stopped talking and he felt the sensation of her warmth as their skin united. Nearing his lips toward hers, he reassured, "That was perfect." Softness filled the emerald shining back at him. Though his tone was soft, a certain part of his body was becoming painfully hard. "I have rules, Claire. Sometimes I need to be assured of your dedication to your job. To do that, I've presented you with tests, and there will be more in the future. Sometimes you'll pass those tests; sometimes you won't. What happens if you don't?"

"There will be consequences."

He grinned. "And what happens if you pass?"

Her expression brightened. "There will be consequences—good ones."

"Very good." His fingertips slowly traced an invisible track from her ear, down her neck, over her shoulder, down the curve of her breast, to her stomach, and back up the other side. With each pass, the track dipped lower and lower. A hint of sultriness entered his authoritative tone. "When we're out in public, your behavior is a reflection of me. How do I feel about public failure?"

Her hips lifted toward his touch, yet she obediently responded. "You … don't like it."

"I don't." He nibbled her neck. "If that would happen, I'd be disappointed." He reached for her chin. "Claire, do you want to disappoint me?"

"No …" Her legs opened, accommodating, allowing, and inviting his actions.

Tony couldn't continue this conversation much longer. "Open your eyes." She obeyed. "You should know, that reporter wasn't a planned test." She nodded. "But if it had been, you would have passed. That's why I believe you've earned the right to have more responsibilities and independence." He had her full attention. "On your table is a wallet. Inside that wallet you'll find your driver's license and a credit card. They're for you to use when I'm not around."

The sudden shock at his gift was evident. "What do you mean, when you aren't around?"

He chuckled. "No, Claire, I'm not setting you free; you have more debt to pay and you need my guidance. You've learned so much in this short time, and you have much more to learn. You won't leave the grounds alone. If you aren't with me, you'll be with Eric, and even then, it'll only be with my permission, but I need to travel to Europe for at least a week next month." He grinned. "You've behaved well." The track he'd been tracing suddenly extended over her buttocks and thigh. "Very well, and you've followed my instructions much better than I would've given you credit for a few months ago." His hands roamed. Claire's eyes closed and she willingly responded to his slightest inclination. "As a matter of fact …" His tone became playful. "… I believe that right now you would do as I say."

Her lids opened, veiling her eyes with her lashes. "I would," she purred.

Tony wondered if Claire knew how totally erotic her accommodating tone was to him. Was it real, or was she performing for her job? He didn't know. He did know that he had needs and desires, and if she was in this accommodating of a mood, the instructions were on the tip of his tongue. Grinning, he said, "I think we should continue to test that theory, but first, I believe you've earned the ability to do some shopping for yourself."

For a moment she seemed lost in thought.

"Claire?" Her gaze focused. "Let's see how well you can do with instructions tonight."

Shall we go to the movies? – August 2010
(Consequences – Chapter 11)

Everyone can be manipulated.
It's most successful by people who're closest to you.
– Aleatha Romig, *Convicted*

Tony looked up from his tablet and peered toward Claire as the car in which they rode wound around the twists and turns of the country roads near his estate. She was staring out the window, quieter than normal. Tony figured that the reason was his preoccupation with his work. Since they'd touched down from New York, he'd been busy with the onslaught of emails, and she knew better than to interrupt him when he was working. Sneaking another glance, he tried unsuccessfully to read her thoughts or decipher her mood. It was something that he didn't particularly like; he owned her—all of her, including her thoughts. Most of the time, his acquisition was an open book. The fact that she could, at times, successfully hide or mask her true emotions irritated him. Usually, he could look at her and intuitively know exactly what she wanted or needed. Her eyes were the key. Sometimes they held a fire of confrontation even when her lips spoke obediently. It was quite the sight to witness, her battling with herself. Tony found her internal struggle very entertaining; however, what he currently witnessed was a newer phenomenon. Claire's expression, including her eyes, was of complete contentment—no, perhaps, indifference. There was something about her body language that didn't match.

Maybe he'd pushed too far during his celebration yesterday? He remembered going back to his New York apartment and finding her asleep on his bed. He hadn't intended for the afternoon and evening to go as it had, but one thing led to another. Besides, it didn't matter. He had the right to push as hard and as far as he wanted. Claire had a job to do, a role to play, and her satisfaction with her job was inconsequential. She would do what was required of her, or she'd face the consequences. Perhaps that was what she was thinking about as they approached his estate—how her life was truly out of her hands, in every way. Oh, if only he could confirm that. It would please him to no end, to know that she had finally succumbed completely to his obvious authority.

Exhaling, he realized he'd lost interest in the information on the screen of his iPad. Closing his eyes, he defined the woman next to him. She was his acquisition, *his prisoner*—a sacrificial lamb for the sins of her forefathers. She was his; he needn't concern himself with worries over her emotional well-being. After all, her physical needs were more than being met. He'd spent a fortune to rid her of debt. She lived on a multi-million-dollar estate, and her clothes, as well as food, were amply supplied. She also had an active sex life. While pleasing her wasn't his top concern, she obviously enjoyed herself quite a bit of the time.

Tony worked to push his thoughts away. He had a lot to accomplish before he left for Europe, and truly, Claire Nichols' happiness, or lack thereof, needn't clutter his radar. As they neared the estate, he remembered his last conversation with Catherine. He knew that she didn't mean her comments the other morning. After all, she'd apologized for them. Glancing again at Claire, he questioned if his behavior yesterday afternoon and night was incited by that conversation. He tried to deny it, but Catherine's concerns ate at him. Even now he was thinking about that conversation:

At a little after 3:30 AM, there was no need for formalities. Catherine didn't knock or address him with any sort of conventionality as she opened the door to his office, secured her bathrobe, and began speaking, "Just because you can't sleep, doesn't mean that I don't. Tell me why on earth you summoned me here at this ungodly hour. Besides, don't you need to leave for New York this morning?"

"Good morning, to you, too. I will be leaving in a few hours, and I woke you because I'm taking Claire. You need to pack her things."

Catherine shook her head. "You're what? Have you lost your mind?"

"I'm taking Claire with me to New York, and I believe that perhaps it's you who's delusional. This early hour has taken your candidness to the extreme. Do you have a problem with my decision?"

Catherine sat on one of the chairs by his desk and shook her head from side to side. "First, you start sleeping in her suite. Then, you take her out on public appearances. Now, you're going to take her to New York? They're already speculating about the two of you in the press. Are you trying to put her in the spotlight?"

Tony shrugged his shoulders as a faint grin emerged.

Catherine cocked a brow. "Explain yourself. Tell me, are you falling for her?"

"No. How about you? Is she fulfilling some unmet motherly need?"

Catherine suddenly stood and the chair where she'd been sitting pushed against the wall. Her gray eyes glared in response. "Anton, that isn't even possible. You know I don't want to discuss that."

"Fine," he agreed. "I won't make assumptions about your motives, if you don't make assumptions about mine."

"My motives. My motives!" Her volume increased. "I'll tell you my motives. They're to keep the two of us out of jail. I mean, seriously, if you'd stayed with the plan, the one we've had for a long time—if you'd stuck to that, there would be no witnesses, no connections, and we'd be safe. This—" she waved her hands toward the ceiling, "—was not our plan, and now you want to make her even more publicly visible?"

"My dear Catherine Marie ..." he said, using her middle name was his way of calming her. She no longer used the name Marie, yet it reminded them both of his grandfather and, therefore, usually helped to soothe her temper. "... it's all about appearances. I'll admit that I've been spending most of my nights in her bed." He leaned forward. "If you were in my shoes, or out of them, I believe you'd do the same. It has more benefits than sleeping alone. Besides, technically, it's my bed, in my house, on my estate, and I can sleep anywhere I damn well please."

"I believe you're putting too much emphasis on those benefits. They're affecting your thinking."

He chuckled. *"You see, that's where you're wrong. I know exactly what I'm doing. I've taken her out in public. She's been seen with me. While we're in New York, I've told her that she'll shop."*

Catherine resumed her seat. *"Shop? So you want her to be visible?"* She sat for a moment and contemplated. *"Do you believe she'll be noticed? I'm not sure that the press will recognize her. Not without you, I mean."*

"Maybe not, but Eric will. He'll get pictures." Tony's grin grew. *"I consider it part of our insurance policy."*

"She'll need to spend more money than she did last time. If you want to convince the world she's after your money, she'll need to buy more than a few blouses and a book."

"I'll emphasize that in my directive." He leaned back. *"Faith, Marie, have faith."*

"All right, since you've already put her out there, the more insurance the better. I just think it would've been better to not have had her out in public with you in the first place." She stood and walked toward the door. *"I think it would've been better to stick with the original plan."*

"She's not on a vacation," Tony reminded in a low, yet direct tone.

"Really?" Catherine turned toward him. *"She dresses in the best clothing, she doesn't lift a finger, and now she's traveling. So she's satisfying your needs. I don't think she hates that—anymore."*

He smirked. *"Are you surprised? For your information, I could provide a long list of references who ... don't hate it."*

"Do I really care? No, I don't. I'm concerned."

"That?"

"That you're letting down your guard. I mean, who's really in control? How much is you, and how much is her manipulating you? You're a man. Men ... well, men forget sometimes what part of their body should do the thinking." She softened her tone. *"Anton, I don't want you to be swayed."*

As Catherine went on about her concern, Tony remembered the night before in Claire's suite. It was the first time she'd willingly offered herself to him—and he allowed it. He didn't direct her movements or give instruc-

tions. He'd allowed her to seduce him, and now he's taking her to New York. Could Catherine be right?

When Catherine quieted, Tony replied, sounding more confident than he truly felt. "That's ridiculous. I didn't wake you for a debate. I woke you so that you could do what you do, and have her ready to board my plane by 6:00 AM. Do you think you can do that? Do you think you can do your part of this project?"

"Yes." Her neck stiffened. "I can do that." She rubbed her hands over the softness of her robe. "I'm sorry. You're right. I'm sure Claire Nichols isn't manipulating you. You're in much more control than that. I know you wouldn't want to disappoint Nathaniel that way. Besides, it sounds like this public appearance thing is well planned and thought out."

Tony nodded as Catherine disappeared around the partially open door.

So what? He liked sleeping in Claire's bed? That wasn't Claire's manipulation; it was *his* domination. He could wake her at any hour and expect complete compliance. Those were his thoughts as they passed through his gates and he placed his tablet in his briefcase. Moments later Claire's words refocused his attention.

"Tony, you said you built your house about fifteen years ago?"

"Yes, why do you ask?"

She continued to gaze toward the house. "I'm not used to seeing it from the front—it's beautiful."

"Thank you." He looked out the window as Eric stopped the car. It *was* a beautiful structure, an architectural wonder.

Claire continued, "But it looks older than fifteen years to me—the style I mean."

He nodded. "I patterned it after my family's home from when I was a child." His thoughts went to Nathaniel. *He wasn't disappointing him; this house was a testament to that.*

As they both exited the car, Claire's eyes widened with wonder. It was as if she were seeing the house for the first time, not as if she'd been living there for months. "I thought you built your fortune from nothing. How did your parents have a house like this?"

He looked at the combination of rock and stone—memories of an earlier time threatened to come forward. He pushed them away. "It was my grandfather's, not my parents. My father was weak. However, my grandfather's house and money were all lost over twenty-five years ago. My grandfather trusted the wrong people." Tony wasn't sure what propelled him to share that bit of information. He'd blame it on his recent thoughts of Nathaniel. No matter, it was true, and there was no way Claire would know her connection—but he did. Walking toward his office, Claire followed a few steps behind. Her sudden acknowledgement of the place wherein she'd been living for so long was amusing.

"It truly is amazing," she said. "Did you pattern the inside after it, as well?"

He shrugged. "Mostly. I even found and purchased some of the original artwork and antiques; however, I wanted my home equipped with all the modern conveniences and security equipment. Every inch of this house is under constant surveillance. I won't make the same mistake my grandfather made." Tony looked up from his desk to a bewildered expression. Suddenly, her placid veneer was gone. The wheels of understanding were visibly turning in her head. Tony continued, "Haven't you ever wondered how the staff knows exactly when to enter your suite?"

Her voice quivered, "Y-you mean *my suite* is under surveillance? L-like there are cameras?"

Revulsion emanated from her pained expression. When their eyes met, his grin widened. "Yes, of course. It's all video-recorded and saved." Claire visibly paled as she backed toward the wall and sat on the nearest chair. Basking in her newfound discomfort, Tony added, "Perhaps we could have a premiere viewing and critique? Then we could work on revisions."

"Tony, please tell me you're joking, some sort of *sick* joke."

He felt his power and control return. It was as if he'd just received a transfusion of domination. Yes, yesterday and last night he'd taken her body, but he'd done that before. This was so much more—her mind and her spirit. This was what she'd successfully kept from him. He stood taller with the revelation: it was now his for the taking, or it soon would be.

"But, my dear Claire," he cooed with mock adoration, "I am *not*. Now, the staff doesn't have access to the view of your bed—only I have that. They do have a view of the sitting area and the doorways to and from your dressing room and bath. That's how they've been able to come and go without your seeing them."

Her eyes filled with tears as she asked, "But why? Why would you do that? Why would you keep it?"

"Because I can—I can watch and decide what I like and what I believe can be improved. You'll understand after you get a chance to view it. Maybe tonight, but now I must be going." As Tony started to walk toward the hall doors, Claire sat statuesque. He reiterated, "It's time to exit my office." When she still didn't move, he casually added, "and in case you're wondering, yes, this room, too, is under surveillance—except for my desk. I do have a great view of the sofa and this open area." He gestured toward the place where he'd administered her first lesson in *actions and consequences.*

While her sudden look of desperation inspired him, he needed to go into Iowa City. The work at his corporate office wouldn't wait. "Claire, I need to go. Get out of the chair now."

Apparently, she was still capable of obeying, as she silently walked past him toward the stairs. Closing the door to his office, he smirked. *Who's manipulating whom?* He couldn't wait for the viewing.

As Tony went about his business at his corporate office, his mind continually looped back to his video library—there were so many. Between phone calls, spreadsheets, and meetings, he debated about which would be best to show Claire. He knew that she didn't want to see them—or star in them—or acknowledge them. It was obvious by her reaction. Until she responded so vehemently, he had no idea she'd detest the idea that much, but once she did, he knew he'd found that missing piece of the puzzle. That made the viewing all that much more special. Now, as he departed for ten days in Europe, he could leave confident, knowing without a doubt that he was in control.

It was Tony's idea to eat on the patio. He called Catherine from the car and told her to have dinner served outside. He wanted the distractions of the outdoors. He hadn't been this excited about his plans for Claire in a while. That wasn't to say he didn't enjoy all of the uses he'd invented for her, but this was new. Concentrating on eating dinner in her suite or in the dining room with only the two of them would've been too difficult. The outdoor setting worked as a distraction—for him. Claire seemed to be another story. She wasn't her normal chatty self. She looked the part, dressed appropriately for dinner, nodded and responded at all the right times as Tony talked about New York, her shopping, his meetings, and his impending European trip, but her mind was obviously elsewhere. As much as he wanted to broach the subject of their movie night, he didn't, partially out of curiosity. He wondered if she would bring it up. There were times when she surprised him by jumping headfirst into conversations he was confident that she'd rather avoid. That candor and resilience amazed him. Tonight was different; Claire emanated an aura of defeat before the battle even began. No, he wouldn't bring it up; it was too enjoyable watching Claire push her food around her plate and sip her iced tea. Perhaps, he pondered, she hoped that by avoiding the subject it would go away. That would not happen! His anticipation was palpable.

"You haven't eaten much of your dinner," Tony assessed.

She shook her head. "I guess I'm not hungry. I think traveling wore me out. I believe I just need to get some sleep."

He smirked. "You napped today."

Her eyes widened as they immediately looked to him. He loved the mixture of emotions that he witnessed flashing before him. Behind the green, he saw the realization that she'd just been caught in her attempt to sway the course of the evening. As a bonus, she also received confirmation of his ability to visually intrude into all aspects of her life. In all actuality, it had been Catherine who'd told him she'd napped, yet if Claire thought it was another example of his omnipresent power, who was he to dissuade her?

Softly, she replied, "Yes, I did; however, I'm not feeling well."

He grinned as he pushed back his chair and extended his hand. "Then, my dear, let's leave dinner behind."

Her eyes lightened as she placed her hand in his and stood. "Thank you."

"Oh, there's no need to thank me. I do, however, find it interesting that after all of these months, you believe you have the power to manipulate me and alter my plans."

"I don't know what you mean," she said, peering at him through her lashes.

When they walked through the sunporch and into the house, Claire turned toward the foyer. Tony's touch redirected her movements. "No, my dear, we aren't going upstairs." She inhaled and looked down. Tony lifted her chin. "I am a man of my word. I promised you something special tonight, and I fully intend to deliver."

"Tony, please ... I-I'm really not feeling well. I think it was the trip. It was great to go someplace, but I'm not used to being away from here. I'm sure I'll feel better tomorrow."

"But you see," he mocked, "I won't be here tomorrow, so our movie night can't wait."

He felt her tremble as they changed direction and headed for the lower level. "Are you cold?"

She shook her head and took a ragged breath. "N-no, I don't want to do this."

As they walked down the stairs, he pulled her close. When his lips grazed her ear, her neck stiffened. Seductively, he whispered, "You've said that before. Has it ever stopped my plans?"

Her shoulders sagged. "No."

"Then, my dear, experience should tell you that it won't change my plans for tonight. I want you to see what an amazing future you have in movies. You're a star! We can be like those reviewers on television, both saying what we like and what we don't like about each scene. Of course, that'll be from a totally outside objective view. What we like while making the movies, our subjective preferences, will be incredibly obvious. Oh, you'll see in a few minutes." He released his hold, allowing her to settle onto one of the large, overstuffed seats. Although her eyes were downcast, wetness covered her cheeks, and her shoulders shuddered in silence. He chuckled. "Since you didn't eat, and this is like a premiere, would you like me to call the kitchen for popcorn?"

She shook her head. The movement was so slight. Had it not been for the movement of her hair hanging over her face, he wouldn't have seen it.

Tony cleared his throat, reached for her chin, and brushed the renegade strands away. He wasn't going to allow her to hide her thoughts from him. There was too much happening behind those damn green windows. His words came slowly, deliberately, and with painstaking control. "I asked you a question. Do you really want me to repeat it?"

"No, I heard you." Her voice grew stronger, starting at a whisper and becoming bold. "No, I don't want popcorn. I want this over." She started to stand. "I don't want it over!" She looked him in the eye. "I don't want it to start!"

His chest met hers. "But it will." His tone left no room for debate.

Obediently, her knees buckled and she collapsed back into her soft chair.

As Tony reached for the remote, Claire asked, "Why? What's the point in this? I know what's happened. Why do you want me to see it?"

His sinister smile returned, as did the tightness in his slacks. If Claire hadn't been so preoccupied, she'd undoubtedly have noticed. "You seemed surprised that these videos exist. I want you to understand: I'm a man of my word. If I say something exists, it exists. If I say you will do something, you will do it. There are no gray areas. Do you understand?"

"I do." She wiped her eyes with the back of her hand. "I didn't doubt you." Crying interrupted her speech. "I-I *don't* doubt you." More tears. "I don't need to see."

"That's enough," he growled. He was done talking and done listening.

Tony hit a button on the remote, lowered the lights in the room, and opened the video library menu. He leaned over to emphasize his point. "I'm not interested in hearing any more. Don't push me further." She didn't speak; instead, she swallowed, nodded, and tilted her tear-dampened face toward the screen which now contained dates and locations.

He'd given this a lot of thought. They had all night to view. *So why not start at the beginning?* Tony chose *2010, March 20, S.E Suite,* and programmed the time: *8:00 AM.* Before he hit *ENTER*, he glanced in her direction. The look he saw told him that she knew the date—and already knew what she was about to see.

The screen came to life; it was Claire's suite:

She was wearing a white robe and lay curled up on the floor near the hall door. There was a beep and the door opened. Claire jumped, hearing the sound and seeing Tony enter.

"Good morning, Claire." Claire looked at him.

"Good morning, Anthony. I want you to know, I've decided to go home. I'll be leaving here today."

He couldn't contain the chuckle that rose in the back of his throat. Obviously, things didn't proceed as she'd planned.

On the screen, with his eyes dark, he smiled and spoke, "Do you not like your accommodations?" He didn't wait for her to answer. "I don't believe you'll be leaving so soon. We have a legally binding agreement ..." He took a bar napkin from his suit pocket. "... dated and signed by both of us."

"Please, Tony. I don't want to see this." Claire covered her eyes with her hands.

He'd warned her to stop this ridiculous display. Roughly grasping her wrists, he pulled them away from her eyes. Through clenched teeth he growled, "I promised a viewing. I said you would watch—and you *will* watch."

He tightly held her wrists to her lap as the video progressed in real time:

Claire was speaking, her voice high-pitched and filled with desperation. "It is not the end of this discussion. This is ludicrous. An agreement doesn't give you the right to rape me! I'm leaving."

Tony's hand contacted Claire's left cheek.

Tony released Claire's wrists and her hand moved to her cheek. He watched to be sure she wasn't trying to cover her eyes again, but she wasn't. Looking back to the screen, he saw himself talking:

"Perhaps in time your memory will improve. It seems to be an issue. Let me remind you again, rule number one is that you do as you are told. If I say a discussion is over, it is over, and this written agreement, which

states whatever is pleasing to me, means consensual, not rape. I've decided that it would be better if you didn't leave your suite for a while. Don't worry; we have plenty of time—$215,000 worth of time." Tony looked down. Under his shoes was broken crystal. He continued speaking. "I'll tell the staff that you may have your breakfast after you clean up this crystal."

He left Claire's room.

"Please stop the video!" Claire cried. "Please, I can't watch anymore."

He hit the button and the menu reappeared. "Oh, there're so many videos." His amusement was clear. "We can watch for hours. For example …" The screen read *March 19, 2010.* "… how do you suppose your suite got into that condition? I'm sure we could find out."

"Please!" she pleaded. "Please … you're leaving tomorrow. Wouldn't you rather spend tonight making movies instead of watching?"

When Claire sprang from her chair, Tony was about to follow and reprimand; instead, she fell to the floor and kneeled at his feet. Desperation emanated from every fiber of her being, from her red and puffy eyes to her runny nose. Not since she first arrived had he seen her so broken. Tony smirked. She was a far cry from the confident woman in her suite, just a few nights ago.

He leaned down and teased, purposely pushing her further. "Maybe we should watch some more—find out where you need improvement."

"I'll do anything you say, anything you want me to do differently— just tell me. Just *please* don't make me watch."

He sat back and looked at her. Truly, the dramatics were growing old. "You *will* do whatever I say, even if it is to watch, but," he hesitated to add emphasis, "I don't want to spend my last night here, for over a week, with you in this condition." As he stood, he callously brushed her from his lap, causing her to fall back onto the carpet. "I'll be in your suite in a few minutes."

Claire stood.

Tony continued, "Go up and get ready. Wash your face! You look like hell, and as far as attire … I'm thinking some new lingerie."

When she started to leave the theater, Tony gripped her arm and stalled her steps. His grip tightened as she met his gaze. They'd been through this too many times. "Claire, what do you say?"

Suddenly, he saw the fire from behind the tears as her neck straightened. It took a moment, but finally she was able to articulate the pleasantries he sought. "Thank you, Tony."

Damn her and damn that fire. He loosened his grip. "You may demonstrate your gratitude when I get upstairs."

He watched as she stood motionless. As the silence grew, the fire smoldered to mere embers. It was then that he instructed her movement. "You have been dismissed. You may go to your suite now."

Promises made – August 2010
(Consequences – Chapter 14)

For every promise, there is a price to pay.
– Jim Rohn

Tony wasn't sure what to expect, or even what he wanted to find, as he walked down the S.E. corridor. He didn't need to check the monitors; Catherine had informed him as soon as he arrived that Claire was waiting for him in her suite. Apparently, Claire had asked Catherine about his arrival, and Catherine had said that she didn't know the particulars.

This was the longest they'd been separated since he brought her to his estate. There'd been occasions when he'd left for a day or two due to business obligations, but this separation had been ten days. Before he left, they'd had another *glitch*, and he didn't leave her in the best condition. Oh, physically she was fine. Her acquired cooperation over the last five months had greatly reduced the need for physical assertiveness, beyond what came in the heat of the moment. No, when Tony left Claire, she was emotionally spent.

Breaking her spirit had been his goal, and in true Anthony Rawlings fashion, he succeeded. He remembered every minute, both in his theater and in her suite. Tony pushed Claire to a place she didn't want to go. He'd exhibited his power and watched as the fire behind her green eyes dimmed. Then, he purposely dowsed it some more. He remembered the note he'd left on her table:

> *I believe we have a blockbuster on our hands. It's hard to say, until we thoroughly review the footage. I plan to return a week from Wednesday. Eric is available if you want to visit the Quad Cities. I trust last night's film reminded you of my rules. Don't disappoint me.*

He left that with the intention of quenching any renegade sparks. At the time, it had been invigorating.

Then he left and—almost immediately—the elation faded.

Tony didn't doubt his power—it was obvious. He had the ability to make Claire's world heaven or hell; however, for a reason that Tony didn't fully comprehend, that control didn't satisfy him the way it once had. From the beginning of her acquisition, he'd thought of it like a business deal. He made those every day. Companies were bought and sold. They were expanded or the doors were closed. Employees benefited or suffered—it happened.

Tony told himself over and over that Claire's role was nothing more than that of an employee—maybe less. Therefore, when his procurement was complete, when he'd succeeded and broken her spirit, he should've experienced the euphoria that accompanied a hard-fought gain. In the case of this acquisition, taking Claire's mind and spirit had been more difficult than taking her body. It would seem as though his jubilation should've lasted longer than the car ride to the plane. It didn't.

Without warning, uneasiness settled in.

It wasn't that Tony missed Claire while he was in Europe; nevertheless, she continually infiltrated his thoughts. After a day or two, he decided to check the feed from her suite, believing it would satisfy his curiosity and allow him to concentrate on the matters at hand. Since there was a seven-hour time difference between Switzerland and Iowa, the morning that he peered into his iPad, he found Claire peacefully asleep in her bed. Obviously, she wasn't having the same insomnia issues that had plagued him.

The small peek helped. Although he wasn't able to keep Claire out of his thoughts, now those thoughts were images of her sleeping. He'd be negotiating or discussing something with someone and the satin strap of her nightgown, which had been barely visible on his small screen, would come to mind. He'd close his eyes and see her relaxed expression. If he concentrated long enough, Tony was sure that he could smell her scent, a fragrant mixture of perfume, hairspray, and sex. He'd imagine what it was like sleeping with her and removing the satin and lace from her soft skin. Although he enjoyed the way the negligees hugged her curves, they were merely for show. When he was home, she rarely spent the night actually sleeping in them.

Then, as his day progressed, his newfound peace faded. Each time he checked the feed from her suite, even late into his evening, he found the room empty. With time-lapsed speed, he saw the cleaning staff, but Claire was absent. The last image he found of her was before 9:00 AM in Iowa.

As he was about to retire, around midnight in Geneva, Claire's suite was still empty. It didn't make sense. It was almost 5:00 PM in Iowa City, and she should be there—it was her job! Nevertheless, she wasn't. Tony checked the library, the theater, the pool, and the gardens. He couldn't locate her on any monitors.

Then he remembered his note. He'd told Claire that Eric was available to her while he was gone. Assuring himself that she was only out shopping and safely with Eric, Tony tried to go to sleep. Behind his closed eyes, images of her sleeping with her sun-lightened hair fanned over her pillow and that damn satin strap fought for contention with his new worries and concerns regarding her whereabouts. Finally, he gave into his curiosity and called Eric.

"Yes, Mr. Rawlings?"

"I was checking to see where you've taken Ms. Claire in my absence, and to learn if you're nearly back to the estate."

"Sir?"

Uncharacteristically, Tony's voice reflected his concerns. "Ms. Claire. I told her that you'd be available if she wanted to leave the estate. You have accompanied her, haven't you? You know not to let her out by herself."

"Sir, I do know her limitations. However, she's not requested to leave the estate. I haven't taken her anywhere."

"She wasn't with you today, for most of the day, and currently?"

"No, sir," Eric replied. *"I can go to the main house and locate her for you, if you'd like?"*

Tony decided to go another direction. Dismissing Eric, he disconnected the line. His chest felt tight as he fought to inhale. Ignoring his physical discomfort, he walked down the hall to the small liquor cabinet in the sitting room of his suite. The bottle clinked the crystal as his unsteady hand poured two fingers of bourbon into the tumbler. The smooth amber fluid numbed his throat and calmed his nerves as it disappeared in one swallow. He poured another glass and reached for his phone. With steadier fingers, he retrieved Catherine's personal number and hit CALL.

Catherine informed him that Claire was spending her days hiking.

Hiking? What the hell? To where? To whom?

Catherine only said that Claire took a lunch and returned each day by 6:00 PM.

That night, he tossed and turned until he had visual confirmation of her return. It was nearly 2:00 AM in Geneva, and Tony wasn't sure who deserved to be reprimanded for this breach, Claire or Catherine. The next evening, Tony cut a dinner engagement short, claiming an exorbitant amount of work with a deadline quickly approaching, to sit in his suite and review days of video. Upon further investigation, he found what he wanted. Starting on the Monday after he left, and each morning following, at approximately 9:00 AM, Claire would walk along the garden path and quietly step through the perimeter of trees. Something in his chest clutched each time he watched her disappear into the shaded darkness.

On the fifth day he called Catherine again. It was after 11:00 PM in Switzerland, and he may have had more than a few fingers of bourbon. *"Is she back?"*

"Isn't your Internet working?"

"Don't be a smart-ass. I'm concerned that you're becoming lax in your judgment."

"May I remind you that you were the one to approve the hikes in the first place? She reminded me of that."

"Walks into the woods—not day-long excursions!"

Catherine's response was more of a sound than a word.

Tony's liquored tongue enunciated perfectly, and his words dripped with sarcasm. "I watched the exchange between the two of you on the day I left. Weren't you just the sweetest?"

"I can be," Catherine responded. "Would you have rather I did nothing and she went mad?"

This time Tony made the noise. "It wasn't that bad," he scoffed.

"It was. She was on the edge of a very dark place. I know the signs. I just helped her see that she could survive."

"I didn't think that was your goal."

Catherine allowed the line to go silent. Finally she replied, "I've grown used to her."

"Used to her? Like a pet?" He knew better than to bring up the motherly comment again.

Catherine murmured under her breath. Apparently, she didn't see his obvious restraint. He changed his tone. "What if she decides to leave the property?"

"She's returned every day, with minutes to spare."

"Hmm." He assessed. "At least she's a well-trained pet, but why? Why is she doing this, and where is she going?"

"I can only assume to gain some sense of personal freedom. She knows that her suite is monitored, and she feels she can have some time to herself beyond the perimeter of the grounds."

Tony thought about Catherine's response. It made sense, but he didn't like it. He didn't want her to have that freedom. He wanted all of her. Perhaps it was the liquor, but his tone softened. "Do you think it's helped her?"

"I do. She seems different, resigned to her fate, yet I don't know— stronger."

"And do you know where she goes? My property goes on for miles."

"I don't know. The laundry staff has informed me of bathing suits. Perhaps she's sunbathing?"

"She can do that at the pool," Tony answered, as images of Claire, wearing one of her many bathing suits, lying near the pool, paraded through his consciousness.

"Do you want me to tell her that she's no longer allowed to go on her hikes?"

He contemplated. "You said she's home every night by 6:00 PM. Why not 5:00 PM?"

"I told her 6:00 PM. You aren't here. She dines alone."

He nodded. "All right, no. Don't stop her as long as she follows your rules. Catherine?"

"Yes?"

"On the day of my arrival, do not tell her when I'll be in. Don't even remind her of my day of arrival. I want to see if she'll be ready. I want to know that she'll be following my rules. She knows that if I'm to be home, she's to be available. Let's see what she'll do with this new personal freedom and how far she'll take it."

"All right, Anton. If that's what you want."

"I do."

He hit DISCONNECT.

As Tony's hand touched the lever of Claire's door, he took a deep breath. Perhaps, just perhaps, what Anthony Rawlings feared was that ten days ago he *had* succeeded. There was something about Claire's resilience, something about her strength in the face of his tyranny, that intrigued him. It was a game and he enjoyed the invigorating play.

Ten days ago, Claire seemed defeated even before he showed her the videos. *If he had totally broken her spirit, would the game be done? Then what would he do? If she were emotionally as accommodating as she was physically, would the challenge be over?*

Tony couldn't remember another time in his life when he wanted so desperately to have failed. Opening the door, he panned the suite and found Claire seated on the sofa with a book. Exhaling, he stepped forward, knowing that he'd have to face the consequences of his actions. Their eyes met and his back straightened. Tony knew. He could see it in those damn green eyes—her fire was back!

"Good afternoon, Claire."

Her movements were deliberate and slow. She placed her bookmark in her book, laid the book on the end table, and stood. "Good afternoon, Anthony. It's nice to have you home. How was your trip?"

He stepped forward, wanting—no needing—to gauge her reaction. The scent of her perfume intensified with each step. When he was mere inches away, he stopped. This proximity required her to look up to main-

71

tain eye contact. Without direction, her chin rose defiantly, her lips held the perfect smile, and her eyes screamed with the intensity he sought. As much as he wanted to pull her into his arms, he heard himself bait her. It was his game and he couldn't stop. "My trip was long. I'm pleased with your greeting. Does this mean your temper tantrum from before my trip has reached its conclusion?"

"Yes, I believe it has. I apologize for my behavior. It was childish and unnecessary."

He had failed to break her—or so it seemed; nevertheless, Tony need- ed to push and learn if Claire was truly as fragile and on the edge as Cathe- rine said, or if her spirit was renewed. He grinned. "As I recall, a great deal of your behavior was far from childish ..." he paused—no reaction, "... but my memory could be failing me. It has been a long trip. I know how we could find out ..." another pause—no reaction, "... or review?"

She didn't take his bait. Instead, she responded, "You're right. It was very adult. I'd be glad to do whatever it is you tell me to do again. I believe I have a debt to repay. My goal is to make that happen sooner rather than later. Fulfilling my contract is the means to that end."

He couldn't fight the urge any longer. He had failed—and he'd never been so relieved. Swiftly, he pulled her against him and watched the fire rage. Oh, she smiled, said all the right things, but her damn eyes were fighting. It was better than he'd dared to hope. Bending down, his lips cap- tured hers. *Did he sense hesitation?* If so, it was briefly lived. Suddenly, she was pressing back with equal force. He lifted her petite frame and held tight to her firm, round behind as her arms encircled his neck.

All of the trepidation he'd felt walking the gauntlet from his office to her suite morphed into unbridled desire. He didn't want to make her watch movies; he wanted to make them. *Would he watch them?* Probably, but that wasn't what he was thinking as he backed her against the beige wall and her legs encircled his torso. He was silently cursing her choice of attire. Tony would give his entire fortune for her to be wearing a skirt.

It didn't take long and the damn white slacks and slippery blouse were history, lost somewhere on the floor of her suite. His suit followed, as Claire met him move for move. She was careful not to initiate, but whatev- er he suggested, whether it was verbal or otherwise, she met him head-on. As the afternoon progressed, he silently questioned if the Claire he'd hope to find was back, or if this was someone different, someone stronger? He wasn't sure, and he didn't waste too much time wondering.

About 6:30 PM, he used his cell phone to call the kitchen and have dinner brought to her suite. The flight had been long and their reunion exhausting. It was about 9:30 PM when he finally succumbed to sleep. In the moment before sweet nothingness prevailed and Tony slept better than he had in over a week, the satin strap he'd seen in the video feed crossed his mind. Taking one last glance toward Claire, he saw her bare shoulders and grinned. Tonight she wouldn't be wearing a nightgown to sleep.

Tony's shoes echoed against the marble floor of the long corridor as he made his way toward the front staircase. Inklings of crimson seeped into his vision as each step pounded more determined than the last. All day long, he'd thought about his reunion with Claire and her change in demeanor. As the day progressed he'd convinced himself not only of her acceptance of her situation, but the obvious pleasure she derived from it. Then, as if to prove him wrong, he went to her suite to retrieve her for dinner, and she was gone. Catherine had assured him that Claire knew dinner was at 7:00 PM. *Where the hell was she?*

Reaching the bottom of the stairs, he was about to call out to Catherine, when Tony stopped. In the sitting room, waiting calmly, dressed appropriately for dinner, was Claire. He stood for a moment and watched as he remained hidden from her view. She had her shapely legs crossed at her ankles, just above her high heels and her hands rested serenely on her lap. The dress she'd chosen to wear was blue and sleeveless, accentuating her tanned, firm arms. She didn't appear anxious, yet she wasn't overtly relaxed—she just *was*. As he stared, the red faded from his view. Tony reasoned that Claire hadn't disobeyed; it was only different. She'd never before taken the initiative to come down to dinner on her own, but there she was. Taking a deep breath, he straightened his suit jacket and stepped into the sitting room. Her eyes immediately went to his. "Good evening, Claire."

She stood and walked toward him. "Good evening, Anthony."

Offering his arm, she rested her small hand in the crook of his elbow, and they walked to the dining room. As they entered, he said, "I went to your suite expecting to find you there."

Her painted eyes widened. "I apologize. I was told dinner would be in the dining room at 7:00 PM; *I didn't want to be late.*"

As he pulled out her chair and she sat, Tony studied the ringlets of hair that teasingly grazed her neck. He reminded himself that the blonde hair emerging from her brown was an outward sign of the new woman he was creating. Her obvious emphasis of obedience was because it was what he demanded—the old Claire wouldn't have done that, perhaps not even recently. This Claire knew her place, and after their glitch a week ago, she was being extra careful.

He sat and studied his creation. He wanted to believe her; yet the red loomed nearby. He found his businessman's tone. "Your punctuality is duly noted. It seems my absence has helped you remember who's in charge and what guidelines you are to follow."

"Yes, your absence was advantageous on many counts."

He stared. *What the hell?* Unable to form a rebuttal that would facilitate their dinner conversation, he waited.

Finally, she spoke again, "I believe it helped me recognize I owe you much, not just the money to repay my debt, but the confidence you've shown in me ... the confidence to trust me with your intimate beliefs." She paused. "I will not betray that confidence."

While Cindy and Carlos entered the dining room and filled the table with food and drinks, Tony continued to stare. He looked for any sign of manipulation. *Truly, what did she expect to gain?* Once they were again alone, Tony said, "Claire, if you're sincere, you never cease to amaze me. If, however, you're playing me, you will regret it."

"Tony, what would I gain by playing you? I'm aware my present, future, and release are solely in your hands. I'm sorry for my behavior before you left."

He broke their gaze as he contemplated her words. Her eyes had been in agreement: he saw spirit, but not fight. Tony didn't accept her declaration, but he didn't rebuke it either. He changed the subject and they ate.

After dinner he escorted her out to the gardens for a stroll. As they approached the area in the path where he'd watch her disappear, he stopped. The underbrush was down trodden. He gazed into the trees. With the setting sun, the woods appeared dark and unknown, yet he knew she'd been there every day. *Why?*

She looked from the point in the border of the trees and then up to him. When she didn't volunteer, Tony asked, "Tell me about your walks. How far do you go?"

"I'm not sure ... in miles. At first, I just walked."

"At first?"

"At first, I was trying to get a feel of your land and would go in different directions. I found the most beautiful clearings, right in the middle of the trees. There were flowers, wild flowers, and ..." He listened to her words, but there was something else, a sense of discovery or wonder that he'd never heard or seen before—in anyone. They were just damn trees and bugs and things that existed wherever man had yet to build something truly spectacular; however, as she described the clearings, the insects, and animals, her eyes—no, her whole damn face—lit up like she was describing the most beautiful monuments in the world. "... that's when I found the lake. Oh, Tony, it's beautiful. It isn't big, but it isn't small. There're fish and a beach. I've been taking books and reading and enjoying the sun."

"A lake?" he questioned. "I remember seeing one, years ago, when I did flyovers of the land to help me decide where to have the house built."

Her look of wonder morphed into one of blatant concern. "I-Is it still on your land?"

He took her hand in his. "Yes," he reassured. "That's still on my land. You haven't broken my rules."

Claire's obvious relief was the final shove to push the red away. Maybe it was as Catherine said, *he was used to her, or maybe he had missed her? Had she missed him? He didn't want to ask. Even if he did ask, could he believe her answer? If she were truthful and the answer wasn't what he wanted—it was better not to ask.*

Tony reached into his breast pocket and brought out a black velvet box. "I found these for you in Italy. I thought they made a nice complement to your necklace."

Claire hesitantly accepted the small box. Before she opened it, she peered up at him through her lashes. It struck him again how different she was from the other women he'd dated. They would've never hesitated;

they wanted gifts, the more the better. Then again, he and Claire weren't dating—were they?

She opened the box and revealed the pearl earrings he'd found at a small jewelry store in Florence. He'd seen them in the window and immediately thought of Claire's necklace. They weren't exactly the same; however, the pearls were very similar and they were offset on white gold circles. He explained, "Your necklace is a cross, which is an X on its side. Now your earrings are O's—X's and O's." He smiled.

"Thank you, Tony," she said as she closed the lid. "It was very kind of you to think of me during your busy trip."

He placed her hand back into the crook of his arm, and they continued to walk about the garden. The sun was setting and he was home.

A day with friends – September 2010
(Consequences – Chapter 15)

A single moment of misunderstanding can be so poisonous that it can make us forget the many loveable moments spent together.
– Melchor Lim

"**I** won that one," Tony said, as he handed Tim the pool cue. "You'd better keep the winning streak going against Tom in this next game, or I may have to look for a new vice president."

Tom heard Tony's jovial tone and joined the fun. "It's all right, Tim: Tony'll give you a good reference," he laughed, "as long as the company isn't looking for a pool shark."

Tim smiled. "Oh, I'm not worried. You haven't seen my mad skills. I'm pretty sure I'll be gainfully employed come tomorrow."

Brent nudged Tony and whispered, "I like his confidence."

"Yeah, the kid's got something. I'm glad Courtney let you invite him."

Brent shrugged.

Eli called from the poker table on the other side of the room. "Hey, who's ready to lose some money? Chance and I have the chips ready."

Brent cocked his eyebrow toward Tony. "I think it's time to show them who's the real master of the cards."

"Maybe we should go easy on them?" Tony suggested.

"Nah," they both said in unison.

When they neared the poker table, Tony hesitated. "Deal a few hands without me. I'm gonna go upstairs for a minute."

"There's more beer behind the bar," Brent offered.

Tony looked down at his nearly full bottle. "I'm good. It's your wife's great cooking—I'm gonna go grab some of that cheese dip."

Brent eyed him suspiciously. "Sure, you know the way, but hurry back after you check on your gal. We'll be waiting."

Tony stared at his friend for a moment. *His gal? Not even close. "Companion." That was the description he'd decided upon.* "Whatever." He shrugged. "I like cheese dip."

With that, he set his beer on the nearest table and walked up the stairs. As he rounded the hallway toward the kitchen, the sound of voices stilled his progress. From his vantage, he could only hear the women. All at once, MaryAnn's voice prevailed as she went on at some length about one of Eli's clients—some movie star who apparently had a body *to die for.* Tony waited and listened as other voices added their opinions. With each passing comment that wasn't Claire's, Tony thought more and more about her restraint. He wasn't sure that the woman he acquired in Atlanta would have remained quiet for so long. The longer her voice remained absent, the more his newfound pride gave way to a growing wave of panic. *What if she wasn't speaking because she wasn't there? What if she'd found a way to leave—a way of escape? Would she do that?*

Determinedly, he turned the corner, hoping for visual confirmation of her presence. Though she was sitting facing out to the backyard, he immediately saw her profile. Nestled in the corner of the wicker loveseat, she was tracing the rim of her wine glass with her finger and listening as everyone discussed the sexy movie star. As he watched, she kept her eyes focused on the women and attentively followed the conversation. For a split second he thought of the woman he met at the Red Wing. The two Claires seemed worlds apart. It wasn't just appearance, although this Claire was toner, tanner, and blonder—all qualities he appreciated. The streaks of yellow that highlighted her hair were probably his favorite change; that's why he'd offered to take her to Chicago. The sun would soon lose its intensity, and that blonde would need help. This Claire was also more refined and genteel: she didn't burst into conversations or talk excessively. Well, she did talk more when they were alone, but the woman on the sunporch knew her role. Just as he was about to step further into the kitchen, he heard her name.

"So, Claire, what's your opinion? He's pretty hot, isn't he?" There was something about Bonnie's voice that grated on Tony's nerves. He wished that Eli and MaryAnn could have made the trip without these ta-galongs.

Tony saw Claire's smile; it wasn't as genuine as the one she flashed him earlier in the car, but that didn't detract from its beauty. She had no idea he was watching or listening as she answered, "Oh, yes, he's hot! But I haven't seen the movie." Looking toward MaryAnn, she apologized: "I'm sorry. I'm just not much of a moviegoer."

Tony knew that was true now, but when he'd watched her in Atlanta, she used to go to the movies frequently with her friends. He remembered taking her to a movie—their private viewing—about a month ago. He quickly pushed the memory away. It wasn't as pleasant as it had once been.

"Is Tony?" Bonnie pried. "Is he a moviegoer? What do you two like to do?"

Before Claire could answer, Sue chimed in. "Well, let me tell you—I saw the movie last week. It isn't Tim's kind of movie, so I went with a friend ..."

Tony quit listening as an arm brushed his waist. Turning, he saw Courtney as she leaned toward him and whispered, "So, where did you find her?"

"What?"

Courtney stood back and looked him straight in the eye. "She's not your type," her serious expression turned joyous, "and that's a good thing. I like her a lot."

"You do? And what do you mean—*my type*? I didn't know I had a *type*."

"Well, you do, and most of them wouldn't be caught dead sitting on my sunporch chatting. Claire's sweet. I'll admit, when Brent told me that you took her to New York for business, I was skeptical." She put her hand on his. "I mean, you know we care about you. It's just that, well, some of the women you've dated—"

Tony interrupted, "So, you're now telling me that you don't approve of my choices?" Though his words could be considered accusatory, his tone was soft and playful.

"Well, it probably isn't my place, but someone has to keep you in line." Her smile twinkled in her blue eyes. "Claire's young, but I think she might be a keeper. I've never seen you like this before."

"Like what?"

"Look at you. You're up here checking on her. What's the matter, are you afraid she's gonna learn some of your dark secrets and bolt?" Courtney leaned closer. "Don't worry, she's safe with us."

"I wasn't checking on her. I-I was getting something to eat." As soon as the words rolled off his tongue, he realized the food had all been put away.

"Oh, my mistake." Her grin clearly displayed her disbelief of his cover story. "I guess it was your swooning and eavesdropping that had me confused."

Courtney didn't know how wrong she was, or perhaps *why* she was wrong. Tony *was* checking on her—her *presence* and her *behavior*. After all, it was the first time he'd allowed her this much freedom with anyone other than his house staff, and it was more than a bit disconcerting. Even when they were out at fundraisers, or she was shopping, she was never with anyone long enough to discuss her situation. He sure as hell didn't want her discussing it now. He shifted his glance back to Courtney who'd quickly moved to the refrigerator. As she opened the large door, she asked, "Now, what was it that you wanted to eat?"

He knew he'd been caught; there was no reason to go on with the charade. Laughingly, he replied, "Don't go to any bother. I think I'm fine."

Claire must have heard the sound of their voices; when he turned back toward the porch she was looking right at him. Her lips smiled; however, her eyes questioned—seeking his approval. Without thinking, he smiled. Claire's shoulders relaxed as she placed her glass on the table, still looking in his direction, and started to stand. Shaking his head, he waved her off. Obediently, she picked up her glass and sat back against the cushion. He'd heard enough of the conversation to know she was performing well, and he didn't want to interrupt the ladies' discussion.

When he looked back at Courtney, she was staring at him.

Before she could speak, he said, "Um, I'm going back downstairs."

"Yes, you do that. I hope you liked your snack."

If it were almost anyone else, Tony would have been upset—but not with Courtney. He truly did value her and Brent's friendship. When he told Claire they were some of his *closest friends,* he'd been sincere. There was something about Courtney that lit up a room. While others seemed nervous or apprehensive in Tony's presence, she never did. He admired her for that.

Walking toward the lower level, he thought about Courtney's assessment of Claire. It both puzzled and pleased him. He'd been apprehensive about bringing Claire to this barbeque—not that he doubted her ability to perform; over the past almost six months she'd improved exponentially. It was more a concern that Courtney would see through the facade. The fact that she didn't *and* she approved of Claire was food for thought.

He entered the lower level just in time to watch Tim lift his pool cue and point. "Eight ball, corner pocket."

Seconds later, the black ball bounced from one bumper to the next, successfully avoiding the scattered striped balls, and fell effortlessly into the corner hole. Shaking his head, Tom said, "I believe I've just been schooled by the schoolboy."

Feeling easier about Claire's behavior, Tony slapped Tim on the back. "Good job, I believe you can be assured your position is safe. Just don't start thinking you can challenge me to a game of eight ball to move higher in Rawlings. I'm not planning on handing over the reins any day soon."

The evening sky began to darken as everyone sat around Brent's fire pit. As much as Tony enjoyed the camaraderie of the day, he couldn't stop thinking about getting Claire home and telling her what an amazing job she'd done. Yes, *telling* wasn't the only thing on his mind. He fully intended on *showing* her. It wasn't a plan of appreciation. She'd done what she needed to do. It was a plan of positive reinforcement. In a few short hours, she'd seemed to charm not only Courtney, but all of his friends.

Courtney had been right when she said that most of the women he dated weren't the type to sit contentedly around a fire pit and listen to stories. They were women who liked to be wined and dined and who enjoyed all that his money could buy. The people present had no way of knowing that this outing meant more to Claire than a diamond bracelet. They had no way of knowing that it was her first experience in a long time that involved this many people. Squeezing Claire's shoulder, he couldn't help but smile when she looked his way. The day had been truly more than he imagined or expected. He whispered, "We should be going."

Although Claire showed a twinge of disappointment, a microsecond later it turned into a complying nod and smile. She knew better than to argue, especially in a non-private setting. The other voices from around the fire were the ones who chimed in with their disappointment. They all wanted Tony and Claire to stay longer.

"It has been wonderful to get to know all of you," Claire said seconds before Courtney swallowed her in a hug.

"Thank you for coming, and make sure Tony brings you around more often," Courtney said as she peered over Claire's shoulder and winked at Tony. When the two women ended their embrace, Courtney continued speaking to Tony, "And don't scare her off. I like her."

While he shrugged innocently, he looked up in time to see Sue hand Claire a piece of paper. As Claire opened it, Sue said, "Call me; we can do lunch."

The next few minutes were a blur. Tony's need for appearances kicked in, and his actions and words were on autopilot. As he remained polite and said his goodbyes, his mind swirled with thoughts about the note. *What did it say? What had Claire and Sue talked about?* He walked Claire to the car and opened her door. *Did he assist her in getting in?* Tony couldn't remember. The moment he maneuvered the Lexus off Brent's property, his ingrained concern with appearances evaporated—it was just Claire and him. They were no longer among others. Though the sun had set, the fall evening filled with a hue of red as they drove silently along the country roads. He made no attempt to rein in the threatening rage. *How had the perfect day changed so drastically?*

Tony didn't know how far or how long he'd driven before he abruptly pulled the car onto the shoulder. Dirt and rocks pelted the underside of the convertible as he slammed his foot on the brake and threw the gearshift into *PARK*. There were too many things running through his mind, too many questions, and too many possibilities. He imagined the conversation between Claire and the wife of his vice president.

"I'm not his companion; he kidnapped me. Can you please help me? He isn't like you think!"

The prospects were limitless. Instead of speaking, Tony held out his hand—he couldn't even look at her, not after what she'd done.

"Tony ..." she began, as she handed him the piece of paper.

He didn't give Claire the chance to continue. With the hand that held Sue's note, he seized her mouth and squeezed her cheeks. If he covered her nose ... no, that wasn't what he wanted. At the moment he didn't know what he wanted. He just knew the perfect day had gone to hell in a matter of seconds.

"Not now," he managed through gritted teeth. "We'll discuss this when we get home." Prying his hand from her face, he resumed his grip on the steering wheel. They rode in silence until they reached the front door of the estate.

Before they arrived at the Simmons' house, Tony had made Claire a deal. *Was it a deal—or perhaps a threat?* Either way, he'd promised her a day at the spa in Chicago—*if* she behaved. When he stopped the car, he didn't bother to open her door. *This wasn't a damn date.* He kept his eyes fixed straight ahead and said, "Go up to your suite. I'll be up soon; in the meantime, I have things to do, like cancel a spa appointment."

Though he didn't turn, he knew she wanted to speak, possibly explain. It took her a few seconds, but soon, Claire opened her door and walked toward the house—out of the corner of his eye, he saw her head high and shoulders back. Her arrogance in the face of his power only fueled his thoughts. *If she were brazen enough to respond like that when she knew she was about to be punished, what would she risk to get free?*

He'd watched her for over an hour on the monitors. Catherine had even come into his office and tried to learn the reason for his change in demeanor. He couldn't or didn't want to explain. He couldn't tell Catherine that she'd been right all along, that Claire had just been holding back, waiting for the opportunity to get free and take him down in the process. Tony didn't want to admit that to himself, much less someone else. After all, he'd taken her to his friends—*to his best friends*—and now look what she'd done!

His decision was made. Behaviors had consequences and she needed to be punished. *How?* He debated, until he realized that punishment wasn't something to be thought out; it was something to be delivered swiftly when necessary. It was a means by which to curb unacceptable behavior. What she had done or said while with Sue was undoubtedly unacceptable. Claire knew the rules: no divulging of private information. If Sue wanted to have lunch—there would obviously be sharing of private information, if there hadn't been already.

By the time Tony stepped through the door of her suite, he'd decided to allow Claire to choose her penalty: a time-out or corporal punishment. By making her part of the decision process, she was forced to accept her responsibility for her actions, ultimately admitting to her insubordination and agreeing to the consequences.

Tony knew from the monitors that Claire was out on the balcony. The sound of the door must have gotten her attention. He didn't speak, but he stopped and stared in her direction. It was an unspoken command, and she heard it loud and clear. With her back straight and her eyes locked on him, she boldly walked within inches. He lifted her chin, leaned forward, and bathed her cheeks in his warm breath. Tony didn't want there to be any misunderstanding: she had failed to maintain her side of this agreement, and there would be a price to pay. "What did we discuss just before we arrived at the barbeque?"

Her eyes flashed fire, but her words sounded respectful. "I told you I wouldn't let you down and I didn't."

"Actions have consequences; I've told you that. Why is that difficult for you to understand?"

"Tony, it isn't. If—" He didn't want excuses. The control he'd tried to gather during the drive and in his office evaporated. His open palm struck her cheek. It wasn't powerful enough to knock her down, yet it accomplished his goal—she stopped speaking.

"Actions have consequences," he repeated. As the evidence of his persuasion began to rise on her cheek, her moist eyes stayed fixed on his, and he continued, "I've been thinking quite a bit about an appropriate punishment."

"Tony, if you would please let me speak. I know your decision is set, but allow me to talk."

Her strength was commendable. More out of awe, he nodded and said, "Fine, make it quick." Her words wouldn't matter; his decision was set.

"I was nervous about going to this barbeque today, but I had a wonderful time. Courtney was the perfect hostess and very charming. Everyone was nice to me. I really didn't know what to expect." Her words were barely spaced. "Well, everyone except Bonnie. By the way, I overheard Bonnie and MaryAnn talking and everyone there had your back. That includes me. Sue—well, Sue's lonely. She told me that Tim works long hours, which she mentioned he enjoys, but she's lonely. At some point, she asked me for my number. I don't have one—as you know—but I thought that sounded dumb: everyone has a cell phone. So I just said I didn't have it with me and I didn't know my number. I never call myself. So, I'm guessing that's why she gave me her number. I really didn't know she was going to do it. If I had, would I've had her do it right in front of you?"

He didn't want to hear this—it wasn't the way he had imagined.

Claire went on. "When Courtney introduced me to Tim and Sue, I told Tim I'd heard good things about him—from you. I can only guess that made Sue and I instant friends. Women love to hear good things about their husbands. I would've told you if I'd gotten the number without your knowing. I have no way of calling, and if I just didn't call, it would appear rude. I know how you feel about appearances." Her tone softened. She'd stated her case; this was more of a plea. "I really did well today; this was just a misunderstanding, and your friends were very nice."

Tony looked down into her eyes and tried to retrieve the red her explanation had muted. He wanted to punish her; she deserved it, *didn't she?* He went on with his plan. "I've decided you may choose. Perhaps you would like to know your choices?"

Defeat filled her green eyes. It was the expression she'd had during their dinner, before he showed her the movies. The window into her thoughts disappeared. For the first time since he entered the room, she looked away as helplessness filled her voice. "Tony, your decision is made; I don't care."

"The first option is a two-week time-out in your suite."

Suddenly, the fire was back. She glared, stood, and met him face-to-face. God, her strength captivated him. The defeat was gone. If there was a punishment coming, she wanted to choose. "Then I choose number two."

He didn't respond. The silence grew. He wanted her. He wanted to tell her he was sorry—he overreacted—but that wasn't him. He couldn't.

"Very well, undress."

She didn't hesitate; she obeyed his command and started by unbuttoning her blouse, one button at a time. Then she shimmied out of her slacks; she didn't argue or complain and maintained eye contact the entire time. Tony's arousal was becoming difficult to conceal. As her body trembled slightly before him, he searched for the red. Like his fury, it was gone. Tony's angry demeanor dissolved.

"Come here," he commanded.

She did. He held her shoulders and looked into her green eyes. "Damn you, Claire." He pulled her close. "I make snap decisions based on the visible evidence. Appearances are important. I assumed you had something planned with Sue—something I hadn't approved. I was wrong. Your speech," he lifted her chin, gently this time, as his tone softened, "was very brave." He watched her expression. "It helped me see that I'd jumped to the wrong conclusion." He put his head down on her hair and the odor of burning wood reminded him of Brent's fire pit. He encircled her body with his arms. She was still trembling and he wanted to warm her.

The memories of the day resurfaced—her smile, the things Courtney and Brent had said, even the fact that Sue wanted to have lunch with her. He was painfully aroused by those thoughts, as well as the soft, naked body in his arms.

Tony's voice continued to mellow. "Up until the moment Sue handed you that note, I was extremely proud of you. You were amazing. Courtney told me that about ten times." He felt the tension leave her body as she became liquid against his chest. Claire lifted her eyes and smiled. He went on. "There's something I'd like us to do."

"Whatever it is—yes."

He'd been wrong, yet instead of being upset, Claire was relieved. He wanted her more than he'd ever wanted her. He no longer tried to subdue his grin as he said, "Your hair smells like smoke. I'd like us to shower."

Returning his grin, Claire took his hand and led him to her bathroom. Once there, she reached for the buttons of his shirt, but before she undid them, her questioning eyes found his. It was a simple unspoken request, and he longed to grant it and more. As she removed his clothes, he undid her braid. Under the warm spray of the shower, he wet her hair, added shampoo, and gently massaged. "Your hair is beautiful, but it needs trimming, and the weather is getting colder, so maybe some highlights. I believe you'll enjoy the spa. It has a great reputation."

Her expression of innocence and surprise about did him in as she turned and asked, "You didn't cancel my appointment?"

"No, I guess I hoped something would change my mind." *Was that true? Had he hoped for that?* Or had he realized that the spa wouldn't be open until the next day? Either way, as he lathered her hair with conditioner and the floral scent replaced the odor of smoke, he was glad he hadn't had the opportunity.

Soon his slippery hands found their way to the curves of her breasts. Despite the warm water, her nipples were taut and hard. Each caress found his hands lower and lower. Turning her around, he lifted her body and held her against the shower wall. She was so light and fit just right. When her legs wrapped around his torso he worked to create the same frenzy in her that he felt burning within. His tongue and teeth taunted her nipples while his fingers increased their pace. By the way her nails gripped his shoulders, he knew she was close to finding the ecstasy that he too wanted to experience.

Adjusting her slightly, he found the place he wanted to be. Her wordless moans filled the shower and pushed him deeper and deeper. All of the day's energies erupted as their bodies quaked in the aftermath of their union. When she laid her head on his shoulder and he heard her ragged breathing, Tony wanted nothing more than to hear those moans of pleasure again.

Through the night, he got what he wanted, and he made sure that Claire did too.

Tony woke before his alarm. Hearing Claire's soft and delicate breathing, he saw her covered with only a sheet and curled into a ball on the far side of the bed. With the pale light of the lingering moon, he noticed her hair fanned around her head, damp and wavy. The sheet did little to hide her petite, soft, and supple body. He carefully lifted the blankets and covered her. As he watched, the warmth of the blankets allowed her to unconsciously relax and settle into a deeper slumber. He wanted her again. He knew he could wake her, and she would accommodate his demands. Laying his head back on the pillow, he remembered the sex they experienced and wondered *when did this happen?* He no longer wanted to dominate but to satisfy.

He hadn't realized the true depth of his feelings until he heard himself apologize. Anthony Rawlings could count on one hand the people to whom he'd apologized. Now this woman—a piece of his plan—was on that shortlist.

Instead of relishing his new realization, he berated himself. Catherine was right: he should have stayed indifferent, dominant, and in charge. *But, wasn't he still in charge?* He was. Even Catherine had said she was used to Claire—so was he.

Maybe he did apologize, and admittedly that was going a bit too far. Words from his past echoed in his memory. "Only the weak apologize." Tony vowed to not allow that to happen again. Glancing again at the woman only a few feet away, he considered waking her. If he did, he could demonstrate the indifferent, domineering qualities that would verify he wasn't weak. He could prove that he was in control.

Seeing her peaceful expression and thinking of her giving and surrendering herself over and over, Tony quietly got out of bed, put on his jeans, and left her suite. Stepping into the corridor, he decided to work out.

AUTHOR'S NOTE

This POV was originally written at the request of my amazing readers and appeared in the Goodreads Group: The Consequences Series Group Reads, Therapy, and Hugs. That version has been tweaked and edited for BHE- Consequences. The "Accident" scene in *Consequences* was tragic, difficult to read, difficult to write, and often resulted in my being asked, *"What was Tony thinking?"* I decided to share. This POV was in no way intended to condone abuse or physical violence, but was meant as insight into the troubled mind of a man who experienced pain and betrayal for the first time in his life.

Thank you for joining me on this dark and insightful journey.

~Aleatha.

Seven

The Accident – September 2010
(Consequences – Chapter 19)

There is no such thing as accident; it is fate misnamed.
– Napoleon Bonaparte

The whole damn deal hung by a thread. How many hours and millions of dollars had been wasted researching and reviewing this investment and securities firm to have it fall apart over some stupid disagreement about benefit buyouts? Sitting at the head of the long conference table, Tony listened to the debate until he couldn't take it any longer. "Ladies and gentlemen," he spoke above the fray, "you have my offer. Your company won't stand as it is another six months. You can either take the deal or file Chapter 11. With my offer your employees will receive appropriate compensation in exchange for their loss of benefits."

"Mr. Rawlings, with all due respect, you're offering pennies on the dollar."

Standing, Tony adjusted his jacket and ignored the vibration of his private cell phone as he replied, "Yes, Mr. Collins, I am. I've also spent over a year learning the ins and outs of your company. You have no other prospects. I suggest you take the offer. The federal bankruptcy courts won't be as generous."

While the murmuring at the conference table intensified, Tony placed the documents and his laptop into his leather briefcase and nodded to his team. Addressing the assembly, he announced, "I expect an answer by tomorrow at noon, or I'll assume that you're taking your chances with the courts. Good day, ladies and gentlemen."

The room fell into a stunned hush as Anthony Rawlings and his protégés gathered their belongings and walked away from the bargaining table. Once they stepped beyond the glass doors and neared the elevator, Tony heard Tom exhale. The team that accompanied him consisted of Tom Miller, his associate, Sharon Michaels, and David Field, one of Tony's negotiators. Only their private assembly entered the small elevator. When the doors shut, Tom leaned toward Tony and spoke in a hushed tone. "I know you know how much it'll cost if this falls through. We're talking about—"

Remaining professional, Tony's eyes met Tom's, interrupting his words. Tony hissed. "I am well aware. We can discuss this further in the office." The conversation was officially stalled. Tony didn't care that it was still early in the afternoon and that their meeting was scheduled to last until much later. He could only present the same information in so many different ways. He had neither the patience nor the inclination to entertain the assholes in that conference room upstairs another minute. They wanted what he wasn't willing to give. He knew that their company needed him more than he needed it. At this point, he needed a few minutes to decompress. If he didn't, he'd be willing to take the whole damn thing as a tax write-off.

The silence continued as they entered the waiting car. They weren't scheduled to return to Iowa until the morning, and they all knew that they'd spend the rest of the day and possibly the night dissecting every last document in their arsenal. Despite Tony's comments, too much had been invested; somewhere there was a definitive piece of information that would insure this deal's success. By all estimations, they had a long night ahead of them.

Just as Tony's nerves began to calm, he again felt his pocket vibrate and reached for his iPhone. Touching the screen, he saw: *TWO TEXT MESSAGES*

Further investigation told him that they both were from his press secretary, Shelly. He read the first:

MR. RAWLINGS PLEASE READ THE ATTACHED PRESS RELEASE THAT JUST CAME ACROSS MY FEED. IT WILL NOT APPEAR FOR A FEW DAYS. IT HAS BEEN PURCHASED BY ROLLING STONE AND PEOPLE. I DON'T THINK I CAN STOP IT.

The car moved in jerky bursts. Tony hated New York City traffic. That was one of the reasons he chose to live in Iowa. Of course, there was traffic there too, but it wasn't this stand-still shit. Instead of reading the attachment, he read the second text, also from his press secretary:

MR. RAWLINGS I'VE CONFIRMED THE SALE OF THE RELEASE TO BOTH MAGAZINES. IF I ATTEMPT TO STOP PUBLICATION IT MAY BACKFIRE. PLEASE ADVISE IMMEDIATELY.

"They're bluffing." Tom's voice broke the silence within the car.

"I don't bluff," Tony replied. "I'd rather lose the preliminary costs than deal with those assholes. I won't be at their mercy. We'll find something that'll make them beg for my offer, and we'll find it tonight."

Tom didn't respond, nor did anyone else. Tony didn't expect responses. After all, he wasn't asking. There was a mission and it would be carried out. When the car stopped in front of the tall office building, Tony and his associates silently entered the building. It was another quiet elevator ride as they made their way to the sixty-second floor and the New York satellite offices of *Rawlings Industries*.

The pretty brunette receptionist immediately stopped her work as Tony and his entourage entered the lobby to the executive offices.

Before she could speak, Tony said, "Kelli, we're planning a long night. Call for food. We'll need sandwiches and coffee delivered."

"I'll get right on that, Mr. Rawlings." Kelli handed him a small stack of papers. "Sir, Shelly has called multiple times. She's very anxious for you to read a press release. I took the liberty of printing it for you."

Taking the printed pages, Tony thanked her and walked into his private office; only Tom followed. He started to sit behind his desk when the title on the page caught his attention. Suddenly, his body ceased to move and the air left his lungs.

"Questions Answered—the Mystery Woman in Anthony Rawlings' Life Agrees to a One-on-One Interview."

His cheeks paled as the blood drained from his face.

"What's the matter?"

Tony heard the concern in Tom's voice. Although their relationship wasn't just that of business, Tony didn't feel like sharing. Prying his eyes away from the article in his tightening grip, Tony forced himself to make eye contact with his longtime friend. "I ..." he hesitated. "I-I need a minute. I'll call you when I'm ready to get started."

"Are you sure? Is there something I can—"

"A minute—now," Tony cut him off. It wasn't the volume of his voice that demanded action; it was the authority.

Tom nodded and headed for the door. Within seconds, Tony was alone with the press release that Shelly had tried so desperately to share.

He scanned the pages. Words and phrases jumped out from each paragraph: *Since May of 2010—Anthony's special woman—she agreed to sit down—freelance writer—Meredith Banks—Claire Nichols*—Tony's blood boiled. The tips of his fingers blanched and lost feeling as his grip upon the helpless pages intensified.

More scanning: *long-time friendship is why Claire finally agreed to sit down and discuss her relationship with one of the world's top bachelors.*

Slowly his knees buckled and Tony's tall, muscular body perched on the edge of his large leather chair. He continued reading: *Anthony Rawlings has long been seen as a wonderful catch for that one deserving woman. He dated such women as supermodel Cynthia Simmons and recording artist Julia Owens. However, none of his previous relationships lasted long. That is until now, now that Rawlings and Nichols have been together. These two were first seen together in late May (see picture) at the Quad City Symphony not far from the large wooded estate of Anthony Rawlings. And since that time, they have been spotted by curious onlookers at various charity events, as well as taking on two of the nation's biggest cities, New York (see picture) and Chicago (see picture).*

Intermittently, he flipped back and forth between the pages and the photos of Claire with him. With each word and each picture his vision blurred. Red seeped from every direction, threatening to cover everything in its wake. The pages, his office—hell, his life were all dripping in red.

Such basic rules—*how could Claire have been so stupid as to break the most basic of his rules?* It wasn't like he demanded that much from her.

There was still more article to read, but Tony's eyes couldn't focus. He envisioned Claire the other night at dinner in Chicago. He remembered the dress—it was tan and had sequins, even her jacket had sequins. They caught his attention because of the way they reflected the lights as they walked along the street from Trump Tower to the Cadillac Palace Theater.

Refocusing on the story, he saw the dress—it was in a picture of her with him—on the page before him, prepared for the world to see. *Privacy! Why was that so fuck'n hard to ask?* It wasn't just the damn reporters taking their picture. No, that happened all the time. This was betrayal. *This was disloyalty—insubordination!*

Tony tried to reason. The other day at the barbeque, he'd jumped to conclusions. *Could this be another misunderstanding?* He looked at his watch—2:37 PM, East Coast time. He could be home before 6:00 PM.

He quickly folded the pages and placed them in the inside pocket of his jacket. Next, he dialed the phone on his desk. "Tom, I have to fly immediately back to Iowa."

Tom was understandably shocked. They hadn't reached any resolution on their deal, and they had hundreds of millions of dollars at stake. Tony wouldn't give Tom specifics—only that something had happened back in Iowa, and he needed to be there. Tom assured his boss and his friend that he'd work diligently to keep the deal afloat.

Less than forty minutes later, Tony was airborne and headed west. The three-hour flight gave him ample opportunity to read and reread the article. Each time something new latched onto his consciousness:

Why Claire? What makes her the woman for a man like Anthony Rawlings?—She didn't deny living in the Iowa City area—Claire and Anthony enjoyed the performance of "Wicked."—Ms. Nichols spent the better part of the day enjoying all the comforts money could buy at one of the most exclusive day spas in Chicago—shopping at such stores as Saks Fifth Avenue, Anne Fontaine, Cartier, Giorgio Armani, and Louis Vuitton—Ms. Claire Nichols was ushered to the eighty-ninth floor of Trump Tower, the private city dwelling belonging to none other than Mr. Anthony Rawlings.

By the time the plane touched down in Iowa City, Tony knew he'd need to print another copy of the press release for Claire. The one in his hand was nearly shredded by the fervor of his grasp. He hadn't been willing to let it leave his hand the entire flight.

Each time he told himself to be reasonable, Tony remembered Claire sitting at the dining room table a month ago, pledging her loyalty. He hadn't asked for it. First, because he rarely *asked,* but more importantly, he never assumed he'd get it; nevertheless, on that evening after he'd returned from Europe, she'd offered it.

At the time, he questioned her motivation. After all, they'd just been through an *episode*, a *glitch* of sorts, and Claire had emerged stronger and more compliant than ever—a very appealing combination. He remembered thinking that perhaps *glitches* were an advantageous element in producing the woman he was creating.

That night in the dining room she'd volunteered, "Your absence was advantageous on many counts." He remembered staring at her, stunned by her candor and unsure of where she was going. Finally, she broke the looming silence. "I believe it helped me recognize I owe you much, not just the money to repay my debt, but the confidence you've shown in me."

He watched for signs of manipulation, yet she never faltered.

She had continued, "The confidence to trust me with your intimate beliefs ..." She added, "I will not betray that confidence."

Tony remembered allowing the silence to prevail as food came and the staff went. Once they were again alone, he replied, "Claire, if you're sincere, then you never cease to amaze me. If, however, you're playing me, you will regret it." Anthony Rawlings wouldn't be a successful businessman if he couldn't read people, yet as much as he tried to see Claire's deception—he couldn't.

As Tony entered the front door of his estate, he realized his own mistake. It wasn't that he *couldn't* see Claire's deception. It was that he *wouldn't*. He wanted to trust her—hell, for the last month or more, he'd wanted to do more than that. He'd wanted to—dare he admit—have feelings. Now it was clear; Catherine was right: Claire had fuck'n played him!!!

Tony's body trembled with the revelation as he walked toward his office. He needed to print a readable copy of the press release before he confronted Claire. He was done being a push-over. Forget her resolve and bravado. Screw her green eyes, soft skin, and sexy smile.

He brought Claire Nichols to Iowa for one reason—she had a debt to pay. Not the goddamn money. Tony didn't give a rat's ass about $215,000. No, Claire Nichols was the proverbial sacrificial lamb for the entire line of Nichols descendants—a child of a child. The vendetta rang in Tony's head. He'd heard it over and over for twenty years. *So what if he'd extracted some pleasure from her consequence?* That was acceptable; however, her blatant disregard for his rules, her insubordination and disloyalty, were intolerable.

The ridiculous idea running through his mind these past few weeks, that there was anything more between them than business, would end today. Tony would stay strong and deliver the consequences Claire deserved.

When Tony initially entered Claire's suite, he knew his mission: confront her about the interview, entertain the idea of a misconception—at least superficially, and deliver the appropriate punishment. It was a solid plan; however, that was a long time ago. As he sat in the chair near Claire's sofa and minutes turned to hours and hours passed like days, Tony's restraint evaporated. With each tick of the clock, his body stiffened and the red colored his vision.

Three hours! He'd been waiting in her suite for three fuck'n hours!

Catherine told him that Claire had gone to her lake for the day. Tony glanced toward the windows, as darkness fell over the land and enveloped her suite. He told himself, *the damn day is done!*

During the entire three hours that he'd been there, Tony hadn't moved or turned on a light. Truly, he thought it was interesting how well his eyes adjusted. Never before could he remember experiencing each moment of diminishing illumination. As the darkness prevailed, the crimson hue grew.

He worked to contain the fury in his chest and soul. It had been years since he'd experienced this depth of rage. Honestly, he hadn't moved because he feared if he did, he'd break something or some things. That's what used to happen when he was younger. He would break an object or punch a wall. There was one time at Blaire Academy when he punched another kid. The kid deserved it. He had said something about Tony's grandmother. The damn teachers broke it up and no one was seriously hurt; nevertheless, his grandfather didn't care about the why. He warned Anton to never let it happen again, and he hadn't. It was surprisingly easy—remain detached. That was how he could buy companies and fire a roomful of people. They weren't people: they were marks on a ledger.

Initially, this technique worked with Claire, but with each day she'd become more than that. Now, in the quiet suite, with time standing still, his thoughts ran together: *He'd allowed her to become more than that—more than just a Nichols! He'd trusted her—hell, he sent her to the spa, allowed her to shop, and even allowed her to remain in Chicago without him. For what? So that she could spit in his face? So that she could publicly discuss their relationship? What else had she told Meredith Banks? Maybe she had the whole thing planned. Of course, it was her plan to get away from him.*

That was probably it ... she arranged it from the spa—hell, he never thought about her using a phone from the spa, or maybe she used a pay phone? He'd supplied her with enough cash. What if she bought one of those disposable phones? The release said Claire and Meredith were sorority sisters. Claire probably contacted her for this purpose!

There were so many possibilities of how she'd betrayed him. It was true—he didn't know the exact mode, but he knew the final result. The papers were lying on her table—the black and white evidence of her deceit! She'd never meant a word of what she said that day in the dining room. The whole damn speech about trust was a sham, and he was a goddamn fool for falling for it.

Tony's train of thought came to a screeching halt as the sound of the opening door filled the otherwise silent suite. While the moonlight pooled in rectangles on the soft carpet, Tony stepped into the dark shadows and neared the woman who'd consumed his thoughts for the last eight hours— no, for years!

Before she could turn on the light, he stepped behind her. With the redness nearly beyond penetration, her presence and her scent fueled the fury and pain within him. He wrapped his arm around her throat while pulling her ponytail with his other hand. Nearing his lips to her ear, he attempted speech through gritted teeth. "Where the fuck have you been?"

Tony heard the desperation in his voice as it filled the dark room. That desperation poured more crimson onto the fire of his rage. No damn woman, especially a *Nichols*, would have this much control over him!

She didn't speak!

He spun her around—he wanted to see her face, see her lying eyes. Gripping her shoulders, he questioned her again. "I asked you a question. Where the fuck have you been?"

"Tony," she gasped. "I didn't think you were coming home until tomorrow."

His patience expired hours ago. He wanted answers and he wanted them now. He slapped her cheek. *Damn her, why wasn't she apologizing for her disloyalty? Why wasn't she answering his fuck'n question?* "I have asked you a question twice. I will not ask again."

His palm stung as it once again connected with her cheek and temple. The red behind his eyes obscured the growing physical evidence of his more forceful contact. Truly, he didn't even see the tears as they began to fall from her pleading eyes.

"Tony, please stop. I was hiking in the woods."

Letting go of her shoulders, he shoved her onto the sofa and followed. Leaning over her petite body, his words sounded too desperate for his own ears. "Do you expect me to believe you were in the woods until this time of night?"

"I was in the woods"—*lies*—"The sun was setting"—*bullshit*—"It was so beautiful."

He couldn't take it anymore! He wanted the truth! "Shut the fuck up! You were out there because you knew I was coming home, and you didn't want to face me after what you did!"

"I don't know what you mean. You told me you were coming home on Saturday—this is still Friday. I haven't done anything."

She was lying. He struck out again. Claire reached for her cheek as she tried to hide her face. He pulled her chin toward him; she wasn't looking away! His breath bathed her tear-drenched face. "Liar!"

He searched her eyes. *Why weren't they contrite or smug? She'd successfully humiliated him, broken his rules—why wasn't she assuming credit for her deceit?*

Tony stepped away. He couldn't look at her expression another minute. Inhaling deeply, he pushed the sound of her sobs from his ears and stepped toward the light switch. While the light filled the suite, Tony concentrated on inhaling and exhaling as he walked toward the table. *Maybe if she read the release she'd accept responsibility.*

The sound of her whimpering on the sofa tempered the red, causing it to wane, but when the tips of his fingers touched the pages of the news release, the crimson violently resurged through his veins. He didn't want the red to be so intense—if he didn't keep it down, he knew it had the ability to control him. Tony didn't want to give in to it, but he sure as hell wasn't giving that control to Claire. His neck stiffened. He refused to proceed lightly; it was his choice. Claire's damn emotions weren't going to deter his quest for truth. Stepping toward her, he held out the pages and steadied his voice. "Then tell me—tell me how this is a misunderstanding." The pages in his hand shook. Despite his best effort, his words came out too close together. "I jumped to conclusions last time. Tell me how I'm doing that now."

Tony wondered why he was giving her the chance to talk her way out. Maybe he wanted to push that bravado. *Would she try to talk her way out of this?* Most people would know better—they would accept the consequences and leave him alone. *Should he even allow it?*

Claire's voice interrupted his internal debate. "Tony, I'm sorry. I really don't know what you are talking about."

He threw the pages toward her and watched as they scattered on the floor near her feet. He didn't move; instead he stared and watched as Claire moved to the floor. Tony knew every word—hell, he'd read it fifty times. He watched as she fumbled with the pages, and her breathing became ragged.

"Tony, oh my God, I did *not* agree to an interview."

He was once again beside her. *What kind of pull did she have on him?* He pointed to the picture. "So you're telling me that the picture of you talking to this woman is a print shop fabrication and this is a colossal misunderstanding?"

"It is me, but—"

He seized her shoulders, lifted her from the floor, and pinned her against a wall. The falling picture and fear in her eyes didn't register.

Her voice begged for understanding. "I wasn't giving an interview."

She was lying to him! He slapped her again! If he had to, he'd force the truth out of her. He leaned down until their noses almost touched. *Would she have the audacity to look him in the eye and continue lying?* "Then what in the hell were you doing?" He shook her again. "Claire, I trusted you! You told me I could trust you, and I believed you. I sent you to a spa day. This is how you thank me? This is how you repay me? By breaking all my rules? By public failure?"

Abruptly, he released her shoulders. He wasn't going there. He refused to reveal how betrayed he felt. That would give her too much power. *She didn't have the power, he did.* And he would prove it!

When he turned around, Claire was scurrying to pick up the papers. The sight of her face finally registered: it was red and blotchy, yet her voice fought for steadiness. "What is this?"

Fine—he could be steady too. "It's an exclusive Internet release of an upcoming story. It'll run simultaneously in *People* and *Rolling Stone*."

In an effort to control the emotions he didn't want to feel, he stepped away, went to the bookshelf, picked up a book, and threw it into the fireplace. The release served as a small vent. After a deep inhale, he answered, "Shelly, my publicist, found it today and immediately forwarded me a copy. I flew home as soon as I could."

While she read, Tony walked to the sofa, sat, and watched. The pages in her hand trembled as tears fell onto the printed words. *What the hell did she think—that he wouldn't find out? That he wouldn't know she'd betrayed his trust?*

"Tony, I did go to school with Meredith. She did come up to me the other day and start talking. I didn't know she was a reporter. I wasn't giving an interview. I didn't say anything about you." She cried, "Your name was never mentioned!"

Tony didn't speak; instead, he nodded toward the pages. Claire continued reading. When it appeared as though she were finally done, she didn't move. She didn't look up, or speak—or anything. Tony waited. The only sound in the suite was that of their breathing. Tony's was getting louder while Claire's became shallower. Eventually, she laid the pages on the carpet and kept her eyes downcast.

His fury had ebbed. On much steadier legs, he walked toward her. "Appearances, Claire. How many times have I told you? Appearances mean everything. There's a picture, right here, of you sitting with her, the author. It doesn't matter if what she writes is accurate. It's believable because she's seen talking to you."

He wasn't yelling; he'd regained some control, yet the aura of rage remained. Claire still didn't look up. He wanted to see her face; instead, all that he could see was the top of her head. Some of her hair had come loose from the ponytail and hung in front of her eyes. "Get up," he ordered.

She didn't move—not a flinch.

His volume increased. "Claire, get up!"

Still looking at the carpet she begged, "P-please, Tony, I-I'm so sorry."

He reached for her arm, lifted her, and said, "The entire way home I was praying that somehow this was another misunderstanding. You wouldn't do this, not after I put my trust in you, but I knew if it wasn't a misunderstanding, there had to be consequences. There had to be punishment for this blatant disregard for the most fundamental of rules."

Claire wouldn't look at his eyes. When he reached for her chin, she moved away from his touch. The red returned and filled every molecule of the suite. *How dare she pull away from him!* He moved again, not to lift her chin, but to strike her face. If she were going to pull away, he'd give her something to pull away from. His hand caught her pearl necklace, and Tony watched as the small pearl charm flew across the room.

He would do more than punish her physically for her betrayal. Next time, she would remember to follow his rules. Tony emphasized his control over her liberties as he continued, "I believe some time away from people, some time alone in your suite, will help you remember who and who not to talk to."

The betrayal combined with the fear in her eyes was too much. She was speaking, but he couldn't hear. She was fighting him or protecting herself. Tony wasn't sure anymore. Nothing made sense.

It was like the boy at the Academy—only multiplied. It wasn't right, but he couldn't stop. Claire's behavior caused him pain. At the moment, the only thing he could think to do was return the favor.

How long did he hurt her? Tony truly didn't know. It wasn't until she stopped fighting, stopped begging, and stopped moving, that the red disappeared.

When it did, the only thing that remained was Claire.

"Claire, get up." She didn't move. "Claire?" Tony reached for her shoulder as she lay upon the floor. Blood trickled from her lip, and her face was beginning to bruise.

Tony fell to his knees and shook her. She still didn't respond. He tried again. This time his touch was soft and gentle. He wanted to shake her harder and wake her from this sleep, but he couldn't. The rage and fury, which seconds earlier had consumed his entire being, faded into nothingness. Momentarily, his soul felt empty. Then, slowly, the void within his chest filled. It filled with fear—a fear like he'd never known.

"Oh, my God, what have I done?" he murmured. Reaching for her pulse, he said a prayer. Tony really wasn't sure to whom, but at that moment he knew the thing he wanted more than anything else in the entire world was for her to live. Not because he didn't deserve to pay for what he'd done. He prayed for her to live, because Claire didn't deserve to die or to suffer as he'd made her suffer. "Please, don't be dead. Oh God, help ... Claire ... please, please, let her wake up ..."

Before his fingers found her pulse, the suite door opened.

"What have you done?"

His eyes met Catherine's, but words failed him.

She knelt beside Claire and pushed Tony's hand away. Finally, she said what he'd prayed to hear. "She has a pulse." Catherine stood. Her stance straightened as her expression turned stoic. There was no understanding or compassion, only determination in her steel-gray eyes as she looked down at him. "Anton, you need to think straight. What are we going to do?"

Tony didn't answer. His mind couldn't process. *Did Catherine actually think he wanted this to happen? Had that ever been his desire?* Seeing Claire's crumpled body, he couldn't remember what they'd wanted or planned. Instead of answering, he scooped her petite, unconscious frame into his arms and carried her to her bed. Catherine exhaled audibly, followed, and pulled back the blankets. Tony gently laid Claire upon the soft mattress and watched as she lay still, exactly as he placed her. Sitting next to her, his shoulders heaved as his head fell to her chest. Catherine waited.

After a deep breath, Tony sat straight, turned toward Catherine, and said, "Call 911. She needs medical care."

"No! You can't do that. Don't you know what will happen to you?"

Slowly, he covered Claire's body with the blankets and tenderly placed her hands above the covers. Taking her hand in his, he momentarily caressed her soft skin with his thumb. Next, he smoothed her disheveled hair away from her battered face and gently kissed her forehead. His thoughts moved much slower than before, as if all his adrenaline were gone. Even his words sounded far away. "She looks like she's sleeping." He looked to Catherine for confirmation. "That's it, isn't it? She's sleeping?"

"We can take care of her, like I took care of—"

"No," he interrupted. His determination was back. "She needs a doctor."

Catherine moved near Claire's head and touched her cheek. This situation wasn't negotiable; he wouldn't compromise. After a moment of obvious internal debate, Tony saw Catherine's shoulders droop and heard the slightest hint of compassion. "Then we need a story. You helped me. I'm here to help you."

"Well, there's a difference. When she gets better, she'll be able to tell someone the truth. Unlike before, *they* never got that chance." Tony reached for his cell phone.

Before he could dial, Catherine touched his arm. Her voice was calm and reassuring. "Listen to me and listen carefully. Claire went for a walk. The ground was wet; she slipped; she didn't come home. I called and told you. We were worried. You rushed home. You went looking for her and found her—like this. Maybe someone else was out there?"

Tony looked around the suite. It was as if he were looking at the path of a tornado. *How did this all happen?* The picture that usually hung near the fireplace was lying on the carpet. The pages of the news release were scattered near the sofa. Shaking his head, he replied, "No, I deserve whatever she tells the authorities."

"*If* she's able to tell them."

"She will be. I'll spare no expense. We'll get her anything she needs. One day, she'll have the opportunity to send me away for this."

"And maybe she won't. Why confess now? Let's see what happens first."

Tony caressed Claire's right cheek; the left one was turning a darker shade of purple by the minute. "I need to get her help. She didn't deserve this."

"Then call Dr. Leonard. If you call 911, the police will come. Just call him directly."

Tony nodded. Telling the authorities would be Claire's decision. He needed to get her well enough to do it. Searching his contacts, he found the doctor's number. Moments later he heard a voice on Dr. Leonard's private line. "Hello, Dr. Leonard, this is Anthony Rawlings. I need you to come to my estate immediately. There's been a terrible *accident* …"

Eight

The days and weeks that followed – September 2010
(Consequences – Chapter 21)

You usually have to wait for that which is worth waiting for.
– Craig Bruce

Tony stroked the side of Claire's arm as he mindlessly listened to the conversation behind him. Dr. Leonard spoke softly. "Ms. London, I'm obligated to call the authorities."

"Doctor, Mr. Rawlings has already contacted the Iowa City police department. They currently have officers combing the grounds for signs of the assailant—if there was one. We don't know for sure what happened."

He cleared his throat. "Then Mr. Rawlings won't mind if I speak with them, too?"

"You'll need to discuss that with him. However, I don't believe now is a good time. As you can see, Mr. Rawlings is very distraught over Ms. Nichols' condition."

"Yes, I see that."

"Can you tell me again what you believe happened?" Dr. Leonard inquired.

"We don't know. Nothing like this has ever happened before. Ms. Nichols likes to go for walks in the woods—she does it frequently. When she didn't return, I became worried and called ..."

Tony blocked out their voices; he knew each word before Catherine said it. He'd told the same story multiple times. After summoning Dr. Leonard, he'd called the police. While the doctor assessed Claire, two seasoned officers arrived at the door and took Tony's statement. He met with them in his office and gave them his statement: got home—woods—found her—unsure. They'd worked for ICPD for years, were well aware of Anthony Rawlings, and unquestioningly took Tony's statement at face value. When they asked to speak to Claire, Tony explained that she was with the doctor and unconscious. They thanked him for his time, shut their notepads, and promised to comb the grounds for clues. Tony explained that his security team was already searching, but the ICPD was more than welcome to join the hunt. There were probably more footprints in the back woods than there'd been in a decade.

Not surprisingly, nothing was found; however, each time the contrived story was retold, the fiction became more plausible. At some point, even part of Tony began to believe it—until he looked at Claire.

The police said that they'd do another search of the grounds once it was light. As Tony peered toward the heavy drapes, he realized that despite the longest day of his life, the sun had yet to rise—but he knew it would. That happened every morning. What ate at him—nagged at the depths of his soul—was Claire. Would she rise? It had been over six hours since her *accident*, and Dr. Leonard remained evasive at best, regarding her diagnosis. Even after all of his tests and examination, she remained the same— suspended in time. The only change was her appearance. The areas on her face and body that had at one time been red were darkening and swelling— distorting her facial features in a way that Tony would never be able to forget.

After Dr. Leonard's initial examination, he'd said that Claire's vitals were strong, but he wanted to run more tests. He recommended an MRI and other procedures that had acronyms instead of names. Tony agreed to any test or any treatment that could be done on the estate. He refused to move her to a hospital, but instead offered any amount of money to bring the hospital to her.

Although that apparently couldn't include an MRI, it did include portable ultrasound and x-ray machines. The images those machines generated confirmed that a few of Claire's ribs were broken. The doctor suspected that she also suffered a concussion, but without all the tests, he couldn't confirm that diagnosis. A large needle was inserted and held in place on Claire's left arm delivering a combination of fluids and pain medication. Even though she appeared blissfully asleep, Dr. Leonard said that if she were conscious, she'd be in a lot of pain. The doctor warned repeatedly about brain swelling—something about the brain being trapped within the skull and unable to heal. He mentioned the possibility of long-term damage, side effects, possible death. Tony listened, he did. For someone who could retain figures and information, what the doctor was telling him proved too overwhelming. He couldn't retain the prognosis if he wanted to—and he didn't. It wasn't possible. Just seven hours ago, she'd been fine.

Repeatedly, Tony cursed the bastard or circumstance that did this to his *companion*.

Tony's shoulders ached and his head throbbed as his eyes opened and his blurry world began to focus. It took a few seconds for reality to register—but when it did, it hit with a vengeance. Sometime after 4:00 AM, he'd fallen asleep with his head on the side of Claire's mattress and his hand over her arm. She wasn't sleeping in their bed. No, Dr. Leonard had done as Tony wished and brought the hospital to her. That included a motorized hospital bed and monitors that beeped. Tony scanned her petite frame looking for any sign of movement: there was none. She lay exactly as she had before he'd fallen asleep.

Wisps of sunlight reddened the outside sky and still Tony had yet to take any calls from Tom or Tim, or anyone at Rawlings Industries. At the moment, he wasn't even sure what he'd done with his cell phone. The big deal in New York seemed like a million years ago. He no longer cared if it worked out or if it didn't. All that time and all that money suddenly seemed inconsequential. Tony didn't care about anything other than seeing

Claire's eyes open. Once, late last night, when they were alone, he lifted one of her eyelids to try to see the green, but he couldn't. He lifted the lid, but all he saw was white, and it was full of red. The other lid he didn't dare touch. It was swollen and dark, as was the area surrounding it.

Tony's stomach lurched at the sight of her bruises as they colored and swelled. He convinced himself to look beyond her exterior and see the real Claire underneath. With time, he no longer saw the bandages or the discoloration. When Tony looked at the woman before him, he saw the vivacious, strong-willed woman whom he loved to bait. He saw the woman who could look him in the eye when most would turn away. He saw the beautiful blonde highlights and the emerald-green eyes. He saw the refined woman he'd created—the one who fit perfectly on his arm at social gatherings and perfectly beneath him on a soft mattress. He imagined the fire—he wanted the fire. The images gave him a false sense of hope as the blissfulness of sleep once again took him to a better place.

The next time Tony woke, it was due to Catherine's hand on his shoulder. "Anton, Dr. Leonard will be in here in a few minutes. Do you want me to sit with her while you clean up?"

Tony glanced at his watch—after 8:00 AM. The morning sun streamed across Claire's makeshift bed and accentuated the bruises he didn't want to see. It wasn't just her face: her arms were discolored too. It didn't take a forensic pathologist to recognize that one bruise on her left arm resembled a handprint.

Where had he been for the last few hours? He'd awakened once, but then he began remembering and scenes floated in and out. He remembered Claire describing the lake on his property. He remembered her excitement and joy. It was almost contagious as her eyes and expression glowed. Maybe he could take her there? Maybe then she'd wake?

No, she'd been there—yesterday.

Tony squeezed Claire's hand. *How could that have only been yesterday?* Her cold unresponsive skin caused the bile in his empty stomach to bubble and surge upward. He nodded his approval to Catherine and moved quickly to Claire's bathroom. He had just enough time to close the door before he was headfirst into the toilet. It wasn't like he'd eaten recently, yet his memories wouldn't give him a reprieve.

Claire had been to her lake. That's where she was—while he was in her suite. She was there, among the flowers and water and beach and trees and all of the things she talked about. She wasn't plotting to leave him. She wasn't basking in some sense of betrayal. No, she was finding solace like only she could. She'd tried to tell him, tried to explain—and what had he done?

His stomach heaved again and again. It was as if his body were trying to expel a part of himself—a part that was deep inside and needed to be gone, a part that Claire didn't deserve.

With a pounding in his temples like he'd never before known, Tony laid his head on the cool porcelain and closed his eyes. Time passed—he didn't know much, but eventually voices could be heard from beyond his cloud. Painstakingly, he rose and walked to Claire's shower. Turning on the water, he disrobed. As the steam filled the bathroom, he stepped under the scalding spray. Liquid fire assaulted his skin. He didn't turn down the temperature. No, Tony wanted the pain—he needed it, he deserved it. When his body adapted, he turned the temperature up. It wasn't until he heard the knock at the door that he even considered the amount of time he'd stood helplessly accepting the spray's punishment.

Stepping from the glass enclosure, he realized he'd not considered fresh clothes. It was then he heard the knock again accompanied by a voice. "Anton, I brought you some clothes. Dr. Leonard went downstairs to eat breakfast. If you're done with your shower, let me give these to you and you can go down and join him. He's finished his most recent examination."

Tony leaned his head against the wall and exhaled. *Thank God he had Catherine. He'd never felt so helpless. Maybe that was how she'd felt at one time; he didn't know. He just knew that if it were not for her, he'd be in a jail cell, or out on bond. Either way, she was his rock and he was so thankful they'd supported one another.*

When he opened the door slightly, he met Catherine's gaze. "Thank you," was all he could manage.

She didn't respond, other than to nod. It was enough. He couldn't have taken her gloating nor her telling him that he'd let the whole thing with Claire get out of hand. He knew that. He needed Catherine's support, and seeing her steady steel expression, that was exactly what she offered.

Wiping the steam from Claire's mirror, Tony's reflection peered back at him. The unfamiliar image with reddened skin, cheeks and chin covered by a day's beard growth, and tired eyes, wasn't what taunted him. It was the tremendous invisible weight crushing his shoulders. The anxiety surrounding Claire's recovery was more than psychological. It was physical, making standing difficult as his knees flexed. For a moment, Tony laid his head on the vanity and debated if he could go on. Then he remembered Claire's fight—the fire he longed to see. The fire he knew was somewhere inside of her. If she could fight to get through this—no, as she fought to get through this—so would he. She needed him to be strong, needed him to be there for her—to help her. He wouldn't let her down, not again. After a few minutes, Tony was down in the dining room, drinking a much-needed cup of coffee, and listening to Dr. Leonard.

Over the next days, Dr. Leonard moved onto the estate. Catherine gave him a bedroom near Claire's, which served as his makeshift office. He told most of his staff that he'd taken an unexpected leave to look after an ailing family member, and another private practitioner graciously agreed to see his patients. Only one member of his staff was enlightened to his true endeavor. She was his trusted nurse and assistant. Both medical professionals agreed to total confidentiality; however, Dr. Leonard maintained his legal responsibilities. Although he didn't come out and say it, Tony knew exactly what he meant: if he could prove that Claire had been harmed by someone on the estate, he would report it.

Dr. Leonard's nurse didn't stay at the estate, but she came and went with some frequency, bringing Dr. Leonard whatever he wanted from his office or from the hospital. She also assisted him with much of Claire's care. She changed IV bags, gave medication, moved Claire so that she didn't stay in one position too long, gave her bed baths, and changed her gown. At first, Dr. Leonard insisted on a hospital gown: it was easier access for his examinations, but Tony hated the sight of it. He immediately sent for nightgowns that buttoned up the front with long sleeves. Dr. Leonard could still have access for his exams, but Claire didn't look as much like a patient.

Even without the MRI, the doctor concluded that Claire's initial unconsciousness was due to a blow to her head. There was no way of knowing the cause of that blow, only that evidence suggested that it had occurred. He immediately put her on additional medication to reduce swelling of her brain. Her medication also included something to keep her sedated. The doctor explained that it was for the best.

Day after day, either Tony or Catherine sat by her side. They only left the room when Dr. Leonard or his nurse insisted. Even then, it was only for a short duration. The doctor couldn't confirm that Claire could hear the world around her; nevertheless, Tony talked as much as he could. Everything felt wrong. Usually the suite was filled with the sound of Claire's voice, and Tony found the silence deafening. Often he'd ask her to wake. "Claire, talk to us. Open your eyes." Sometimes he'd read—usually things related to Rawlings Industries—but he continued to speak. The only time Tony allowed the blanket of quiet to cover the room was at night. He no longer slept with his head on her bed; instead, he had a large recliner brought to her bedside and slept there.

For over a week, Tony relinquished full control of Rawlings Industries to his vice president, Tim. Tony asked Patricia to not contact him, unless it was a dire emergency. He received emails, and those, too, he'd read aloud. That was how he'd learned that the New York negotiations had finally resulted in a deal. Truthfully, he wasn't happy. It was that *deal* that took him out of Chicago; it was that *deal* that left Claire alone. It was that *deal* that Tony held responsible for the condition of the woman before him. Despite years of work and hundreds of thousands of dollars, Tony emailed Tim and told him to sell off the investment and securities firm and to do it as soon as possible. He didn't care what happened to the damn employees, their pensions, their benefits, or anything else. Anthony Rawlings wanted the damn firm out from under the Rawlings umbrella.

As time passed, Claire's bruises began to fade. Tony hoped and prayed that if the swelling on the outside was decreasing, that meant that the swelling on the inside was too. Claire's IV now contained some kind of nutritional supplement. In essence, the nurse explained, Claire was being fed from the tube in her arm, and Tony hated it. Claire wasn't that big to begin with; yet each day she seemed to shrink behind the nightgown and blankets. Multiple times a day he'd move her arms and legs as the nurse taught him to do. Each time he lifted her limbs, they felt lighter in his grasp. It was also during those times that he saw her otherwise covered bruises. The areas that used to be red first faded to blue/purple, and were turning green and yellow. Each time he was faced with these markings,

Tony made himself see beyond the green discolorations. The only green he wanted to see was behind her lids.

Although, Dr. Leonard warned that she might not ever wake, Tony refused to believe that. Claire's eyes would open and when they did, she'd be coherent. The possible traumatic brain injury that the nurse discussed was nonsense. Claire was too strong for that.

It took almost two weeks, but finally it happened. Slowly, Dr. Leonard had discontinued the medicine to keep Claire from waking. Since that time, there had been small signs of movement. Sometimes her lids fluttered or her fingers twitched, but then one afternoon with both Catherine and Tony present, her eyes opened and she looked right at Tony. He could hardly speak through his relief. Finally, he found his voice. "Claire, are you awake?"

Catherine must have heard the change in his voice, because immediately she was at the other side of Claire's bed. "Ms. Claire, please come back to us."

Tony spoke fast. "She opened her eyes. I saw it—just a second ago." He reached for her hand—it was still so cold. "Claire, can you hear me?" He continued speaking to Catherine, "Go get the doctor. He's getting something to eat in the kitchen. Let him know she's finally waking." With a different tone, one of desperation and affection, he pleaded, "Claire, please open your eyes."

She obeyed, just as he'd taught her to do, but when she did, she immediately squinted. He jumped up and shut the heavy drapes. With only the light from the bedside stand, the colors within the suite muted, making her bruises less visible. Tony smiled as tenderly as he could and prayed that she would be able to talk. He didn't want to think about the nurse's warnings. Fighting back those thoughts, he lifted her hand and said, "It was too bright in here. I closed the drapes for you. Is that better?"

Her mouth moved, but nothing came out. His chest tightened as a tear fell from her once again closed eyes.

"It's okay, you don't need to talk," he said, trying to reassure her. "Please open your eyes again. It's so good to see your beautiful emerald eyes." Tony didn't know if it was his imagination, but her hand felt warmer. Her eyes opened and moved to the needle taped into the bend of her left arm. He explained, "That's how you've been eating for almost two weeks, and it has some pain medicine too—to make you more comfortable."

Her expression went from uncertainty to—Tony wasn't sure—terror? With her eyes open wide, he tried to reassure her by talking. After all, he'd been doing nothing but talk for over ten days; now he couldn't seem to stop. "Can you remember what happened? You had an accident."

She stared.

He wanted to know she understood. *Did she even know who he was? What was she thinking?* He continued, "You had an accident in the woods. When we found you, your jeans and boots were all muddy, and you had multiple injuries. Did you fall? Did you slip? Did someone or something out there hurt you? We've had the woods searched. Nothing was found." He leaned toward her. "Claire, we've been so worried about you."

Catherine and Dr. Leonard rushed into the suite. Dr. Leonard pushed forward, toward his patient. Obviously, he was as concerned as everyone else with her cognitive abilities. So far, Tony didn't know what to think. He only knew she was finally awake. He looked to the doctor and silently mouthed, "I don't know."

"Ms. Nichols, I'm Dr. Leonard. I've been taking care of you since Mr. Rawlings found you in the woods. Can you talk to me?"

Claire lifted her right hand to her throat.

They all smiled; Claire was trying to communicate. The doctor spoke, "Catherine, could you please get Ms. Nichols some water?" When she returned, Dr. Leonard put the straw to Claire's lips and commanded, "Drink slowly; your stomach has been empty for a while."

Claire began to sip.

The doctor turned to Tony. "Mr. Rawlings, as you can imagine, this is a very good sign. Due to the length of time Ms. Nichols was unconscious, I was hesitant to make any predictions. I believe we have just passed an important juncture in her care and with that, my prognosis for her has greatly improved." He removed the straw from her lips.

"Please, that was so good," Claire said. The room went silent. Everyone turned to her.

Tony spoke first, "Claire, thank God. How do you feel?"

"I feel—I feel—tired—and kind of dizzy." Her voice quivered unsteadily.

"Mr. Rawlings, I need to ask you and Catherine to allow Ms. Nichols some privacy while I examine her."

Catherine nodded and stood; however, Tony didn't want to let go of Claire's hand. He could gaze into her eyes forever. "Doctor, I can assure you, there is nothing I haven't seen. I don't believe Claire will mind if I stay."

"Mr. Rawlings, I realize you hired me; however, as a medical doctor, I need to see and speak to Ms. Nichols alone. You'll be welcomed back as soon as we're done." Tony stared at Dr. Leonard. The doctor continued, "Mr. Rawlings, she is *not* related to you. We must allow her some privacy."

Tony knew that the doctor was right. It was that, as he released her hand, Tony had the ominous feeling that he'd never hold it again. All it would take was for Claire to tell Dr. Leonard the truth, and the judgment he'd weeks ago been willing to accept, would be his. For so long, he didn't know if Claire would ever be able to tell the truth. Even now, he wasn't sure if she remembered it, but something about the way she looked at him while they were alone, told him she did remember. He squeezed her hand. "I'm sorry, Doctor," he said to Dr. Leonard. "You're right. It's just that it's been so long since she's been awake. I don't want to leave her." Standing, he continued, "I will; I'll be right outside the door. Please call me when you're finished." He then leaned over, kissed Claire on her forehead, and took one last long gaze into her beautiful green eyes.

Catherine was waiting in the hallway. As soon as he shut the door, she said, "What are you going to do if she tells?"

"What do you mean, what will I do? What choice do I have?"

Their voices were a stage whisper as they walked away from Claire's suite. "You have money. You have a lot of money. That money bought silence once before—it can do it again."

"Dr. Leonard already knows what happened. He's all but told me."

Catherine stood taller. "Anton, think! You aren't thinking straight. You refused to silence Claire—silence Dr. Leonard."

His eyes opened wide. "What the hell are you suggesting?"

Catherine shook her head. "Not that. I'm suggesting *money*. Everyone has his price. Pull up the monitor on your phone and learn what she's saying. Be prepared. For God's sake, do you think your grandfather would have wanted you to come this far to lose everything because of one mistake with a Nichols girl?" She reached for his shoulders. "It was an *accident*. They happen. Stop berating yourself and act like the man Nathaniel knew you could be." She took a deep breath. "Anton, I've seen that man. I know he's there. I've watched him succeed against all odds. Look around you. You did this. You made Nathaniel's fortune and more. You are Anton Rawls/Anthony Rawlings. Don't let this derail everything."

He didn't like what he was hearing, but now that Claire was all right, now that he knew she would survive, it was easier to take a step back. It was an *accident*. They'd been working too long and had too many triumphs to let it all unravel. He nodded and pulled the phone from his pocket. As he began to bring up the app, he thought about money. *How much would this cost him? Catherine's accident cost him a substantial payment each year. If he could pay for her mistake, he could pay for his own.* Dr. Leonard did seem like a respectable doctor; nevertheless, money had enticed him to step away from his own practice for two weeks—if it could do that, the possibilities were limitless.

The screen was small, yet when he held it out, both he and Catherine could see and hear. Claire was speaking, "… I'm very tired and my memories are fuzzy."

"It's all right," Dr. Leonard said. "Let me put your bed back." He pushed the button to recline the bed and continued to inquire. "Now, please, what do you remember?"

"Doctor, I'm going to get sick." Claire sat up with a wince. The doctor grabbed a basin, and the water Claire had drunk came back up. Tony felt Catherine's hand on his shoulder.

"Miss Nichols, it's okay. It's normal—your stomach has been empty for too long. Ms. Nichols, your pain medicine has started to wear off. I'll get you some more, but I want you to be thinking straight. Please tell me what happened."

Claire was now trembling and crying. Tony wanted to go back in the room. "I need to stop this. She isn't strong enough right now. Why can't he see that? He can do this another time."

"He can," Catherine said. "That's why he's pushing. He's hoping to catch her at her weakest."

Catherine's words burned deep. She was right. Dr. Leonard came across as nice and trustworthy, but here was evidence of how methodical and dubious he truly was. Tony refocused on his screen. The doctor gave Claire more water but instructed her to only rinse and spit into the basin. She began to speak, "I went for a walk in the woods ... I like the woods ... it rained the day before ... and the ground was slippery in some spots ... I made it into the woods fine ... but I let it get dark ... I watched the sun set ... I remember it being crimson and beautiful." She laid her head back on the pillow and closed her eyes.

"Please continue, Ms. Nichols."

"So it was dark by the time I headed back to the house. I remember getting to the clearing—which is about forty-five minutes from here. The sun ... I mean, the moon ... was bright ... I tried to get back ... Catherine had dinner waiting for me." Her words slowed and slurred.

Tony started to move and Catherine touched his arm. "It's too late," she whispered.

He nodded as his heart pounded rapidly in his chest. Dr. Leonard spoke softly. "Ms. Nichols, did you make it back to the house?"

"I don't remember." Claire's voice became stronger. "I remember slipping in the mud. There were roots and limbs. It was very dark under the trees. After that, I just don't know."

"Please know, Ms. Nichols, anything you disclose to me is said in confidence. I'm bound by complete patient-doctor confidentiality."

"Doctor, I'm not sure what you're asking me or what you're implying, but I can't remember what happened that night. Perhaps I hit my head?" Her eyes were open and brimming with tears. "Please, may I rest?"

The look of surprise that Tony saw on Catherine's face was surely a reflection of his own. For another moment, they both stood in silence.

"Well then," Catherine finally said, "congratulations, you did it. I doubted you, but you did it."

Tony put his phone in his pocket and fell against the corridor wall. "*We* did."

Just then the door to the suite opened. "Mr. Rawlings, Ms. Nichols is very tired, but you're welcome to come back in. Let me explain my find-ings ..."

Nine

Will you—Can I? – November 2010
(Consequences – Chapter 24)

Manipulation, fueled with good intent, can be a blessing. But when used wickedly, it is the beginning of a magician's karmic calamity.
– T.F. Hodge

Tony had been mulling the idea over and over in his head since Claire first woke from her *accident*. At first, it was only a fleeting thought, but then he would remember what it was like to be without Claire, and the idea of making her presence more permanent would seep into his mind. The way he saw it, Claire passed the ultimate test when she followed his rules and kept private information private. She'd had the opportunity to tell Dr. Leonard what truly happened—not just the accident. That would've been the tip of the iceberg—one story would have led to another. Oh, Tony had contingency plans. That's why he purposely created the *gold-digging* persona, but with her injuries, public opinion would've undoubtedly gone in her direction. Tony may have been able to keep it out of the media—he was prepared to pay Dr. Leonard an exorbitant amount of money to maintain his secrets—yet thanks to Claire's obedience, it never went that far. She had the perfect opportunity to expose him, and she didn't.

Starting that day in the hallway, as he listened to her with Dr. Leonard, through her recovery, onto their car ride when he took her to the meadow, confessed his behavior and she responded favorably, Tony began to see that Claire was the woman he wanted in his life. Anthony Rawlings usually got what he wanted. When he carried Claire to his bedroom after their car ride, it was his ultimate invitation. In all the years he'd lived on his estate, he'd never taken a woman to his bedroom. He didn't need to. He could take them to hotels or to their place. On the rare occasion that he brought a woman to the estate, he had plenty of bedrooms. No one, not one other woman, had ever seen his private suite—his ultimate personal space. Claire didn't know that, but Tony did. When he carried her from the car to his room, he opened a part of himself that he'd never shown to anyone else. It was a meaningful gift that she didn't know she'd received.

Months ago, he'd taken a strong young woman and refined her. Tony supposed it was like the process with gold, where excessive heat removes the impurities. In his process, he'd taken Claire into the fire and come away with the perfect companion—wife? Until recently, he'd never imagined marrying—anyone. Until recently, there'd been no one who could handle the job. Claire proved that she could handle it and more. She knew how to appropriately behave in public and in private. She was pleasing to the eye and even more pleasing to be with. Without planning to do so, Tony and Catherine had created the perfect Mrs. Rawlings.

It also seemed that realistically, Tony couldn't hold her prisoner forever. From the beginning, he knew that one day the arrangement would need to end. *What better long-term bind than a wedding ring?* That's what he explained to Catherine, when he told her that he'd finally decided to ask Claire to be his wife. Stoically, Catherine reminded him of the problems that his changes to their plan had already created. He reminded her that all the problems were under control, and assured her that they would remain under control when Claire was no longer a Nichols.

To Tony, that was the best part of his plan. Over the last eight months, he'd successfully removed Claire Nichols from the woman who slept beside him. She was, in actuality, the same woman, but anyone could see, she'd become someone new—from her new even more blonde hair and leaner build, to the most important quality—her behavior. The woman who walked away from her job as a bartender at the Red Wing no longer existed. Tony wasn't sure if even Claire realized the transition she'd been through.

The woman he'd created was as close to perfect as he could imagine. He also felt confident that as time passed, if further refinement was necessary, he was more than qualified to facilitate the change. After all, their paradigm was set. He was the teacher and Claire was the student. That wouldn't change once they were married. The real change would be in the eyes of the world: everyone would know that she was his.

Dr. Leonard had been right to ask Tony to leave the room when she woke. He'd said, "She isn't related to you, Mr. Rawlings." That phrase rang over and over in Tony's mind. The doctor had been right. Tony wanted the whole world to know that Claire *did* belong to him. No one would ever question his presence or right to be near her again.

As Eric drove Tony toward his New York City apartment building, Tony anticipated the evening he had planned. Everything was set, except her answer.

In most cases of business, Tony was sure of the answers he'd receive before he received them. With Claire, he wasn't one-hundred-percent sure. He'd debated his proposal. He had a stunning ring from Tiffany and Company, but it was his wording that he couldn't decide on. Over the course of the last eight months, Claire had been allowed very few choices. He wondered how it would be possible to ask her to choose marriage, without actually allowing her to choose. *If he did that, was that what he really wanted?* Her silence with Dr. Leonard was definitely a passed test. If presented with marriage or continued indebtedness, would he know that she truly wanted to marry him? Of course not. The only real test of her true feelings would be to offer her an alternate choice—her freedom.

The prospect made him nervous as hell.

What if she chose freedom? What if she said she wanted to leave him and never look back? Where would she go? Surely, she realized that there was nothing remaining of her previous life. Her apartment, car, and job were gone. She still had her sister. Even that was part of his plan. Claire didn't know that her family was scheduled to join them for Thanksgiving dinner. *What would happen if she decided on freedom?* Without a doubt, she'd need to maintain his rules—private information could still not be divulged. *Could he let her go?*

Tony didn't know.

When he entered the apartment's bedroom, Tony was momentarily mesmerized by the woman at the mirror. Walking behind her, he nuzzled her neck. As his breath bathed her soft, perfumed skin, he said, "Good evening, Claire. I trust you were successful today with your shopping endeavors?"

Tilting her head to allow him better access, she smiled. "Yes, I was out the better part of the day, and I found a whole new ensemble for tonight's *mysterious* activities. You know," she feigned a pout toward the mirror before continuing, "it'd be easier to shop, if you'd tell me more about our plans."

"All in due time, my dear, all in due time." He kissed her cheek, walked toward the dressing room, and called, "I can't wait to see tonight's ensemble."

When Tony reentered the bedroom on the way to his shower, he caught Claire's fiery gaze in the mirror. He'd learned to read her moods, and the fire he saw in the reflection wasn't a battle of wills—what he saw was desire. The way her cheeks reddened when their eyes met told him that she knew that she'd been caught. She'd been watching him with the expression of a girl looking through the candy store window. Totally nude, he moved behind her, wrapped her in his arms, and maneuvered his large hands beneath her flimsy robe. As he caressed her soft skin, he brushed his lips against her neck and whispered, "Do you think joining me in the shower would be detrimental to your hair and makeup?"

Goose bumps materialized on her arms and legs, as she breathlessly replied, "I think it would."

"Then perhaps we should plan it for another time?" His hands contradicted his words as they continued their descent.

"Or," Claire closed her eyes and tilted her head against his bare chest, "we could postpone your plans?"

Tony's body was obviously up for that idea, and the way she molded against him had his thoughts jumbled, but his mind prevailed. "Oh, God, I want to, but we have plenty of time for that. Tonight, I have special plans for you." He slowly stepped back, but before he relinquished his touch, he said, "And, so far, you look amazing. I believe I like your outfit now better than the one you bought."

With her robe now lying on the floor in a black silk puddle, Claire's cheeks blushed, and she flashed a modest smile. "It's November. I believe I'd get cold as we walk the streets of New York."

"Perhaps, but if I have anything to do with it—cold is *not* what you'd be feeling."

After a lingering kiss, Tony disappeared into the bathroom. He turned on the shower and with a groan, moved the levers to cold. When he emerged freshly showered and shaven, Claire looked amazing! After a little investigation, he learned that she was wearing some kind of hosiery that only went to her thigh. It was ingenious! Each step of obedience, each time she had the opportunity to disobey and didn't, his hope and anticipation for her answer was fortified.

After they'd eaten dinner and seen a play, Eric drove Tony and Claire to Central Park. The night was much cooler than Tony had planned; however, he was prepared for a carriage ride with gloves, scarves, and blankets. The longer the carriage moved, the happier Tony was for the cooler temperatures. It was as if no one else was out, and Central Park was lit up just for them.

He leaned close and began talking. It was something he'd never done to excess, until Claire—well, until her accident. Those days and weeks of talking just to talk had opened something inside of him. He had no desire to talk that much around others, but with Claire, he could. So, he did. As the horse trotted along the deserted paths, he talked about dating other women and how Claire was different. He explained that she knew the real him—the man few people ever get to see. Tony wanted her to understand, he had feelings—more than he'd ever experienced with anyone in his life. For the sake of the conversation and the proposal, he'd call them *love*. It wasn't that he thought his wording was deceitful. It was that he'd never experienced this feeling before, and he wasn't completely sure what it was—but, he believed it could be love.

"Claire, the other night you asked me if I cared about you. Honestly— with our initial arrangement—I never intended to, but without a doubt, I do." Tony looked down and took a deep breath. Resuming their eye contact, he asked, "Do you care about me? Do you enjoy being with me?"

He loved her smile and the way she never took her eyes off of him. "Tony, I do care about you. I want you to be happy, and I would do anything to help that happen, and on a night like tonight, or even a quiet night at home, I enjoy being with you," her eyes glistened in the cold air with the twinkling reflection of the lights from the trees, "more than enjoy; however," her eyes fluttered, "honestly, there are times I don't. There are times I want you away from me, or vice versa." Although her honesty may have been difficult to voice, she did just as he'd taught her and never looked away.

Tony smiled and leaned closer. He needed to kiss her. All he could think about was the taste of her lips. When he pulled away, he held nothing back, wanting her to know that not only did he expect honesty, he craved it. There were too many people in his life who were *yes men,* yet this woman who'd seen the absolute worst in him, could look him in the eye and be totally honest. "You're the most amazing woman. I have vice presidents, presidents, and chairmen of boards who've never experienced me as you have. None of them would have the courage to answer that question as honestly as you just did. It's your strength and determination that have infuriated me. That strength and resilience have also made me fall in love with you. Claire, I experienced life without you—after your accident."

He'd made his decision. Dr. Leonard wasn't the ultimate test: this was. She could walk away—he'd try to allow it. He would try, if that's what she wanted, but he had to know. He had to present the option.

He continued, "I don't want to be without you again, but I want you to make your own decision. Tonight, I'd like to present you with two options: your freedom—you may leave tonight and your debt is paid, or," he removed the ring he'd bought from his jacket pocket, "you could agree to marry me and spend the rest of your life with me, not out of obligation or contractual agreement, but because you want to be with me."

Perhaps Claire would think that his shaking was due to the cold. He waited. When she didn't reply, he said, "You told me yesterday no more black boxes, so I took it out of its box." He grinned. "Could we see if it fits?"

Claire nodded and extended her left hand, covered by a large mitten.

Tony smiled as he removed the fuzzy mitten and placed the ring on her fourth finger. "It seems to fit." Tony looked into her emerald eyes. "The question still seems to be unanswered. Do you want to keep it on and stay with me? Will you please be Claire Rawlings?"

"I-I'm so surprised," she stuttered, "ar-are you seriously asking *me* to marry *you*?"

He grinned and bowed his nose to hers. "Yes, my dear. This entire night has been leading to this proposal. I've watched you with me in private, in public, and with my closest friends. I want you there always. I love you."

"Please," she implored, "please, let me think. I promise you an answer soon."

He did what she asked. It wasn't often that Claire asked anything of him, and now she wanted time to think. As the carriage moved slowly around the frost-dusted park, Tony wondered how much time she wanted. Each moment made him more anxious. Maybe he hadn't thought this through enough. *What if she chose freedom? Could he do what he'd said? Could he give it to her?* As the panic continued to build a defensive wall, her beautiful voice broke through—shattering his doubts and calming his anxiety.

"God help me, yes—Tony, I'll marry you." He wrapped his arms around her and kissed her tenderly. When their lips separated, Claire confessed, "I love you too."

Relief like he'd never known filled his chest. Despite the frigid temperatures, he was warm and satisfied. Her confession of love was the most wonderful thing he'd ever heard.

The next morning, Tony slipped from their bed and made his way down to his office. He didn't care that it was Thanksgiving morning. He had a wedding to plan, and he wanted it done—now. Glancing at the clock, 7:03 AM, he knew who he needed to call first.

He'd discussed his plans with Catherine, and since Claire's conversation with Dr. Leonard, Catherine's opinion of Claire, too, had softened. She even told Tony more than once that she thought Claire was *good for him*. Funny, that was also what Courtney had said. It was more than that. Catherine spent hours and hours working with Claire and helping her recover from her accident. Tony suspected that it reminded Catherine of her own accident years ago. She knew firsthand the difficult path Claire endured, both mentally and physically. She understood it in a way Tony never would. That common experience created a bond between the two women. Of course, Catherine never admitted that, but she did say that when Tony was with Claire, especially during her recovery, Catherine saw Nathaniel in him. Although, Tony hadn't witnessed Nathaniel and Marie's interaction during that time, he knew a compliment when he heard one.

Despite all of that, Tony wasn't sure how Catherine honestly felt about the marriage thing. He squared his shoulders and hit *CALL*. Catherine answered on the second ring. "Yes?"

"Good morning, Marie."

"Anton ... you have heard of holidays, haven't you?"

"I thought you would want to be the first to hear my news—*our* news."

Catherine gasped. "You did it, didn't you? You asked her and she said yes?"

"Yes, and she's very anxious for your reaction."

"You actually *asked* her?" She emphasized the word.

"Yes—I *asked* her."

"And she said yes?"

Tony grinned into his phone. "Should I be offended that you find this so difficult to believe?"

"No, you shouldn't. I'm just—just—pleased. I think you're right. The situation couldn't go on the way it was much longer. This makes perfect sense. Besides, I can tell ... it's what you want."

"I do," Tony agreed.

"Did you offer her an alternative?"

"Her freedom."

"Oh, Anton, what if she'd gone that way?"

"She didn't."

Catherine's tone hardened. "Tell me how this changes things."

"It doesn't. Like you just said, it's a continuation."

"She'll have your name. Things will change."

Although his office door was closed, Tony lowered his voice. "She'll share the name *Rawlings*. You know as well as I, that she'll never be able to share *my* name and we both know why."

"Do you? Do you remember? It's important that you remember."

"Marie, how could I forget? I remember as well as you."

"Are you *in love* with her?"

Tony hesitated. "I believe I am."

"And you don't believe that changes anything."

"Maybe it does," Tony conceded. "Maybe it changes her role, but it doesn't change her debt. Now it has become a debt that she'll pay forever. That's the way this works, right? *Forever*—until death do us part?"

"No, Anton, it goes beyond that. I can promise you that."

He sat taller. "It may not have been the original plan, but once she says *I do*, there'll be one less Nichols."

"You believe that, don't you?"

"Don't you?" Tony asked. "Tell me that we haven't changed her and made her into a Rawlings."

"She has changed. I see that." Catherine conceded.

"I've helped you and you've helped me. Can I continue to count on your assistance?"

Catherine's tone softened. "Yes, of course, Anton. Nathaniel intended for us to work together. I won't be the one to disappoint him."

"I'm glad to hear that. Neither will I."

In a professional tone, Catherine replied, "Mr. Rawlings, please tell the future Mrs. Rawlings that I'm very happy for both of you."

Tony smiled. "I'll do that. Marie?"

"Yes?"

"This has worked out much better than I ever imagined, and I know it wouldn't have without you."

"Anton, I agree with everything, but please don't forget the big picture."

"I've told you that I'm in control, and we've seen that over and over—with Dr. Leonard and with my proposal. Now the whole world will know that she belongs to me—it won't be a clandestine arrangement."

"The whole world?" Catherine asked. "Is that referring to the emails you've been receiving from Emily Vandersol?"

Tony grinned. "As a matter of fact—yes. The Vandersols will be joining us for Thanksgiving dinner. Soon, they'll learn that Claire belongs to me. Her interaction with them will be at my discretion."

"Oh!" Catherine exclaimed. "How I wish I were a fly on the wall."

"My dear Marie, technology is a wonderful thing. Help yourself."

"Thank you, Mr. Rawlings, I believe I will. I'll also show the future Mrs. Rawlings my extreme pleasure upon your return."

Tony smirked. "That'll be interesting to witness. We'll be returning on Saturday. I'll let you know when I know more about the wedding."

"You know me—always at your service," she quipped.

Tony grinned as he hit *DISCONNECT.*

After some coffee and a light breakfast, Tony made the rest of his calls, and within a few hours, he had the whole wedding thing underway. The next hurdle was quickly approaching. Within a matter of hours he'd have the opportunity to meet his future in-laws face-to-face. They weren't exactly strangers. He knew everything about them and had even been at their wedding. Tony smirked; now, they'd be coming to his. Sometimes he marveled at how strangely things come full circle. That wasn't really true. He'd know that they were at his wedding; they'd had no idea.

With a few hours before his surprise guests arrived, Tony decided to go upstairs. He wanted to visit his fiancée, tell her about their wedding plans, and enjoy what was his for the taking. Besides, with their impending visitors, it was never too early to remind the future Mrs. Rawlings that her change of name would not mean a change in his rules.

Just another symposium – September 2011
(Consequences – Chapter 42)

Everyone has to make their own decisions.
You just have to be able to accept the consequences without complaining.
– Grace Jones

R isk versus Failure in the World of Business—that was the title
they'd given him. Tony wondered sometimes how they came up
with this crap! Three years ago the bottom fell out of the damn
economy and he'd survived. It seemed as though some of these symposi-
ums and seminars were trying to tell the up-and-coming entrepreneurs that
the failure was the fault of business. That wasn't entirely true, but voicing
his true feelings wouldn't win him any supporters in the necessary arenas.
So, every now and then, he'd concede to play their game and talk their talk.

Inspirational—that was what the planners called him, as they crooned,
gushed, and requested his presence at their seminar. Shelly received invitations like this all of the time. More often than not, she turned them down.
After all, Tony was a busy man; however, every now and then, she'd ask
him to consider attending. She'd remind him that he needed to do the occasional public-relations outreach. It not only kept his name on the tips of
people's tongues, sometimes he found talent along the way.

As he delivered the keynote address, Tony talked about recognizing and weighing risks. He discussed the importance of knowing your opponents and competitors, as well as your customers and investors—he admonished the audience to be informed. Don't be blindsided—be prepared. The people in the crowd hung on his every word. After all, he was Anthony Rawlings.

The act of delivering the occasional speech wasn't new; he'd been doing it forever. The newness came in that he didn't mind doing it as much as he once had. Looking to his left and seeing the emerald gaze, his business smile morphed into a genuine grin. The way Mrs. Rawlings watched and listened to his every word fulfilled an emptiness that he never knew existed. Many of the magazines and tabloids referred to Claire as nothing more than an ornament to adorn Tony's arm. That wasn't true. She was so much more.

Without a doubt, she was much smarter than the press gave her credit. It wasn't just her education—she was also a quick learner; however, when it came to her degree, Tony was thankful that Claire never mentioned pursuing meteorology. Other than a night a long, long time ago, in a bar, in a faraway land, the subject never came up. As a rule, Tony enjoyed fulfilling Claire's requests. He liked the entire process. He liked being asked and watching her techniques of persuasion. Most of the time, he enjoyed granting her desires; however, if she'd asked to return to the world of weather, he'd have denied it, without thinking twice. Since last December, Claire's full-time job was him. She was his wife—Mrs. Anthony Rawlings—and as such had no time for other endeavors. When he allowed her to enter the spotlight as his fiancée and wife, Tony hadn't realized the many roles she'd be required to perform. He didn't manufacture the responsibilities—they just were. With each new task, Claire succeeded. Whether it was charity work, hosting a party, or being at his side, he was constantly awed by her perfection. Perhaps he shouldn't have been. After all, as a Rawlings, nothing less would be acceptable. Public failure could not be tolerated. She handled her responsibilities well.

On occasions such as this particular seminar, after the speeches were complete, Tony was expected to mingle with the attendees. Claire was the one with that talent. She possessed an uncanny ability to talk to anyone and was the master of small talk. With a smile on her face, she could move people through the process, keep him from being saddled with one person too long, and most importantly, get them out.

Once his speech was done and he sat, Claire's small hand moved to his thigh. No one could see below the table, yet her light touch combined with her beautiful smile gave him a sense of accomplishment as he'd never known. A grin, a touch, and suddenly the evening was not only tolerable, but enjoyable.

Every now and then while the speeches continued, she'd whisper something to him—most of the time it had nothing to do with what was being said. It might be an observation of someone in the audience, or something totally random. It was strange how that, too, could make him relax. Externally, he was calm, cool, and professional, just as he'd always been. Tony recognized the difference—it was internal.

Sometimes he'd think back to a year and a half ago in sheer wonderment. The woman next to him was so different than the woman he met in Atlanta. Claire had exceeded his expectations at every test and turn. Tony knew that the same could be said of Catherine's expectations. Eighteen months ago, Catherine begrudgingly agreed to assist in overseeing Claire's care. Today, she was Claire's biggest cheerleader. As such, she'd articulate accolades at Claire's success with each new test or challenge. Catherine would remind Tony how proud Nathaniel would be of what he'd accomplished. He successfully removed a Nichols—a child of a child—while keeping her in a blissfully unaware state of debt.

With the attendees waning, Mr. and Mrs. Anthony Rawlings stood, still surrounded by a handful of eager entrepreneurs. Claire seemed to know that Tony's personal time clock was about to expire and graciously moved each man or woman on as soon as possible. There were still a few people waiting for their chance to speak with him when a blonde-headed young man approached. "Hello, Mr. Rawlings, I'm pleased to meet you. Your speech was remarkable and inspiring." Tony shook his hand and politely thanked him, and then the young man continued, "I have an unusual request. May I speak with your wife for a few minutes?"

Tony's glare immediately went to his wife. Moments earlier she'd been the perfect companion, yet in a split second, he saw her well-polished mask shatter into a thousand pieces. There was something in her eyes, a look, a feeling, one he'd seen in pictures, and then it was gone.

It all happened so fast. Then, she seemed to remember her place and worked to recover. She placed her hand gently on Tony's arm and stuttered, "O-Oh my," "A-Anthony," "S-Simon." She swallowed. "Anthony, may I introduce Simon Johnson. Simon and I were students together at Valparaiso—a million years ago." Each word came faster than the last. "Simon, may I introduce my husband, Anthony Rawlings."

The two men locked eyes and shook hands again. Tony hadn't seen Simon Johnson in years. He'd actually spoken to him a few times in California. Although he remembered the man was truly gifted in the world of gaming, that wasn't forefront in Tony's mind. He remembered pictures from the private investigators—pictures of two young people, practically children, head over heels in love. Suddenly, Tony's world came to a screeching halt. *Was the love he'd seen in those pictures ever anything he'd seen in the woman who professed her love for him?* Even her smiles today were different. *Was it age and maturity, or did this man possess a piece of Anthony's wife's heart that Tony would never have?* Summoning his most affirmable voice, Tony replied, "I believe that's Mrs. Rawlings' decision."

It didn't take Claire long to choose Simon over Tony. She willingly, without regret, excused the two of them and left him standing all alone. Before he brought Claire to these events, Tony would usually bring Patricia. He didn't enjoy her company nearly as well; however, Tony was sure she'd never have left him hanging in the middle of a room of people all alone.

Anthony Rawlings continued to smile and shake hands. He listened to questions and proposals and said all the right things; however, his eyes and mind were constantly pulled to a table not terribly far away. To Claire's credit, when Simon attempted physical contact, Tony watched her pull away. For what seemed like hours the two of them appeared engaged in a soul-searching discussion. When Claire finally returned, he scrutinized her expression. It was perfect and empty. He never realized that he'd been denied that *look*, until he saw it bestowed on someone else. Stoically he nodded and addressed his wife, "Mrs. Rawlings." They had more attendees to meet, and her name was his subtle reminder of her title and her duty. *She belonged to him!*

Tony glanced at his watch. Claire had only been gone for eight minutes. It was the longest eight minutes he'd endured in a lifetime. The rest of the evening, she performed beyond expectation. She spoke politely and moved people along. It was her eyes: they were far away in another time and another place.

As they stepped to the curb and waited for Eric, Tony's hand rested in the small of Claire's back. He, too, was seeing memories—flashes of photos. He remembered pictures of Claire and Simon on the Valparaiso campus and reports of her staying in Simon's room, or vice-versa.

When they were settled into the limousine, Tony waited. He waited for Claire to talk, to apologize, or to say anything. She didn't. Her normally chatty demeanor was gone; instead she stared aimlessly toward the window, seemingly mesmerized by the lights of Chicago. Time didn't register as Tony's blood boiled. *How dare Simon Johnson approach Anthony Rawlings' wife in a public setting? Claire knew her role; it was that of the perfect companion. How many rules had she successfully broken in a matter of seconds? By leaving him and going off with Simon, she'd not fulfilled her obligation, in essence, not doing as she'd been told. She did it in public! It was public failure!* Tony wondered how many tabloids would jump on this.

Finally, he spoke, "Mrs. Rawlings." He moved closer. Their noses nearly touched when she turned to face him. "What is your name?"

It was as if his words weren't registering. He wanted—no *needed* for her to understand. Tony grasped her chin, not allowing her to turn away, and repeated his question. "Your name. What is your name?"

He watched as the fire in her eyes began to burn away the fog of memories. "Tony, what are you doing?"

He held tight. "I'm asking you a question. One that you seem unable to answer."

Claire's neck stiffened. "My name is Claire ... Claire Rawlings."

"Please, Mrs. Rawlings, explain to me how you can be sitting with me, your husband, wearing the rings I purchased, in the limousine paid for by my hard work, and thinking about another man."

"Tony, please let go of my face. You're hurting me."

Though the red seeped, he remembered his promise and released her chin; however, relinquishing her completely was out of the question. His large hand slid behind her neck, tightly holding her head, and purposely pulling the hair that dangled down her neck. Tony did not like repeating himself, and he'd already done it once since they entered the limousine.

For Claire's sake, he didn't want to do it again. He continued, "Do I need to repeat every question, or do you think you may be able to answer at least one the first time?"

"Seeing Simon caught me off guard. I haven't thought of or heard from him in eight years. Don't you think that deserves some reflection?"

She gasped as his grip tightened. "No," he growled. "I believe the past is just that. It's done and now it's time to concentrate on the present." He stared at the fire that now burnt out of control as the car's cabin filled with his pent-up rage. *How dare she be thinking about another man!* He spoke slowly and deliberately, wanting to give her the chance to hear every word. Anthony Rawlings would not repeat himself again. "At present, I believe you need to concentrate on showing me that *my* wife is first and foremost concerned with pleasing her husband."

With their eyes still locked, Tony reached for the button to close the window between them and Eric. Claire didn't look away until she noticed his next move. With the hand not holding his wife's neck, Tony unzipped the slacks of his tuxedo. He wasn't truly thinking—he was reacting. That didn't matter. When Claire began to protest, he trumped her. Physically she was no match for him, and the idea that she'd attempt to push herself away may have been comical if it hadn't fueled his rage. Tony seized her hand and twisted it back. Holding her neck, he rested his head against the leather seat, entwined his fingers in her hair and directed her movement. It didn't take her long to remember how to follow his number-one rule. Not all demands required audible words. He'd trained her well.

Before they left the limousine, Tony told Claire to fix her makeup; there would be people in the building where they were about to enter. The world didn't need to know that his wife needed a refresher course on appropriate behavior. Dutifully, Claire appeared composed as they walked through Trump Tower's lobby, yet when he gently put his arm around her waist, she tensed. It was enough insubordination to tell Tony that Claire's lessons were not complete. He leaned close and whispered, "I have more ways you can demonstrate your devotion, Mrs. Rawlings. We'll review when we reach our apartment."

Tony woke during the night. They'd be heading to Iowa in the morning, yet his head pounded with the memories of Simon Johnson. Once they were back to the apartment, Claire had done her best to show her devotion. Tony reminded himself that she wouldn't have misbehaved if Simon had not approached her. That didn't absolve her of her inappropriate behavior. He planned to remind her about her duties, again, once they returned to the estate. A breach like what occurred couldn't be repeated. Perhaps she needed some time alone at the estate, showing her devotion to her husband, instead of out with friends or communicating with her sister. Perhaps that would help to reinforce his stance. After all, he couldn't tolerate public failure.

Claire's consequences weren't enough to quell Tony's fury. Simon Johnson was also guilty. He'd had the audacity to approach Tony's wife in a public forum. Tony slipped from their bed and made his way to his apartment office where he pulled out his private laptop.

He began to search Simon Johnson. The man had made quite a success of himself. He was founder of a gaming company in Palo Alto, California, called SiJo Gaming. Though not as wealthy as Tony, he was doing very well. It seemed as though he'd left Shedis-tics, a Rawlings subsidiary, years before. If he still worked under the Rawlings umbrella, Tony thought he could influence Johnson through business. After all, Tony had done it before; however, this was different. Johnson's success made him a potential threat. Tony wanted Claire totally dependent upon him. He couldn't allow there to be an ex-boyfriend with the financial means to help Claire if she asked. By the way Johnson looked at her, and she at him, that wasn't beyond the realm of possibility.

If business intervention weren't possible, Tony needed to look elsewhere. In an unnamed file, he found the cell phone number he sought.

The way he looked at it, it was a business decision. Claire's behavior reflected upon him; he had a reputation to uphold. He'd invested a lot of time and money into his wife. As with anything else in business, he evaluated the facts. Positives were accentuated and negatives needed to be eliminated. If an adversary was identified, it became a liability. Liabilities can hinder the projected outcome—and needed to be removed.

Admittedly, this was different than any other call he'd authorized. Simon Johnson was not on Nathaniel's list. That didn't mean that Tony couldn't justify his decision.

Claire was on his list, and as long as she performed well and personified a Rawlings, Tony was doing his part to rid the world of a Nichols—a child of a child. When she failed, when she exhibited her independence and innate strength in a non-Rawlings matter, she reminded Tony that he'd failed to directly, fully fulfill Nathaniel's directive. In order to avoid this type of a failure in the future, ridding the world of Simon Johnson would work to assure Claire's success. He was helping her.

After the short call, Tony made his way back to their bed. He felt a slight twinge of his conscience when he found Claire sleeping on her edge of the massive mattress. It was how she used to sleep when he first brought her to the estate. He wanted to pull her close and apologize for some of his earlier behavior, but that wouldn't teach her the lesson he needed her to learn. It would only show weakness, and that wasn't acceptable.

When they returned to the estate, Claire's disobedience would result in new rules, and her recently earned liberties would need to be reevaluated. It only made sense: actions had consequences. Nevertheless, by the time he slid under the covers, the sound of Claire's soft breathing and the knowledge of his call dissipated the last hues of red. With a renewed sense of calm, Tony drifted off to sleep.

Eleven

The beginning of the end ... coffee? – January 2012
(Consequences – Chapter 46)

If a relationship is to evolve, it must go through a series of endings.
– Lisa Moriyama

Tony paced the length of his office. Although his decision was set, he couldn't shake the conflicted feeling that nagged deep inside of him. He told himself that this was a test—only a test. He'd presented Claire with more tests than he could count, and when she passed this one, everything could continue as it had been. *Would she pass?* Tony knew in his heart that this wasn't the same as other tests he'd created; this was bigger and potentially life changing. It wasn't a *test:* it was her *final examination*—the fulfillment of a personal deal he'd made a lifetime ago. It started out as an idea, a seed, and like things do, it grew.

Twenty-two months ago, when he brought Claire to his home, Tony didn't know what to expect. He never in a million years planned to have feelings for her—she was the enemy, a Nichols. In hindsight, Catherine had seen and warned him. She knew his interest in Claire was more than that of curiosity. That being said, Tony fought those feelings with all he had. He'd never admit it to anyone, but in a significant way, Claire was his biggest success and his biggest failure. He'd brought her to Iowa to pay the penance of her family's sins, but during her sentence she'd won him over. Oh, he'd changed her, but she'd changed him, too. He was no longer her warden but her husband. In essence, she'd derailed his plans.

Unlike any other failure, and he'd had very few, Tony didn't mind. He enjoyed her—more than enjoyed, he craved her. She fulfilled a part of him he'd never known existed, yet despite all the ways he'd changed her, he knew that she was still a Nichols. She acted, dressed, and looked different, but was it real? After all, deep down, she was still the same woman who he'd acquired. It was a reality he couldn't shake. Maybe it was the way the subject snuck into conversations. Catherine would say something like, *I saw the photos of the two of you in the magazine. Claire is doing so well, and you two truly make a handsome couple. Sometimes I forget that she's a Nichols.*

It would be at times like that when Tony would remember the little seed that had been planted decades ago—the seed which grew tall and deep and reminded him that a *Nichols* helped to condemn his grandfather to twenty-two months in prison. That time period resonated in Tony's psyche. *Twenty-two months*—the length of time that Nathaniel Rawls lost to the state of New York for sins that were saddled on him by Sherman Nichols and Jonathon Burke. With that time period in mind, Claire's sentence was almost up. Originally, it had been the time period Tony had hoped to keep Claire. He and Catherine had even discussed what would happen to her once it was all over.

Since the very beginning, Catherine had reminded him that Tony needed to stay cognizant of his public persona. If Claire failed, Tony need-ed to be prepared to distance himself. If he couldn't, there was only one option. That option may have been viable two years ago, but it wasn't something Tony would entertain now. Claire's *accident* had been too traumatic. He refused to consider her enduring anything worse; neverthe-less, the groundwork had been laid for the option of public disgrace.

From Tony's perspective, the decision was hers. The only way that Claire would be publicly disgraced was if she failed the test he was about to present. If she passed, the time period of her sentence would pass and life would go on. Taking a stiff drink of Johnnie Walker Scotch, Tony re-assured himself that Claire would pass. She'd been presented with the op-tion of freedom once, the night he proposed, and she willingly surrendered her liberties to him. Standing near the highboy, Tony poured himself another two fingers—maybe three—of scotch when he heard his office door open.

"Anton, it's late. Why are you still up?"

He didn't turn around; instead, he glanced at his watch—2:14 AM. He had no idea it was that late. "I'm thinking."

"Where's Claire?" Catherine asked.

"Bed." He spun around. "Where would you expect her to be at this hour?"

"She's in *your* suite, isn't she? You left her alone in there?"

"What's the matter, Catherine? No videos for you tonight?"

Catherine shook her head and sat on the leather sofa. "Anton, you're upset. Are you worried?"

He lifted one finger in her direction and went to his desk. After a few moments and a few codes, he stood and faced his oldest colleague. "No, I'm not worried. I have total confidence in my wife. Tomorrow night you and I'll be discussing how she followed my rules, once again."

"I believe you're right. So, why are you doing this?" Her shoulders sagged. "Why are you forcing her to jump through another hoop?" With more determination, she stood and faced him. "Claire loves you and you love her. Let that be enough. There are other Nichols who can pay. Look what you've done to John." Her eyes glistened. "Oh, Anton, that was brilliant."

Tony exhaled and collapsed on the chair near the sofa. "That had its own perks, but it was also a step of this test. Don't you understand? Now John can't help her—so much for his proclamation of undying devotion. He and Emily are a little busy at the moment."

"I do! I understand, and the Simmonses? They're still out of the country. Right?"

He studied Catherine's expression. "Right. Why would that matter? They're *my* friends. Brent works for me."

"Oh, you're right. It's just that I believe Claire and Mrs. Simmons have become very close."

Tony shrugged. "I don't know. Claire complains about how much Courtney talks." A small grin emerged. "Now, if that's not the pot—"

"Anton, I see how you have this all planned. Nathaniel would be so proud. And you're so brave! You're willing to take the poison?"

His dark eyes darted from his near empty glass to Catherine's questioning gaze. "I am. I don't think it'll be necessary, but if she takes the bait and drives away, I'll drink it." He swallowed the remaining contents of his tumbler. "Are you sure you know what you're doing?"

Catherine nodded. "It's not like I can practice on anyone, but yes. I'm confident you'll go unconscious and nothing more."

"As in, I won't die? Go ahead and say it, Marie. I've momentarily turned off the surveillance to the whole damn house. The whole system's doing a reboot. No one will ever hear what we're saying."

"Anton, I don't want to talk about you dying—that's not going to happen. As you've said, you probably won't even need to drink the coffee. But, if you do—"

"If I do, I'll live to see the repercussions of Claire's decision."

Catherine nodded. "What about witnesses?"

"I have a web conference I'm doing from home tomorrow. If she gets in the car, I'll be live in front of people all over the country."

Catherine reached out and covered Tony's hand. "If you're sure you need to do this, I'll help you. Just like I've helped in the past and how you've helped me. I won't let anything happen to you. We're too close to seeing the fulfillment of our goals." She clapped her hands under her chin. "Just think—the end is so near. Only Emily will be left."

Tony straightened his shoulders and sat taller. "Remember that—only Emily. Claire will be done. Nothing else is necessary; her name is off the list."

"Yes, of course. That's what you'd said, but if she doesn't take the bait?"

His voice deepened. "Then her name is off the list. If she's presented with a clear line to freedom and doesn't take it. No! *When* she's presented with this avenue and doesn't take it, it'll prove that Claire Nichols is gone." He felt his eyes darken as he emphasized his final point, spacing each word. "Claire. Rawlings. Was. Never. On. Our. List."

Catherine stood. "Yes, of course. Now, how much longer until the cameras turn back on? I'll get things set in the kitchen."

Tony glanced at his watch. "You have about ten minutes."

Walking toward the door, she said, "I'll have it ready."

Looking into his empty tumbler, Tony's mind filled with images of him and his wife. They were memories of private times, times of comfort and companionship. He'd never had a person in his life before. He'd never wanted to be near someone or please someone. He had to know that, no matter what, he could trust this person. *Why, oh why had that person been Claire?* Of all of the people in the world, why did it have to be one of the people he'd promised to bring down?

Closing his eyes, Tony remembered Claire after her accident. He had brought her down, but in true Claire fashion, she rebounded. That strength and resilience amazed him. *If she failed this impending examination, would she rebound?*

He didn't want to think about it; instead, he imagined their future. Claire would pass. She wouldn't take the bait.

Feeling a bit more confident, Tony walked back to his desk and searched travel sites. Claire enjoyed travel. She didn't know that she was facing a life-changing test, but when she passed, he wanted to reward her. Maybe England? They'd talked about that. No, it was January. The United Kingdom would be cold. A grin surfaced as he thought about her likes and dislikes—she liked sun. He entered *tropical beaches* into the search engine. Tony would take her someplace warm. If she asked why, he'd say it was because she was upset about her brother-in-law; however, he'd know the real reason: it was her positive consequence.

When Tony crawled back into his bed, he slid behind Claire's sleeping body and wrapped her in his arms. She fit perfectly as he was drawn to her radiating warmth. Gently kissing her hair, he tasted her perfume as his hands wandered her curves, caressing her soft skin. Her soft murmurs filled his heart with hope as she settled into his embrace. Smiling, Tony imagined that in a few days he'd have his wife on a sunny beach with nothing more than a bikini—maybe not even that. Those images and more filled his mind as he drifted off to sleep.

When he woke, Tony lingered longer than usual in the warmth of their bed. Being much too early for Claire to wake, he lifted his head, rested it on his elbow, and watched her sleep. Her lightened hair covered her pillow as renegade strands crisscrossed her cheek. Along with her exposed face, one bare shoulder was visible above the mound of luxurious blankets. Tony leaned closer, kissed her forehead, and watched in amusement as her nose wrinkled. Lightly, he kissed her again. This time he was rewarded with the most beautiful moan as she stretched and turned toward him. Although Claire was still sound asleep, she subconsciously responded to his touch. He wanted to wake her, but he feared that if her warm, soft skin touched his and they connected their bodies, as they'd been connected the night before, he wouldn't be able to carry out his plan.

Brushing the strands of blonde from her face, he whispered, "You don't need to wake yet." When she didn't respond and he was confident of her sleeping, he added, "You have a big day, my dear. You need your rest. Tonight we'll celebrate."

Throughout Tony's morning routine, he avoided thoughts of Claire's impending examination. To him it was merely a formality—the final signature on their life-long contract. The deal was already complete; she belonged to him. His wife wouldn't disappoint.

Anthony Rawlings reassured himself. Claire knew better than to disappoint, because if she did, he'd promised consequences, and above everything else, he was a man of his word.

Tony had finished his breakfast when Claire entered the dining room. She'd obviously just gotten out of bed and in his opinion was the most beautiful woman in the world. It was part of her appeal, a piece of the puzzle that helped Tony realize that he had truly fallen in love. She didn't have to be wearing designer dresses nor have her hair and makeup perfect. Even without the polish, she was stunning. Smiling he said, "Good morning, my dear. You look beautiful this morning."

Claire made a face. "I think you need an eye exam." She wrapped her arms around his neck, and he stared up into the emerald glow of her eyes. Before he could speak, she kissed his cheek and continued, "I just wanted to catch you before you left."

It was then that Tony's attention went to Catherine. She'd silently entered the dining room, and at Claire's comment about Tony's departure, Catherine's lips pursed into a straight line. As Claire sat and Catherine poured her coffee, Claire continued speaking. "I wanted to tell you how much I appreciated talking to Emily. It's a difficult time for them, and I wanted to let you know I'll miss you."

It wasn't just her words that reassured Tony: it was her smile. She knew her contact with her family was at his discretion, and she wasn't fighting, but thanking him for it. He was glad Catherine heard. The crimson that had been threatening faded. Tony proceeded with confidence. "Good news, I'm working from home today." He settled back against the chair as Catherine slipped wordlessly from the room. "So, you won't need to miss me."

"That's great!" Claire replied. "Do you have a lot of work?"

"A few web conferences and phone calls, but don't worry, I know your schedule is free. I have some ideas for us, too." Tony knew that his smile was too big for the circumstances; nevertheless, he couldn't restrain it. Claire would pass her test, and he had multiple ideas for celebration in mind. He couldn't wait to tell her about the surprise trip. He'd found it earlier this morning when he was supposed to be preparing for his web conference. It was a small exclusive resort on Seven Mile Beach on the west side of Grand Cayman Island. Currently, the temperatures were in the mid to upper eighties and the forecast was perfect. He imagined her delight as he showed her the website.

Claire replied, "All right, I need to work out and clean up. I came down here in a hurry to see you."

"When you're dressed, come to my office," he said. As he stood to leave, he reached out. Mindlessly, he touched her shoulder and fought the urge to explore below her soft robe. His desire to speed time and move past the examination was almost palpable.

She tilted her head toward his hand and said, "I'll be there as soon as I can."

Kissing her cheek, he allowed his desire to infiltrate his tone. "Or, you could visit before you dress?"

She touched his hand. "If I do that, you may not get your work done."

Damn, she was right. They would have plenty of time for his plans. "As usual, my dear, you're right. I'll see you in my office, soon." As his lips brushed her cheek, he looked up in time to see gray irises watching from the hall. Reluctantly, he left his wife and walked toward his office.

Before he closed the door, Catherine hurriedly came down the hall. Everything they said at this point would be on video. They both knew what could be at stake. "Mr. Rawlings, you left the dining room before I could check on you. Is there anything you need?"

"No, Catherine, I believe I'm quite satisfied with all that I have."

She squared her shoulders. "You are planning on working from home?" Her tone made the statement a question. "Or have your plans changed?"

"Nothing has changed. I'll let you know if I need anything."

Catherine nodded and turned away.

After a brief visit to the Grand Cayman's website, Tony forced himself to concentrate on the business at hand. He had a web conference with some other investors about a joint endeavor that hadn't yielded the desired results. It was a bold initiative to revitalize manufacturing in Michigan. In desperate need of help, the auto companies and the state had been more than willing to make concessions regarding taxes and fees. The problem centered on the expiration of the original terms. It seemed as though the powers that be in the state of Michigan believed that they had Tony and the other investors over the proverbial barrel. As far as he was concerned, it couldn't be farther from the truth. Reviewing the numbers, Tony knew that he'd gladly take the write-off and shut the doors before he agreed to the exorbitant taxes. He'd already shut the doors of an unprofitable stamping plant in Flint, Michigan. He didn't understand how they could think he was bluffing on this.

It was almost 10:00 AM when Tony heard the faint knock on his office door. Despite his conversation at hand, a grin briefly flew across his lips as he read the time on his screen. His rules regarding Claire spending her days with him in his office no longer existed. She was, after all, his wife; however, it seemed that old habits die hard. When she'd first been told that she needed to spend the days he worked from home, nearby, in the event her services were required, he'd told her to *always* be present by 10:00 AM. Even though he didn't say that this morning, nor did he require her services, her obedience continued to strengthen his confidence. He pushed the button under his desk and his door opened. Before he could acknowledge her presence, he needed to respond to one of the other investors. Claire didn't interrupt; she smiled and sat quietly on the sofa. Later he noticed her reading an article in one of the magazines.

The conference finally finished around 10:45 AM. He'd tried to end it sooner, as he wanted to appreciate every second they had together before her test. She must have heard that his conference ended, because when he turned his chair, she was looking in his direction. Immediately, she placed the magazine on the table and walked toward him. Grinning, he murmured, "Ahh, blue, my favorite color." Tony was suddenly thankful for his loose-fitting sweatpants. "You're beautiful in any color." He drank her in, savoring everything about her. His eyes settled on her diamond journey necklace. He knew why Catherine had laid it out: it helped to create the persona that Claire enjoyed the finer things. Nevertheless, he'd always liked it. Lowering his gaze to the neckline of her sweater, his tone turned sultry. "Or, in no color." Putting his hands around her waist, Tony longed to pull Claire onto his lap and whisper, *follow my rules—I know you can*. If he did, would it ruin the test? He could say it loud and proud. Anthony Rawlings wasn't hiding from anyone; instead, he caressed her trim waist and said, "I have one more web conference at 11:00 AM and then two lunch phone calls. I'd like you back after that." It wasn't a request: it was a demand or a plea. He wasn't sure anymore.

"It's so nice out. I'd like to go for a hike while you're working."

"No." Tony slowed his tone. He couldn't give anything away. "The phone calls may need to be postponed, depending on the outcome of the next web conference. I'd like you here, if I'm done earlier. We can lunch and discuss our possible afternoon activities." He turned back to his computer screen and read while he spoke. It was the message he'd planted, the next step. As he was about to continue, Claire surprised him with kisses to his neck.

Warm breaths instigated chills, as Claire responded. "Well, then, may I just go out back? The sky's so clear, and I could really use some fresh air."

He didn't try to contain his seductive grin. "Okay, just be back by noon, and ..." It was now or never. "... could you get me some coffee before you go?"

Each move she made filled him with hope and desire. His arousal was nicely hidden, but as soon as she left, he definitely needed to reposition his seating. One more kiss to his neck and Claire said, "Yes."

At 10:57 AM, Claire returned to his desk with a warm cup of coffee. When he heard her approaching, he picked up his iPhone and pretended to have a conversation as he rummaged through papers on his desk. When he *hung up*, he turned and faced his wife. Tony's body battled with his mind as he fought his personal desire. It was the confidence of her impending behavior that propelled him forward. "Tell Eric there are contracts at the Iowa City office. I need them here *before* 1:00 PM. He needs to get them immediately." For a moment, Claire stood silently and stared with her big, innocent emerald eyes. A small voice told him that she knew his plan, she was ahead of him and—and—he waited for the voice to tell him if she would pass. Then he remembered her earlier request. Claire didn't know his plans; she wanted to walk outside. Exhaling the building tension, he added, "And after that, you may go for your walk. Just be back by noon."

She smiled and kissed his cheek. "Okay. I'll tell Eric and be back." He watched as she hurried away. The web conference was to begin in two minutes, yet he felt as though his life was literally walking toward her destiny. He adjusted his computer screen and pulled up the house surveillance.

Sitting on the edge of his desk, where she'd placed it, was his coffee. Tony looked at the cup. He'd never asked Catherine the specifics about the contents. He had no reason to distrust her. She said he'd wake after he drank it. Tony knew that Catherine would not disappoint him.

The conference began as each participant introduced him or herself. Tony listened halfheartedly as he scanned their resumes. They were the pages he'd been ruffling through earlier. He heard their voices and put names with their faces; all the while he watched the small section of his screen devoted to the garages.

After he'd introduced himself and given a synopsis of the goals he planned to accomplish during the next thirty minutes, he watched Claire enter the garage. Briefly, she gazed at the cars and then walked toward Eric's apartment door. The small image didn't have sound, but he could see as she knocked and Eric opened his door. It seemed as though Eric answered a little too quickly; after all, he was expecting Claire, but Claire didn't seem to notice.

The exchange between her and Eric lasted only seconds, but as the cup of coffee taunted him, Tony felt as if time were standing still. Then the examination he'd prepared unfolded before his eyes. Eric grabbed his coat and hat, unlocked the key cabinet on the wall, removed a set of keys, and shut the cabinet. Tony held his breath as the small metal door bounced open. It wasn't overt and Eric didn't appear to notice. He was still speaking with Claire as he looked at his watch. Next, the garage door opened to the outside world as sunlight streamed over the camera, fading the color from the corner of Tony's screen.

On the larger image, two participants discussed something about a quantitative summary. Tony didn't care. His attention was on the small corner where Claire wrapped her arms around her midsection and watched Eric drive away. Color returned to the image as the garage door closed. She turned back to the way she'd entered when she stopped and stared toward the open cabinet.

Tony didn't know what was being said on his web conference as he held his breath and waited. Seconds earlier, time had stood still; now he couldn't slow it down. Claire reached into the cabinet and grabbed a set of keys. The ones to the new Mercedes were purposely placed in a more accessible spot. The headlights flashed as she hit the button on the fob.

When the garage door opened again, Tony didn't notice the loss of color. His vision, his office, his life was red. The disappointment was overwhelming. The pain of betrayal washed over him as the crimson-colored memories sped through his consciousness. Everything—all twenty-two months—was a lie. Claire never loved him. If she had, she wouldn't have jumped at the first opportunity to leave. She'd played him, used him, and manipulated him. He'd been a fool to believe that love existed. He'd never seen it—not the *love* they talk about in songs or in books. Not the look she'd given to Simon Johnson. None of it was real. It was a fictitious emotion created for saps who wanted to believe, an illusion—like Santa Claus. The *idea* brought people joy, until they were faced with the bitter reality and disappointment of betrayal. Hadn't Tony learned the truth a long time ago? Numbers were real. Money was real. Emotions were for the weak.

As the garage door closed, Tony reached for the ceramic cup. The liquid had cooled, yet as he used one hand to make the web conference fill his entire screen, his other hand tentatively touched the rounded handle as if it were potentially scalding. He didn't know how long it took to pick up the cup, or to take that first drink; however, as soon as he did, redness exploded, extreme pain clenched his chest, and blackness prevailed.

Twelve

Consequences were promised – January 2012
(Consequences – after Chapter 46)

Consequences are unpitying.
– George Eliot

Voices infiltrated the smothering darkness. Tony fought to find the surface, to break free of the blackness that surrounded him. It was as if he were at the bottom of a deep pit filled with water, swimming toward the air, pushing upward with all of his strength. *Where was it?* As the voices became clearer, he focused on and used them as his new goal. With all his might, he pushed toward the sound. A few more attempts and he'd break free.

The voices were clear. "Doctor, his vitals are stronger. The medicines have gotten his blood pressure back within the normal range."

"Have there been any signs of regaining consciousness?"

The first voice sounded less confident. "His physical response has been encouraging. The results of the EEG are in his chart, but we haven't had any signs of voluntary movement."

Tony pushed forward, *I'm here. I can hear you!* The darkness wouldn't allow him to speak. Unrelenting, it wrapped about him, filled him, and held him tight.

"Doctor, do we know the substance he ingested?"

"Not completely. The preliminary tests of the coffee found at the scene, and the contents removed from his stomach, confirm that the coffee was the source; however, due to his physical reaction, we believe the list is inconclusive."

"There was more than one toxin?"

"Yes, whoever did this, wanted to be sure it …"

The voices drifted farther away, taking with them Tony's audible goal and disorienting him in the darkness. Exhaustion prevailed and the blackness momentarily won.

Tony blinked his eyes, trying to focus on the world beyond the black. The room was bright, too bright, as people spoke. Keeping his eyes open was too difficult; instead, he settled into the darkness of his closed eyes and tried to listen. He heard voices, but their words were unfamiliar. Slowly they began to register … *his heart*—they were talking about his heart: it was beating.

That was reassuring, and he was glad to hear that, but he had to wonder: had it *not* been?

When he felt someone touch his forehead, he opened his eyes. It was one of the people in scrubs. Tony blinked toward her.

"Doctor, the patient is conscious."

Suddenly, another face was before him. This face had bright eyes that were acutely alert. "Hello, Mr. Rawlings, we're glad you decided to join us."

Tony tried to talk, but he couldn't. There were unknown sensations in his chest and throat that ached. The sensation was more of discomfort than pain. He tried to block it and searched for a new goal. Somewhere in the chaos he found a consistent beeping—somewhere beyond the people and discomfort. Closing his eyes, he concentrated on the steady rhythm.

"Mr. Rawlings, don't leave us again. We need you to stay with us." It was the voice of the bright eyes.

He looked toward her and blinked.

"Can you hear me?"

Since he couldn't speak, he blinked.

"You had us all worried."

Tony's mind scrambled. *What happened? Where was he? Why were they talking about his heart?*

His heart.

They said it was beating, yet agonizing emptiness made him doubt its presence. As Bright Eyes stared, the memories rushed back. He couldn't think of anything except Claire's examination. She took the bait, drove away, and failed his test. How these people could possibly be right? How could his heart continue to beat when Claire had ripped it out of his chest and shattered it beyond repair?

Bright Eyes spoke again, "Mr. Rawlings, it seems that you ingested a poison. Do you remember what happened?"

He blinked again.

"You do? Did you take this toxin knowingly?"

He fought to keep his eyes open.

"Mr. Rawlings, relax. You'll be able to talk with us soon."

Soon? *Why couldn't he talk now?* Then there were people—more people—in his line of vision. They scrambled about pulling and prodding. He didn't want to think about what they were doing; instead he closed his eyes and listened to the beeps.

It was sometime later, the bright-eyed woman returned.

"Mr. Rawlings, can you speak?"

"Y-yes," he managed.

"Do you remember what you ingested?"

"Cof-coffee." His voice sounded unfamiliar—scratchy and weak.

"Yes, the police collected the coffee. It contained poison. The police want to talk to you. However, I believe you need your rest first. How are you feeling?"

"My chest and sides hurt."

Bright Eyes nodded. "We had to restart your heart. Whatever you ingested has had a negative effect on your heart muscle. We'll have to ensure that there's no permanent damage. We have a cardiologist who'll be in to talk with you regarding future treatment."

Tony blinked and tried to concentrate. "Treatment? What do you mean? There could be long-term effects from this?"

"I don't want to worry you unnecessarily, but yes. Mr. Rawlings, you're lucky to be alive—to have survived this. I'm guessing that either you were too healthy for this toxin, or the dose was misjudged."

"Are you saying that I could have died?"

Bright Eyes smiled. "I'm saying that you'll survive, and if treatment is necessary to facilitate that, we'll find what is best for you. In the meantime, the Iowa City Police have stationed officers outside of your door."

"Why?"

"Mr. Rawlings, someone tried to harm you. We don't want to give that someone another opportunity."

"I have my own security. I don't need policemen outside my door," Tony said.

"You can discuss that with the ICPD but not right now. I'm going to give you something to rest."

Tony looked around the room and saw the source of the repetitive beeping. "Nurse, what is all of this? Why is it beeping faster? Where's my doctor?"

Bright Eyes' smile returned. "First, your IV is flushing your body with fluid. It's helping to rid your blood and organs of the toxins. These are monitors that tell us what's happening inside of you. The one beeping faster is telling me that you are stressed, and the medication we just added to your IV will help alleviate that. Your heart doesn't need any unnecessary stress."

She had no fuck'n idea!

Tony tried to sit up, but Bright Eyes' small hand pushed against his shoulder. He couldn't believe that this tiny woman could overpower him. He'd never felt so weak. "Mr. Rawlings, listen to me. You need to rest. Let me introduce myself: I'm your doctor, Doctor Logan, and I want you to follow my rules."

His eyes opened wide. "Oh ... I didn't realize. I just assumed ... oh shit ... I should probably just shut up."

Doctor Logan smiled again. "Yes, Mr. Rawlings, I think that would be a good idea. Soon the medicine will take effect and you'll feel sleepy. I recommend you rest. Then, when you wake, we'll see about you talking to the police."

"D-doctor?" His words began to slur.

"Yes, Mr. Rawlings?"

"W-where's my ... wife?" Tony slipped back into the darkness.

The next time Tony woke, he wasn't alone. Eric was sitting in a recliner near his bed, reading a magazine. After a few swallows to moisten his throat, Tony found his voice. "Eric, why are you here? What happened to Claire?"

Eric dropped the magazine and moved swiftly to Tony's bedside. "Mr. Rawlings, um, Mrs. Rawlings is on her way back to Iowa City."

Tony's chest ached. He didn't know if the pain was from the medical treatment or the confirmation in Eric's voice. "How far, Eric? How far did she drive?"

"Mr. Rawlings, I'm here to assure your safety."

"Are the police still outside?" When Eric looked puzzled, Tony continued, "The doctor, she told me about them—before."

"Yes, sir, they are. There're some FBI agents here too. I promised I'd alert them as soon as you woke. Do you want me to get them?"

"Eric, damn it! Answer my question. When Claire left the estate, how far did she go?"

Eric leaned forward and lowered his voice. "Sir, I don't believe the FBI want me to say anything."

"Since when do I give a fuck about anyone else's directives?"

Still whispering, Eric said, "Mr. Rawlings, Mrs. Rawlings was found, and she's been arrested in connection with your attempted murder."

Tony closed his eyes. Everything was in motion. It had proceeded just as they'd planned, and damn, his plans never failed. Well, once, but that was over—Claire finished it. Opening his eyes, he stared. "Go tell the damn police or FBI or whoever the fuck wants to listen, I'm ready to answer their questions."

During the few moments that Tony lay alone in his hospital room, he remembered a scene in Claire's suite. It was before they were married. They'd been discussing the prenuptial agreement. He remembered telling Claire why there wouldn't be an agreement. He said it was because they would not divorce—he would not leave her, and she would not leave him. He asked her if she knew what would happen if she did. She said she did.

As the law enforcement officers entered his room, Tony pushed the button, raised the back of his bed, and squared his shoulders. He bet Claire had no fuck'n idea of the consequences of her failure! She would soon find out what would happen!

Anthony Rawlings' statement was straightforward. "There was nothing special about the morning. I got up, worked out in my gym, showered, ate breakfast, and began working."

"Working?" the officer asked.

"Yes, that's what I do—I work."

"Mr. Rawlings, did you go to your office?"

Tony pressed his lips together and momentarily stared. "Officer, I may be lying in a hospital bed, but I'm not crazy or stupid. Don't ask me questions when you already know the answers. I don't deal with incompetents and I don't intend to start."

The man bristled in his seat and rephrased his question. "Could you please be more specific about where you were working?"

"I have an office in my home. On occasion, I work from there. On the morning in question, I was working from my office within my home."

"Sir, who else was in your home?"

"My wife and my staff." Tony shook his head. "No one unusual."

"Did—" The officer immediately rephrased, "What did you eat and drink that morning?"

Tony tried to recall. "I had a bottle of water after my workout. I think I ate eggs and bacon for breakfast. There might have been fruit, I don't remember." He paused. "Oh, I had orange juice and coffee with breakfast."

"Was that all?"

"I had coffee again in my office, late in the morning."

The officer's shoulders stiffened. "Did you get your own coffee?"

"No." Tony didn't offer more.

"Sir, how do you take your coffee?"

"Black—sometimes with cream."

The man wrote more in his notepad. "Who brought your coffee to your office?"

"My wife," Tony mumbled.

"Did you say it was your wife?"

"Yes, my wife, Claire Rawlings, brought me coffee that morning, but if you or anyone else is suggesting that she would knowingly try to poison me, I believe you're mistaken."

It wasn't the young officer taking notes who responded. It was the older gentleman who'd been watching from the perimeter of the hospital room. "Mr. Rawlings, we aren't suggesting anything. We're trying to gather the evidence."

Tony was obviously feeling much stronger. Dr. Logan had been in earlier and authorized the questioning, and the cardiologist was scheduled to visit later in the afternoon. Tony leaned forward. "I'm at an obvious disadvantage," he spoke to the older gentleman. "You know my name, but I don't believe we've been introduced."

"Agent Hart, FBI."

"Well, Agent Hart, would you mind sharing that evidence with me?"

"Once our questioning is complete, we'll be glad to share with you. First, we want to know what you remember."

"I remember being with my wife the night before the morning in question. I remember a lot about that night and none of that would hint toward hostility. I'd share more, but out of respect for my wife, I won't. I remember talking with her on multiple occasions during the morning and making plans for later in the day. I remember booking a surprise vacation for the two of us. We're supposed to be in the Grand Caymans right now. I remember asking her for a cup of coffee and her bringing it. Tell me now, why you believe the woman I share my name and my bed with is being suspected of this crime."

Agent Hart nodded toward the young officer who'd been asking questions and taking notes. The younger man gathered his things and left the room. Once alone, Agent Hart swung the officer's chair around and straddled the seat. Leaning forward on the chair's back, he spoke quietly. "Mr. Rawlings, your wife was found yesterday driving near St. Louis."

He appeared genuinely shocked. Eric hadn't told him her destination. "St. Louis? Why?"

"Yes, Mr. Rawlings, why? Why would your wife leave your home in such a rush as to not take a coat? It is, after all, January in Iowa. Why would she leave without a purse, without her ID, and without any cash or credit cards?"

Tony couldn't respond if he'd wanted to. *St. Louis! She'd really left him. She'd taken the car and driven as far as she could.* Finally, he asked, "How did you find her?"

"Her car has built-in GPS. Your driver was kind enough to share the information, and we were able to track the vehicle."

"What did she say?"

"She hasn't said much. She's denied harming you, vehemently."

Tony closed his eyes. "Where is she? I want to talk to her."

"She's on her way back to Iowa." Agent Hart looked at his watch. "She may be back. The Iowa City prosecutor has secured a warrant for her arrest, and she's being arraigned this afternoon."

Shaking his head, Tony worked to contain the swirl of emotion: disappointment, betrayal, anger, hurt. It was a potent mixture. "I believe I need to speak with my legal team."

"Yes, Mr. Rawlings, I believe you do." Agent Hart stood. "I'll ask your driver to come back, if you'd like?"

"Agent?" Tony's voice hardened. "I don't want to believe any of this."

"I understand."

"I doubt you do. No matter what, find out who did this, and I want that person to pay. There has to be consequences for this. Do you understand?"

"Yes, sir, that I can assure you, I understand."

Once Agent Hart was gone and Eric was back, Tony began making calls. His first was to Tom. Tom and Brent headed up Tony's and Rawlings Corporation's legal team. Tony told Tom that under no circumstance would any of his legal team be used to defend Mrs. Rawlings.

Tony said, "If she did this to me, I don't intend to throw her a lifeline—she sure as hell didn't throw one to me!"

It is MY decision – January 2012
(Consequences – Chapter 48)

When a good man is hurt,
all who would be called good must suffer with him.
– Euripides

With each day that passed and Tony wasted in the hospital, his disappointment grew and festered. Every hour of work lost, every time someone entered his private room and performed some duty that was not to his liking, every time his personal space was invaded or the police came with more questions—every minute of each day was a reminder of how Claire had failed. Her failure didn't only affect her—no, Tony suffered as well.

He suffered physical pain as the toxins exited his body. Every time Tony took a deep breath or moved, he suffered piercing pain from the repercussions of the CPR. Two of his ribs were broken along with excessive damage to the cartilage in his chest. Then, there was the psychological suffering as he endured the humiliation of test after examination after test. Never had he been so exposed to so many people. Even his money couldn't save him from the prying eyes and hands of doctor after doctor.

After he regained his strength, Tony convinced the Iowa City Police Department and the FBI that he was safe with the help of his own security team. He explained that it was senseless for the people of Iowa to be burdened with the financial responsibility of his protection. The powers that be agreed, and Tony was at least free of the twenty-four-seven prying eyes of law enforcement.

The Simmonses cut their vacation short and hurried to Tony's bedside. Although he was happy to see them, they entered his hospital room right after Tony had finished another round of examinations and blood draws. His demeanor was not pleasant.

Their expressions were a mix of sadness and exhaustion. The trip from Fiji to Iowa had been long. Courtney was the first to speak as she rushed to Tony and swallowed him in a hug. He flinched at the discomfort. With tears in her eyes she said, "Oh, Tony, thank God! We've been so worried about you."

Brent gently slapped Tony's shoulder. "Hey, we rushed home because you're supposed to be at death's door. You look good to me."

"You missed the good part," Tony replied. "Apparently, I was more than at death's door—I passed the threshold. The doctors said they had to restart my heart."

Tears flowed from Courtney's eyes as she hugged him again. "Oh! I can't believe this. What happened? With all the traveling, we've only heard small snippets."

Brent cleared his throat. "We heard that Claire's been arrested. Man, tell us that isn't true."

Tony sat straighter and watched *his* best friends. "It is."

"No!" Courtney stood. "Claire wouldn't do this! There has to be some mistake."

"Do I look like there's a mistake?"

Using the voice Tony had heard in courtrooms and conference negotiations, Brent said, "Courtney, let's hear what happened before jumping to any conclusions."

"She poisoned me!" Tony lowered his volume. "In front of a live web conference, I took a drink of coffee that Claire brought to me and I died! My damn heart stopped. Last I heard that's the definition of death. The police have reviewed all of my in-house surveillance and everything points to her. Marcus Evergreen has been here a couple of times. They have

Claire locked up." When neither of his friends commented, Tony added, "She's being held on charges of *attempted* murder. Apparently, even though my heart stopped, the fact it restarted gets her out of a murder rap."

Brent wrapped Courtney in his arms as she hugged her midsection and her shoulders shuddered. Finally, she broke free and asked, "Why? Why would she do this? What happened? What did you do?"

Tony stared as red seeped into his peripheral vision. First, there were the damn doctors who poked and prodded, and now Courtney had the audacity to accuse him! It was all he could do to keep his lips pressed together in a tight line. When he looked away from Courtney, his eyes met Brent's. By his friend's expression, Tony believed that Brent knew what he was thinking. Tony didn't intend to say too much in front of Courtney, but he sure as hell would tell Brent.

Taking a deep breath, Tony winced and said, "I've spoken with Tom. No Rawlings money will be used for her defense. That means personal or corporate. No members of the Rawlings legal team will assist her, and that includes *you*," he looked to Brent, "and *your wife*."

Courtney shook her head and turned away.

Tony went on. "I personally hope that a trial can be avoided. I hardly want the world to know that I married a psycho who wanted me dead ... nevertheless, the evidence is straightforward. I believe we should start thinking about a divorce."

"Tony, please," Courtney pleaded. "Please think about this. Please don't make decisions that you'll regret."

"Brent, I'd like to speak with you privately." Tony had never treated Courtney with anything other than respect. He didn't want to start now. To facilitate that—to avoid a possible confrontation, Tony needed her to leave. "Courtney, I've had nothing to do for the last few days but lie in this bed and think. I've thought this out multiple different ways. You two have been traveling and are obviously exhausted. I promise this was not a rushed decision. Now, I'd like to speak to Brent for a moment."

Brent nodded to Courtney as she picked up her coat and purse and headed toward the door. Just before she reached the handle, she said, "Tony, I'm really glad you're all right. You know how much we care about you, but you were the one who brought Claire into our lives. I don't abandon friends. Don't ask me to do that."

"I'm not. I'm asking you to support *me*."

Her shoulders lifted and dropped before she looked down and left the room.

Trying to keep his voice in check, Tony glared at Brent and waited for the door to shut. Once they were alone, he said, "Control your wife! That's not a recommendation nor a suggestion—I'm fuck'n serious. Claire did this to me. Neither you nor Courtney will visit or help her in any way!"

Brent nodded. "I hear you. Let me talk with Cort."

"Talk to her, do whatever you need to do, but I'm not backing down on this!"

Brent feigned a smile. "I guess we don't need to worry about you anymore. You're obviously feeling better."

Tony nodded. "Check in with Tom and get up-to-date. Evergreen seems to have everything under control, but I don't want a trial. I'm willing to do anything to avoid that. You know what I think about the damn press—they're already having a field day. I don't want to give them any more ammunition. I have no idea what my wife was thinking or why she did this. She'd been acting strangely since that old friend of hers died. Then, after she heard about John, she must have snapped."

"John?" Brent swallowed hard. "Did the shit hit the fan?"

"Yeah, a few days ago. His firm pressed charges."

Brent closed his eyes and shook his head. "Damn, I didn't know it would happen so soon."

"Focus! This isn't about him or even her. I'm getting out of here soon. Find out exactly what Evergreen's planning. He just trips over himself whenever I talk to him, with all his damn *yes sirs* and *no sirs*."

"I'll find out what's happening. Would you drop the charges to avoid a trial?"

"That's just it. I never pressed charges—the state of Iowa did. I fuck'n lost control of this, and I want you to get it back for me—yesterday."

Brent nodded and looked at his watch. "I'll see what I can do. Do you have your cell?"

"Yeah."

"I'll call you later tonight. When are they letting you out?"

"If I had my way it would've been yesterday. My doctor's this little five-foot firecracker who refuses to release me until some damn numbers drop in my blood."

Brent smiled. "So the administrators don't give a damn about your donations?"

"They do, and *they're* making sure I get the best. Apparently, that's her and she's not interested in my donations or cash on the side—I've tried. Maybe I should pay off the damn lab techs. I'll pay for the fuck'n numbers to go down."

"Jesus, Tony! Listen to the damn doctor. I'd bet they want you out of here as much as you want to be out."

Tony couldn't help but smile. "You're probably right, but I might look into the lab tech angle."

Brent walked toward the door. "I'm leaving. I'll call you after I talk with Evergreen."

"Brent." Tony's tone lowered. "Do what I said. Control your wife. Don't disappoint me."

Brent nodded as he stepped through the door. Tony saw members of his security staff standing just beyond the open frame. Closing his eyes, he remembered Catherine's words: *Claire and Mrs. Simmons were getting close?* Memories of Courtney's question increased his discomfort. *Close—how close?* Had Claire said anything to Courtney that would cause her to suspect him of pushing Claire to the extreme of attempted murder? Shit—he needed to feel that out. *Could it be that Claire had disappointed him without him even realizing it?* He opened his eyes. The monitor near his bed was beeping faster and faster as new red flooded the empty room.

The damn numbers finally confirmed Tony's health. That didn't mean the pain was gone. His ribs hurt every time he breathed, and the cardiologist warned that Tony could have long-term effects. His heart would require further monitoring, but the signs for his long-range recovery were positive.

Riding up the drive of his estate, Tony pushed his emotions away. With Claire gone, his house seemed so empty. He'd spoken with Catherine on multiple occasions and, thankfully, she'd never boasted about Claire's failure. As a matter of fact, she was genuinely saddened by the outcome and worried about Tony's well-being. Whenever Tony mentioned Claire, Catherine would steer the subject to him and his recovery. He reassured her that he would get well, and he never doubted that he would.

Focusing on his responsibilities at Rawlings, which Tim had been assuming for too long, Tony entered his front door determined to ignore the obvious emptiness. His staff fell over themselves as they fulfilled his every need. It wasn't until he'd been home for a few hours that he wandered into the sitting room. He didn't mean to look above the fireplace—but he did. Tony wasn't looking for the green eyes; however, when he saw the large mirror that had hung there for years, fury overtook his being.

"Where the hell is the wedding portrait?"

There was no one near; the house was as empty as it felt. When he screamed his question again, Cindy came running. "Mr. Rawlings, are you all right? Can I help you?"

"No! I'm not all right! Where is Mrs. Rawlings' portrait?" He'd paid a fortune to have that portrait commissioned. He'd purposely had it painted by Sophia Rossi. No, not Rossi—Burke, and now it was gone!

"Sir, Catherine had it removed. She believed that you wouldn't—"

"I don't care what she believed! Where is it?"

"Sir, I-I don't know?"

"Where is Catherine?"

Suddenly, Catherine appeared, hurrying in from the hall. "Cindy, I'll help Mr. Rawlings. Thank you."

Cindy looked to Tony and waited. When he nodded, she turned away.

Catherine's voice tried to reassure. "Mr. Rawlings, you are supposed to rest."

He waited until Cindy left the room. "Where the fuck is the picture?"

"I thought that you—"

He glared. "I didn't ask you what *you* thought. I don't care what *you* think! Tell me where the fuck the painting is!"

Catherine's shoulders squared. "It's in her suite."

Tony closed his eyes and exhaled. Reestablishing his glare, he spoke slowly. "Don't you fuck'n touch any of her things. Don't make any damn assumptions about what I want and what I don't want. This isn't negotiable. Her things belong to me. Only I will decide what happens to them. I don't want to have this conversation again—ever. Are we clear?"

"Yes, sir." He heard the contempt in Catherine's voice, and at that moment Tony didn't give a damn.

"Have the portrait moved to my suite and hung over my fireplace. It'll stay there until I decide. Clear?"

"Yes, sir." He turned on his heel and stepped deliberately from the sitting room. Fighting the urge to go up to Claire's suite, Tony went to his office and contemplated his most recent revelation. If the state of Iowa wouldn't allow him to decide Claire's fate, then his most recent idea could. He called Brent.

Brent picked up on the third ring. "Yes, Tony?"

"What if she's insane?"

"Excuse me?"

"I told you that she'd been acting more and more detached since Johnson died. What if she lost it?"

Brent waited and then he said, "Evergreen said she's been very quiet, not saying much of anything."

Tony smiled. *This could work!* "If she pleads insanity, what could happen? Can we avoid the trial?"

"Let me look into it," Brent replied. "Do you want the state to sentence her to an institution?"

"No!" Tony's answer came too fast. "I want to pay for it. There's no sense having the people of Iowa pay her expenses."

"And when ... *if* ... she gets better?" Brent asked.

"We'll cross that bridge, but if I'm paying, it should be my decision." Everything about her had been his decision, even before she knew his name. He wasn't losing that control now.

"Tony, I'll investigate and get back to you. Evergreen said there's a preexamination scheduled for the day after tomorrow."

"I should be there."

"That isn't the customary practice."

"I don't give a shit what's customary. You investigate the insanity plea and I'll call Evergreen."

Tony didn't wait for Brent's answer before he hit: *DISCONNECT.*

Tony had Judge Reynolds' written decision in the breast pocket of his jacket. He didn't care if Evergreen didn't want him at this preexamination. Tony wanted Claire to plead insanity, and he needed to tell her. Honestly, he didn't expect any resistance from her or her counsel. Evergreen had said she received court-appointed attorneys, and apparently her draw hadn't been the best. Paul Task was fresh out of law school, had recently passed the bar, and was still wet behind the ears. His co-counsel was Jane Allyson. She'd spent a few years in the defender's office before and during law school. Evergreen said she was tenacious, but unestablished and unknown.

As Tony entered the hallway of conference rooms in the courthouse complex attached to the Iowa City jail, he was met by multiple law-enforcement officers. No one questioned his presence or commented about his wife's behavior. Everyone greeted him as if he were a long-lost friend. "Hello, Mr. Rawlings." "It's nice to see you, Mr. Rawlings." "Can I help you, Mr. Rawlings?"

It didn't take him long to find the conference room occupied by Evergreen and his team, as well as Claire and her legal team. There was a small window in the door. As soon as he looked in, he saw her. She looked so small and frail sitting at the cluttered table flanked by her incompetent counsel. Taking a deep breath, and remembering the pain of his broken ribs, he opened the door. The room, which had been full of murmuring, went silent. It was Marcus who finally stood and approached. "Mr. Rawlings, I thought we discussed this, and you weren't to attend this conference."

"Mr. Evergreen." Tony forced himself to look at the prosecutor as they shook hands. Every instinct in his body wanted to look at his wife. Feeling the green of her eyes penetrating his facade, he pushed on. "I appreciate everyone's concern for my safety. I'll repeat what I told Judge Reynolds. I don't believe my wife is a threat to my well-being. I believe if we can have a few moments alone, we can save the taxpayers of Iowa the cost of a lengthy trial, and this court, some time. Judge Reynolds has agreed to my request."

Marcus nodded and turned toward his team. Immediately, they began to move their chairs and stand. Claire's counsel whispered to one another and then to Claire. Next, Paul Task stood to meet Tony chest to chest. It was almost comical. Tony tried not to smile as Mr. Task stuttered, "M-Mr. Rawlings, I-I'll need to confirm that Judge Reynolds has indeed approved this visit. In situations such as this—"

Grinning, Tony reached into his jacket and passed a paper to Claire's frightened attorney. "Of course, Mr. Task. I would have expected no less. Here's the good judge's written approval."

Tony tried not to notice Paul Task's shaking hands as he took the paper and began to read. Once he was done, Tony smugly nodded as Claire's attorney turned toward her and confirmed, "Mrs. Rawlings, it appears to be in order."

As most of the room's occupants began to leave, Claire's co-counsel sat unmoving. Tony's gaze centered on the woman to Claire's right. Finally, Jane rose and met Tony's eyes. "Mr. Rawlings."

"Ms. Allyson." They nodded.

"Mr. Rawlings, this is unexpected. I'd like to speak to our client for a few moments and determine *her* desire regarding this meeting. If you'd please step into the hall with Mr. Evergreen and his team, Mr. Task and I will discuss this new situation with Mrs. Rawlings." *Who the hell did this woman think she was?* Tony started to respond, but Jane continued, "And then *if* Mrs. Rawlings agrees to your meeting, it may proceed under her conditions."

Before Tony could speak, Marcus placed his hand on Tony's arm and nodded. Tony turned toward Claire. This woman thought that she could stop him? He didn't need words, not with Claire. He wanted Claire to know that soon they'd be speaking, it wasn't open for debate. When he saw her expression, Tony's cheeks rose and his grin grew. She understood his unspoken promise. He turned back to her co-counsel. Accommodatingly, he said, "Why of course, Ms. Allyson," and stepped from the small room.

Once in the hallway, Marcus looked him in the eye and took a step backward. "I'm sorry, Mr. Rawlings, this is highly unusual. Ms. Allyson is—"

Tony squared his shoulders and smiled affirmatively. "—doing her job. I respect that, but as I've stated, I'm not frightened of my wife. I believe she was merely overwhelmed."

Marcus looked at his colleagues and then back to Tony.

Tony had everyone's attention. "You see, I've given this a lot of thought. Despite the evidence, I don't believe my wife wanted to kill me. The doctor said that the dose was wrong, and she's too intelligent for that. I'm a busy man. Perhaps it was nothing more than a cry for help."

"Mr. Rawlings, the state of Iowa—"

Tony put his hand on Marcus's shoulder. "The state of Iowa has done a remarkable job building a case. You've said that she's remained mostly silent. Is that still the case?"

Marcus nodded.

"Very well, I've had my attorneys working on this case day and night."

"But ... it isn't up to *your* attorneys." Marcus answered, somewhat puzzled.

"No, it isn't. However, if ..." Tony turned to address the entire group, "... if my wife pleads insanity—we can call it *temporary*. If my wife pleads temporary insanity and the state accepts that plea, I believe she'll receive the treatment she needs and deserves. Mrs. Rawlings isn't a criminal: she's ill. I want her to get the best care possible."

Marcus looked confused. "But, we have a solid case."

"I'm sure you do. I'm sure it wouldn't hurt your career, or any of your careers, to add this gem to your résumé. I can assure you though, that supporting the insanity defense, keeping this out of court, and allowing my wife to enter a private treatment facility, will also benefit your careers. You have my word."

Tony glanced toward the small window and saw Jane Allyson talking as Claire nodded. He wanted in that damn room.

"You realize," Marcus said, "it isn't enough for her to plead insanity. It must be clinically verified."

Tony grinned. "Yes, Marcus, I realize that. I have a plethora of psychiatrists ready to evaluate her."

"We have state-appointed—"

Before he could finish, Tony said, "I have their names, and I can assure you, they're on my list."

"It's customary for the courts to determine the amount of time and treatment—"

The door opened and Paul Task and Jane Allyson stepped from the room, interrupting their discussion. "Mr. Rawlings," Mr. Task said, "Mrs. Rawlings is ready to speak with you now."

Tony's smile broadened. "There are always exceptions, Marcus. I know this can be worked out."

Marcus Evergreen nodded as Tony stepped from the hall to the room. Closing the door behind him, he stared at his wife. Her eyes watched his every move. He sat down across the table from her. Bravely, she reached out and said, "Tony, I'm so glad you are all right." He took her petite hands in his and felt their coldness. For a moment he wanted to warm her, then she continued, "You know I'd never hurt you?"

He fought the red. *She'd left him. Driven to St. Louis. Made a public laughingstock of their marriage!* He tempered his tone. "My dear Claire, it certainly appears you did. You handed me the coffee. There was poison in the coffee."

"You told me to get you coffee." Although her voice was strong, he saw the tears that threatened to spill from her glistening eyes. She continued, "I've thought about it a million times. There must've been poison in the coffee already ... or in the cream. I just don't know. I don't know who would do this. The only other people at home were staff—staff you've employed for years—but it should be on surveillance. You have cameras in the kitchen—"

He interrupted, "All evidence points to you. Then, there's the way you ran to the car and drove away."

Suddenly, the emerald was gone as she looked down at the table and mumbled, "I'm sorry." She paused. Still looking at the table, she continued, "It was impulsive. I knew not to take one of the cars, but I saw the keys. I hadn't had the opportunity in so long, the sky was so blue, and you'd been—well, life had been unpredictable. I felt like I was suffocating and just needed a reprieve, a small break. Honestly, Tony, I was about to turn around to come home. I wanted to be home—I want to be with you."

He lifted her chin. "Claire, how are your accommodations?" His voice was low yet strong. "Consequences, appearances, I thought you'd learned your lessons better."

"Tony, please take me home. I promise I'll never disappoint you again. Please tell them you know I wouldn't—*couldn't*—do this."

It was the pleading he wanted, and once she was in the mental facility, he'd allow her to expand upon her remorse. In the meantime, he needed to push forward.

Claire continued, "I know there'll be consequences and punishment. I don't care, as long as you're all right. I just want to go home. Please, please, Tony, they'll listen to you."

He looked deep into her eyes. He'd trusted her and she'd failed him. He spoke softly, "The entire thing seems to be a colossal *accident.* However, I've done some research and it seems you can plead insanity and receive *treatment* instead of *incarceration.*"

She sprung from her chair and started to pace. "What are you saying? I'm not pleading insanity! That means guilty and crazy—I'm neither! And this wasn't an *accident.* I didn't try to kill you!"

He stood and moved very close. Looking down, he whispered, "Claire, listen. I've found a mental hospital that is willing to accept you. I'll pay the expenses so the taxpayers aren't responsible for your lack of judgment."

"I've been here for over a week. I've been questioned over and over. I haven't divulged any private information. I've followed all the rules. The only rule I broke was driving a car. That's it!"

She was too loud. He kept his voice low, trying to make her understand. "This plea will avoid a trial. The entire unfortunate incident is understandable. You came from a modest background. The life we shared had pressures and responsibilities—with entertaining, charities, and reporters. It's understandable. You just couldn't handle it."

Claire sat. Tony walked to her and bent down to maintain eye contact. "I should've recognized the signs. Perhaps, I was too busy with work. When you recently canceled your charity obligations, I should've realized how overwhelmed you felt." He fought the disappointment that fueled an unneeded rage. Although he tried to sound reassuring, authority prevailed in his tone. This was too important. Claire needed to listen to every word. It was what he'd done after her accident; he planted the seed and she obediently embedded its roots. He wanted the same outcome. Just as she'd responded to Dr. Leonard, he needed her to respond to her attorneys. "You wanted out, and in a moment of weakness—no, in a moment of *insanity—*

you decided the only way out was to try to kill me. I'm only thankful that you underestimated the amount of poison needed or you may have succeeded. After all, if you'd succeeded, I wouldn't be here to help you now." He pulled out a chair and sat facing his wife. "Aren't you glad I'm able to help you? And, Claire ..." He leaned nearer. "... I hear the rooms at the mental facility are larger than the cells at the federal penitentiary."

Tony expected a sign of recognition. He expected her to grab the lifeline he was throwing and hold on with both hands. It was a gift. She'd disappointed him—failed his test, publicly and privately—yet instead of walking away, he was offering her an out. This solution would help her and fulfill his need for control. Claire was his—her belongings, her portrait, and most importantly, her. He was angry. She had a long way to go to earn back his trust, but nonetheless, he was offering her an out. Claire needed to understand that he was helping her.

When she straightened her neck and met his eyes, he immediately realized—she wasn't taking his offer. The fire he loved to see was burning a blaze brighter than he'd ever seen. Didn't she understand? He loved that strength, but now wasn't the time. Now she needed to redeem herself.

Tony stood in amazement of the defiance before him. He wouldn't beg her! *Damn her.* This was crucial! He continued, disappointment audible in his tone, "Utilize the time you have to think this over. Don't make another poor, impulsive decision. This is your best offer." He knocked on the door. "Goodbye, Claire."

She didn't respond as he stepped back into the hall.

"Mr. Rawlings?" Marcus asked. "Is everything set?"

Counselor Allyson spoke, "This decision cannot be made without our input."

Tony turned toward the outspoken attorney. "Then I suggest that you convince your client that *she* has been offered a gift, and *she* should take it." With that, he nodded and walked down the hallway, leaving the group momentarily silent. The voice in his head cursed Claire's independence and stubbornness, pushing Tony to walk faster and faster.

Damn her! Damn her! A reprieve? A small break? Claire had left him! And now she was being obstinate!

Tony reasoned that she just needed time to consider his offer. A grin emerged as he reached the door of the courthouse. Yes, *time,* that was what she needed, time alone to think.

It had worked before. It would work again.

Damage control – Two days later – January 2012
(Consequences – Chapter 49)

Reputation is rarely proportioned to virtue.
– Saint Francis de Sales

"Mr. Rawlings, Mr. Evergreen is calling." Patricia's voice came through the speaker.

Tony turned away from the computer screen. "I'll take it."

"Yes, sir, I'll send it through."

It had been two days since Tony had visited the courthouse, two days since he'd given Claire the gift of an out. He knew she was upset at the time, but he had faith that her better judgment would eventually prevail. This was the first he'd heard from the prosecutor since that afternoon.

"Marcus, I assume you have some good news for me."

Marcus Evergreen cleared his throat. "Um, not exactly, Mr. Rawlings."

Tony's grip tightened on the receiver, yet his tone remained affable. "Would you like to be more specific?"

"Can you come to my office?"

Tony contemplated his schedule. He'd already wasted too much of his time on this whole mess. "I just returned back to my work, and things are backed up. Are you sure this can't be handled over the phone or by email?"

"Well, I think … see … I believe it would be in your best interest—"

"Marcus, spit it out. Time is money."

"Mr. Rawlings, j-just moments ago, I received Paul Task's preliminary brief. I haven't had a chance to read the entire document. It's quite long, but I've read enough—"

Tony interrupted, "Tell me that she's taking my offer."

"That's the thing, sir. She isn't. She's made allegations …" Marcus continued to speak, but his words faded into the buzz of seeping crimson. "… why I thought you might prefer if I didn't email this?"

"Marcus, I told you she was crazy. This is ridiculous!"

"Do you want me to email—"

"No! I don't want you to email or show it to another soul! I'll be there in less than thirty minutes." Tony hung up the phone before Marcus could respond.

Tony contemplated his response to whatever was in Claire's statement. As soon as Tony hung up with Marcus, he called for Eric. When he learned that Eric was at the estate, Patricia willingly offered her car. The entire drive, Tony's mind was on Claire. *What had she said? Would she really divulge private information?* His leather gloves strained from the grip on the poor car's steering wheel. He wouldn't allow this information to go public. Hell, he didn't even want his attorneys to be involved. Tony debated his options.

Taking a deep breath he entered the prosecutor's office. It bustled with people—men and women in suits coming and going all different directions. Mr. Evergreen's secretary, a young blonde woman with a nameplate that read Kirstin, stood at the ready. As soon as she saw Mr. Rawlings, she immediately escorted him to the unimpressive office. Marcus stood as Tony entered, and the two momentarily stared in silence. The frightened young lady took one last look at the two men and backed out quietly, shutting the door and allowing them their privacy.

Once alone, Marcus offered his hand and began somewhat sheepishly, "Thank you for hurrying over. I realize you have a very busy schedule."

Tony shook the prosecutor's hand and stared intently. "Tell me, who else has seen this testimony?"

"It isn't really testimony. It wasn't said under oath." Marcus shook his head as he walked around his desk and motioned to a small table. "Please, have a seat. No one on my team has seen it. Only me."

"On your team?" Tony asked, as he laid his overcoat on one chair and sat.

"Paul Task and Jane Allyson obviously took Mrs. Rawlings' statement," Marcus replied. "I don't know who prepared the document."

"Find out."

Marcus nodded. "Mr. Rawlings, there're some serious allegations. Legally this should be forwarded to—"

Tony sat back against the chair and squared his shoulders. "If you planned to do that, you wouldn't have called me."

"It's just," the prosecutor began, "I don't want the mad ravings of an angry spouse to bring down the reputation of such an esteemed man, such as yourself."

"Thank you, Marcus. I appreciate your candor and your discretion."

"Would you like to read what she's said?" Marcus asked as he booted up his laptop.

Tony shook his head. "No ... to be honest, I wouldn't. It saddens me. I can't imagine what she's said, but it must be something terrible for you to have been this concerned."

"It isn't flattering," Marcus admitted.

"I don't want this made public." Tony's tone was not up for debate. "I don't want anyone to know that the woman I married has become delusional and irrational." Tony leaned forward. "I'm sure you've seen the media coverage. Let's not add to the frenzy."

"I totally understand. If only she'd have taken your offer—"

"Obviously," Tony said, "another sign of her mental incompetency. I want you to do whatever it takes to keep this out of a courtroom."

Marcus nodded. "Sir, some of these allegations seemed very farfetched. May I ask if your wife had access to others?"

Tony's brows came together. "What kind of a question is that? This is 2012—everyone has access to everyone."

"Cell phone? Email?"

Tony nodded. "Yes," he sounded puzzled, "doesn't everyone?"

"May I have her number and email address?"

"Yes, of course. Whatever you need, I'll be glad to provide. I'm sure you can find many things just by searching the media. They do seem to like to write about my wife's latest purchases ... or ... hair color." Tony looked down.

"Mr. Rawlings, I apologize. I'm sure this is extremely difficult. It's that, we'll be meeting with Mrs. Rawlings and her attorneys in the morning. The more prepared I am for this preexamination, the better chance we have of stopping this from going to full trial."

Tony took a deep breath; his ribs ached. He reached for his side, and said, "I suppose this'll get worse before it gets better."

"I'll be in touch. I promise to keep you up-to-date."

Tony stood, his dark eyes downcast before settling on the prosecutor. "Marcus, I promise that you'll not regret this. I know you won't disappoint me, and I won't disappoint you. The state of Iowa has excellent opportunities. I believe there are great prospects in your future."

Marcus's shoulders went back. "Thank you, Mr. Rawlings. I'm truly saddened by this string of events. I'll keep the casualty list as short as possible."

"Tony," Tony said. "Please, you've been to my wedding and by my side as it all fell apart. Please, call me Tony."

"Thank you, Tony. I'll also let you know the full list of who's seen this information and promise to keep that list manageable."

Tony put out his hand. "I don't doubt your abilities. That's why I believe you have true possibilities for great aspirations. Both of our futures will be much brighter. I look forward to hearing from you."

Tony gathered his overcoat and stepped from Marcus' office, confident of the containment of Claire's disobedience. Fine! She didn't want to take his offer. Tony wouldn't be derailed by a Nichols! Let her rot in a damn prison. Let her experience the consequences of her decision—at least Tony would know where she was. One day her little reprieve would be over, and she'd be free—from the state of Iowa, that was, but never from him.

Tony could promise that!

Above anything else, Anthony Rawlings was a man of his word.

BEHIND HIS EYES

Reading Companion to the bestselling Consequences series

TRUTH

New York Times and *USA Today* Bestselling Author

Aleatha Romig

Prologue

And it begins again –March 2013
(Truth behind the scenes)

Nothing is so painful to the human mind as a great and sudden change.
– Mary Shelley, *Frankenstein*

As the car slowed, Tony looked up from his tablet. He'd been so lost in the document that he hadn't realized they were almost home. Sighing, he watched as his house came into view. A man's home was supposed to be his castle. *Why, then, did he dread coming home each night?* It was the same as it had always been, and this evening would be the same as the one before. When Eric would open his car door, his staff would be ready to greet him. Dinner would be warm and ready whenever he desired. If he wanted a drink, it too would be prepared. Anthony Rawlings had all the comforts money could buy, and he couldn't remember being more miserable.

At first the doctors attributed his lethargy to the lingering effects of the poison. The cardiologists ran every test and scan possible. They concluded that Tony's heart muscle was as healthy as that of a man in his thirties and reassured him that physically everything was repaired; nevertheless, Tony felt an unfillable void deep within his chest. It was like nothing he'd ever known. As time passed and his divorce finalized, Tony decided that dating would help to fill that void. Shelly agreed, saying it was a sign of strength to the world. It showed that Anthony Rawlings was invincible and able to overcome any obstacle. She also said it would be good for Rawlings Industries: the CEO was back to his old self. It helped that Catherine also encouraged dating. Her reason was less business-oriented. One evening she came to his office and told him without hesitation that he needed to stop spending so much time alone. Tony agreed. He was ready for some companionship.

When the invitations to benefits, galas, and other social gatherings began to trickle in, Anthony Rawlings returned to the dating scene. Each outing was similar to his dates before *her*. Most of the women who accompanied him were high-profile and high-maintenance. They looked perfect and knew the importance of appearance. It didn't take long for Tony to realize that these dates felt more like business meetings. He listened to the women's words, responded appropriately, and smiled for cameras—but it was all superficial and meaningless.

Tony never took any of these women to his friend's home for a barbeque. He didn't sit with them for hours and talk nor go on long walks hand-in-hand. He didn't know or care about their lives or a book they'd read. They fulfilled one need—appearance. These women were nothing more than an ornament to dangle from his arm. Everything had come full circle: he was living the life he created before *her*. It was a life that used to satisfy—it no longer did. The outings left him feeling more hollow than his empty house.

How could something—like a house, a date, or a life—that was virtually the same as it had been when it had been fulfilling, now seem empty?

He was Anthony Rawlings. He ran a billion-dollar industry. The ornaments—women—who accompanied him offered more than just public companionship with no desire of commitment. He had every man's dream.

Lately, it had become worse, and Tony knew why. Had Tony realized the time of year and mentally prepared, he wouldn't have been so affected. However, with all of his work and recent travels to Europe, he hadn't given the pseudo-holiday any thought. Then without warning, at a large benefit in Chicago, with a beautiful blonde on his arm, he heard her say, "Anthony, you should have worn a green tie."

He acknowledged her words with his infamous grin, yet he had no idea why she'd commented on his attire. Apparently, she noticed his confusion, because she giggled and said, "You know—because it's Saint Patrick's Day."

After weeks and months of consciously *not thinking* about his ex-wife, an invisible dam broke. In the presence of hundreds of donors, at a $10,000-a-plate dinner, memories flooded his mind. He carried on for the rest of the evening, shook hands, and made small talk, but his thoughts were three years in the past, at an Italian restaurant in Atlanta, Georgia.

Over the course of the next week, Tony tried diligently to push the memories away. When he'd wake in the middle of the night with his healthy heart beating erratically and his body covered in perspiration, Tony would stare toward the portrait veiled in darkness and remind himself that it was Ms. Nichols who'd failed her test. She was the one who chose to drive away and leave him. Before they were married, he'd promised her consequences if she ever left him, and being a man of his word, he delivered. Well, actually, the state of Iowa delivered; nevertheless, her absence and consequences were the result of *her* actions, not his.

When Tony stepped through the door to his home, Cindy stood ready. "Mr. Rawlings, may I take your coat?"

As he handed it to her, she said, "Dinner can be ready as soon as you like. Sir, are you going to eat in your office again, or would you like to eat in the dining room this evening?"

Tony squared his shoulders. "The dining room. I'll be there in half an hour. First, I have business in my office."

Cindy acknowledged him and walked away as he headed for his office. Despite the number of staff that Tony employed, silence loomed omnipresent, allowing the sound of his footsteps to echo through the vacant corridor. Once inside his office, Tony poured a finger—or two—of bourbon into the crystal tumbler. The decanter was waiting for him on the highboy, as much of a welcome to his home as his staff—safe and dependable. Tony despised eating alone, especially in the dining room. That was why he often chose to take his meals in his office or in his suite, but he was tired of hiding from the memories. The only way to stop them was to meet them head on. Swallowing the liquid courage, he relished the burn as the amber liquid soothed his nerves. He'd eat the *damn* dinner in the *damn* dining room and then spend the rest of the night going through a stack of new proposals. If nothing else, his renewed dedication to work had been beneficial to Rawlings Industries. At least something in his life was thriving.

After one more tumbler, Tony proclaimed that he'd shut the door on his memories. He'd done it before and would do it again. Leaning back in his leather chair, he removed his jacket and extracted his phone. The blinking light alerted him, reminding him that there were always people trying to reach him—calls, text messages, or emails. A quick brush of the screen told him that besides the plethora of emails, he had two missed calls with voice mails. The first telephone number was the governor's office. Tony didn't know why Preston, the new governor, would call, unless he was looking for a favor. Tony had fulfilled more than a few of those, especially for Marcus Evergreen, Iowa City's prosecutor. As much as it irritated Tony to be at the man's beck and call, the prosecutor had done his part to help Tony by ridding the world of Ms. Nichols' accusations. *Quid pro quo.* The missed calls grated on Tony, reminding him that some debts may never truly be repaid; nevertheless, if keeping the new governor happy would one day benefit Tony, he would endure the imposition.

Being after 7:00 PM, the Iowa state offices were obviously closed until tomorrow. There was no need to bother with the voice mail now. Tony made a mental note to call Governor Preston in the morning. As he was about to check the second message, a bit of news on his computer screen caught his eye, and he mindlessly laid his phone on his desk, his thoughts overtaken with the information on his home screen. A subsidiary of Rawlings Industries had a substantial jump in stock price. The attached article stated that the upswing was due to the proposed quarterly revenue reports; the actual revenue reports wouldn't be released until early next month. Wondering if the reports would support the assumptions, Tony began accessing data. Within seconds, everything else was forgotten. Even dinner slipped his mind until Catherine knocked on the door.

After he ate, Tony turned off his private line and told his staff that unless the house was burning, he did not want to be interrupted. Minutes turned to hours, and the March Iowa sky darkened, as Tony continued to work, read, and make notations. The memories that plagued him earlier found themselves successfully locked behind a wall of figures and reports. It wasn't until nearly midnight that he noticed his phone. With the ringer muted, he'd forgotten about the voice mails and texts. Illuminating the screen, he saw that the alerts from before had multiplied. Scanning the list of numbers, Brent Simmons was the most recently missed call. He'd also sent the last received text.

"GOVERNOR PRESTON HAS CALLED ME SEVERAL TIMES TRYING TO REACH YOU. I DON'T KNOW WHAT HE WANTS. HE SAID HE MUST TALK TO YOU TONIGHT. I'VE CALLED AND TEXTED. ARE YOU OUT? PRESTON SAID TO CALL HIM NO MATTER THE TIME."

Tony shook his head and accessed the voice mail from the unknown number.

"Mr. Rawlings, er, Anthony, this is Sheldon Preston. I hope you get this message. I must discuss something with you tonight. I don't care how late it is. Please call me. This is my personal cell. You can reach me here at any hour."

Tony sighed, wondering what possible favor was so damn important. Scrolling the list of missed calls, he saw Sheldon's private number repeatedly, as well as Brent's. Fine, if the governor wanted to speak to him so damn bad, he'd call him at this ungodly hour.

Governor Sheldon Preston answered on the first ring. "Mr. Rawlings, thank you for returning my call."

"It's late, Governor. What do you need?"

"I wanted to tell you—before you saw the news tomorrow—Claire Nichols is out of prison."

Tony leaned forward, his mouth gaped in disbelief. *How could she be out of prison? She had only served fourteen months of her seven-year sentence.* "What in the hell do you mean she's *out of prison*? Did she escape? What kind of facility is this state operating?"

"N-no, Mr. Rawlings, she didn't escape," Preston stuttered.

"Then what happened? She had over five years left on her sentence."

"Yes, she *did*."

"Did?" Tony asked.

"Well, you see, Governor Bosley pardoned her."

Tony's pale world seeped with crimson. "What the hell?"

"Er—"

Tony didn't let the man speak. "Bosley resigned before I left for Europe. How did he grant her a pardon—*now*?"

"That's the thing. Governor Bosley granted her a pardon two weeks ago. Somehow her name escaped the newspapers. I wasn't informed until today. I'm not sure where the mix-up occurred; however, I intend to find out. Mr. Rawlings, please know that I'm very sorry. You should've been notified immediately. You should know that my entire office has been in an uproar. I'm very upset about this. I promise I'll get to the bottom of it."

Tony listened as his hand clenched the small phone. He couldn't contain the fury in his voice. "Two weeks ago! Two weeks! The woman who tried to kill me has been out of prison for two fuck'n weeks and I'm just now learning about it!"

"I'm very sorry. That's why I wanted to speak with you before the story hit the media tomorrow. I've been informed that there's a news blitz coming out first thing in the morning about how her name escaped the earlier press release. They're insinuating a cover-up. You can understand how as a new governor—"

"You think you're upset? What about me?"

"Yes, I'm sure you..."

Sheldon's words faded as Tony tried to think rationally. *Damage control. There must be damage control.* "My publicist should be involved in this news blitz. Who's running it?"

"The Des Moines Register had the initial story, but I believe the AP picked it up this evening. It'll be everywhere by tomorrow morning."

Shit! "I don't like this at all." There were so many thoughts. Tony struggled to keep them all straight. "Governor, where is she? She *is* in Iowa," his baritone voice lowered another octave, as he added, "isn't she?"

"Mr. Rawlings, a pardon is different than a parole. With a pardon the entire crime is erased—expunged. It officially never happened, the arrest, the sentencing—none of it. We don't know where Ms. Nichols went. She doesn't need to check-in or be accountable to anyone."

Tony reached into the top drawer of his desk and pulled out an old key ring. Unconsciously, he threaded the relic through his fingers and steadied his voice. "This is completely unacceptable. I want details. How did this happen and who petitioned for her pardon?"

"I don't have all of the details. At this time, all I know is that Jane Allyson, formally Ms. Ni—"

"I'm well aware of who she is."

"Yes, well, she submitted the petition to Bosley's office. Apparently, she also was the one who went to the penitentiary and sought Ms. Nichols' release. Again Mr. Rawlings, I'm very sorry—"

Tony interrupted again, "Yes, Governor, I'm sure you are. I'm sure there will be other people who are *sorry* when I'm done with them." Tony hit the *DISCONNECT* button. *Free. How in the hell could she be free? And not only that—missing!* Tony needed answers. *Fourteen months! Expunged!* Tossing the old key ring, Tony hit Brent's number.

As the phone began to ring, energy surged through Tony's body, forcing him to his feet. He paced the confines of his office as he waited for Brent to answer. Tony didn't care that it was the middle of the night or that Brent or Courtney may be sleeping. This was a damn emergency. Claire was missing! As the phone continued to ring, he thought back. *When was the last time he hadn't known her whereabouts?* Years. He'd known where she was before she knew him, and now suddenly she'd walked away—no, not suddenly, two weeks ago!

Brent answered with a hushed tone. "What is it, Tony?"

"She's gone! She's fuck'n gone!"

"Who? Who's gone?"

"Claire! Bosley pardoned her—two weeks ago!" Tony's knees gave way as his tired body collapsed on the sofa. He'd thought about her. He'd received updates on her, but until that moment, he hadn't said her first name—not since he learned of her allegations. Her blatant violation of his most basic rule relegated her back to the world of *Ms. Nichols.* Whenever she was mentioned in his presence, he required that she be discussed as Ms. Nichols, even before their divorce; however, tonight everything changed—*his Claire* was gone!

Brent stuttered, "T-Tony, I don't know what to say? I mean, I read the names of the people Bosley pardoned. That list didn't contain Ms. Nichols' name."

"That's what Preston wanted to tell me. Somehow her name wasn't disclosed, but now the press has it. Tomorrow the whole damn world will know that she's been pardoned."

"Where is she?"

Tony ran his hands through his hair. "I don't know. Shit—Preston doesn't know. Jane Allyson did this. I want her in my office first thing tomorrow morning, and I want Claire found."

Brent sighed. "Because..."

"Because..." Tony stammered. He couldn't tell Brent the truth—that he'd never lost track of her in ten years. "Because, she tried to kill me. What if I'm in danger?"

"Of course. Have you notified your security team?"

No, he hadn't. He hadn't done anything. "I called you first. How long will it take for you to hire a private investigator from your list and track her down?"

Brent replied. "I'll get on it first thing in the morning—"

"Now!" Tony yelled. "I want her found by morning!" He heard Courtney's concerned voice in the background.

"Okay, Tony," Brent reassured. "I'll get right on it. I'll also call Patricia and have her get a hold of Jane Allyson."

"There has to be some legal recourse, right? I mean, you can fight this—legally?"

Brent hesitated. "I'll need to see the paperwork. If Jane made any mistakes in her petition, maybe—"

Tony shook his head. *If? Maybe?* "That's unacceptable! I want something done immediately. This injustice needs to be rectified."

"Tony, Courtney wants to know if you're all right?"

"Tell her that I'm fuck'n great." The energy that had momentarily fueled Tony's rage faded into the black night. Holding his head, Tony sighed. "The damn press will have a field day."

"Patricia will contact Shelly. She'll do all she can."

Tony nodded. He had a great team. His people would rally around him. "Give me an update in the morning." Not having the strength to wait for a response, Tony hit *DISCONNECT. Two weeks—where in the hell was she?* His mind searched for possibilities: people, places, anything.

"Indiana?"

Tony looked up at the sound of Catherine's voice. His dark eyes glared, daring her to say another word as she eased her way through the partially open door. "What in the hell are you doing in my office?"

"I heard you yelling, and, well, you've been acting strangely lately. I wanted to be sure you're all right. Are you?"

He forced an unnatural laugh. "That seems to be the question of the day. No, no, I'm not. I'm also not prepared to talk about it, especially with you."

Catherine relaxed her stance and sat on a chair near the sofa. "Why not me? You can talk to me. I'm the only person you can talk to about *her*, and besides, I'd like to know more."

Tony's darkening eyes burned toward her. "How do you know this is about *her*?"

"Like I said, I heard you yelling. You said her name."

Tony ran his hands over his stubbly face and exhaled. "Not tonight, Catherine. I don't even fuck'n know what to say." He stood and walked to his desk. Turning back around, his tone regained its earlier intensity. "Claire is gone, but since you just offered a possible location, you probably already knew that. When did you find out?"

"Just moments ago." Her eyes opened wide. "Like I said, I heard you speaking to Mr. Simmons."

"You don't seem too concerned."

She shrugged. "I am. I'm concerned about *you*, about the fact that you still have her picture hanging in your suite, and that you look more worried than upset."

Tony glared. "Then looks can be deceiving, because I'm definitely upset—no, I'm outraged!" His volume increased. "Richard Bosley screwed me over. He pardoned her two weeks ago and hid it all."

"Pardoned?"

"Yes! Did you miss that little bit of information during your eaves-dropping endeavor? She was *pardoned*. Her crime, plea, and sentence are gone! It's like it never happened. Like suddenly I was never lying in a hospital bed fighting for my life."

Catherine bristled slightly in her chair. They'd had more than a few words over his condition following the poisoning. "Anton," she said, soft-ly, "what are you going to do?"

"I'm going to find her!"

"Remember, she left you. You offered her an alternative, and she dismissed it. Do you think she wants to be found? And even if you find her, what will you do then?"

With his jaw tightly clenched, Tony poured another drink. Silence enveloped the regal office as Catherine's gray eyes stared, and Tony contemplated his answer. *Did Claire want to be found?* Obviously not, or he would know her location. *What was he going to do after he found her?* Tony didn't know the answer to that, either. Closing his eyes, he fought the bombardment of emotions. There were too many, coming too fast and too conflicting. Rage, uncertainty, worry, anger, hurt—the list could go on and on. Tony couldn't identify what he was feeling, much less discuss it.

After he swallowed the alcohol, Tony slammed the helpless tumbler on his desk and glared. "If I remember correctly, I told you that I didn't want to discuss this—with anyone. That includes *you*."

Catherine pressed her lips into a straight line, stood, and walked toward the door. As she reached for the handle, she looked back. "In case you don't know… the answer is *no*. But you could change that."

His brows knitted together. "What answer?"

"Does she want to be found?" Catherine answered.

"I said that I didn't—"

Catherine interrupted, "I asked you if Claire wanted to be found. The answer is no, but she's good for you. Despite the fact that she's a Nichols and she left you… at one time, she was good for you."

Tony collapsed into his chair. The emotions and liquor were taking hold. "Good for me? What about *me*? Was I good for her?"

Catherine diverted her gaze to the floor. When she resumed eye contact, she shrugged. "In some ways, but you could be better for each other. I know you could. You just have to show her that."

He closed his eyes. He and Claire could be good together. Tony knew that—they had been. When he opened his eyes, Catherine was gone.

Answers—March 2013
(Truth Chapter 3)

If you are looking for answers, you'd better choose the question carefully.
—Javier Bardem

E ven before sunrise, the corporate offices of Rawlings Industries buzzed with activity as people swarmed about. Tony nodded to his assistant and motioned toward his office as he passed her desk. Moments later, he listened as Patricia updated him on their progress.

"Shelly has been working since the middle of the night, but it doesn't seem as though she'll be able to stop the media blitz regarding Ms. Nichols' release. It's already started."

Tony's indifferent expression failed to hide the displeasure radiating from his dark eyes.

Patricia looked away and removed a page from a file. "Here," she said, as she handed it toward her boss. "This is what she's been able to add to the public information."

Tony read:

Mr. Anthony Rawlings is stunned by this turn of events. He has no further comment at this time.

He looked up and met his assistant's gaze. "What about Jane Allyson? When will she arrive?"

"I've left numerous messages, both on her office voice mail and her personal cell phone. I'll let you know as soon as I learn anything."

A knock on the door's frame refocused their attention. The circles under Brent's weary eyes and his wrinkled shirt said more about his lack of sleep than he'd ever admit.

"Do you have news?" Tony asked.

Brent nodded. "Some."

"If you'll excuse me," Patricia interrupted, "I'll keep working to get a hold of Ms. Allyson."

"Let me know as soon as you do."

"Yes, sir," Patricia replied, as she closed Tony and Brent inside Tony's office.

Making his way to one of the chairs across from Tony's desk, Brent collapsed and wearily began. "The media is running with the story. It was first announced, very early Eastern Time, and every morning news program has enhanced it since. I understand why Preston was so anxious to talk with you. He hasn't even been in office for two weeks, and they're calling for an internal investigation. They're saying that you paid to have her release covered up."

"That's ridiculous." Tony ran his hand through his hair. "I can't cover something up that I didn't know happened. Maybe Shelly should emphasize that?"

"It's up to you, but you might want to stay with *no comment*. I mean, the more you say, the more they'll infer."

Tony stood and walked to his conference table. In the center of the table was his usual morning decanter of coffee and two cups. "Coffee?" he asked, as he poured the rich, dark liquid.

"Yeah, man, I haven't slept since you called."

Tony's dark eyes peered over the rim of the ceramic mug.

"I know," Brent added. "You haven't either. Courtney's worried about you."

"Well, I'm fine. I want to know about the private eye. Who did you hire and has he or she found her?"

Brent sighed as he filled his cup. "I hired a man named Phillip Roach. He's good. I've used him before, and he's never disappointed me. He has a great resume—military as well as private. Give him some time and he'll find her."

Tony shook his head. Although he was too tired to sound hostile, determination rang loud throughout his tone. "Time is the one thing that he can't have. Money—fine. Resources—fine. Time—no." He set the mug down and leaned forward. "What information have you given him?"

"The Internet was full of pictures from when the two of you were dating and married." Brent looked sheepishly toward his friend, obviously trying not to overstep his bounds on this sensitive subject.

Pressing his lips into a straight line, Tony nodded.

Brent continued, "So I forwarded him some pictures and links. I also sent him Emily's information—her address, phone number, place of work. He said he'd start there. I mean, it made sense to Cort and I that she'd go there."

"Yes, that was mentioned last night. I agree. She doesn't have any money or any other resources. She has to be in Indiana."

Before either of them could continue, Patricia knocked and entered. "Excuse me, Mr. Rawlings, I spoke with Quinn, Ms. Allyson's assistant. Ms. Allyson will call back in a few minutes, and I'll find out how soon she can arrive. She's just now getting to her office."

Tony glanced at his watch, 7:46 AM. "If she gets into her car now, she can be here by 10:00 AM."

The ring from Patricia's phone caused her to step hastily from the office with only a nod.

Brent leaned forward. "Well, here's the thing. Roach has been working since I contacted him last night. He learned that on the date of her release, March 9th, Ms. Nichols had a first-class seat booked for San Francisco on American Airlines; however, less than an hour before boarding, her ticket was cancelled with no further record of her traveling."

Rubbing his cheeks, Tony asked, "How? How could she possibly have a first-class ticket? Who paid for it?"

"The airline refused to disclose customer information. Roach is working on another avenue. He also found a number linked to one of those disposable, untraceable phones that has called Emily's cell phone every day since Cla—Ms. Nichols' release. Some days they've connected multiple times."

Tony tried to comprehend this new information. It seemed very James Bond. "Can he tell where the calls originated from?"

"He's working on that. He did call Emily during the night," Brent grinned with a shrug, "or early this morning. It's a matter of perspective. Anyway, Emily refused to divulge any information."

"Of course she did." Tony said curtly, distaste for his ex-sister-in-law thick on his tongue.

"Apparently, Emily said she didn't know her sister's whereabouts, had no further comment, and hung up."

Tony squeezed the bridge of his nose. "Where was the phone purchased?"

"California."

"That doesn't make any sense. She doesn't know anyone in California. Maybe it's some trick and she's really in Indiana."

"Well, like I said, Roach is good. He'll—"

Patricia reentered. "Excuse me, again. I just got off the phone with Ms. Allyson. She claimed that her schedule is very full. She's working on a few big trials and can't possibly come to Iowa City for another week."

No longer able to restrain his emotion, the room echoed with the sound of Tony's fist contacting the hard, shiny table. Coffee sloshed as the cups jumped. "Today! I said I wanted to speak with her today—in person—and that was what I meant. Call back. Talk to Quill or Qu—her damn assistant, and find out the details of *Esquire* Allyson's schedule. If she has court today, learn the name of the presiding judge. It's obviously in Iowa, so get the trial or hearing rescheduled. Ms. Allyson will be talking with me sooner rather than later. I'm already two weeks behind on this catastrophe. I'm sure as hell not waiting another week."

Patricia hurried away as Tony looked toward Brent. "That's bullshit!" He paused for a drink of coffee. "Did Roach tell you any more?"

"No, that's all he had at last check. Do you want me to stay in contact with him, or would you prefer that he contacts you directly?"

"Give him my personal cell number and email. I want to know what he knows, when he knows it."

Brent nodded. "I'll get a hold of him so that he can contact you." Brent stood.

Tony looked at his watch. "This is ridiculous. I'm not going to get anything done until I at least talk to Jane Allyson."

"The woman was just doing—"

Tony's glare stopped Brent's words. "If you're about to say that she was just doing *her job*, then I want to know who hired her."

Brent feigned a smile. "I guess we wait."

"Hell no, *I* don't wait." He stood and straightened his jacket. "Get your things. We're headed to Des Moines." Yelling toward the door, Tony called, "Patricia!"

"Yes, sir." She peered around the frame.

"Call the hangar and have my plane ready in thirty minutes. Mr. Simmons and I are flying to Des Moines. Then clear Ms. Allyson's schedule, and tell her we'll be there by 10:00 AM."

The tension within the cabin of the plane was palpable. Tony wanted to blame his stretched nerves on his excessive intake of caffeine, but that was only the tip of the iceberg. Wondering if he weren't teetering on the edge of sanity, he tried to concentrate on his work and the documents before him. Instead of words, images filled his mind. They weren't images of real life, not memories, but a dream—perhaps a nightmare.

After Catherine left his office the night before, Tony went to his suite and tried to sleep. He knew it would be fitful, yet he had to try—for his sanity. He needed a break from the tornado of emotion whirling within him. It was in those moments of unconsciousness that memories of *her* came back to him.

The pale green walls of the visitor's room were exactly as Tony remembered from his visits to his grandfather. Tony stood helplessly under the fluorescent light and watched the only door. Momentarily, he believed he'd been transported to another time. Intellectually, he knew that wasn't possible, but what if—what if maybe—he could see Nathaniel once again? He looked down at his hands. They weren't the hands of a twenty-three-year-old; no, he wasn't waiting for them to bring his grandfather. He was waiting to see her!

Even in the dream state, Tony's knees wobbled. He reached for a chair and felt the cool metal beneath his forty-eight-year-old hand. How did he get there? He didn't want to see Claire, not here. He couldn't face her in a prison.

The hiss of the light magnified as he braced himself. Why hadn't he thought about this? Why did he wait until he had only seconds to prepare? She was in prison. Had she survived? Did this place break her spirit—the spirit he loved to bend? Or had he wanted it broken? Hadn't that once been his goal?

Tony's stomach churned with the turning of the knob.

Before the door opened, Tony remembered that this—prison—was Claire's doing. She accepted this consequence, not him. Maybe she didn't poison him, but she left him, their home, and their marriage. If she were a broken shell, she had no one to blame but herself!

His shoulders squared as the door opened.

An unfamiliar man entered. "Mr. Rawlings, the woman you seek—is gone."

Tony's chest ached as the void grew, yet he stayed steady. "I'm not seeking anyone."

It was as if he hadn't spoken. The man continued speaking and handed Tony an envelope. "She left this for you." Before Tony could reply, the man went on, "She knew you'd come for her."

"I didn't come for her. I don't know why I'm here." On the front of the envelope, in Claire's handwriting, he read For Anthony Rawlings. *It wasn't prison-issued stationery. No, the thick linen envelope was lavish with an embossed "N." Tony tried to reason, an "N"? Shouldn't it be an "R"? "Where did she get such nice—" Tony looked up and the man was gone. He hadn't heard the door, but he was definitely alone.*

Sliding his finger under the flap, Tony opened his message and peered inside. There was nothing. As if to be proven wrong, Tony tore the expensive paper searching for something—still nothing.

He looked up and gasped.

"Boy, you got what you gave." Nathaniel's pallor was evident under the cheap lighting.

Tony's neck straightened. "Sir, that's not true. I di—"

"Are you calling me a liar?" Nathaniel bellowed.

"No, sir." Instead of a confident, successful businessman, he was suddenly Anton, young and seeking approval. *"I did what you expected, what would make you proud."*

"Then, my boy, you failed. They took my family and now you've allowed them to take yours. That empty envelope and your empty life are your consequences."

"No! Sir, I didn't fail. I don't fail! I don't..."

Tony woke to the sound of his own voice. With his body drenched in perspiration, he threw back the covers. "It wasn't real. It was a dream," he whispered.

There was no one to hear.

With sleep an impossible goal, he made his way through the dark corridors, past the indoor pool, to his gym. If he were going to sweat like a damn pig in his own bed, he might as well get a workout in the process.

Tony couldn't talk to Catherine about his dream, and he sure as hell couldn't talk to anyone else. While running mile after mile on his treadmill, he attempted to decipher its meaning. He hadn't failed his grandfather. Tony's whole life proved that he'd succeeded. Anthony Rawlings was wealthier and more influential than Nathaniel Rawls had ever been. Rawlings Industries was legitimate in all of its dealings. It would never face the public scrutiny that Rawls Corporation had endured. He'd listened to Nathaniel's advice and kept up appearances, and he'd stayed true to his word. *How could he have failed?*

Tony's eyes darkened and his jaw clenched with the memories. He couldn't recall having a more vivid dream. He'd felt the damn chair, heard the fluorescent light and the voices, tasted his shame at his grandfather's words, yet, intellectually, Tony knew that it wasn't real. As they neared Des Moines, Tony pushed the dream away and concentrated on the present. *How could Bosley pardon Claire?* If the man weren't dying of cancer, Tony would make sure that his career was over—Anthony Rawlings was capable of making and breaking people. Then, there was Jane Allyson. It wasn't good for his thoughts to linger on her for too long. Tony wanted someone to blame—a head on a platter, so to speak. That counsel had been a thorn in his side ever since he laid eyes on her at Claire's pre-examination at the Iowa City courthouse. Since he would be meeting with Esquire Allyson in a matter of minutes, Tony needed to remain calm.

Of course, the blame could also be shared by his ex-wife. When it came to thoughts resulting in rage, Claire wasn't immune; she never was. There was something about her—something that ignited him like no one else. His entire body stirred with an energy he fought to control. Despite the negativity, for the first time in a long time, he felt alive.

Tony didn't want to admit it, but along with the anger and disappointment, he was concerned—maybe that was part of his dream? *Was Claire all right? How was she living? Was she destitute?* Those thoughts would temporarily derail the anger until he'd remember that this—all of this—was all her fault. She left him. Now she'd done it again. *How could she be so stupid?* He would find her. Then, he would—he didn't know, but he knew he would find her.

A driver waited at the Des Moines private airport to whisk Tony and Brent to Ms. Allyson's downtown office. Once they were inside the car, Tony asked, "What about travel? Could she have left the country? I still have her passport."

"Roach doesn't believe that she could get a passport this fast. Homeland Security would never allow her to leave the country without one. Well, he said they would never allow her to *reenter* the country without one; leaving is a possibility."

Tony shrugged. "Has anyone spoken to Bosley?"

"No. He's undergoing chemotherapy. According to his assistant, the cancer has metastasized to his bones. The treatment is extremely taxing, and he's not available for comment."

"I want to know why in the hell he signed that pardon. I supported his campaign. He was at my wedding!" Each statement became more emphatic. With the last comment, he realized, it was *her* wedding, too. "I want to know every name associated with this injustice."

Brent nodded. "We'll have more answers soon."

When they arrived to Ms. Allyson's office, a little before 10:00 AM, Quinn immediately called her boss. "Ms. Allyson, Mr. Rawlings is here, accompanied by his attorney, Mr. Simmons." After a moment, she smiled and said, "Please, follow me gentlemen, Ms. Allyson will see you now."

Claire's former attorney met them at her office door and ushered them inside. "Hello, Mr. Rawlings, Mr. Simmons, please have a seat."

Tony and Brent sat opposite her desk.

Before they could speak, she said, "Now gentlemen, to what do I owe this honor?"

Brent spoke first. "It has just recently come to my client's attention that on March 8th you filed a petition with then Governor Bosley, requesting a pardon for Claire Nichols."

"Yes, that's correct."

"My client would like to know why this was filed, on what grounds, and who approached you to make this request."

"Gentlemen, Ms. Nichols was never convicted of a crime. She pled *no contest*. That was *not* an admission of guilt. She's had an impeccable record during incarceration..."

Her words faded into the all-encompassing red. Tony didn't give a damn for Ms. Allyson's legal drivel. When she paused, he asked, "Why was I not notified?"

"Why would you need to be notified?"

He wanted to slap the smug expression from her face. "For my safety. She tried to kill me!"

"Have you been threatened since her release?"

"No." Tony bristled. "I just learned of her release last night."

"It *appears* as though you needn't be concerned. She's had two weeks to finish what *you* claim she started, and it seems that you're still with us."

Mentally, Tony gripped the arms of the chair. The words flowing through his head wouldn't be beneficial to the conversation. Perhaps Brent sensed Tony's demeanor, since he continued the inquiry. "Do you know where Ms. Nichols relocated? For my client's safety, he should be informed."

"I do not. As I'm sure you're aware, with a pardon, the criminal record is expunged. Ms. Nichols does not owe the court a thing. She is *free* to go wherever she chooses. Furthermore, she is *not* required to keep the court or the state of Iowa informed of her whereabouts. I took her to the airport and left her at the gate. There is *nothing* more I can tell you."

"She had a ticket for San Francisco," Brent said, "but prior to boarding the plane, her reservation was cancelled. Do you know where she went instead?"

Jane appeared genuinely surprised. "I don't know anything about her reservation being cancelled, and as I said before, I don't know where she is now."

"Ms. Allyson, she had a first-class ticket. Do you know how Ms. Nichols could afford such a ticket?"

"As I mentioned, some things are confidential." Standing, Jane said, "Now, gentlemen, if that is all? I have work—"

How dare she? Tony hadn't flown to Des Moines to be flippantly dismissed. He stood to meet her glare. "Ms. Allyson, I'm not happy with the recent turn of events. I plan to learn of *all* individuals involved in this miscarriage of justice, and it's obvious that you played a role."

Her gaze never faltered. "Mr. Rawlings, I was your ex-wife's co-counsel during her trial. I represented her then, and I would gladly do so again. If you have complaints about her pardon then I recommend you take them up with Richard Bosley. His signature alone opened the door of her cell, and I'm certain that a man of your stature did not intend for his concern regarding self-preservation to be misinterpreted as a threat. That wouldn't coincide with your benevolent image and—I'll add—is illegal."

Standing to join the rest, Brent interceded, "You're correct, Ms. Allyson. My client is obviously distraught over the recent turn of events. You can understand his alarm. After all, Ms. Nichols tried to harm him once. It's only natural for him to be concerned she may try to do it again."

"Yes, Mr. Simmons, I see how *your client* would be concerned that *my client* would cause him harm."

Tony didn't appreciate Ms. Allyson's thinly veiled implication. He wasn't going to allow her to bring up Claire's accusations in front of Brent. Inhaling deeply, Tony summoned his most affable voice. "Thank you, Ms. Allyson. I'm glad you understand my concern, and I hope you didn't misinterpret my alarm. If you remember anything else regarding Ms. Nichols' departure or learn of her location, I would appreciate being informed." Well-ingrained manners took over as Tony extended his hand.

Shaking it firmly, Ms. Allyson replied, "Mr. Rawlings, you will be among the first I call. Are we done?"

"Yes," Tony said, with a genuine smile. "I believe we are." As they exited her office, Tony's lips remained turned upward as he contemplated various possibilities of derailing Ms. Allyson's career. Someone would take the fall for this travesty, and right now, she was at the top of his list.

With nightfall, Tony's energy plummeted. The surge that had been propelling him for nearly twenty-four hours was gone. He stared once again at the text message he'd received from Phillip Roach.

"I'M CONFIDENT THAT THIS IS MS. NICHOLS' NUMBER. AMONG OTHER NUMBERS, IT HAS BEEN IN CONTACT WITH EMILY VANDERSOL, ON MULTIPLE DAILY CALLS, SINCE THE MIDDLE OF MARCH. I'VE NARROWED THE ORIGIN OF THE CALLS TO PALO ALTO, CALIFORNIA. THE NUMBER IS: XXX-XXX-XXXX. I WILL CONTACT YOU AGAIN WHEN I LEARN MORE."

Tony had waited all day for more information and was tired of waiting. He'd learn for himself. Walking the corridor back to his suite, Tony entered his private haven, his *sanctuary*. He didn't want to be interrupted—or overheard—like the night before.

His suite held more memories than Tony cared to recall. There were those that he should abandon, both literally and figuratively, and ones that he treasured. The literal memories were items relegated to a box in the back of his closet. Some of the items, his ex-wife never knew he possessed. There were the photographs he'd taken from her Atlanta apartment, and her old laptop. He doubted the old dinosaur even worked. It hadn't been booted up in almost three years. Tony searched the box for the one item he treasured. It was one of Claire's belongings, one that he couldn't bear to include in the auction. Catherine had encouraged him to purge it all, break free and move on. She even insisted on redecorating Claire's suite. He wanted to move on, but he couldn't get rid of this item. Anthony Rawlings may be a lot of things; however, he wasn't a man who would donate his wife's—or ex-wife's—most sentimental possession to a fund-raising auction. Riffling through private investigative reports, pictures, and papers, Tony found the black velvet box and grinned. Peering inside, he gently touched the delicate white gold chain and cream-colored pearl. The necklace had belonged to Claire's grandmother. Closing his eyes, he remembered the night he gave it back to her—the night of the symphony.

Glancing at the numerous pictures from his years of surveillance, Tony wondered if he and Claire had come full circle. *Would it be like this again? Would his only connection to her be through this new investigator? Would he only see Claire in two dimensions?* Tony searched for their contract, the beginning of their personal journey together. He knew it wouldn't be that easy again. If he were to get her back to Iowa and into his life, it wouldn't be because of a signature on a napkin.

Then he shook his head. He didn't want her back, did he? Hell, the lack of sleep was making him sentimental. He stopped his search. The damn contract was no longer valid; it never had been—legally. Pushing the box back into its hideaway, he contemplated throwing it all away. Having her back wasn't his goal; learning her location was. She had no right to disappear.

With the necklace in his hand, Tony settled upon the soft leather sofa in front of his fireplace. If Phillip Roach were correct, in a few moments he'd hear the voice that used to fill his suite and his house. When her voice came through his phone, Tony wanted to *feel* her presence. He imagined the sound as he looked up at her wedding portrait and saw the emerald green that haunted his dreams. *What did he want to hear?* He wanted to know she was safe and unharmed. He wanted to know where she was, and he also wanted to bring her back to Iowa—because that was where she belonged.

It didn't make sense. To the world she was the woman who tried to kill him. To Tony she was more than that. The past twenty hours had proven it. She was his drug. Claire Nichols ran through his system like ecstasy, sending him on otherwise unobtainable highs. He reasoned that lows followed highs, and she'd given him those, too; they'd given them to each other. Nevertheless, without the right stimulant, the euphoria could never again be achieved. Whether it was elation or misery, neither would be obtainable without the exhilarating potency of Claire. He didn't want an empty envelope. He wanted her. Nathaniel was wrong: Claire wasn't gone; she was just misplaced.

For the last twenty-four hours, his entire being had surged with anticipation. Claire may not understand it—hell, Tony didn't understand it, but he couldn't deny it. Now that she was gone, he needed her back in his life, and he would have her.

Tony shook his head. He was acting like a heartsick schoolboy. He squared his shoulders and exhaled. The telephone number from Roach was already programmed into his phone, and of course, his number was blocked. The clock read 9:47 PM. Tony honestly didn't know for sure where he was calling. Roach suspected California, and if that were the case, it would be two hours earlier there. Momentarily, Tony contemplated a drink to calm his nerves. No, the only drug he wanted was unknowingly waiting for his call.

The small cream-colored pearl swung from his finger like a pendulum, keeping rhythm with the ringing phone. When the ringing stopped, time stood still. The anticipation was over. Claire's voice came through loud and clear.

"Hello?"

It electrified him from head to toe.

Relief. Hurt. Love. *Loss.*

Her greeting was a torpedo hitting the dam he'd built around his memories. His mind flooded. He was back in time to her first coherent night at the estate. Even in her shocked condition, Claire stood tall—for her—and defiant. No longer was Tony seeing the woman in the designer wedding gown. No, behind his closed eyes, he saw Claire Nichols—his acquisition.

"Good evening, Claire." He greeted her in a tone drenched in debonair swagger. As he awaited Claire's response, Tony heard other voices. When she didn't respond, he continued, "Now Claire, we've been through this before. It is customary for one person to respond to the greeting of another. I said, *good evening.*"

"Hello."

He grinned at the change in her tone. Undoubtedly, his call took her by surprise. "Very good," Tony praised. "I thought perhaps we would need to review common pleasantries."

Momentary silence gave way to her stronger declaration. "Good-bye, Tony."

His cheeks rose higher, listening to her rediscovered strength. Tony pictured his ex-wife squaring her shoulders with fire blazing in the depths of her emerald eyes. She wasn't broken. "Claire, you should know that I learned of your release less than twenty-four hours ago. As you can hear, I already have your telephone number. How long do you think it will take for me to learn your location?"

"It seems as though *you* have lost the ability to perceive meaning. *Good-bye* means this conversation is over. For the record, that includes future conversations. I'm sure you remember, once a discussion is closed, reopening it is not an option."

A hearty laugh resonated through his suite. Tony couldn't contain his amusement. "I have always admired your strength. Such a brave speech from someone hiding across the country..." He didn't know for sure when she disconnected her phone. All Tony knew was that the line went dead. In a previous life, at a different time, he would've been irate that Claire—or anyone—would have had the audacity to hang up on *him*. Times change; Claire's action was a challenge, one he gleefully accepted.

Once again, Tony dialed the number. This time it went to voice mail. *No, her spirit wasn't broken.* If anything, she was stronger than before. He sent a text.

"ONLY I CLOSE DISCUSSIONS. THIS ONE IS STILL OPEN. I LOOK FORWARD TO RESUMING IT IN PERSON..."

And oh, he did! Tony didn't know when, but he knew for sure that one day soon he'd be seeing the fire in those beautiful eyes and not in a picture. He would witness it firsthand.

Sighing, he reviewed their findings: the cancelled airline ticket to San Francisco and a California area code on the cell number. Tony scrolled through his recent calls for Phillip Roach's number and called. The investigator answered on the first ring.

"Mr. Rawlings?"

"Mr. Roach, I wanted to confirm that the number you gave me is indeed Ms. Nichols'. It seems that the trail is pointing west. I'll cover all your expenses. I want you to find Claire Nichols, and I want her found yesterday."

Disconnecting the line, Tony sat silently and stared at the portrait. He hadn't expected her early release from prison, but now that she was out, he was ready to reclaim what was his. Smirking, he considered her cell number, *her* cell number. *Could she have her own computer or car? Perhaps she's accumulating debt?* That tool had worked well before. He mused, "My, only two weeks removed from prison and so independent."

Love versus Hate – April 2013
(Truth – Chapter 10)

Step One: Admitting that one cannot control
one's addiction or compulsion.
– Twelve-Step Program, Alcoholic Anonymous

"**M**r. Rawlings, I sent you an email. I can resend," Cameron Andrews, private investigator, said.

"Yes, do that. Sometimes things are blocked." Tony knew that probably wasn't the case. He hadn't been paying attention.

Andrews continued to report, "Mrs. Burke closed her art studio in Provincetown and moved to Santa Clara."

Tony shook his head against the phone. "Closed it?!"

"Temporarily. That's what the sign said."

If Sophia were willing to follow her husband across the country, she obviously didn't recognize the future she had in the art world. Not every artist received an invitation to exhibit her work at the Florence Academy of Art. Tony remembered Italy, watching her from afar. Her poise and confidence were evident as both art enthusiasts and patrons praised her work and her new, bolder pieces. Tony couldn't understand why she'd put that life aside to take a backseat to Derek's ambitions; after all, Tony had spent a lot of money paving her way to fame and fortune. Derek's *job opportunity of a lifetime* was supposed to emphasize their differences, not bring them together.

"When did she move?" Tony asked.

"Yesterday," Andrews replied.

"Keep an eye on her." Tony's mind swirled. There were more options; he just needed to concentrate. "Get me a list of names. I want to know all the art curators in the Santa Clara area. Perhaps we can get her connected to that local art world."

"Yes, sir, I'll get back to you with that."

"I don't believe she's in danger. She doesn't need constant monitoring. Just keep me up to date. And Andrews?"

"Yes?"

"Run some financial background checks on those curators and their studios. Let's see if anyone is having difficulties during this recovering economy." Tony added with a smirk, "I've always wanted to diversify into the world of art."

Andrews chuckled. "Yes, I'm sure that will be a great investment. I'll get back to you with some numbers in a day or two."

"That'll be fine." Tony disconnected his phone and pinched the bridge of his nose. Damn, after all the time and money he'd spent on Catherine's daughter, it seemed like every time he looked away for a minute, her life spun in another direction. Derek's job offer was no surprise; Tony had weaved that bit of manipulation personally. When the parent company's CEO made a suggestion, presidents and vice presidents of subsidiaries listened, at least ones who enjoyed employment. Apparently, Roger Cunningham fell into that category. Sophia moving to California *was* a surprise. The last thing Tony had heard, Shedis-tics offered Burke the opportunity to fly east most weekends.

To Tony, it seemed like the perfect scenario: Burke alone in a new city with a pretty little assistant who was willing to make extra money. Tony never considered the possibility that his plan would fail.

Sophia deserved better than a *Burke*. Even if he was only a distant cousin from the Burkes on their list, he was still a Burke. She also deserved to flourish in her chosen career. Tony didn't know much about art, but he knew how he felt about the portrait that graced his suite. Sophia had captured Claire's eyes perfectly. Tony should know: he'd spent hours looking at her work. On more than one occasion, when the sweet burn of Blue Label couldn't stop the bottomless pit of memories, he would stare at Claire's wedding portrait and recall scene after scene, some good, some not.

Then he would remember her failure. Tony had experienced loss—most significantly, his family. He had seen his parents, covered in their own blood; however, the video footage of Claire driving away tore at him like nothing he'd ever known. His parents didn't *willfully* leave him. The reports of murder/suicide were false. His grandfather didn't *willfully* die in a hellhole of a prison with inept medical facilities. No, that blame fell on Jonathon Burke and Sherman Nichols. Claire *willfully* seized the first opportunity she found and left him. She failed his ultimate test.

Over the past year, on the rare occasions when Tony allowed the memories and thoughts to flow, he waged an internal war—love versus hate. At one time, he thought he loved her. *What the hell was love?* It wasn't something he'd ever witnessed in real life, except perhaps on occasion between Marie and Nathaniel. He recalled moments—when they didn't know he was present—when Tony saw an unfamiliar side of his grandfather.

Usually the man was in total control of everyone and everything, except during those moments. *Did Tony ever give that to Claire—control?* He'd never given that to anyone. With Claire, he needed control. He yearned for it, and she'd flourished under it. Obviously, when given a choice, she'd failed. Claire needed his guidance.

While she was in prison, Tony knew she was safe, secure, and unable to make poor decisions.

Now things were different and public.

Her damn picture wasn't just showing up in his inbox from Roach. No, she was gracing magazine after magazine. In the new world of Internet frenzy, she was fuck'n *trending*. Tony didn't know what to believe. Many articles claimed that she was penniless and destitute. Tony knew for a fact that wasn't true. Roach reported a $100,000 windfall. It'd come from a cashier's check that Roach traced back to a bank in New York. Unfortunately, it had been purchased with cash and the trail died. *Who would give Claire that kind of money?* Whoever it was didn't have the balls to man up. If they had, Tony would have found a way to cut them off.

Tony's anger at the initial source of funds was minimal compared to his rage when he learned that Claire had sold her jewelry—more specifically, her wedding rings. The sentence in Roach's email seemed so benign, yet the moment the words registered, Tony was filled with unprecedented fury. Thankfully, the email came while he was in the privacy of his home:

I have traced the source of Ms. Nichols' newfound wealth to a reputable jewelry broker in San Francisco. He has kept her sale confidential, out of the media, and well hidden. He utilizes offshore accounts to pay his customers, but after a few dead ends, I was confident that Mr. Pulvara was the source of Ms. Nichols' nearly $800,000 windfall. To that end, I paid Mr. Pulvara a visit. After some persuasion, he admitted that he purchased a necklace, earrings, and wedding rings from Ms. Nichols.

The room exploded in red. In the love-hate battle, Tony's barometer shot toward hate. *How could she so casually sell the representation of their union, their visible contract?* After the mental chaos faded and Tony's mind cleared, he thought about her rings. He couldn't—no, wouldn't—allow another woman to wear those rings. They'd been designed and purchased for Claire. The thought of anyone else wearing them infuriated him more than the idea of her selling them. Tony didn't respond to the email in kind; instead, he picked up his phone and barked orders. Saying them aloud helped to dull his overwhelming sense of impotency. "I want the damn rings, and I don't care how much you have to pay to get them. If this Pulvara man sold them, find the buyer and get them. Don't disappoint me. I want them in Iowa tomorrow!"

Roach didn't disappoint; he even delivered the rings in person to Tony's office. Now, within the confines of his suite, Tony possessed her rings and her grandmother's necklace. During less lucid moments, he'd imagine returning the rings to their rightful owner. He'd envision her smiling, emerald gaze as she'd extend her petite hand. The eyes in his imagination swirled with a combination of desire and happiness, as he'd slip the platinum band and sparkling diamond back onto her finger. Those were the moments when love overpowered hate.

Tony looked through his inbox and found Cameron Andrew's emails. He clicked and reread the last few weeks of reports. If he hadn't been so preoccupied with his ex-wife's release and new life, he'd have known about Sophia's move. *Would it have mattered?* Maybe this move would streamline his life. Tony chuckled as he pulled up a map of Silicon Valley. Perhaps he should fire one of his private investigators. The red arrows said it all: Sophia and Claire were living mere miles apart.

Exhaling, Tony minimized his screen. He was going to California. After over eight years of—on again and off again—watching Claire from afar, he wasn't going to do it any longer. He clicked on Roach's most recent email and exhaled at the displeasure of seeing Claire's life unfold in pictures. With a fresh tumbler of bourbon, he stared at the screen. Before him he saw Claire and Harrison Baldwin dining at some restaurant. The hair on the back of Tony's neck bristled as he observed their level of comfort. Roach had many attributes: one was the ability to take pictures in rapid succession. By activating the slideshow program, Tony could watch as if it were a movie, and like a real video from his surveillance, he could also pause and stare at each frame.

Weeks ago, Roach had sent background information on Amber McCoy and Harrison Baldwin. It was pretty straightforward: they were siblings—same mother with different fathers—who were both were on the payroll of SiJo, and both lived in the same condominium complex in Palo Alto. What his research didn't answer was... *why? Why would Claire turn to Amber McCoy, Simon Johnson's fiancée, for help? How did they become friends?* Tony met Amber at Simon Johnson's funeral, the same time Claire met her. It didn't make sense.

He paused the slide show at the sound of Catherine's knock. As he looked up, she entered. "Have you learned anything new?"

Tony didn't want to discuss Claire with Catherine. Claire was his, and he didn't want to share; however, he acquiesced, knowing it was he who had brought Claire into Catherine's life. "I just opened an email."

Catherine walked around the desk and peered over Tony's shoulder. "Hmm, I don't think you need to worry." She smirked. "She seems to be rebuilding her life quite well."

Tony minimized the screen and turned to glare. "I could use less innuendo."

Sitting down, Catherine shrugged. "I didn't realize I was insinuating. I'm being honest. She looks happy."

He hated to admit that Catherine was right. "Roach said they're *friends*. He hasn't seen anything to indicate—"

"That's not what the articles are saying. I saw one that said she was living with—"

The muscles in Tony's neck flinched. "Catherine, I think we both know that reporters like to sensationalize things."

"So you believe that she's living with Simon Johnson's fiancée?"

"That's what I said."

"Maybe they're all one big, happy family living under one roof."

"No," he responded adamantly. "Roach said that Baldwin's apartment is on the same floor as his sister's. Claire *is* living with the sister."

After a prolonged silence, Catherine asked, "Why?"

Shrugging his shoulders, Tony admitted he didn't know. He couldn't figure it out. "But," he added, "I guess that we should be happy she has a place to live."

"We should?"

"Do you want her living on the street?"

"That's not what I mean. She has a sister."

"I'm not defending her choice."

"I would hope not," Catherine quipped. "We both know that *choices* aren't her strong suit."

"Then perhaps she needs guidance."

"And I suppose you know a willing teacher?"

"I have work in California next week."

She lifted a brow. "Work?"

"Yes, I have subsidiaries on the West Coast that need my attention."

Catherine nodded. "I'm surprised it took you so long."

"I'd go now, after these latest pictures, but Claire's going out of town tomorrow—to Texas."

"Texas? By herself?"

"That's what Roach said, but of course, he'll be there, too. So we'll find out exactly what she's doing."

"And when you're in California...?" Catherine probed.

Tony straightened his shoulders. "Do you want me to say it? Do you want to hear it?"

"Anton, I want you to admit it to yourself."

"Fine! I want to put her on my plane, bring her back here, and convince her that this is where she belongs." He sighed. "I want her to *want* to be here, to admit that she's miserable in California. I want..." His words trailed away as he maximized the pictures on his screen.

As he gazed at Claire's expression in picture after picture, Catherine's voice infiltrated his thoughts. "She's all over the Internet. If she suddenly went missing, it would be noticed."

He ran his hand over his cheeks, rubbing his stubbly growth. "I know. I know that I can't do that again. She needs to realize it on her own, and I don't know..." He couldn't complete the sentence. Anthony Rawlings rarely admitted lack of knowledge, but he honestly didn't know. He didn't know what to do to make her understand. He looked up at Catherine's gray eyes and knew that she saw through him. The two of them had been through too much together.

"She knows you." Catherine's voice softened. "Perhaps better than you know yourself. You need to help her understand what she knows."

Tony nodded. "What if... if she doesn't want to know?"

"She does. She wants to know more about you and why things happened the way they did."

His brows lifted. "How do you know that?"

"I know you don't see me as one, but Anton, I'm a woman."

"I know you're a woman. What does that have to do—"

"I know what it's like to be an outsider in this household. She lived here for almost two years, and yet never knew the family secrets. She never knew the *why*."

"She'll hate us forever if she knows. I can't—"

Catherine's head shook from side to side. "You underestimated her ability to survive. You underestimated her ability to get to you. Don't underestimate her ability to understand." She started walking toward the door.

"Marie."

She turned toward him with an unspoken question.

"I want her back." His voice was barely audible as he choked back unwanted emotion.

"I know."

"She's mine."

Catherine smiled. "Remind her."

He looked back at the screen. Baldwin's hand was on Claire's lower back. If she weren't leaving for Texas in the morning, Tony would fly to Palo Alto immediately; instead, he emailed his personal shopper and instructed her to order Claire a new outfit. He'd have it delivered with a note informing her of their impending date. He'd given up trying to reach her by phone—she refused to answer the number Roach had given him. That was fine. He'd sent flowers to let her know that he knew her address. Now, he'd send this. Tony would get through to her one way or the other.

Good evening, Claire – April 2013
(Truth Chapter 15 & 16)

The best thing you can do is the right thing; the next best thing you can do is the wrong thing; the worst thing you can do is nothing.
– Theodore Roosevelt

inding a plausible excuse to visit the West Coast wasn't difficult. Rawlings Industries had subsidiaries all over the world. Tony was aware of these companies, followed them, and contacted them regularly, mostly from a distance. No doubt, some of the directors sitting around the conference table in San Francisco were less than comfortable with the parent company's CEO's sudden personal interest. It didn't matter. Anthony Rawlings could conduct the web conference from Rawlings headquarters, his estate, or a conference room in California. He could do whatever he damn well wanted.

He'd made that clear to Shelly, his publicist, during an earlier telephone conversation.

"Mr. Rawlings, you—we—have worked diligently to distance you from Ms. Nichols. In case you forgot, she was incarcerated for your attempted murder. Besides, you've moved on. I mean, just a little over a

week ago you were photographed with Dr. Newman's daughter, Angela. The acceptance numbers in Iowa were through the roof. The people of your home state were abuzz with the idea of Anthony Rawlings with Angela Newman. The two of you are both considered Iowa royalty."

"Shelly, while I appreciate your hard work, and I pay you extremely well to do your job, my personal life is my business."

"Sir, you know that's not true. Everything you do is watched. Right now, everything Ms. Nichols does is watched. I've been following the reports and even have a continual search running. Mr. Rawlings, her Klout score is through the roof. Everyone is talking about her. She was even mentioned on one of the late night—"

"Perhaps you misunderstood my call. I didn't call to seek your permission to see my ex-wife. I called to inform you that I will be seeing my ex-wife. I'm taking her to dinner tomorrow night."

"Please, if I may be so direct, be discreet."

"Didn't you just say that we're both watched people? How discreet do you expect me to be?"

Shelly sighed. "Mr. Rawlings, I believe that if you set your mind to something—even the seemingly impossible—you will accomplish that goal."

"I wanted you informed, and I'll do what I can on my end. You do your job and spin it however it needs to be spun."

"Thank you for the advance notice. I'll do my best."

"I'm sure you will, Shelly. You never disappoint."

Tony didn't appreciate Shelly, Catherine, or anyone else telling him what he should or shouldn't do with his private life. Granted, it was Shelly's job, and that's why he called her in the first place. Catherine, on the other hand, was family—dysfunctional and totally messed up—but as close to family as either one had.

Truthfully, Catherine did have family, even if she wasn't ready to admit it. Another goal of Tony's trip to California was to do his part to bring Catherine's daughter into the art fold of Northern California. If Catherine was family, then so was Sophia. Tony had made a promise to Nathaniel to watch over Sophia and help her. He'd tried, but too often Tony's personal life had gotten in the way. Now he intended to help her focus on her talent and career. After the web conference concluded, Tony had a scheduled meeting with Roger Cunningham of Shedis-tics to discuss one of his newest employees, Derek Burke. Perhaps Sophia believed that she needed to follow Derek to California because of his new income. Today, Tony would decide if Burke would be allowed to continue that new position. Surely, enticing Derek Burke to California just to take it all away would be difficult on their marriage. Maybe that would be the way to rid her of the man who didn't deserve her.

There was also another plan in the works. After the meeting with Cunningham, Tony had an appointment in Palo Alto with the curator of a small art studio, Mr. George. Sophia Rossi Burke had already received worldwide recognition for her art. Unfortunately, recognition didn't always equate to financial freedom. With Mr. George's assistance, Tony had a plan to help Sophia achieve both. It was an offer that Mr. George couldn't refuse.

Cameron Andrews had unearthed Mr. George's dubious past. Apparently, he'd made more than a few bad business dealings. One major misstep resulted in the loss of a larger studio and his home in southern California, as well as a divorce. When it was all said and done, Mr. George was left with a small studio in Palo Alto. Currently, that business hung by a financial thread. If Mr. George didn't receive assistance—or a savior— soon, his life's work and passion would be gone, just like his wife and children. While Tony had no influence over Mr. George's past, he believed he could impact his future. This afternoon, Tony would take a personal interest in learning how far Mr. George was willing to go in order to save the remaining pieces of his life.

With a busy day ahead of him, the *pièce de résistance* were his plans for dinner. It had to be perfect. In the event of paparazzi, Tony had sent Claire a stunning outfit from Neiman Marcus. It was delivered prior to her trip to Texas and included his dinner invitation. Tony waited to hear from her, some acknowledgement of their reunion. When he didn't, he decided that the absence of a refusal was the equivalent to an acceptance.

He had the entire evening planned from the wine to the dessert. On *The Embarcadero*, in San Francisco, was a restaurant with a sweeping view of San Francisco Bay and the Bay Bridge. It was consistently busy with both locals and tourists. Patricia booked the private upstairs dining room. Although the facility's private area sat sixty, tonight it would seat two. There was a car scheduled to pick Claire up at her condominium and bring her to him. Even Phillip Roach had been given the night off. Tony had thought of everything and didn't want their reunion interrupted.

The last time he saw Claire, in person, was at the Iowa jail. To say he was upset at that meeting would be an understatement. She'd asked him to take her home, and instead, he'd offered an alternative to her impending prison sentence. That *alternative* had been the perfect option. It covered all bases—Tony's fulfillment of his obligation to Nathaniel, as well as his promise to love and keep Claire. As a psychiatric patient at a private facility, Tony would have been able to facilitate her release. When he first mentioned divorce to Brent, it was a gut reaction to Claire's failure to pass his test. If she'd accepted his offer, taken the insanity plea, Tony wouldn't have divorced her. Their legal bond would have allowed him to control the length of her treatment.

Refusing his offer, pleading no contest, and continuing her disappointing behavior further fueled his rage. For appearances alone, Tony distanced himself from *Ms. Nichols* and her reputation. It worked. The world pitied the lonely, wealthy man who was deceived by the gold-digging, treacherous woman.

Tonight, Tony would explain that he wanted that distance to end; he was ready to forgive her for the past and move on. It was quite a gift. After all, Anthony Rawlings didn't easily forgive, but he would. She'd failed a test and paid the price. It was time to go on with their lives—together. Claire was his. She had been his since she was eighteen years old. He wouldn't tell her that, even though it was true. Together they would rebuild the trust that she'd severed.

As the web conference neared its end, and the table of directors listened to Anthony Rawlings' every word, the cell phone that he'd laid on the table before him began to vibrate. Glancing down, intending to turn it off, he saw the screen flash with an unexpected name—*CLAIRE*.

Tony stopped mid-sentence and reached for the phone. Addressing the directors, he apologized, "Ladies and gentlemen, this is rude and highly unusual behavior; however, I'm sure that you understand that I have many fires burning. I need to take this call and will be back to you in just a moment." Not waiting for acknowledgement, Tony stepped from the room and hit the green button. "Hello, Claire. I hope you're not calling to cancel our plans."

She responded immediately, "I wouldn't do that, Tony." At the sound of her voice, blood rushed through his veins quickening the beat of his heart. "That would be rude, to cancel something at the last minute."

"I must admit, I'm surprised to receive your call... on my private cell, no less."

"I presume you are. I wanted to contact you about tonight."

"Yes?" He mused.

"You see, I've been living in this area for a while. There's a lovely French restaurant that I believe you'll enjoy." Before he could comment, she continued, "I realize you made reservations, but so have I. I'd be glad to meet you at *Bon Vivant* on Bryant, at 7:00 PM."

Hearing her spirit made his cheeks rise; nevertheless, he'd made plans. "Well, there's a car coming to pick you up—"

She interrupted, "I appreciate that. It's very kind of you; however, I have my own car and am more than willing to drive."

He chuckled. Fine, Palo Alto it would be. Tony would let her win this battle, as long as he won the war. "If that's what you prefer."

She exhaled. "I do."

He couldn't remember a time that he'd wished he could forget his work and talk on a telephone. What propelled him was the promise of speaking in person. "Very well, I must return to this table of directors and web conference. Until tonight."

"Yes, good-bye." The phone went silent. Before reentering the conference, Tony shook his head, tried to suppress his grin, and sent a hasty text.

"CANCEL TONIGHT'S RESERVATIONS. CONTACT BON VIVANT IN PALO ALTO AND SECURE PRIVATE DINING."

Hitting *SEND*, he reentered his meeting. "Ladies and gentlemen, let's carry on..."

Bon Vivant didn't offer private dining; therefore, not wanting to disappoint her boss, Patricia did the next best thing. She explained that *Mr. Anthony*

Rawlings wanted to enjoy the delicious cuisine and not be disturbed. If *Bon Vivant* could accommodate his wishes, Mr. Rawlings would compensate the restaurant as well as the employees generously for any potential loss of revenue. In an effort to avoid any backlash against *Bon Vivant*, Mr. Rawlings would also compensate any customers with reservations by purchasing their meal on another date. After a few minutes of discussion, Tony and Claire once again would be dining in private.

As Tony parked his rental car and approached the Civic Center Art Studio in Palo Alto, he noticed the quaint businesses all nestled on tree-lined streets. This was where Claire lived, and he hated its welcoming appeal. He'd left her alone for too long.

His earlier meeting with Roger Cunningham had proved informative. Derek Burke was an asset to Shedis-tics. They were very happy with the recommendation. Without a plausible reason to suggest Burke's dismissal, that left Tony with Plan B.

Once inside the studio, Tony studied the works of art. To him, art was an investment, and that was his goal for this meeting. He wanted to make an investment—perhaps not so much in art or an art studio, as in an artist.

A short man with ruddy cheeks came from the back of the store. "Hello, I'm Mr. George, the curator of this studio. May I help you?"

Tony extended his hand. "Hello, Mr. George, I'm Anthony Rawlings, and I believe that we can help one another."

On Tony's drive back to his hotel in San Francisco, his thoughts volleyed between his meeting and impending date. It was true that everyone had a price. Mr. George was no exception. What separated the world into two distinct groups were the people who strived for more and those who were willing to settle for less. Tony had been willing to spend more than he offered to elicit the curator's help; however, the strange little man had jumped at the first offer without as much as a hesitation. No matter. Soon, Mr. George would lure Sophia Burke into his studio. From there the plan would proceed. Although Tony would need to talk with Mr. George again, he had no intention of ever meeting again face-to-face. As a matter of fact, today's meeting never occurred.

Bon Vivant, too, was nestled into the Palo Alto landscape. The bright red sign with black letters was unassuming, yet Tony's heartbeat quickened as he parked the car. He was almost an hour early for Claire's reservations. Slipping into the lobby, he confidently approached the *maître d'*. Within moments, Tony had confirmation of his plans. Many customers had been notified by phone; those who couldn't be reached would be addressed at the door. Earlier customers had been accommodated; however, the *maître d'* promised the dining area, as well as the lounge, would be empty by 7:00 PM.

With time the only hurdle keeping him from his ex-wife, Tony took a seat at the bar, listened to the piano music, and ordered a drink. As time passed, couple after couple were led away. At twenty-five before seven, a waitress approached. "Mr. Rawlings, your companion has just arrived. Would you like her to join you?"

"No. I'd like to wait elsewhere until the restaurant is empty."

"Very well, I was told to invite you to the back offices. You're welcome to bring your drink, and we can get you another if you'd like…"

He followed the woman through a doorway and down a hall. After a few minutes, Tony made his way back down the corridor and peered through the small window in the door to the lounge. Time stood still as his peripheral vision muted; through the frosted glass he saw *her*.

His ex-wife, *his Claire*, sat alone near the middle of the lounge. The back of her dress dipped low, revealing her tanned skin. Although he couldn't hear, she appeared radiant as she spoke confidently to a waiter. Until her call, earlier in the day, Tony had wondered if she'd truly come— if she'd follow his instructions. Seeing her, with her hair piled high and ringlets grazing her long, proud neck, he swelled with pride. She was so strong, so proud, and still so obedient.

Tony was so enthralled in the vision that it took some time before he realized she wasn't wearing the dress he'd sent. His buyer had sent him pictures. She wasn't wearing any of the outfit. Pushing away his irritation, he softly chuckled. Damn, she was the challenge he needed in his life.

Just before 7:00 PM, Tony took a back hall to the front of the restaurant. Squaring his shoulders, he entered the lounge. The blue lighting that accentuated the chic ambience and the piano music both faded as he focused on the only remaining customer. If there had been others, he wouldn't have noticed. It was only Claire. As Tony approached, he watched her expression. Though she wore a mask of calm, in her emerald eyes he saw the fire he'd so desperately craved. With each step, he relished the warmth, like a frozen man in the wilderness coming upon lifesaving flames. Her heat radiated throughout the empty room pulling him closer. When he stood before her, her neck straightened. With a nod he said, "Good evening, Claire."

"Good evening, Tony. Won't you please have a seat?"

Refusing to lose sight of her eyes, he maintained their gaze and replied, "Thank you."

As he sat opposite her, he tried to read her thoughts. Before he could evaluate, she said, "It was nice of you to accommodate my change in plans." Gesturing toward a bottle of wine, she continued, "I took the liberty of ordering us a bottle of wine."

Lifting the bottle, he assessed the label. "Excellent choice."

Before their conversation could continue, a waiter appeared at their side. "*Monsieur* and *Mademoiselle*, your table is not yet ready. May I open your wine?"

Tony knew that there was one remaining couple in the dining room. As he was about to reply, Claire spoke, "*Oui, merci.*" Her French was Americanized, but French nonetheless.

Once the waiter departed, Tony said, "My, Claire, you continue to amaze me. I see you're trying to show me the new, independent Claire Nichols." When she didn't speak, he continued, "You don't need to work so hard. I've been observing you from afar and am already impressed."

"Tony, my goal isn't to impress. My goal is to show that I don't need your observation. I'm doing quite well on my own."

"I believe you have surpassed my expectations, once again."

"And for the record, I was independent before our encounter."

215

"Yes," he paused. "I can see how you would think that." He sipped his wine. "Now tell me, what was the point with the change in venue?"

"There was no point. I've eaten here before, and I thought you'd enjoy the cuisine."

"I see." He continued to sip the wine. "That's good. I was afraid you were trying to manipulate our visibility—"

Before he could continue, the *maître d'* approached their table. "*Excusez-moi*, but your table, it is ready."

"*Merci*," Tony replied as he stood. While Claire gathered her handbag, Tony politely helped her with her chair.

As they walked through the empty lounge, Tony nodded to the pianist and reached out to direct Claire's movement. His fingers contacted the warmth of her exposed back, and he fought the urge to explore below the draping material. Oh, it wouldn't be an uncharted expedition. He knew every inch of her body, but it had been too long. Leaning down, placing his lips near her ear, he inhaled her scent. With every ounce of restraint, he kept his lips from contacting her skin. Instead, he said, "I'm glad visibility wasn't your goal for this evening. I would hate to disappoint you."

As they stepped from the lounge into the dining area, Claire's neck stiffened and she gasped. Meeting him eye to eye, she boldly asked, "What have you done?"

He smirked, "I wanted to spend time with you, without the diversion of others."

"Where are the other people?"

"I believe they accepted an unbelievable offer. In essence, I rented the entire restaurant. After all, you said it was delicious, and I wanted to enjoy the food and your company."

"You bought out the entire place?"

He suddenly feared she'd run. Keeping a calm façade, he answered, "Yes, Claire. Shall we sit? I believe you requested this central table."

Overwhelmed with relief as she settled upon the cushioned seat, he gently pushed her chair under the table. Before they could resume their conversation, the waiter was present, delivering their wine and glasses to their new location. It may only be one person, but they both knew the importance of appearances. Once he was gone, Tony lifted his glass of wine and proposed a toast. "To you, the only person in this world who can keep me on my toes."

Taking a sip, he watched intently as Claire waged an internal war. He hadn't realized how much he'd missed watching the battle of wills behind her eyes. As she began to take a drink, he laughed at the outcome. She'd just lost and he'd watched it all.

"I hope you're amused." She placed the glass back on the table without drinking. "I believe I'm getting a headache. We'll need to postpone this dinner for another time."

As she began to push herself away from the table, his heart raced. Tony wouldn't allow her to leave, not now, not after so much time. He reached across the table and covered her hand. Summoning his most gentle touch, he *explained*. After all, that was what Catherine had said to do—to have faith. Let Claire decide. She couldn't decide if she didn't know his intent. Sheepishly, he implored, "Claire, I'd like you to stay. Your plans are to be commended. You probably know, but even without the clothes I sent, you're stunning. Now, if we're done with this ridiculous posturing, I'd like to talk with you for a while."

"This wasn't meant as posturing!" Her tone was hushed and harsh. "I assure you, my head *does* hurt."

"I have missed you terribly." He didn't intend to say it so bluntly, but he had to let her know. "I have missed your voice, your strength, your smile, and mostly, your eyes. My God, Claire, you have the most amazing eyes!"

"Stop it."

"Excuse me?" *Had she just ordered him to stop talking? Didn't she realize how hard this was?*

"I said, stop it!" The emerald fire intensely burned. She continued, "The last time we spoke in person, I begged to go with you back to your home, *our* home in Iowa City. As I recall, you offered me a psychiatric institution, so why would I be interested in listening to your drivel today?"

His mind spun. Explain yourself—that was what Catherine had said. He tried. "Well, first, because you accepted my invitation."

"I accepted your invitation for one reason, to convince you to leave me alone. We are done!"

"My dear, it isn't that simple." His tone was flat, leaving no room for debate. He wasn't going to argue the concept, no matter how ludicrous it was. She was his forever. *Done* wasn't an option.

"It is." Yet he heard the uncertainty in her voice, until her next emphasized word smashed his world to smithereens. *"Anton."*

The floor fell from the room. Or perhaps it was the ceiling that fell. Tony wasn't sure what just happened, but as prepared as he had been for the evening, nothing could have prepared him for that. Straightening his neck, he fought the red. Through clenched teeth, he replied, "My name is Anthony, but you may still address me as Tony."

"That's very gentlemanly of you. Do you not think that, as your wife, I deserved to know your true name was Anton Rawls?"

He fought to stay seated. It was like coming out of the effects of the poison: he clawed to reach the surface—the place where his world was intact. Those two words—Anton Rawls—spoken by Claire, ripped away the veil separating his past from his present. With a semblance of calm, he asked, "Where could you possibly have come up with such a story?"

"Why, *Anton*, it was in your box of confessions."

What the hell was she talking about? His voice gained strength with each syllable. "I assure you, I have no idea what you're saying."

"The information you sent me in prison."

Before they could continue, a waiter appeared beside their table with menus. Placing the binders in front of them, he asked if they were interested in hearing about the specials. Concurrently, they answered, "No." The waiter apologized for the interruption and meekly backed away from the table. Tony worked to process her words. Box. Confession. Prison. He squeezed the menu tighter.

Claire's voice pulled him from the whirlwind of questions. *If she knew that, what else did she know?* "Are you saying you didn't send me a box of information?"

Looking her in the eye, he confirmed, "I can assure you, I did not send you anything while you were in prison, and speaking of prison, congratulations on your early release." He made no attempt to suppress the sarcasm that saturated his final statement; he was too busy processing.

"Thank you, I promise that I was as surprised as you must have been."

Tony *harrumphed* as he took another drink of his wine, wishing it were bourbon. Once, he emptied the glass he poured another. After a hearty drink of the second glass, the calming effects began to settle his nerves and he replied, "That, my dear, is debatable."

He concentrated on the menu as Claire mentioned entrees that she'd enjoyed. Slowly, the tension began to subside as they superficially chatted about the options. Tony worked to control his thoughts and actions and salvage their reunion dinner. Her information, knowledge, and depth of that knowledge would all need to be assessed. Of course, he hadn't sent her information in prison. *But if not him—who?* That wasn't even the question; Tony knew *whom*. The question was *why?*

As he ordered their meals in French, he noticed Claire smile. He'd meant to surprise her with her entrée for it was the one she'd mentioned; however, it was obvious that she understood everything he and the waiter had said. Once they were alone, he tested his theory. Speaking in French, he said, "I see that you've broadened your language portfolio."

Also in French, she replied, "Yes, I decided to capitalize on my gift of time."

He smiled. *How could he not?* She was talking casually about prison, as if it had been a vacation. He leaned forward. "Claire, how's your headache?"

Taking a sip from her glass, she smiled. "I believe the wine is helping."

"That's good. Tell me about San Antonio."

If he expected her to be surprised by his knowledge of her activity, she disappointed him. Then again, he suspected that she knew he was watching her. Claire didn't miss a beat. She immediately began talking about sunshine, books, and relaxation. They fell into easy conversation. He remembered the *Red Wing* and talking with her for the first time. Even then, she'd impressed him with her confidence and knowledge. Her strength hadn't waned over the last year and a half. It emanated from every pore of her being, like an aura that pulled him nearer. She possessed knowledge, of language and of him. It intrigued, as well as frightened him. *What would she do with her new power? Could he stop it? Did he want to?* As the dinner progressed, her smile became less forced and her tone rang with the occasional laugh or giggle. It was music to his ears, and he didn't want the evening to end.

Neither one of them mentioned his birth name or the box again. The subject had been closed—temporarily. Tonight was about reconnecting. Maybe it was about something else. Tony wanted her to see that he was still in control; after all, he'd manipulated her plans. However, there was no doubt that her revelation created a shift in their game.

He couldn't wait to continue the play!

AUTHOR'S NOTE

This POV was originally written at the request of my amazing readers and appeared in the Goodreads Group: The Consequences Series Group Reads, Therapy, and Hugs. That version has been tweaked and edited for Behind His Eyes Truth. The "Dream" scene in *Truth has been interpreted in various ways. My initial intention was to show that from Tony's POV it wasn't what many have claimed it to be; however, like the rest of my story, his intent is still your decision.*

Thank you for joining me on this dark and insightful journey.

~Aleatha

A dream you dream alone is only a dream.
A dream you dream together is a reality.
– Yoko Ono

T he luxury of the upscale condominium escaped Tony's notice. Nothing mattered, other than making his way to Claire. Since their dinner the night before, he'd been unable to concentrate on anything or anyone else. As the elevator moved upward toward the fourth floor, Tony closed his eyes and envisioned his ex-wife. He remembered the white dress, the way his hand touched the skin of her back, and the slight whiff of perfume as his lips neared her long neck. He recalled the fire in her eyes as she called him *Anton*. Though he had tried to hide his reaction, Tony knew he'd failed. Claire saw him as others never could. She knew that her declaration affected him, and she knew when a subject was closed.

The woman he'd shared a meal with last night was more like the Claire Nichols he'd watched from afar—the one before his acquisition. Sometime during his refining process, she'd muted qualities that he now longed to explore. She was different. He could see it in the pictures, but more vividly in person. For the first time, he wanted to know the *real*

Claire Nichols—the one who could stare him down, and the one who would attempt to manipulate their dinner plans. Tony didn't just want to converse with that woman: he wanted to know her intimately. The woman he created knew his wants and needs; did he truly know hers?

As he neared the door of her condominium, he pushed away his carnal thoughts. Tony wouldn't do what he'd done before. He'd had his reasons, but they were done. She'd paid her price, or rather her family's price, for their past sins. Now it was time to move on. Tony needed to help Claire see that for herself.

After they'd parted ways last night, Tony started to call Catherine—he almost did—but he decided he needed more information. Perhaps the contents of that box would help him understand why Catherine sent it. Then, during the night, the revelation hit him: Claire's new knowledge was the stepping-stone he needed. That box would facilitate a path to her understanding. First, he needed to know what Claire knew. He also needed to emphasize that her newly acquired knowledge was private. Their roles may be evolving, but some rules would never change. Private information could not be divulged.

Tony went to her condominium to learn and to experience. Besides learning her level of knowledge, he couldn't go back to Iowa without spending more time in her presence. He hoped that a more private setting would bring out the woman with the fire in her eyes. He wanted to see those flames, feel the heat, and inhale her smoky aroma.

Before knocking on her door, his surroundings registered. He'd definitely waited too long. Claire was becoming established in Palo Alto. It was a double-edged sword. Negatively, she was making a life without him; however, the positive aspect was that she wouldn't likely disappear from him again. Phillip Roach's watchful eye guaranteed that. The private investigator was how Tony knew that Claire was currently home and her roommate was out of town.

With his knuckle ready to strike, Tony took a deep breath. *What if Claire refused to talk to him?* A rush of anxiety flowed through him. *Why hadn't he thought of that before?* She could refuse him entry. No, he reasoned, Claire wouldn't do that. Exhaling, he allowed his hand to rap on the door.

The voice from within rang with unabashed glee as the door opened. "Did you forget your key?"

Her happy, carefree expression morphed before his eyes. The dazzling smile disappeared and her neck straightened. He watched as his presence registered. The fire he loved in her emerald eyes ignited, as she worked to contain her swirling emotions. Watching that spark, seeing it before him, filled every empty space of his existence. The last fifteen months had been pure hell. He wanted that spark back in his life. Tony would move heaven and earth to make Claire understand that she belonged to him.

Reining in his desire to pull her into his arms and elicit another type of spark, Tony replied, "I don't have a key, but I'd be glad to get one. Just tell me where to sign up."

Her stance straightened and her tone hardened. "How did you get up here? You can't be on this floor without a key."

Trying to keep the conversation light, he requested entrance. "Perhaps you could invite me in and we can discuss it?"

"Tony, why are you here?"

He smirked, "If we're playing one hundred questions, I admit defeat. May I come in?"

After a prolonged silence, during which her eyes never left his, Claire took a step back and nodded. He tried to contain his relief as he walked into her foyer and glanced around. "My, Claire, you're living much better than I expected. When I first learned of your release, I pictured you destitute."

"I'm sure you enjoyed that scenario. I'm sorry to disappoint."

He snickered. "Disappoint? On the contrary, your ingenuity is to be praised." Although he hadn't foreseen an alliance between Claire and Amber McCoy, Amber was obviously helping Claire make a life—without him. His heartbeat quickened. Without him was *not* acceptable.

Her words brought him back to reality. "Tony, I'll repeat myself at the risk of being redundant. Why are you here, and how did you access my floor?"

"I gained access by the security guard on the first floor. He tried to call you, but you didn't answer. I explained that we're old friends, I'm leaving town, and since I had recently talked with you, I knew you were home and expecting me—"

The ringing of her phone interrupted his explanation. After glancing at the screen, she said, "This is security. I'll tell them I don't want you here, unless you quickly tell me why you're here." The phone rang again.

He didn't hesitate. He was inside her new home and didn't want to leave—not yet. "I want to know more about your prison delivery."

She didn't respond, at least not to him; instead, she answered the phone and decided his fate. With each word his body eased—she told the security guard that he could stay. While she spoke, he drank in the woman before him: casual and comfortable, with her dark hair pulled back, wearing soft slacks and a big shirt. There was a wide neckline that exposed a shoulder revealing the strap of a camisole. It was a stark contrast to the woman in the white dress, yet equally as sexy.

When she finally turned back to him, he noticed the determination in her voice. "I have plans today. Please make this quick."

His cheeks rose and his breath quickened. The aroma of shampoo and jasmine filled his senses. "Yes, I see you're dressed for business. What do they call that, business casual?" While she debated her response, he lowered his voice and added, "I'm not complaining. I always found the casual Claire as sexy as the one who rocked designer dresses."

Claire crossed her arms over her chest and exhaled. "Please, I have lunch plans, and I'd like to change. Question what you want and go."

Lunch plans? With whom? He'd seen pictures of her with Harrison Baldwin. *Could that be whom she was planning on seeing?* While these questions and many more ran through his head, he managed to ask, "Do you only entertain in the entry, or may we sit?"

"We may sit," she replied, and began walking toward the living room. As they sat, her next sentence caught him completely off guard. "I know you enjoy coffee. I'd offer you some, but the last time I got you coffee, it didn't work out so well for me."

To his amazement, he found her brazenness titillating. "God, Claire you're something else. I can't imagine anyone else joking about that."

"Well, see, you misinterpreted. I wasn't joking. I'm actually still pissed as hell."

"Good for you." He leaned toward her. She didn't look away. He loved her tenacity! "Your ability to admit your displeasure is refreshing. It encourages me to be honest, too."

"Honesty? That would be an invigorating change."

He worked to maintain his expression and keep his tone soft. "You should know that I'm sorry."

The battle once again raged behind her eyes. *Would she voice her thoughts or stay quiet as she had when they were married?* He waited. Her volume raised exponentially with each phrase "What? You're *sorry?*" It was as if she filled the room with her presence. "Well, Tony, I believe I need a little clarification. Tell me what exactly you're sorry about. I'll gladly give you a few options."

She suddenly stood and paced about the living room, her chest heaving with each exaggerated breath. When she neared the large windows, the sunlight muted her features. Tony much preferred having her close to watch her emotions unravel, and at the same time he yearned to calm her, seize her shoulders, and make her forget what she was about to say. He couldn't; she deserved to tell him exactly what she thought. He prayed that after she was done, they could move forward.

Finally, she spoke, "First, you're sorry for invading my privacy for years, years before I even knew you existed. Second, you're sorry for kidnapping me, isolating me, controlling me, and manipulating me. Third, you're sorry for lying to me, pretending you cared, and, oh yeah, marrying me. Fourth, listen carefully, Tony, this is a big one. You're sorry for framing me for attempted murder, resulting in incarceration in a federal penitentiary." She sat back down and once again crossed her arms over her heaving breasts.

One doesn't deal with people as successfully as Anthony Rawlings without understanding confrontation. If he chose to retaliate, this scene would escalate to a place he didn't want to go. As he fought to allow her this release, she added, "I would prefer the words, but you are welcome to say one through four, if that's easier for you."

Tony leaned closer. Avoiding his stare, she looked down at her trembling hands. *Had her speech caused her hands to shake, or was it him?* His fight for control evaporated into a need to reassure. *From the very beginning of his acquisition, hadn't he asked for honesty?* Though her words were painful to hear, they were her version of the truth and she'd delivered. When her green eyes finally peered at him from below veiled lids, he watched the tension fade.

Tony gently reached for her hand and spoke softly, "I am deeply sorry for one and four." He rubbed her hand with his thumb. "I did provide you with an alternative destination for number four."

Claire exhaled audibly.

"I'm not proud of two, but three would never have happened without it." His tone deepened and slowed. "I am *not*, and never will be, sorry for three, and for the record, I never lied about loving you, or pretended to love you. I didn't realize it at first, but I have loved you since before you knew my name." He bowed his head, kissed the soft skin atop of her hand, and continued, "And you forgot our divorce. I'm sincerely sorry for that. Had I known you would be released so soon... we could still be married." Placing her hand once again on her knee, he touched the fourth finger of her left hand. "You could still officially be mine."

Her wedding rings came to mind. This wasn't the time to bring up that she'd sold them. While he waited for her to respond, his gaze went to the table. Laying on the shiny surface were two phones. Before Tony could comment, Claire reached for the smaller phone and slid it into her camisole between her breasts. He closed his eyes and gently shook his head. "If I didn't want to see that phone before, I sure as hell do now."

"It's my *work* phone," she answered too quickly.

"Oh, I was unaware of your employment."

"Really? I guess I forgot to inform you or your spies."

"Claire, I want to show you that I can change. Have as many damn phones as you want. Two seem excessive, but go for it."

"Thank you for your permission. I don't need it. I can have fifty phones if I want."

Tony nodded. Her spunk seemed to be without bounds. *Why had he not allowed it to shine before?*

Claire continued, "It's documented, when people are forbidden something, once it's made available, they tend to overindulge."

His tone turned sultry. "Before it is made available, a person may dream of it, long for it, and fantasize about it. Especially if he once had it and knows how amazing it is."

"I don't recall availability being an issue for you."

His pulse quickened. If she only knew how close he was to being that person again. Not because he desired to harm her. On the contrary, his desires were totally and completely centered on pleasure—his and more importantly hers. Tony warned, "Be careful, Claire. That could be interpreted as an invitation."

She stood. "Then once again, you would be misinterpreting."

He stood and stepped toward her, yet she didn't move. *Was it self-control or unabashed determination?* Whatever she possessed flooded his system like no chemical aphrodisiac ever could. Though their bodies didn't touch, electricity sparked between them. The inches of separation were but a conductor for the energy that couldn't be contained. *If he moved nearer, would they be burnt?* His words came from somewhere deep in his throat. "I believe you want what I want, as much as I do."

"If you're suggesting I want you to leave, you're absolutely correct. If you're suggesting anything else, it couldn't be farther from the truth."

His head bowed slightly. Her words said one thing, but every ounce of her being said something else. Perhaps it was a subtle scent, the way her cheeks reddened, or the hardening of her nipples under the light shirt. He wasn't exactly sure, but Tony knew his desires were shared.

He wanted to kiss her and take her newfound boldness to the next level. *How would it translate to their bed?* Then he reminded himself that they no longer shared a bed or a life. As she lifted her chin and her lips neared his, Tony summoned all of his restraint to not bend and taste what was right in front of him. Instead of a kiss, he reached for her chin and bathed her cheeks in his warm, sensual breath. "You, my dear, have never been a good liar."

If he leaned forward, he'd be able to feel her hard nipples against his chest. Before he could move, she stepped back, sat, and crossed her arms over her chest.

"You're right. Your deceitfulness far exceeds my modest attempts at dishonesty. I bow down to your superior duplicity."

It was a small victory, but a victory nonetheless. Tony worked unsuccessfully to hide his grin. She'd just confirmed she still had feelings. Exhaling, he retook his seat. Refusing to relinquish contact, he allowed their knees to touch.

"I know you have no reason to believe me, but I thought you should know why I came to California."

Her gaze was too innocent as she asked, "Why?"

He couldn't lie. "To take you back to Iowa."

Claire stared. Finally, a smile briefly fluttered across her lips. He wondered what it meant. She replied, "Well, since this time I have a choice, I'm going to say *no*."

Tony tried another route. "Catherine misses you."

"I miss her, too." With a hint of hesitation, Claire asked, "Does she believe that I tried to kill you?"

God, he hated this. It was just one of the many things he'd done to her, one of the many things he couldn't take back. The anguish in Claire's voice tugged at his heart. He couldn't tell her the truth, not now. If he told her that Catherine not only knew, she was also involved, it could alienate Claire forever. Trying to focus his thoughts, Tony carefully worded his response. It wasn't lying; it was more a minimization of facts. "I'm not sure. We've never discussed it. I know at first she was worried about me. Then once I was well, she was upset, but I don't know for sure if it was at you or at me. The subject's never come up."

"Then how do you know she misses me?"

"I just do. When word came of your pardon—"

Claire interrupted, "You were angry."

Red knocked at his thoughts—memories of his rage when Preston called, the impotency of not knowing her location. This time it was Tony who stood and paced, avoiding her gaze. Stopping at the large windows, the beautiful view was lost behind the impending veil of red. She was pushing him, testing him. He couldn't lose his temper; he wouldn't. He knew what he'd done to Claire—and so did she. If she were ever to trust him again, he needed to be honest. Perhaps someday the whole truth could be revealed, but Claire wasn't ready for everything, not yet.

Forcing restraint, he weighed his words and began. "I was. I admit, I was… stunned. Governor Preston informed me of your release *two weeks* after it occurred. I was angry at everyone: at you for being pardoned, at Jane Allyson for presenting the petition, at Governor Bosley for signing it. Hell, I was even mad at the clerk who filed it." He turned toward her, continuing to maintain control. She didn't turn away. The intensity of her stare frightened him as much as it exhilarated him. No one else in Tony's life had ever glared at him, not like Claire. He went on, "I finally figured out that the person I was the most upset with was me. For the first time in years—yes, more than three, you know that now—I'd lost track of you." His volume increased. "My God, you were gone!"

He waited as she remained silent. Only her stare intensified and prodded, as if she could see deep into his soul. The sudden vulnerability chilled his skin. *Could she see his pain?* Yes, he was responsible for her consequences and pain that she'd endured, but he had pain, too. With all his heart he wanted to make them both forget it all—the pain, the past, every-thing. Stepping toward her, he saw anxiety in her expression increase. His chest ached at the realization that she was frightened of him. He would do anything to change that.

Exhaling, he maintained his distance and forged ahead. "Damn it, Claire. Nothing has been the same without you. The house is just a big, empty hole."

"Tell me why," she demanded.

"Why is it empty? Because you're not there."

"No, Tony. Why did you do it to me? Why'd you set me up—worse, arrange my entire life to look as though I was after your money, setting you up for the kill? You know I continually told you I didn't care about the money. But everything, from the beginning, was manipulated to make me look guilty. Now you say you loved me. You don't do that to someone you love. Tell me why you did it."

"It isn't past tense, Claire. I still love you. And I thought you knew why."

"I want to hear it from you."

"What was in the box you said you received? What information did you think I revealed?"

Suddenly, he envisioned her in prison, receiving the package. It wasn't a thought he'd entertained before his dream. He'd convinced himself that prison was her fault, but now having her before him, he thought about the time she'd endured in a cell—months, a year. Thirteen days in her suite had nearly broken her. Damn, he deserved anything she said to him and anything she did with this newfound knowledge.

Her words rushed together, glued by years of suppression. "There were pictures, articles, and a letter. It explained that your birth name was Anton Rawls, and that you changed it after the death of your grandfather and parents."

Perspiration threatened to dampen his veneer, as his hidden past came rolling from her tongue. "Was it handwritten? Where is it? I'd like to see it."

"Yes, the note was handwritten. I thought it looked like your writing. It wasn't signed, but you never signed anything." Her fire-filled gaze dis-appeared as her eyes dropped to the floor. "You can't see it. I burned it."

His anxiety lifted as a relieved laugh escaped his lips. "You what?"

Her stare once again found its target as the intensity grew. "I burned it—all of it. I took it to the incinerator at the prison and watched it burn."

He couldn't believe his ears. "You're serious. You have no proof of anything you just said? You burned it." A smile momentarily flittered across his lips. "I don't know who sent it to you. I did confirm, today, that you received a box in October of last year. The prison said the return address was Emily's."

Claire nodded. "Yes, I assumed it was books or something."

"Burned it. Why?"

She shook her head. "I've asked myself that same question a thousand times. I believe it was a cleansing of sorts, my way of removing you from my life."

Tony smirked, "How's that working for you?"

Claire's grin filled his heart. It was more real than any last night, and he didn't want it to stop. "Not as well as I'd hoped." Looking about, she added, "I really do need to get ready for my lunch date. If we're done, I'd like you to leave."

Date? He didn't want to leave—ever. "I would like to ask you one more thing."

Claire nodded.

"Who was the expected recipient of that dazzling smile?"

Her head tilted and brows furrowed. "What are you talking about?"

"When you first opened the door, your smile was earth-shaking. Who were you expecting?"

"A good friend."

Tony raised his eyebrows, but Claire didn't respond. *A good friend. Could it be Harrison Baldwin?* He would or could have a key; after all, he's Amber's brother. *Or did someone else have a key?*

Claire stood. "If you'll follow me; I'll show you to the door."

Tony followed. "I will not give up my quest." He wanted to be honest, too. He wanted her back in every way possible, by his side, united in everything.

When they reached the door, Claire said, "Please give Catherine my love. If you have truly changed, as you claim, you'll respect my decision. If that's the case, you're wasting your time."

"I have invested much more. One last thing," he paused as his words slowed. "Do not share your unsupported theories with anyone." He'd kept this part of his life hidden for years. The repercussions of it becoming public were too far reaching.

Claire's neck straightened. "I'm sorry. It's too late for that."

Though her words set off alarms, her proximity incited desires, pushing the warnings temporarily away. Wanting one last morsel of contact, Tony reached for her hand, lowered his lips to soft skin, and brushed her palm with the tips of his fingers. Despite her demeanor, her acceptance and arousal were evident. If he could just take her back to Iowa—there were so many things he wanted to do.

With her hand still in his, he warned, "Be careful. You don't want to disappoint me."

Her posture grew and her voice feigned strength. "That—is no longer my concern. Good-bye, Tony."

Nodding, Tony turned and strode through the door toward the elevator. Behind him, he heard Claire's door shut. The sound reverberated through the unoccupied hallway, returning the emptiness of the last fifteen months to his soul. Part of him wanted to turn around and tell her that, no matter what, she could never disappoint him.

Then he remembered her question, why? *Why did he choose her?* He lowered his head and debated the answer. It was because of the vendetta; she should have figured that out from the box. Tony knew in his heart that it was so much more. She was part of him. Maybe that was the real purpose of the vendetta: it brought them together in the most unlikely of circumstances. Fate. No matter of the why, the truth was that he needed her. He was incomplete without her, and he didn't want to live another moment without knowing she would once again be part of his life.

Suddenly, he turned on his heels and returned to her door. He would tell her!

Before he could knock, the crash of something breaking came through her door. Tony inclined his head and listened. With each passing minute of silence, his anxiety grew. *What if she were hurt?* He knew Amber was out of town. Claire might be injured and in need of help.

Tony reached for the handle, expecting it to be locked; however, it turned under his grasp. Hesitantly, he opened the door and slowly entered the foyer. Straining his ears, he heard only silence.

Walking in the opposite direction from the living room, he neared a partially open door. Pushing it wider, he found a bedroom. Immediately, he knew it was Claire's. It wasn't one thing in particular, although he did see a picture of Emily and John; the space was filled with her presence—her scent and her aura. Searching the room for his ex-wife, he allowed his fingers to touch the sheets of her unmade bed. Instantaneously, images of her sleeping upon this bed filled his thoughts—or better yet, not sleeping.

His loafers echoed on the wood floor of the silent condominium as he walked back toward the living room. When he turned the corner, he saw Claire was lying on the sofa, and on the table, was the small cell phone she'd put into her camisole. He picked it up. The screen was cracked. When he tried to access the numbers, nothing happened. Perhaps that was the sound he'd heard.

His heartbeat quickened. Tony knew that he should show himself out. Claire was all right, just sleeping. He should leave and not look back.

He couldn't. Though she wasn't speaking or moving, her presence pulled him closer. Her slightly parted lips looked perfect for kissing. Before he could stop himself, Tony knelt beside his ex-wife and touched his lips to hers. The decadent sweetness aroused him; he yearned to taste more than her lips. With her eyes still closed, Claire's body moved toward him. He expected her to tell him to leave; instead, a soft moan echoed throughout the condominium. The sound was magical, like a switch turning on the feelings and emotions he'd tried to hide.

Tony didn't know what was going to happen, but she looked wrong sleeping on the couch. Her bedroom was so close; he decided she needed to be in there.

"Claire, put your arms around my neck."

He waited. *Would she respond?* She moaned again with a slight shake of her head. Tony tried for another kiss. This time when their lips united, hers were no longer soft, but firm and puckered as they pushed against his. When her mouth parted slightly and her tongue searched for his, he couldn't control himself any longer. Conscious reasoning disappeared as primal instinct took over. Before he could repeat his demand, her arms encircled his neck, fanning the heat of his desire. His mouth searched for hers, hungry for more. This wasn't just him. He'd felt the mutual attraction earlier. They were both willingly surrendering. Claire's breasts heaved against his chest as her arms tightened their embrace. He gently lifted her from the sofa causing their lips to momentarily disengage.

The sound of her purring unrecognizable words as she nuzzled her cheek into his shirt made her room suddenly seem too far away. Tony wanted to ask if she were sure, if she wanted this as much as he did, yet, as he lowered her onto her bed, he feared her response. If he didn't ask, he could claim innocence. Gazing into her bedroom eyes, he slowly removed the clip from her hair and fanned the long brown tresses over her pillow. The scent of shampoo filled his senses, as her back arched and the most beautiful smile lit his world.

His fingers lingered at her collarbone as his lips found the sensitive skin of her neck. Piece by piece, he removed her clothing. At times he directed her movements, asking her to lift her arms or arch her back. Each command was met with compliance. When he lifted her camisole over her head, he watched as her pink nipples hardened before his eyes.

Tony couldn't stop his fingers from caressing the hard nubs. Claire's body responded as she pushed her breasts toward his hands and whimpered his name.

The sound of Claire speaking his name—dripped with need—threatened his resilience as he eased her soft pants over her hips and toward her ankles. Before he could remove them completely, Tony saw her panties and gasped. The small piece of black lace was Claire's ultimate display of independence. The panties both fascinated and intrigued him. Curiously, he encircled her hips with his large hands as his thumbs teased the small bow directly above his destination.

Lost in his own sensations, he didn't notice the change in Claire's breathing until he saw the goose bumps upon her skin. When he tore his eyes from the delicate lace, he saw her alarm. Tony couldn't comprehend the change; instead, he breathed deeply in anticipation and displayed a reassuring, devilish grin.

She sighed as her eyes mellowed, and she lifted her hips for him to remove the panties. When they slipped over her ankles, she said, "This isn't real. This is a dream."

"Do you want it to be a dream?"

She shook her head, and repeated, "It isn't real."

Tony smiled at her justification. There was no way this wasn't real. He'd dreamed about her, her scent, and the taste of her soft skin. He'd imagined her body and fantasized about her responses... this was all of that and more!

After he removed his clothes, he climbed upon the bed and watched her eyes for approval. Tony wanted this more than he wanted life, but he wouldn't take it from her unwillingly. He'd done that before and swore to never again. With her petite body radiating immense heat, he eased himself over her. The tips of her hardened nipples pressed against his chest as he lowered his lips once again to her shoulder.

"Please," was all Claire could seem to manage as his lips moved from shoulder to neck and down to her breasts. As he suckled each nipple, Claire's fingers wound through his hair and pulled his mouth tighter against her chest. When his lips moved past her flat stomach, her pleas became louder and less coherent. The scent of her arousal intoxicated Tony as he gently spread her legs.

"God, you are so amazing." He needed to hear her approval. If she denied him, he didn't know if he could stop, but he needed to know that this was consensual. "Are you sure?" Once again, he held himself above her body as their eyes made contact. "Claire, are you sure?"

"Oh, God, yes, please!"

She didn't need to repeat herself. His fingers delved as gasps and moans filled his ears. Her petite hands seized his shoulders as her body quivered at his touch. When the time came and they reunited, Tony couldn't remember anything, *anytime*, feeling so right.

Claire was his. He'd made terrible mistakes and done awful things, but as they moved in sync, he saw hope for a future. He told her over and over how beautiful she was, how magnificent she was, and how much he wanted her. He knew it wouldn't be easy—hell, he wasn't supposed to be seen with her in public—but it would be. He knew every inch of Claire, inside and out. He knew that the woman with him was there willingly. She may keep making comments about reality and dreams, but he understood. This was his dream, too.

Her time away hadn't changed the magnificent woman she was. She still excited him. Her hands, lips, and body could bring him to heights he'd never approached with anyone else. Her lack of inhibition proclaimed her newfound independence. She willingly pleased him while allowing him to fulfill her every fantasy. They fit together like two pieces of a puzzle. There was no question: in dream or reality, they belonged together.

After every desire was fulfilled and every height exceeded, they collapsed in each other's arms. Claire's breathing slowed as she nuzzled against his chest, and her fingers swirled through his chest hair. Within moments, she was sound asleep.

Tony lay with her for a while, drifting in and out of dreams. Maybe Claire was right. Maybe this wasn't real. As he held her sleeping body, he wondered if reality could truly be this amazing.

When he finally eased himself from her bed, he saw her black panties upon the floor. Picking them up, he fingered the delicate lace. He'd never imagined underwear could be so erotic. Inhaling her scent, he eased the panties back over her feet and up her sexy legs. Seeing her asleep, wearing only underwear made him hard again.

Tony shook his head. He was getting too old for this multiple-orgasm sex. Nevertheless, he couldn't deny his obvious arousal. He covered the panties with her soft pants. Surprisingly, she didn't wake as he dressed her. It wasn't that he didn't enjoy seeing her naked. It was that he needed to leave. If he didn't cover her, he wasn't sure he'd be able to walk through the door.

Once they were both clothed, she was sleeping soundly, and he was ready to leave. He brushed her lips with a light kiss. Claire didn't wake, but he watched as the tips of her lips turned upward, and she nuzzled into her pillow.

Perhaps this was wrong on many levels, yet as he walked from her room toward the door, wrong wasn't the feeling he entertained. They were both consenting adults. They could pretend it wasn't real, that their feelings didn't truly exist, but he would know and she would know that it was real and despite everything, they were and always would be one.

Tony made sure the door to her condominium was locked.

Confrontation – April 2013
(Truth Behind the scenes)

The wise man doesn't give the right answers, he poses the right questions.
– Claude Levi-Strauss

Tony hadn't called home during his trip to California. He wasn't sure what to say. Had he called the night he and Claire dined, he would have laid Catherine out. Each moment his thoughts lingered on Claire's prison delivery, the darker the consuming crimson became. He didn't want to believe that it was Catherine, but yet, it had to be her. There truly were no other options.

While his mind searched for answers on the night of his and Claire's dinner, sleep remained an elusive goal. Tony utilized his insomnia by messaging his contact at the Iowa State Penitentiary. Surprisingly, he received a quick response. Over the course of Claire's incarceration, she received multiple packages and letters. The senders of those mailings were constantly either a J. Findes—someone with a Chicago P.O. Box number—or Emily Vandersol. Initially, Emily's packages came from New York; later, they came from Indiana. One package, in October of 2012, had Emily's return address, handwritten—as opposed to her customary label—and the scanned image showed a Cedar Rapids postmark. Tony had no idea who J.

Findes was, although he wanted to find out, but he believed the one from Cedar Rapids was the delivery that Claire mentioned. His mind went into overdrive, questioning the contents and intent.

Catherine had been so concerned when Tony altered the course of their plan. She warned that bringing Claire onto the estate was dangerous. She mentioned more than once that Claire was a liability they shouldn't have taken on, yet over time, she came around. Tony mused, it was Claire. She did that to people—penetrated shields and infiltrated thoughts. When Claire failed her final test, Catherine never gloated. On the contrary, she was as disappointed as Tony and was genuinely concerned about Tony's condition. Her actions to rid the estate of Claire's things were solely meant as an aid to help Tony deal with the situation.

He didn't agree, but he understood.

Then, when Tony learned from Claire that the box she received contained *pictures, articles, and a letter* explaining *his* change of name and association with *his* grandfather and parents, anger intermixed with curiosity.

Why would Catherine send Claire information about his past? What did she hope to accomplish? Had she confessed her role? What did she expect Claire to do with that knowledge locked away for her entire sentence of seven years?

Not only did Tony want answers, he wanted to see Catherine's reaction when he confronted her. If he'd called ahead, she would've been prepared for his arrival. *Would she even suspect that Claire would share her knowledge?* Tony intended to tread lightly.

After spending part of Saturday afternoon in California, it was quite late when Tony returned home to the estate. Once he did, he went straight to his suite, more specifically, to his closet and *his* box of memories. Claire had said there were pictures—he wondered if they came from his stash. As he removed the box, he marveled that this was the second time in as many months that he'd rummaged through these mementos. Other than to remove Claire's grandmother's necklace, Tony hadn't touched any of its contents the entire time she was under his roof. After she failed her test, he didn't *want* to look at it or remember any of it. He never planned to dispose of this record of his acquisition, but for the longest time he couldn't bear to view it.

Setting the box near his sofa, Tony began to pull from its depths. Everything appeared in order as he removed file after file, each containing private investigative reports. There was a time when it seemed safer for his updates to be transmitted on paper, with photos that were glossy or matte. Paper clips connected envelopes to folders; each contained various numbers of pictures. When he turned over any given picture, Tony saw his own writing, as he'd painstakingly scribbled names on each back. With every envelope, Tony reminisced. Before long, he was lost in the past—Claire's past.

Tony hadn't taken the photos at her parents' funeral, although he'd been there. He did take the ones at Emily's wedding. Smirking, he remembered how easy it was to work his way into the church and reception. No one questioned a man taking photographs at a wedding—everyone was doing it. The majority of the photos and reports in the box were mostly taken by private investigators; nonetheless, Tony was the one to label subjects.

After a while, he realized that he wouldn't be able to tell if the pictures Claire received were from him. There were just too many. One or two or—hell—even ten taken from this file or that envelope wouldn't be missed.

Then he remembered the *Red Wing* napkin. He'd looked for it last month and given up. Digging farther into the treasures of the past, Tony again pulled from the box. Once everything was sprawled across his floor, he realized the napkin was gone. *Did Claire say it was in her prison delivery? Could he have left it in a suit-coat pocket? Did its absence prove beyond a shadow of a doubt that Catherine was the sender of the box?*

Claire had also said articles. *What articles?* Tony didn't have articles about his past.

Each moment and each revelation churned Tony's stomach. The sender had to have been Catherine. He'd worked too hard to distance his current life and persona from his past. Though his curiosity remained, red seeped around the edges. Tony's jaw clenched as he envisioned Catherine going through his personal belongings.

He put everything back, except a snapshot taken at Claire's college graduation. It was taken from a distance, but you could see her in her cap and gown surrounded by people. On the back, it read: Claire (with Emily),

Valparaiso Graduation—2007. Sighing, he folded it in half and placed it in his shirt pocket.

Instead of confronting Catherine, Tony decided to let her come to him. He knew she would, out of curiosity about his trip. With each step toward his office, he battled the red. Instinctively, he wanted to bang on the door of her suite and demand answers. Yet, years of experience with Catherine told him that wouldn't be the best means to learn her motives. He needed to surprise her without confrontation.

Tony had only been within the confines of his office long enough to pour a few fingers of Blue Label when he heard the knock. With each rap, his muscles tensed and the hair on the back of his neck stood at attention. Easing himself into his desk chair, Tony hit the button and watched his door open.

It was late, but not late enough for all of the staff to have retired to their rooms. He watched as Catherine played her role. "Excuse me, Mr. Rawlings. I was just informed that you were home. May I speak with you for a minute?"

He could say no and make her wait. Her unmet curiosity could be her punishment; however, if he made her wait, then he would have to wait. Tony was tired of waiting. "Certainly, Catherine, shut the door and have a seat."

Her gray eyes narrowed as she approached his desk. "What is it? Did she refuse to speak to you?"

"What is what?"

"You look... I don't know, upset? And you didn't call."

He shook his head. "No. She spoke to me."

"And?" Catherine leaned forward. "Tell me, how is she?"

"She's doing well—too well."

"Anton, don't make me pry each word out of you. I want to know all about it."

There was no way in hell that Tony planned on telling her *all* about it. His and Claire's reunion had gone better—much better—than he'd dared to imagine. He wouldn't tell anyone about what happened at her condominium. That memory would be theirs alone. It would sustain him until he held her in his arms again, until she was where she belonged—in Iowa.

He suppressed a chuckle as he recalled Claire's power play. "I had reservations for our dinner. A few hours before, she called my cell."

Catherine gasped. "How did she get the number? She didn't try to cancel, did she?"

"I don't know how she got my number. I wondered the same thing. Although I'm curious, the subject never came up." He shrugged and suppressed a grin. Since something else had come up during their reunion, he no longer cared. "Perhaps, she remembered it from before? And, no, she didn't cancel; she'd made reservations of her own."

Catherine's eyes widened. "What did you do?"

"I let her believe she was in control. I went to her destination."

"You see, Anton, she's much stronger than you gave her credit for."

He didn't usually think about the way Catherine addressed him. She'd called him Anton ever since the two of them were very young. That would change. Nodding at her statement, Tony leaned forward and looked her in the eye.

Uncharacteristically, she pulled away. "What is it?"

"My name is *Anthony* or, better yet, *Mr. Rawlings*. It is not, nor has it been for a long time, *Anton*."

"What? Of course it is. You'll always be Anton to me." When he didn't respond, she added, "That was how you were introduced to me, and what Nathaniel—"

"Don't go there." He abruptly stood and walked toward the highboy.

Catherine's voice softened. "Did something happen... with her? Is that why you're acting this way?"

"I think it's time to move on. *Anton Rawls* is gone." He lifted his brow. "And so is *Marie Rawls*."

She shook her head. "Stop it. Why are you saying this?"

"Because of you."

"Me?" Catherine asked, stunned.

"You said that Claire lived in this house for two years and never knew its secrets. I think it's time to put those secrets to rest. Our list is done— we're done with the past. After all, no one knows about it but us." He watched as she smoothed nonexistent wrinkles from her skirt. When she failed to respond, he asked, "Isn't that correct? No one but us."

Lifting her chin, she swallowed before she spoke. "I-I think I might... I might know..."

"What, Catherine? What do you know?"

Squaring her shoulders, she stood. "*Mr. Rawlings?* Really? After everything that we've been through, you suddenly want to be addressed as *Mr. Rawlings*—in private? And what respect do I get? After all, I was Nathaniel's wife."

"You were," Tony agreed. "But since Rawls was taken from you, I suppose it would be London."

Her eyes screamed with retorts, yet her lips remained pressed together in a straight line. Finally, she nodded. "Very well, *Mr. Rawlings*, I hope that you feel better in the morning. I believe this conversation is deteriorating faster than either of us is willing to admit."

Tony chuckled and pulled the picture from his pocket. Thrusting it toward her, he asked, "What can you tell me about this?"

Slowly, she took the photo and unfolded it. "It's a picture of Claire and Emily at Claire's graduation." Meeting his eyes, she asked, "Why?"

"Because apparently it was just part of a prison delivery that Claire received."

Catherine stepped back. "I didn't include... I don't know... she *told* you?"

"She blindsided me. You didn't think it would have been helpful to let me know about your little package before I went to see her?"

Her hands ran over her skirt as she sat and perched on the edge of the chair. "Anton-thony, I should have." She nodded. "I should've told you when I first did it. It was just that... well, I saw how much you were hurting."

"And telling Claire my birth name would help that—how?" Tony's baritone voice echoed throughout his regal office.

"It would help her understand *why* you did what you did."

"What about you? Did you add your autobiography to this delivery as well?"

"She didn't share all of the contents?"

"If you are asking if she invited me to her condominium to see for myself, no." When Catherine didn't reply, Tony went on. "She knew the name Anton Rawls and that my parents and grandfather were dead."

"Anton, you have to understand."

He raised his brow.

"Anthony," Catherine corrected. "She wasn't supposed to be released for a long time. I thought that maybe if she knew some of your background and if she had time to think about it, she would understand you better. She would *want* to understand you better."

He stepped closer and his words slowed. "I don't want you or anyone else going through my private things."

"T-that picture, I didn't send it."

"But you did send pictures, and they had to have come from my information."

"You're right. I'm sorry." Catherine went on to talk about the articles she included. They were selected to create an accurate timeline designed to lead Claire to the right conclusion.

"And what *exactly* was the conclusion you wanted her to find?"

"I wanted her to know that you'd been obsessed with her far longer than she realized. I hoped that would show her that you did love her and had for a long time. I wanted her to understand that you are a man of your word, and you had a promise to keep. I hoped that if she understood all of that, she could forgive you and... I don't know... help you."

Tony sunk back in his chair. Running his hand through his hair, he asked, "Forgive *me*? She's the one who left me."

"Yes, An-nd she knows that she didn't try to kill you. She knows that she spent over a year paying for a crime she didn't commit. I had hoped that she would stop hating you for that consequence and start to understand you."

His eyes closed as he processed her explanation. It wasn't at all as he'd imagined it. *Had Catherine's plan worked? Did that information help to propel her to become the woman at the restaurant and in her condominium?* Finally, he stared back at the steel-gray eyes watching him. "It wasn't your place or your right to share."

"It wasn't your right to take her, either."

"But it was all right to have her killed? That's what you wanted."

"No, Anton, that's not what I wanted. I wanted the children of the children to pay, just as Nathaniel asked. I didn't want to get to know them, reassure them, and tend to them. I didn't want to nurse them back to health and have a personal relationship with them." She stood. "You did that." Her voice grew more determined. "You changed the rules and so did I."

"I should fire you—kick you out of my house."

"Do you think so?" Her cold tone sent a chill through the office. "Do you think Nathaniel would approve? Do you think your grandfather wanted me out on the street? Perhaps you're just not willing to admit that if Claire knows you, really knows you, she might understand you. Is it that difficult to admit that *I* had a good idea?"

Their nearly thirty-year history fast-forwarded through Tony's mind. Images of his grandfather were a blur to the years of planning and manipulating. "You're not fired. Just stay the hell out of my private things! That means my closet, my suite, and my files. You know?" His brow rose. "She could send us both to prison if she fully unravels your trail. Do you still think that it's a good idea?"

"She won't share."

"What if she already has?"

Catherine's brows peaked in question.

"I don't know if she has or not. I told her not to, and she said it was too late."

"What does that mean?"

Tony shook his head. "I don't know." His dark gaze penetrated. "And, to be honest, I'm tired of discussing it."

Her gray eyes swirled with unasked questions. Finally, she stood and walked toward the door. Just before reaching her destination, Catherine stopped. "Just one more thing, *Mr. Rawlings*. Did my name enter the discussion?"

"We talked about you—but not in the context of her delivery or my past. She said to tell you hello and that she missed you."

Catherine nodded, obviously wanting to ask more, but recognizing that her time had expired. Wisely, she slid behind the door, leaving Tony alone with his whirlwind of thoughts.

Loophole – May 2013
(Truth Chapters 23 & 24)

The confession of evil works is the first beginning of good works.
– Saint Augustine

Tony waited—and waited—and waited. With his cell phone on his lap and his head against the cool car window, his mind spun and slipped into scenarios, possibilities, and dreams. It was strange how a thought can transform into a full-out movie played behind closed eyes. Tony's flight from Iowa City to San Diego took less than four hours. He'd had pressing matters that delayed his desired departure; nevertheless, he was once again on West Coast soil by 6:00 PM, PST.

By the time he was seated behind the steering wheel of a rented car, he had the confirming text message from Phil Roach:

"MS. NICHOLS HAS ORDERED TWO MEALS TO BE DELIV-ERED TO HER SUITE. HER GUEST RECENTLY ARRIVED. I'VE CONFIRMED THAT SHE TOO IS A GUEST AT THE U.S. GRANT. HER NAME IS MEREDITH RUSSEL. SHE'S A JOURNALIST. FOR PUBLICATION SHE USES THE NAME BANKS."

Every muscle in Tony's body tensed. Blood coursed through his veins and echoed in his ears; the reverberating sound kept beat as splashes of red infiltrated his vision. The innocent steering wheel received the brunt of his displeasure as he struck it repeatedly with his clenched fist. After a few loudly yelled expletives, the red faded enough for his vision to register. He was still in the parking lot of the private airstrip. Running his bruised hand through his hair, Tony inhaled deeply and began to text his reply.

His shaky fingers didn't want to cooperate with the small keypad. Finally, he said, "Screw this," and dialed Roach's cell. "I fuck'n knew that was what was happening. Keep watching her suite, and let me know the second something changes. I'm at the airstrip but should be there soon."

"I have a camera set on her door," Roach replied.

Tony paid him well enough; he should have damn cameras *in* the suite. "Text me every ten minutes. I want to know the exact moment that woman leaves Claire's suite. And text me her room number."

"Yes, sir."

This damn nightmare felt like it had been going on for weeks, but in reality it only been happening since late the same morning. Shelly had sent an email with a copy of Meredith Banks' planned retraction. It was a seemingly benign article stating that in 2010, she'd used her journalistic prowess to connect the dots of her story about Claire Nichols, and that Ms. Nichols never mentioned or alluded to her involvement with Anthony Rawlings. Apparently, Meredith submitted the short article to various publications. Thankfully, Shelly had connections—connections who understood Anthony Rawlings' desire for privacy. Someone from *Rolling Stone* alerted her. She'd been able to dissuade a few avenues of publication, and the Rawlings legal team was diligently working to stop more. With each mile toward the U.S. Grant Hotel, Tony's disappointment grew.

It wasn't the retraction that bothered Tony, other than the fact that it confirmed Claire's innocence during the supposed interview nearly three years ago. He tried not to remember that night or the horrendous weeks that followed. Nevertheless, the parallels to his current situation were ironic. Once again, he was waiting, just as he'd waited for her that night in her suite. In 2010, she was at her lake, unaware of the circumstances of his rage. Tonight, she wasn't innocent. Claire was willfully, willingly divulging private information. She was in that damn hotel, eating and talking with Meredith Banks. She was breaking his rules with no regard for the consequences!

Last time he flew home from New York, this time it was from home to San Diego. As the sky darkened and he sat silently watching the people come and go from the grand hotel, Tony imagined the conversation occurring floors above in the luxurious suite. He wouldn't have it—this was not debatable.

The part of the article that upset Tony, sent off alarms, and caused the Rawlings legal team to scurry was the last paragraph. Tony had it memorized:

She has, however, promised me exclusive rights to her story, promising an enlightening view into the world of her true relationship with one of this country's wealthiest men, as well as the truth behind her arrest, plea, incarceration, and unconventional release. Please stay tuned. The wait will be worth it!

The one variable that was dissimilar to 2010 was the intensity of the redness. There were moments as he waited that it deepened, blinding him to the world outside of the car, but then he would remember Claire—her lying on the floor of the suite, battered and unconscious, the doctor and nurse's prognosis before she regained consciousness, and the bruises that took forever to fade. Each memory worked to lessen the crimson. He wouldn't allow another *accident*, but he would confront her. Tony would make sure that she understood that this alliance with Meredith Banks would not continue.

Initially, Tony had hoped that he could stop her impending rule-breaking with a call. Claire didn't answer; however, she did return his call, barely under the time limit he'd proposed. That was what propelled his spontaneous flight west. When he first called, she was on a damn plane. He knew that Claire was in San Diego for one purpose, and Tony intended to put a stop to it, once and for all. His phone buzzed.

"NO CHANGE"

It was the exact same as the last eight messages. The confines of the car were closing in all around him. Stretching his weary legs, Tony got out of the car and slammed the door. Of course, Claire couldn't have booked a room at an out-of-the-way, secluded resort. No, she was staying in the center of San Diego's Gaslamp Quarter, a location filled with tourists. Although he wasn't wearing his customary Armani suit, he was Anthony Rawlings, and as such, was potentially recognizable. It was a part of his life that Tony detested. More often than not, he longed for anonymity—the ability to enter a restaurant or bar without the potential of seeing it as a news piece. He imagined tomorrow's headline: ANTHONY RAWLINGS FOLLOWS EX-WIFE ACROSS THE COUNTRY. Hell, that plus Claire's little exposé unfolding floors above in the historic structure could ruin everything he'd taken a lifetime to accomplish. Shelly would do her best to spin it the right way, but Tony needed to stop it before it went any further.

He considered going to Claire's suite, interrupting the interview, and putting an end to the foolishness, but better judgment told him to stay clear. Meredith was a reporter. She'd plaster that shit all over the media in seconds.

A walk up Broadway and back loosened his overly tense muscles. Tony settled back into the plush leather driver's seat and continued to wait: One hour. Two hours. Three hours. Finally, the text arrived:

"MS. BANKS JUST EXITED MS. NICHOLS' SUITE."

Again, Tony responded with a call. "You're done for the day. I've got it from here."

"If there's anything you—"

"I said you're done!" Tony growled into the phone before hitting *DISCONNECT*. No one approached him as he entered the stunning lobby and made his way across the tile floor. Each step was more determined than the last. His reasoning for calm dissipated with each floor as the elevator went up and up. By the time the doors opened, memories of Claire's *accident* were muted by the displeasure of her current blatant disobedience. He knocked once upon her door. Within seconds she opened it wide. He glared as her stance morphed before him. Seconds earlier she'd worn a smile; now he saw a woman who knew damn well she'd made a disastrous mistake. Through clenched teeth, he managed, "Let me in. We need to talk."

"I don't think we have anything to discuss. You made an unnecessary trip. Please go."

He blinked as Claire's words registered. *Had she just refused him?* Tony took a step in her direction; his eyes narrowed. "We are *not* having this discussion in the hallway. I'm coming in."

Her lips pressed together in protest, but as he stepped across the threshold, Claire silently backed away, allowing him to enter. Tony immediately closed the door. This would be private; he didn't want their confrontation on tomorrow's news. Briefly he took in her accommodations and the stunning view of San Diego through the large windows. She sure as hell was reaping the benefits of selling her rings—*his* rings, the rings he'd bought—*twice.*

Claire's strengthening voice refocused him. "We're not married, and I'm not your prisoner. You can't just bully your way in here."

Dumbfounded, he stared. *Didn't she understand that her behavior was unacceptable—that there would be consequences? Hadn't she learned anything during their time together?*

She continued, "I want you to leave."

Tony circled the living room, his mind a tornado of thoughts. He came for one reason—flew across the country for it—and he wasn't leaving without reassurance that this farce was done. Tony turned around and made eye contact. "What are you doing with *her*?"

Claire shrugged—*she fuck'n shrugged!*—and casually replied, "I'm having an overdue reunion with an old college friend. Besides," she added flippantly, "it's really none of your business. You shouldn't even be here."

For a moment he stared at the woman who'd been his wife. He was teetering on the edge of sanity, and she was spurring him on, pushing him, when she knew damn well what he was capable of doing. She was either incredibly stupid or incredibly brave. He decided to learn which. In a microsecond, he was before her, seizing her shoulders, and invading her space. Their faces nearly touched when he growled, "Do you think I'm stupid? You're talking to *her* about *me*, and I won't have it."

Claire stared, fire burning in her damn green eyes. He'd asked a question. Common sense would tell her to answer, but no. Instead her glare burned his soul, daring him to push her further.

"Damn it, Claire, you infuriate me!" He released her shoulders and stomped toward the windows. With his back towards her, he closed his eyes and exhaled. Exhaustion overpowered his anger as he tried to explain. "I flew across the damn country and have been sitting in a damn car, waiting for your little reunion to conclude."

"Tony," her voice was still strong, "you need help. I can't believe you're watching me that closely. Get over it!"

Her words made no sense. *How could she even pretend that he could stop?* "Don't you understand?" he asked with all sincerity. "I can't. You know from your prison delivery that I've been watching you for a very long time."

"And I think it's beyond creepy. Why? Tell me why. You didn't answer my question before."

The tension in his jaw severed as the corner of his lips inched upward. "Creepy? I've been called many things, but I think that's the first time someone has called me *creepy*."

"To your face," she retorted.

His grin felt foreign after the tension of the past few hours; nevertheless, it was real. In a matter of seconds, Claire had taken him from fury to fancy. Her ability both amazed and scared him. "Touché. That may be true."

"I guarantee it. Now, if you're going to burst into my hotel room, answer *my* question. I don't owe you answers if you're not going to give them to me."

He looked toward the sofa and back to Claire. "If you're asking me questions, does that mean you aren't throwing me out?"

Her arms folded across her chest, and her lips pursed as she contemplated. Finally, she said, "I don't recall ever having the ability to *throw you out* of anywhere. Maybe times do change?"

"People change, too," he murmured as he sat. Suddenly, there was a knock on the door. "Are you expecting company?"

"I ordered wine from room service."

When she peered through the peephole, he smirked, "That must be why you opened the door earlier. You obviously didn't look the last time."

"You're right; it's a habit I need to work on."

He exhaled and leaned his head against the plush upholstery. It'd been one long day, and he didn't see it ending anytime soon. When he looked up, Claire was signing the receipt and handing the waiter a tip. In the past, he'd always been the one to handle everything. Sitting back and watching was odd, yet surprisingly refreshing. Before the waiter left, he opened the bottle. Tony nodded when the waiter looked in his direction. *How did the two of them appear to this man? A husband and wife? A couple dating? A man on the verge of insanity and the woman who put him there?* For once, Tony didn't care.

Tony started to stand when Claire's gaze captured his attention. She was giggling—*giggling*? He shook his head and asked, "Did you order two glasses?"

Through muffled laughter, she replied, "No, but since they're here, would you like some Merlot?"

He stepped toward her. "You know, you're the only person who can have me pissed off one minute and completely dazzled the next. Why are you laughing?"

Claire shook her head. "I don't know, shock, absurdity? It seems I never know what's coming. As much as I plan, I'm continually blown away."

Tony poured wine and spoke without a filter. He'd spent much of the past five hours recalling their past; the wine returned one particular scene to his mind. Handing her a glass, he asked, "Do you remember when we had wine at the *Red Wing*?"

Claire closed her eyes and nodded. "I do."

"I'd been watching you for years. I was so nervous that night. I thought I was planning your acquisition." He looked into his glass. *Was it the wine that was making him confess or his need for Claire to understand?* Either way, it was liberating.

"If you're using business metaphors, may I suggest *hostile takeover*. It's more appropriate."

He took a sip of wine and exhaled. "Yes, Claire." Standing close, he looked solemnly down into her emerald eyes. "And I have apologized for that." He paused for a moment, silently encouraging himself to go further, to tell her exactly what he was thinking. "What I didn't know, as we sat talking, despite all my research, was *you*. I mean, I knew everything about you." He shook his head reflectively, walked back to the sofa, and sat down. "Yet, I didn't know *you*. Truthfully, at first, I had no desire to."

"Oh, *really*? Because I recall some pretty up-close-and-personal contact."

Tony smirked. She wasn't going to make this easy. "Yes, I wanted *that*. I didn't want to *know* you—the real you. I fought it for months, but you were this light that kept sucking me in. It wasn't supposed to be that way. *We* weren't supposed to happen."

"What was supposed to happen?"

He shuddered at the fleeting thought of Claire being another name crossed off of their list. Even before he knew the depth of his feelings, Tony knew he never wanted that. "Well, the *takeover* was supposed to stop you. I never expected anyone to flourish under such circumstances." She eyed him suspiciously, yet all he saw was the strongest, most beautiful woman he'd ever known. "You didn't just flourish, you conquered." He took another drink of his liquid courage, though he'd rather it have been bourbon. "I've continually underestimated you, or perhaps I should say, you've continually exceeded my expectations. You still do. You're the only person who has ever derailed me, and more than anyone, you know me, not *Anthony Rawlings*—me."

"The real you. Would that be *Anton*?"

Something in his chest clenched. It wasn't the anger he'd been feeling earlier; this was painful and solemn. He detested hearing that name from her lips. He exhaled. "I suppose, yes, but not anymore. I had it legally changed. So, you see, I didn't lie. My legal name is Anthony Rawlings, and it has been for a long time."

Claire stood as she responded, each phrase hitting him with painfully accurate aim. "You share this with me now, but not when we were married. That tells me that you never trusted me, *the only person to really know you.* Plus, you threw me away and left me to rot in prison." Her hands slapped her sides with exaggerated movements as her volume increased. "You say you love or loved me, past or present. You don't know what *love* is. You have an obsession, and it really needs to stop. Stop watching me. Stop having me watched. Your fun is done. It's over."

He couldn't continue meeting her stare. If he did, he'd surely confess more than he was ready to admit. Instead, Tony concentrated on the swirling red liquid in his glass and weighed his response. His tone held none of the anger she'd directed at him. "I don't know how to explain it. It was a loophole. Don't you understand?"

Her eyes widened, filling his vision with green.

When she didn't respond, he elaborated, "I tried to help you. Anyone else would have jumped at the insanity plea. I had a hospital all set; your commitment time would've been negotiable. But no." Energy returned with each word. He stood and walked back toward the windows. "No! You refused! By doing that, you took your sentence away from *me* and gave it to the state of Iowa. I no longer had influence over your release." He turned to face her, and his volume increased, "Why did you have to be so damn obstinate?"

"Me? You're accusing *me* of being obstinate? I didn't want you in control of my life any longer. I was willing to let the state of Iowa decide, rather than you."

He tilted his head. "It was the only way to save you."

"I have no idea what you're saying." She closed her eyes and sighed. "Save me from what?"

"Me."

Claire resumed her seat as his one-word confession silently loomed larger than life, saturating the suite like a gas, filling the room, seeping into every crevice, and stealing the very air from their lungs. Tony had just admitted that the man he'd once been was someone he no longer wanted to be. *What would Claire do with this revelation?* His entire world hung by a string as he awaited her reply. Suddenly, their bubble shattered; her phone vibrated and flashed on the table before them. Without thinking, Tony read the screen: *HARRY CELL.*

His heart twisted. "Are the news stories accurate?"

"You should know the accuracy of news reports."

The phone continued to vibrate. "Perhaps I should answer it?" he offered, the earlier sentiment in his tone now replaced with clipped sarcasm.

"No, thank you. I'll be just a minute." Claire reached for the cell phone and stepped into the bedroom. Before the door closed completely, he heard her say, "Hi."

The difference in her tone was painfully obvious. With only one word, she'd thrust a knife deep into his chest. It was his fault, all of it. He'd done terrible things. *How could he ever expect her to understand?*

Tony poured another glass of wine and walked back to the dark windows. He'd come to San Diego for one reason. Neither reminiscing about the *Red Wing* nor making monumental confessions had been on his agenda. Besides, Roach had confirmed that Baldwin was still in Palo Alto; therefore, if Claire told *him* that Tony was there, their private time would more than likely be cut short. A part of Tony relished the idea of confronting the mighty *president of security at a two-bit gaming company.* It wouldn't even be a contest; nevertheless, that confrontation was also *not* why he'd come to California. Tony heard the bedroom door open and watched Claire's reflection in the window as she walked toward him.

"I apologize for the interruption," she said as she neared him.

"Do you now, *Ms. Nichols?*"

Her fiery gaze penetrated his composure. "I do. You're correct; I *am* Ms. Nichols, not Mrs. Rawlings."

Tony faced his ex-wife. The knife in his chest twisted. Her name was his doing and he knew it. Although she was merely inches away, the expanse suddenly seemed massive. At this late hour, he didn't have the energy to attempt to lessen it. He replied, "I'm sure you're busy. If I were *he*, I'd be getting on a jet right now. According to my calculations, that gives us about ninety minutes to discuss what I came to discuss."

Claire walked toward the sitting area, refilled her glass, and sat. "What do you want to discuss?"

"You *will* discontinue your discussions with Meredith Banks and any further plans you've entertained regarding speaking with the media."

She leaned back and smiled. "Will I now?"

"Don't push me. I'm tired and suddenly not in the mood."

"Well, I'd like to discuss something else."

His neck tensed. "I would like to stay on topic."

"Then it seems we're at an impasse. Perhaps you should go. We can continue this another day—or not."

"You're not changing the subject." Tony's volume increased. "The nondisclosure of our relationship is non-negotiable."

"I don't recall signing anything—well, other than a blank napkin. We didn't even have a prenuptial agreement, so I have no legal restraints on what I can and cannot disclose."

Tony stepped closer. "Legal, no, but what about ethical or moral?"

"Did those concerns come into play during your *acquisition* or our *relationship*?"

"I have tried to explain—not at first, but they did."

"Tony, I'm tired, too. I don't have the energy to figure out your puzzles. I don't plan on disclosing anything about your true identity to the media, if that's part of your concern. I have, however, learned of many misconceptions regarding *me* during our relationship. I do plan on correcting those errors."

"Why?" he asked.

She sat straight. "Because I can."

Hearing his own words spewed back at him turned the metaphorical knife. Shit. *How many times had he said the same thing to her?*

Claire continued, "The world wants to know, and I'm willing to disclose."

"It won't happen." He sat his glass on the table and leaned forward. "I came here to emphasize *this* is a waste of your time. Currently, my legal team is working diligently to stop any information regarding our marriage or relationship from public media. If anything appears on the Internet or anywhere else, a civil suit will immediately follow, against you, Meredith, and the offending sites." He watched and waited. Red seeped and flowed, yet the woman before him appeared amused.

Finally, she retorted, "Well, at least this time you have the nerve to deliver the ultimatum in person, instead of sending Brent."

His shoulders pulled back—damn. The knife had done a three-sixty. "I was angry about the plea."

"You've made your point, but now it's my turn."

"Yes," Tony quipped. "I recall, you did like your turn."

Instead of taking his bait, she went on. "I want a promise from you."

"What promise do you want from me?"

"I want a guarantee that the people in my life, my associates and friends, the people whom I've *acquired* aren't in harm's way."

"My, Claire, you give me too much credit. I'm a businessman. I don't have the ability to cause harm to anyone, much less those associated with you."

"Simon, John... do these names mean anything to you? How about my parents, your parents? Are there more? I can't seem to process right now."

He bristled. *How much did she know?* "I don't take responsibility for that entire list, and explain exactly what you're requesting."

"Actually, I don't believe I'm *requesting* anything. I'm saying, beyond a shadow of a doubt, if anything happens to me, or my friends, or associates, my story and the truth behind our relationship will be made public. I will continue to work on the articles and stop production before everything is public; *however*, if anything happens to me, or my friends, everything will become public knowledge. You're welcome to do damage control, but that'll only be after the initial public response has been made and broadcast globally. As you know, once a perception is set, it's difficult to change."

He squeezed the stem of his glass. Through clenched teeth he confessed, "I don't want you with anyone else. You're mine and have been for a very long time."

"That isn't your choice. You sent me away!"

"No. You left; *you* drove out of our garage."

Claire stood. "Tony, I'm done with this conversation. I'm tired; however, I have a few other demands." Before he could respond to her candor, she continued, "John's out of jail. I want his law license reinstated. You took it away—don't deny it. Now, bring it back. I will consider that proof of your commitment to this agreement."

"I never liked him."

"I'm pretty sure the feeling is, and always has been, mutual. Nonetheless, he never deserved what you did to him."

Tony walked toward the door. He was done, too—drained from an exhausting day and their exchange. He'd flown to San Diego to make his point; the ridiculous behavior with Meredith would stop. He hadn't traveled to accept *her* petitions. Anthony Rawlings made demands; he didn't receive them. That was how it had always been—not just with Claire, with everyone.

Claire's question stilled his steps. "By the way, do you know who sent me the box?"

"Yes, my dear." He gazed down into her questioning eyes, trying to block the green from registering. "That information wasn't known by many. My list of candidates was quite limited. It didn't take long to confirm my theory."

She followed him to the door. The confidence she displayed only seconds earlier vaporized into the trusting woman he'd married—the one who knew that only he held the answers and only he made mandates. "Who?" she asked.

"Good-bye Claire—for now. May I have your hand?"

Her eyes narrowed. "Why?"

He didn't answer; instead, he held out his hand and waited. Reluctantly, she placed her right hand in his upturned palm. Tony bowed, touched his lips to her knuckles, and turned her hand over. "Close your eyes." She obeyed. "Keep them shut," he whispered. She nodded as he reached into the pocket of his slacks, brought out her grandmother's necklace, and placed it into her hand. Closing her fingers, he squeezed. "My sign of commitment. End this stupidity with Meredith." Kissing her closed fingers, Tony opened the door and stepped from her suite.

Exhaustion consumed him as he strode toward the elevators. It was nearly midnight in San Diego, and Tony had a three-and-a-half hour flight back to Iowa. He closed his eyes. This flying back and forth to the West Coast was already getting old, and he needed to be back to this part of the country for a keynote address in two weeks. Thank God, he had a private plane. Perhaps if his concerns over Claire's *depth of knowledge* didn't plague his thoughts, he'd be able to get some sleep.

Reunification – May 2013
(Truth Chapters 33 & 34)

Reunification: *verb. To cause group, party, state, or sect to become unified again after being divided.*

Though the San Francisco St. Regis Hotel was large and stately, Tony didn't notice, and more importantly, he didn't care. The charity gala taking place there was a fiasco and getting worse by the minute. Initially, he'd planned to attend to have an opportunity to speak with Derek Burke. It was all arranged. The CEO of Shedis-tics, Roger Cunningham, promised Burke's presence. The only issue was Derek's wife, Sophia. Tony wasn't ready to come face to face with Sophia quite yet. He'd been to too many of her art exhibitions, and they'd crossed paths more times than he was sure she realized. Tony didn't want her to have a revelation in the middle of a huge charity function.

That was why he'd ordered Mr. George, from the Palo Alto art studio, to send Sophia back to Provincetown. It was a legitimate story. Tony had spent a fortune on her paintings, and he wanted his purchases. He also wanted to see more of her collection. What neither Mr. George nor Tony expected was for Derek to fly with Sophia to the Cape and help her gather her collection. Together they'd managed to accomplish her mission in days instead of weeks. Now, at this ridiculously expensive Friday-night celebration, both Mr. and Mrs. Derek Burke were present and awaiting Anthony Rawlings.

If that weren't enough to send Tony's private life into overdrive, there was plenty more. As was common practice, Patricia had requested the guest list for the gala. The Rawlings Industries' security personnel customarily reviewed these lists prior to events. It was one of the many mundane steps that assured their CEO's safety. This time the list was far from mundane. The name that caught Patricia's attention was *Claire Nichols.*

When Tony read his ex-wife's name, his figurative floor dropped out from under him. Not only was Claire attending, but she was being escorted by Harrison Baldwin; they were the official SiJo Gaming representatives. As luck would have it, SiJo Gaming and Shedis-tics shared a table. Tony's head ached with the thought of Claire and Sophia at the same table. He wondered how that conversation would go. *"My, you look familiar. Oh, yes, I painted your wedding portrait. How do you like it?"* The coincidences were too numerous not to raise suspicion.

Tony made his decision. He would attend the gala, and *he* would escort Claire. He had no intention of being at the same function with his ex-wife and another man. It didn't matter that he could have a damn *Sports Illustrated* swimsuit model on his arm; Tony was not sitting at the head table and looking out to a room of donors and seeing Claire with *anyone.*

He thought about calling her, discussing the event, and proposing his idea. It was a fleeting thought. After their conversation in San Diego, Tony didn't believe that Claire was ready to willingly make the appropriate choice. According to Roach and his time-lapsed cameras, after Tony left Claire's suite in San Diego, Baldwin showed up at her door after 3:00 AM with the police in tow. Tony understood; he would have done the same. What reassured Tony about Baldwin's visit were the pictures that Roach took of the inside of Claire's suite with the couch made up like a bed. Tony wasn't happy that Baldwin spent two nights there, but those photos made it much better.

Since their meeting, Tony had asked Brent to start working on having John's law license reinstated. It was a painful task. Tony didn't like John, and helping him went against Tony's nature; nevertheless, he told himself he wasn't doing it for John—it was for Claire. He'd also signed Claire's damn agreement and paid Meredith a stipend. Claire's memoirs would stay hidden as long as her criteria were met. The agreement stated that Claire, her friends, and her family would remain safe—a rather broad statement. *What if one of them stepped in front of a bus?* Tony's legal team reworded it to something more specific about *questionable causes of harm or disappearance.* The loophole in the agreement, the one about to be exploited, was the lack of specifics about harm done to a *company.*

Every company had at least one employee with a price. SiJo was no exception. The virus that infected SiJo's network a few hours ago was essentially harmless. It was the public repercussions of such a breach that could be potentially damaging; whether that breach became public depended upon Claire's response to Tony's new declaration.

Against Shelly's better judgment, she wrote a news release to Tony's specifications. The release was ready to publish. Tony was just waiting for word of Claire's arrival to the St. Regis. Once she was in the building and out of the range of media, news of their reunification would hit the wire.

Associated Press – May 24, 2013

Mr. Anthony Rawlings, CEO of Rawlings Industries, asks the public for patience at this difficult time. He believes that two years ago he and the world were deceived. Despite circumstances and appearances, he is now convinced that his ex-wife, Claire Nichols (Rawlings), was erroneously accused of attempted murder.

This realization came to Mr. Rawlings through a series of personal and private encounters with Ms. Nichols. Listening to instinct and following his heart, a combination of resources that have successfully helped to create his global empire, Mr. Rawlings is now certain of Ms. Nichols' innocence.

In an effort to correct the wrongful prosecution by the state of Iowa, Mr. Rawlings attempted to reverse the ruling of the judge, to no avail. In a moment of inspiration, Mr. Rawlings personally contacted Governor Bosley and requested Ms. Nichols' pardon. With the assistance of Jane Allyson, Esquire, and the signature of the late Governor Richard Bosley, the innocent Claire Nichols was pardoned and released from prison on March 9, 2013.

Mr. Rawlings regrets initially denying connection to her pardon. He also refuses to speculate as to whom he believes was responsible for the poisoning, which resulted in his near death and led to the false accusations. He will only respond, "It is a personal issue."

It has been reported that multiple long-time employees of Mr. Rawlings have been relieved of their duties.

At the current time, Mr. Rawlings is concentrating on renewing his relationship with Ms. Nichols. He confirms that theirs is a complicated and passionate bond and asks for privacy at this important time of healing.

The entire world would learn of their new relationship—before Claire.

At a little after 7:00 PM Tony received notice of Claire's arrival, sent Eric to retrieve her, and texted Shelly:

"PUBLISH THE PRESS RELEASE."

The fact that the gala had already begun, Tony's impending tardiness, as well as Sophia's continued attendance worked to exacerbate Tony's already unpleasant demeanor. He paced near the large windows and punched Mr. George's number in his phone.

The curator immediately answered, "Mr. Rawlings, I-I've texted and called her. Ms. Burke isn't responding."

"I'm not sure if you can fathom the depth of my disappointment regarding your inability to perform to my liking. You have received exceptional compensation for your services. I don't believe I have been as kindly reciprocated."

"I am *here*. If I have to drag her from the gala, I will."

"Do you truly believe that will go unnoticed?"

"No, sir. I'll think of something."

"I have taken care of it. My associate, Mr. Hensley, has a suite here at the St. Regis. I want you and Ms. Burke in that suite. Tell her that *the buyer*—I assume you know better than to use my name—wants to meet with her. Do not leave that suite until my associate releases you. Is that clear?"

"W-what if she wants to bring her husband?"

"That's not an option. Mr. George, don't make me repeat myself."

"Yes, sir, when it comes to the gala—"

"She's not to be there. And, only *he* is to remain."

"I'll do my best."

"No, that isn't acceptable."

"Mr. Rawlings—"

"This has been the plan forever. If you aren't capable, I'll find someone who is." Tony turned at the sound of footsteps and saw Eric entering with Claire. At least someone could do his job.

"Twenty minutes—I'll be waiting." Tony said as he disconnected the call and slid his phone into the pocket of his slacks. "Thank you, Eric. Ms. Claire will remain with me. Please take care of our other issue. I'm late for the benefit, and that's very upsetting to me."

"Yes, Mr. Rawlings. Twenty minutes?"

"Not a second more."

Eric nodded as he backed toward the door. "Yes, sir."

Tony stood and glared. This wasn't how he wanted their reunion to go down, yet desperate times called for desperate measures. The closing doors echoed through the suite; silence filled the room, until Claire's shoulders straightened and she swallowed. "Tony, please explain to—"

He didn't allow her to finish. Instantly, he was across the room, his chest pressed against hers and her chin in his grip. Forcing eye contact, he leaned down and bathed her cheeks in his warm breath. "I have no intention of being at a social gathering, or anywhere else, with you and another man. You're a fool to consider such a thing."

Her face trembled below his grasp, yet her words sounded strong. "I agreed to attend this gala weeks ago, and I didn't learn of your attendance until this evening."

Tightening his hold of her chin, he replied, "Then your informant is as incompetent as the firewall at SiJo."

Fire ignited behind her glare. "What did you do?"

"Nothing—and as long as your friends don't have an overwhelming sense of conscience requiring them to inform the public of their near breach, no harm will come."

"Why?"

He released her chin and continued to stare. That damn fire burned right through his overwrought nerves. He'd made the right decision. Claire may not realize it, but they belonged together. No one else could do what she was doing. No one else could continue to maintain eye contact as well as question his motives.

She repeated her question. "Why did you do this?"

"I told you, Claire. I know your weakness; it's your concern for others. God only knows why, but for some reason, Amber McCoy has been kind to you. Her company won't be harmed." He paused and walked toward the window. The darkening sky reminded him that he was late. The gala was starting without him, and he'd yet to learn of Sophia's location. Exhaling, Tony turned back to Claire and continued. "*If* you follow my rules."

He waited. Claire didn't respond, yet her complexion blanched as she lost footing. It wasn't what he'd expected. Fight? Argue? Tears? Instead, she suddenly appeared ill. "Are you not feeling well?" Tony asked. Concern overtook his displeased tone "You're pale."

"I need to sit down."

Wrapping his arm around her petite waist, Tony helped Claire to the nearest sofa. As she sat, her beautifully painted face glistened with a sheen of perspiration. He watched in horror as she lowered her head to her knees. Tony noticed a crystal pitcher of iced water and poured Claire a glass. When he returned, he knelt before her and handed her the glass. The domination in his voice was replaced with something softer and reassuring. "Here's some water, drink."

Only her head moved as she shook it slightly from side to side.

"Dinner will be starting downstairs in about an hour. Have you eaten recently?"

Claire's cheeks were flushed as she looked up. "No, I-I haven't. I don't want to go down there with you." Her strength seemed to be returning. "I'm here for SiJo, for Amber and Simon."

Harshness returned. "Then you'll do as I say."

Lowering her head once again to her lap, she obediently replied, "What do you want me to do?"

Tony closed his eyes. With his plans blowing up right and left, her response was exactly what he needed to hear. He touched her knee. "Claire, what the hell was that? Are you sick?"

She shook her head. "I'm not ill. I'm sick of *this*. Please, just tell me what you want me to do so that I can help my friends and go home."

Tony clenched his jaw and exhaled. "I'm ordering you some food. After you feel better we'll discuss your duties."

Exceptional service was only one of the perks associated with the presidential suite. In no time at all, Claire had a plate of crackers, cheese, and fruit as well as a soda to calm her stomach. Tony waited. When she seemed steadier, he asked for her purse. The last thing he wanted was her calling for reinforcements. This night would be about the two of them. Thankfully, she didn't protest. He immediately removed her iPhone, turned it off, and placed it in the breast pocket of his shirt. Next, he began searching each compartment and found only cosmetics and tissues.

Claire asked, "What are you looking for?"

"Your work phone."

"It isn't here; I left it in my condo."

From what he could see, she was telling the truth. He glanced at his watch; still no word on Sophia, but he needed to get things moving. "As you may remember, while at a function such as this, your attention should be on me and your duties at hand. I believe tonight you're representing Si-Jo Gaming. As well as representing it to the masses downstairs, your behavior will go a long way in solving their current situation, or," he paused, "making it public."

"I understand."

"I'm glad you do. You'll get your phone back when this evening is done. I believe you'll have enough on your plate, and you don't need another distraction."

Tony then handed Claire the news release.

"What is this?"

"It's a new release. My press secretary released it moments before you arrived to the penthouse." Smiling, he added, "I just saw a text from Shelly; it's already viral."

He watched as Claire read. After she'd finished, she looked up at him; her eyes glistening with unshed tears. "W-why? Why are you doing this?"

Tony explained, "I've tried to express my feelings for you. I've even apologized for past behaviors and attempted to explain, yet you blatantly flaunt another man at a shared function."

"I was *not* flaunting. We—you and I—are divorced. This..." she picked up the news release, "...is false. You didn't secure my pardon. You had *nothing* to do with it."

"And who's going to refute my claim?" Tony replied confidently. "Governor Bosley? No, he's dead. Jane Allyson? I think not."

"Why, Tony? What have you done to Jane?"

He made no attempt to suppress his grin. "Again, so much credit, I should be honored."

Claire stood and her words slowed. "Tell me what you've done."

"While I may be able to assume some responsibility, it's quite the opposite of what you suspect. Miss Allyson is currently enjoying the honor of an invitation to one of the most prestigious law firms in Des Moines." His phone buzzed. Tony read the text from Eric.

"MS. BURKE AND MR. GEORGE ARE WITH ME IN THE SUITE."

He sighed in relief. "Now, as informative as this conversation has been, we can continue it later. It's almost 8:00 PM. As you know, this gala started an hour ago. You may remember—I do *not* like to be late."

With Sophia securely out of the way, Tony took a step back and evaluated the woman before him. The food and drink had returned the color to her cheeks. His words may be misconstrued as condescending, but his tone bordered on sultry. "My, Claire, you do look lovely. I admit I doubted your financial ability to dress as would warrant my companion for the evening. There's a complete ensemble in the master suite for you, but I like your choice." Scanning her from head to toe, he stepped toward her and lifted the pearl of her grandmother's necklace. Grinning in anticipation, he continued, "Yes, after you touch up your makeup, I believe we'll be ready to attend our *reunion* gala." Gently dropping the cream-colored pearl, he softly brushed the back of his hand against her cheek. Bogus empathy dripped from his words. "Don't look so strained, my dear, this is a happy occasion. You wanted our dinner public, so your wish is my command. Besides, you came here to represent SiJo Gaming. I promise this will bring that small company more publicity and positive public relations than would have originally happened." Reaching for her small hand, he assured her. "This is a win win."

Her lips pressed together as Tony basked in the fire burning before him. He could gaze upon it for hours, but they had a gala to attend. With her neck straight, Claire asked, "Where can I get ready?"

"The master suite is upstairs. Let me show you the way." Tony wasn't sure of the exact cause. Perhaps it was that Eric had Sophia secured away from the festivities, or maybe it was Claire's appropriate behavior; whatever the cause, his night, as well as his demeanor, was improving.

Eight

The Gala – May 2013
(Truth Chapters 35 & 36)

To understand the heart and mind of a person,
look not at what he has done, but at what he aspires to do.
— Kahlil Gibran

Claire was absolutely lovely as she stepped from the master bath. Her green dress accentuated her eyes, and ringlets of hair brushed her proud neck. "You are beautiful, my dear."

She exhaled and placed her hand in the bend of Tony's elbow. "Let's get this over with."

He stilled their steps. "Claire, perhaps a review is in order. It has been a while." Her eyes narrowed, but he continued, "I expect you to follow my rules this evening. If you're to assure SiJo's recovery from their current problem, you'll remember that as my companion, I expect you to do as I say and that public failure is not an option. If you have something to say, get it out now. Once we are at that gala, any misconstrued comment could have far-reaching consequences."

The fire that had been smoldering blazed with new intensity. She squared her shoulders and looked him in the eye. "I assure you that I remember your rules, but if you want me to *get it out*, then here it is. You're a heartless bastard. This is blackmail and I'm angry at myself for letting this happen."

He laughed. "There, now we can proceed."

Just before they entered the golden elevator, Tony lowered his lips to Claire's ear. Inhaling her perfume and sweet scent, he whispered, "You needn't blame yourself. You couldn't have stopped this if you'd tried. Let this *heartless bastard* take all the blame." The pools of emerald mellowed beneath his amused gaze. Claire needed to hear—to know—that she couldn't have stopped it. He grinned, knowing that he could've eased her mind more by letting her know that the problem at SiJo was now fixed and no damage had occurred. Of course, he didn't. That tidbit of information could wait.

Except for a private whisper now and then, Claire performed beautifully. Murmurs and gasps at the news of their reunification rippled throughout the ballroom like waves from a rock shattering the glassy surface of her lake. She smiled and spoke with confidence. Even when Tony spent a few extra minutes with Derek Burke, Claire stayed steadfast. Since Claire was supposed to have been brought to him before she hand a chance to mingle, Tony wasn't happy to learn that she'd already met the Cunninghams; however, her warning was not only helpful, but refreshing.

It wasn't until after his keynote speech that Tony saw what he didn't know he'd sought. It was a look, a stare, something in Claire's expression. Tony couldn't describe it, yet it was there. He hadn't seen it in years, but he recognized it immediately. As he resumed his seat, he reached for Claire's hand and gently lifted it from her lap. This time, his touch wasn't meant as a warning; instead, he intended affection as he lowered his head and brushed her knuckles with a soft sweep of his lips, all the while keeping his eyes fixed on hers. Claire's cheeks blushed as her smile broadened.

Quietly, she whispered, "Very nice speech, Mr. Rawlings."

"Thank you, Mrs. Ms. Nichols, you're mighty remarkable yourself."

Someone else was now speaking from the podium; their voices were a faint whisper against the sound from the nearby speaker. Claire raised her eyebrows and asked, "Mighty?"

It was a word Nathaniel had used, reserved for only the truly special people in his life. Perhaps that was what Tony was missing from his envelope. No, she hadn't been missing, only misplaced, and now she was with him. Although he'd never used that word before, it felt right. Gently squeezing her hand, he repeated, "Mighty."

They both smiled and turned to listen to the next orator, a woman from the Center for Learning Disabilities who was thanking the audience for their support. When the final speaker concluded, the emcee from earlier came to the podium and announced, "Ladies and gentleman, the orchestra will be in place soon. If everyone could please make their way out to the atrium, dancing will commence in less than half an hour."

"Are we staying for dancing?" Claire asked quietly.

His eyebrows rose. "Do you want to dance?"

"No, I really don't; I'm tired, and I'd like to go home. If I could have my phone, I'll call for the SiJo car."

Tony leaned back against his chair. He wasn't ready for this evening to end. He sure as hell didn't want to send her back to Palo Alto—to *him*. Roach had been keeping tabs on Baldwin, and Tony knew from a series of text messages that Baldwin had started to drive toward San Francisco but turned around and was now at his condominium in Palo Alto. Although Tony wasn't sure what made Baldwin turn around; he smugly assumed it was the press release.

Claire leaned in close—too close. Her smile was too large, as threatening tears perched precariously on her lower lids. With a faint crack in her voice, she asked, "Have I done everything you asked?"

"Yes," Tony replied honestly. "But I want more."

"Please, I'm tired."

He broadened his grin. "Then perhaps you should go to bed."

Though her expression remained flawless to a bystander, Tony saw the recognition of his innuendo in her green eyes. "I'm *not* agreeing to sleep with you."

"Sleeping, my dear, was *not* what I had in mind."

After a moment of collection, she replied. "I will go upstairs with you; I will complete this scenario; however, I will *not* have sex with you."

"Why do you fight it?" Pushing her in public was not his plan. Truthfully, neither was sex, although he wasn't opposed to changing his plans.

"May we please go upstairs? This conversation is upsetting me. If you want to maintain this charade, we'd better leave while I can maintain a smile."

Knowing that she was right, Tony stood and offered Claire his hand. "Ms. Nichols, shall we bid our adieus to the appropriate people?"

"Yes, Mr. Rawlings. I'm so ready to close the curtain on this performance."

As she stood, he whispered, "The press release is viral. This, my love, was only the first act."

When they finally reached the golden elevator, Tony removed his phone and sent Eric a text.

"WE HAVE LEFT THE GALA. ALLOW SOPHIA TO RETURN."

Claire broke the silence as they exited the elevator to the penthouse. "May I have my phone?"

Tony looked at his watch, 10:17 PM. "My dear, the night is still young." When she didn't respond, Tony removed her cell phone from his breast pocket. It never occurred to him that she might take the phone and walk away; he'd always listened to her calls. Once she turned it on, the small device vibrated with an onslaught of messages. No doubt the world outside their bubble had seen the news release. Instead of checking her messages, Claire called for the SiJo car. He faintly heard the driver through her phone.

"Hello, Marcus, yes, this is Claire Nichols—"

Tony changed his mind. He wasn't ready for the evening to be over. Taking her phone from her hand, he stilled her words and interrupted her conversation. "Hello, Marcus. Ms. Nichols will not need your assistance this evening."

"Umm, excuse me. Who is this?" Marcus replied.

"This is Anthony Rawlings."

"Oh, okay? Oh! Mr. Rawlings."

"That is correct."

"So, Ms. Nichols is done with the car for tonight?"

"Yes, you are relieved of your assignment."

"Okay. I'll head back to Palo Alto."

"Thank you, good-night." Glancing at the number of messages on her screen, Tony once again turned off her phone and returned it to his pocket.

He watched as Claire walked to a sofa and sat. Momentarily, defeat hung around her like a cloud. Tears coated her cheeks as her emerald eyes met his. Tony didn't want this. He didn't want to see her defeated. It was that the evening had been remarkable. Having her next to him, even the clandestine retorts—all of it was invigorating.

Then it happened, right before his eyes. Claire shifted, sat taller, and asked, "What do I need to do to *leave*?"

Relieved by her forwardness, he sat beside her and softened his voice, "Eric will take you home whenever you want. You may leave at any time."

"Then I want to leave now."

Of course she did. *Why would she not?* He was a *heartless bastard* in her eyes. If only he could make her see that she was right—before, but not now. Now, he knew that his heart beat for one reason. It had stopped when she left him—literally. The reason it restarted was sitting beside him. Solemnly, he nodded and removed his phone. He'd call Eric and send her on her way.

Her soft tone stilled his movements. "Tony?" her voice quivered with concern. "Is SiJo secure? Did they get their problem fixed?"

He placed his phone back in his pocket and ignoring her question, asked his own, "Do you want to know what I've been thinking about all night?" He'd been honest in San Diego. Catherine's box was about disclosure. Surprisingly, there was a strange sense of relief that came with each admission; Tony yearned to tell Claire more. Never could he remember having the desire to share such intimate thoughts with anyone.

She shook her head. "What you've been thinking about? All right, tell me."

"Many things. The first—how amazing you've been." Excitement infiltrated his words. "I've endured many companions since our divorce, but I haven't enjoyed any of those evenings as much as I have tonight, being with you. Shelly wasn't happy with my desired press release, but I decided it was the only answer. Now the world knows of our reconciliation. It's official."

"You say that as if it's beyond debate."

His brows furrowed. "Beyond challenge—it's public."

"SiJo?" she asked.

"The breach has been resolved. It *has been* since about 8:00 PM this evening."

Claire sighed. "Thank you."

He smiled at her relief. Perhaps he should leave this night here. She was happy. "Actually," he said, "I'll have Eric take you to your condominium. It's probably better if you don't know what else I've been pondering."

"Thank you again. I'm ready to leave."

He closed his eyes and nodded. This was better.

Then, without warning, she took his hand and asked, "What else have you been thinking?"

Her pools of emerald concern washed away his doubt. He'd be honest. "Those black lacy panties."

Claire stood abruptly. "What did you say?"

His cheeks rose. "I've been thinking about your black lace underwear; there was a small bow." His smile turned sensual. "I've been wondering what color you're wearing tonight."

Her voice resonated an octave higher. "How do you know about black lace panties?"

Tony stood, grasped her shoulders, colliding their chests as his breath quickened. "Why can't you believe that I still love you?"

"Really? You want me to believe you still *love* me? After an entire night of blackmailing me into being your companion, threatening my friend's company with disaster, and now learning that you... that you..." Her body trembled, tears once again flowed, and her voice broke, becoming a mere whisper. "...raped me."

The floor was once again falling. "No, Claire." Pleading laced his command. "Don't even suggest that." Lifting her chin, he searched her eyes. She'd talked about a dream, but she knew it was real as well as he did. "You agreed to everything. You more than consented: you wanted it as much as I did." When he released her chin, she didn't pull away; instead, her cheek settled against his chest as she wobbled in his arms. Tony kissed the top of her head and scooped her up into his arms.

"No, Tony, not tonight."

"I'm putting you on the sofa. You're about to fall."

She nodded against the silk of his shirt. Together, they sat on a large white sofa, facing the tall windows. Claire removed her high heels and curled her legs onto the plush cushions. With his arm around her shoulder she fit perfectly against his side. The scent of her perfume wafted through the silent air. The scene of the Golden Gate Bridge through the windows was stunning. Tony's mind replayed vistas they'd shared: the beaches of

Fiji, the mountains of Tahoe, and even the view from her suite in Iowa. *How many hours had they spent silently enjoying the beauty that he never noticed without her?*

Tony wanted this to go on forever, to forget their past and the vendetta. He wanted to keep her exactly like this. *Didn't Anthony Rawlings usually get what he wanted?* But he knew that it would never be right if it were forced. With a deep sigh, Tony broke the spell. "Are you ready for me to call Eric?"

Her response surprised him. "What I really want are answers."

"What kind of answers?"

"Truthful ones." Again, she used his words and repeated demands he'd made of her. When he didn't respond, Claire pushed on, "You say you still love me. You're a very intelligent man. Surely, you understand actions speak louder than words."

He turned to her with surprise. "You said no."

"I don't mean sex. I mean actions, like tricking me tonight, and setting me up for your attempted murder."

He exhaled. The past wouldn't go away.

Claire continued, "Tell me why."

"I told you. It was a loophole."

Her head shook against his shoulder. "I don't understand your puzzles."

"You, too, are very intelligent. I don't believe you've spent the past year and a half without suspicions."

"I truly didn't understand," Claire replied. "Until I received that box of information."

"And what did you conclude from that?"

As she contemplated her answer, her fingers mindlessly played with the small buttons down the center of his silk shirt. The familiarity filled him with a new sense of hope. Finally, she spoke, "Well, it's hard to answer. You see, I thought *you'd* sent it, so I thought you were adding insult to injury, you know, rubbing salt in my wounds."

Damn Catherine! That was the exact opposite of what she'd said. Tony pushed aside his anger and concentrated on Claire. Seeing the delivery from her perspective caused his chest to ache. "You thought I'd do that?"

"What else could I think? You set me up and left me."

The hope that moments earlier filled the penthouse evaporated; nevertheless, he tried again to help her understand. "There are few people in this world whom I've cared about. Few people whose opinion of me I value." He cupped her chin and looked into her glistening emerald eyes. "I know you have reason to doubt me—hell, *reasons*—but, Claire, you are one of those people." She closed her eyes, and he continued speaking, "I need you to understand that I made promises, and I keep my word."

"You made *me* a promise, on December eighteenth—"

He interrupted, each word coming slower than the one before, "Two thousand and ten, in our estate, to love you forever—I kept my word."

His lips found hers. She responded with the same unspoken need, primal and raw. It wasn't his imagination or a dream; they had the same desires. Then, it ended too soon. Without warning, Claire stood and swayed. Tony reached out to steady her. "Are you all right? What happened?"

Claire picked up her shoes and smoothed her dress. "I'm fine. I want to go now."

He didn't argue. In another minute they'd have been where they were in her condominium. Tony didn't want Claire to associate tonight's manipulation with sex. The next time they made love—and there would be a next time—she needed to admit her desires. There would be no more dreaming.

His eyes never left her as he called Eric. She looked beautiful, even with her smeared makeup and tousled hair; however, that wasn't why he couldn't look away. From her earlier paleness to the bouts with dizziness, Tony was worried. Perhaps he'd pushed her too far. Whatever the issue, he didn't want her to fall. Once his call was done, he said, "Eric will have the car ready in the private garage in a few minutes." Seeing the question in her eyes, he added, "If we enter the car in the garage, then we can avoid paparazzi."

"Oh, good idea, I need to use the restroom, and I'll be ready to leave." Claire turned to walk away and then turned back. "We? Tony, I don't need you to ride with me," she paused. "I'd prefer you didn't."

"Then I'll escort you to the car, if that's acceptable?"

Claire nodded and walked toward the bathroom. With her shoes dangling from her fingertips, her dress swept the floor. No one else needed to see her in this condition, though he could. To him, it was a gift, a very private view that he didn't want to share. Soon enough the media would intrude upon their world. According to the text messages he'd received, he and Claire were the talk of the town—hell, the country.

When the elevator opened to the private parking area, Eric immediately opened the door to the backseat. As Claire nodded and entered the car, Tony spoke to Eric, "Ms. Claire would prefer to ride back to Palo Alto alone. Please call me when she's safely to her door."

"Yes, Mr. Rawlings," Eric said as he began to shut Claire's door.

"I can get this," Tony said, as he leaned into the backseat and handed Claire her phone.

"Thank you, Tony. Good-bye."

"Don't forget the news release."

"How could I?"

"We'll need to discuss it further."

"I'm discussed out."

"I can tell you're tired," he admitted. "Go get some sleep. We can continue our discussion tomorrow, before I leave for Iowa."

"I have plans tomorrow. Call me after you're back in Iowa."

He wasn't in the mood to debate. "This would be better discussed in person."

She relented. "Let me meet you somewhere."

"Ten tomorrow morning. Text me the location; Palo Alto is fine."

"Tomorrow," she agreed with a nod.

"Tomorrow, Claire." He closed the door, tapped the top of the car, and Eric drove away. Tony watched the taillights of the Mercedes C-Class grow smaller as it left the underground garage. Wearily, he made his way back to the empty penthouse.

As the bourbon burned his throat, his mind cleared. The evening had gone well. Despite Claire's fire, she could still follow his rules. Tomorrow they would talk again and iron out the specifics of their reunion.

Nine

Paving the way – May 2013
(Truth – Chapter 41 & Behind the Scenes)

*What you perceive, your observations, feelings, interpretations, are all
your truth. Your truth is important. Yet it is not THE TRUTH.*
– Linda Ellinor

Common sense would say that Tony's best friends had too much going on with their son's wedding less than a week away to take time for a visit from him; nevertheless, common sense had never been Tony's calling card—especially when it came to his personal life. Fortunately, Brent and Courtney had been his friends for long enough that they were used to his ways. That was what Tony reminded himself as he neared their home on Sunday morning following the gala. They were his first stop. After them, his day would include a visit with Tim and Sue, as well as Tom and Bev.

During their discussions the day before, Tony and Claire agreed that in two weeks they'd meet in Chicago for a weekend of business activities, and reinforce the reunification perception to the world. He hated that she wanted her own accommodations. Yes, he'd offered that, but he'd hoped she wouldn't think it was necessary. After all, they *had been* married, and his apartment held more than one bedroom. Shaking his head, he recalled how adamant she'd been about other issues as well. Claire refused his credit card for clothes, saying that if he didn't like the way she dressed, he could find another companion. She also refused private planes and insisted on flying commercial. On more than one issue, Tony debated his response. He wanted to demand, command, and insist. He was Anthony Rawlings; his gut instinct and intuition had created a billion-dollar industry—he knew best. However, there was something about her perceived strength, the way she demanded and insisted, yet never commanded. It intrigued him. As he listened he found himself laughing. Not because her desires were funny, no. It was the way she did it. She listened and then politely refused many of his proposals. *Had there ever been anyone who had so blatantly and repeatedly told him no?* Definitely no one who knew him as well as Claire.

Of course, there were other issues where Tony refused to budge, specifically his undebatable demand regarding public outings. Neither of them would be seen with anyone in a situation that could be misconstrued as a *date*. It was selfish and Tony would admit that, at least to himself, but when it came to Claire, he was a selfish bastard—not heartless as she'd said, but selfish.

There was little he could do at this time about Claire's living arrangements. As long as she was living with Amber, and Baldwin lived down the hall, Tony knew that Claire and Baldwin would run into one another. His new undebatable rule would at least minimize public outings. If there was something Tony was tired of seeing—both in his email attachments and on his newsfeed—were pictures of her with *him*.

Tony pulled up to Brent and Courtney's, and parked on their brick drive. He'd told them he needed to speak to them about the press release. After spending the past sixteen months refusing to say Claire's name, Tony realized his change of heart might be a tough bill to sell, but he was a master businessman, and talking a good game was his specialty. The thing was, he had an ulterior motive—his visit wasn't only about the press release. Tony wanted to bring Claire to Caleb Simmons' wedding. It was a revelation that occurred to him while he and Claire were sitting at the park in Redwood Shores. He didn't care that he already had a date; he'd cancel. But before he asked Claire, Tony wanted to run the idea past his friends. They needed to know his stance and understand that he no longer believed Claire tried to kill him. Of course, he never believed it, but he couldn't tell them that.

As Tony scaled the front steps, Brent opened the front door. "Good morning, Tony," Brent greeted. "Come on in."

"Thanks," he said, as he looked around. "Is Courtney here?"

"She is. She's kind of going a little crazy right now."

"I know you two must be busy. This won't take long."

Brent led Tony through the house toward the kitchen. "Cort, Tony's here."

Although she greeted him with her customary hug, volumes of unspoken questions filled the room with tension. Tony didn't like it. He had very few people in his life that he considered true friends, and Brent and Courtney were on his short list.

"So," Tony began. "I thought you deserved to question me yourself—about the press release. I'm sure it came as a shock. I would've been here sooner, but I didn't get back from California until late last night."

The Simmonses looked at one another. Finally, Courtney spoke, "I really don't know what to say. I mean, seriously, what the hell?"

Tony pressed his lips together. It was more direct than he'd anticipated.

"I don't understand," Courtney continued. Her voice cracking as her volume increased. "I wanted to help her and *you* forbade it!"

Brent squared his shoulders. "Sorry, Tony, Courtney has a lot happening right now. This caught us both off guard."

"No," Tony hastily replied. "Don't apologize for her." Turning to Courtney, he added, "You're right. You're absolutely right. I was wrong and I deserve everything you just said."

His friends sat silently as a bit of the tension eased. After a few moments, Courtney wiped a tear from her cheek and offered, "Wow, I never expected to hear that from you."

Tony shook his head. "I never expected to say it. I think it was seeing her, talking to her—"

Courtney interrupted, "Wait, would you like some coffee? I think we need more than a brief answer."

Tony agreed.

Courtney started the coffee and excused herself for a moment. When she returned her tears had dried, and the three friends moved to the sunporch. The fresh, gentle breeze from the open windows helped to facilitate a calmer atmosphere. As Tony spoke, he explained how he never wanted to believe that Claire would want to kill him, but the evidence seemed so strong. He lashed out—at her and everyone else. He added, "I'm sorry."

Though Brent didn't respond, Courtney walked to where Tony was seated and wrapped her arms around his shoulders. Tony exhaled. It was a more welcoming hug than the one he'd received upon his arrival. After she moved back to her seat, Brent asked, "How did you secure her pardon?" His frigid tone returned the chill to the spring air.

Tony glared in his direction and the wheels turned. Honesty? Fabrication?

Before he could reply, Brent continued, "I mean, I accompanied you to Ms. Allyson's office. I know you pretty damn well—or so I thought."

"No, you do know me," Tony conceded. "I didn't know who was responsible for her pardon that day—and I still don't. Maybe this will pull the coward from hiding. I don't care anymore. Taking responsibility was Shelly's idea and I agreed to it. She thought it made the story more convincing."

"I bet *she* was excited about this declaration of reunification," sarcasm dripped from Brent's statement.

"She wasn't." Tony's neck stiffened. "However, I'd hoped that maybe you'd understand."

"I do!" Courtney chimed in.

Tony turned his dark glare from Brent and saw Courtney's shining blue eyes. Sighing, he said, "I'm glad, because I'm not exactly sure where this is all going. Claire and I've had the opportunity to hash a few things out, and I'm hopeful that in time we can be back together, as a couple."

"One press release won't change people's perception." Brent stood and paced. "Hell, Tony, we're your friends and I don't know what to think. What about outsiders, employees, and investors?"

"I don't give a damn," his resolve reverberated through the porch and beyond.

"You don't? I've known you for a long time, and that has always been your main concern."

"Listen, I don't have all the answers. What if I'm getting played? What if none of this is real, just some charade?" Tony used Claire's word. "Right now, I want it to be real. And," he paused. "I'd like to have her accompany me to Caleb's wedding."

Courtney gasped. Brent's eyes grew wide, masking the usually present lines.

"I haven't asked her," Tony added quickly. "I'm talking to you first."

Courtney's words came slowly. "Are you *asking* our permission?"

The obvious emphasis on the word *asking* made Tony bristle. Was he *asking*? *Did he ask?* "Yes, I guess I am."

Courtney stood and walked to the window. With her back to them, they could only watch as her head shook slowly from side to side. Finally, she turned on her heels; a new look of determination prevailed. "Here's the deal. It's not up to you, or me, or even Claire. First and foremost, it's up to Julia."

Tony nodded. He hadn't thought of that.

"It's her wedding. I mean we've seen thousands of pictures of that gala in California. I don't want my son's wedding turned into some media circus because suddenly you've had a change of heart."

"If it's the security you're concerned about, I'll gladly help pay—"

Courtney lifted her hand. "You're getting ahead of yourself. First, let me call Julia."

Tony acquiesced—did he have another choice?

Courtney stepped from the porch to make the call, leaving Tony and Brent alone in a cloud of uncomfortable silence. This whole conversation was different than Tony had imagined. In his mind he would come over to their house, explain the press release, and tell them he would bring Claire to the wedding—end of story. Of course, he still needed to convince Claire, but needing to convince his friends never entered his mind.

When he looked up, Brent's tired eyes were bearing down on him. "What?" Tony asked. "I get the feeling there's more you want to say."

"No. I'm just processing. I'm trying to figure out why the hell I went to Mitchellville and threatened *Ms. Nichols* with a civil suit. What has she said or done that has made you do a one-eighty?"

Customarily, a rebuke such as that would send Tony through the roof; instead, he sagged against the soft cushion and exhaled. "I don't know. You know that I was angry when she refused my offer of the mental institution."

Brent *harrumphed*.

"I sent you there... because..." Tony stood and paced. "...I wanted her to know that I was angry."

Brent continued to glare.

"I know, I know. I wish I could explain. Honestly, I don't even know where to start. It's just that when I'm with—"

"She said yes!" Courtney interrupted, filling the room with a ring of happiness like Tony hadn't heard since he arrived.

"She did?" Brent asked. "Does Julia have any idea what this will be like?" Turning to Tony, he asked, "Do you plan on bringing *Ms. Nichols* to the rehearsal reception?"

"You may," Courtney quickly added.

Tony ran his hand through his hair. "*Claire*, her name's Claire, and I don't know. I haven't even talked to her about it. Shit."

"What?" Courtney prodded.

"This has been much more difficult than I anticipated. What about everyone else?"

"I thought you said you didn't care?" Brent quipped.

"I don't, but I'm thinking of Claire." Tony thought out loud. "I wish there was some way to reintroduce her to our inner circle, without all the wedding guests or even the wedding party."

"Have you spoken to anyone else about this?" Courtney asked.

Tony explained that he'd been waiting to speak to them. Then, he planned to visit Tim and Sue and Tom and Bev. He would call Eli and Mary Ann.

"You do that and then call Claire. Let me see what I can do." Courtney's enthusiasm was contagious.

Tony shook his head. "No, you have too much happening."

"Nonsense." She put her hand on Tony's arm. "Just tell everyone what you've told us. None of us wanted to believe that she was guilty. If Claire's willing to face all of us, the least we can do is make it easier for her."

Tony peered into Courtney's sincere blue eyes. "Thank you."

Once back inside of his car, Tony dialed Claire's number; she didn't answer. Next, he tried Tim Bronson. "Hey, Tim, this is Tony. Are you and Sue home?" "Good, I was wondering..."

By the time Tony made it back to his estate, he was exhausted. He'd stated his case with all of his closest friends; he'd even been able to reach Eli and Mary Ann in California. They all agreed to support his decision, although somewhat apprehensively at first. It was during his drive home that he received the call from Sue. She'd spoken to Courtney and asked if the reunion of the *inner circle* could take place at their house on Thursday night. Momentarily speechless, Tony accepted her invitation. Sue had been the least receptive regarding Claire's return. She rightfully questioned the presence of someone with even the possibility of having attempted murder being around her family. Of course, she meant their son, Sean. Tony assured her that since Sean wouldn't be at the wedding or rehearsal, there would be no need to worry. Since her tone, during the call, still held the slightest bit of trepidation, Tony suspected that Courtney had played more than a leading role in the plans. He wanted to ask if Sue planned on sending Sean out of state; instead, he said *thank you*.

The next step was Claire. He'd tried calling her between Tim and Tom's house and again didn't receive an answer. Looking at the corner of his screen and seeing that it was almost 3:00 PM, he dialed her number.

He was just about to give up when Claire answered, "Tony, this is the third time you've called today. We aren't making any public appearances for two weeks. *Please* give me some space."

A chuckle came from the depth of his throat. "Hello, Claire, so nice to hear your pleasant tone."

"I've got a lot going on. What do you want?"

Tony contemplated her agitation. Part of him feared that allowing her any distance was asking for her to change her mind. He tried to keep his voice light. "Let me say, I would call less frequently *if* you would answer your phone." She didn't respond, so he continued, "I made plans for us, for this coming weekend."

"I agreed to go to Chicago, in two weeks." Each phrase grew a bit louder and more clipped. "I'm not going anywhere with you *next* weekend."

"I believe I might be able to persuade you otherwise."

"Is that a threat? What are you going to do this time, arrange a walk-out of SiJo's employees?"

"No, Claire. No threats," he reassured. "I believe you'll *want* to attend this function."

"Why? What function would I possibly want to attend with *you*?"

"Caleb and Julia's wedding."

Claire gasped. "B-but all of your friends think I tried to kill you."

"The press release says differently."

"That doesn't mean they've changed their opinion. They probably don't want me there—"

"That's not true," he interrupted. "I promise that I've spoken to all of our closest friends. I've explained things to them."

"I-I don't know?"

Tony had put too much effort into this. It was the perfect plan to get Claire to Iowa, not just to be there, but to be there willingly. He wouldn't stop until she said yes. He explained about Brent and Courtney and how Courtney had talked to Sue. There may have been a few details that he forgot to mention: questions and tones of voices, but that wasn't lying—it was omitting. Slowly, Claire began to come around. The irritation Tony heard when he first called morphed to what he hoped could be interpreted as excitement.

By the time their discussion concluded, Claire agreed to fly commercially, but only if she had a return ticket to Palo Alto on Sunday. She also agreed to the get-together at Sue and Tim's on Thursday, the rehearsal reception on Friday, and the wedding on Saturday. The subject of accommodations took a little more persuasion. It was when Catherine was mentioned, and Tony expressed how badly Catherine wanted Claire at the estate, that her undebatable stance began to sway.

Tony smirked at Claire's ultimatum. "My room will need a lock."

"That isn't a problem." It wasn't a problem at all. Tony imagined the electronic lock that could so easily be reactivated on the door of her suite.

Perhaps sensing his thoughts, she qualified, "It needs to be a lock that operates from the *inside*. Also, I *will* keep my phone at all times and have access to your Wi-Fi."

"You drive a hard bargain. I've told you before that you should go into business. You're a master negotiator." Hell, he'd have promised the moon and the stars if it meant she would once again be under his roof—*their* roof.

Thursday couldn't come soon enough.

Honesty – June 2013
(Truth – Chapter 42 thru 44)

The first condition of progress is the removal of censorship.
– George Bernard Shaw

E verything happened in slow motion, from Eric's driving, to the opening of the large iron gates. If Tony didn't get into his house soon, he might combust. It didn't help that his recent conversations with Mr. George and Danielle grated on his already frayed nerves. With Sophia in New Jersey, it was the perfect opportunity for Danielle to convince Derek Burke that he could find comfort elsewhere. Why the stupid girl hadn't gone to China with Burke in the first place was beyond Tony. *Did all of these people need him to micromanage their lives?* He had much more pressing matters with his own life.

Eric had barely put the car in park on the brickyard in front of Tony's estate before Tony had his door open and was halfway up the steps. From his peripheral vision, he saw Eric's head shake. That man knew Tony better than anyone else, probably even better than Catherine knew him. It wasn't that Eric pried, like she did. No, Eric was observant and omnipresent. He didn't comment or judge; he just was. Tony appreciated his objectivity, such as how he concisely described picking Claire up at the airport and taking her to the estate. In every situation, Eric was calm, ready, and loyal. Tony couldn't ask for more.

The grand foyer of his home shone with a welcoming glow that he hadn't noticed in over a year. As Tony entered the grand doors, Catherine turned the corner. "Oh, my, *Mr. Rawlings*, you seem to be in a hurry."

"Come to my office." He didn't wait for her to respond before his quick step and long legs had him safely within the confines of his private domain.

Following closely behind, Catherine entered and closed the door behind her. "Yes?" she asked, the word elongated and her brow lifted.

"Where is she? What was she like when she arrived? Eric said that she was upset. Why?"

Catherine chuckled as she settled on a nearby chair. "She's in her old suite."

Tony's eyes opened wide before he narrowed them questioningly. "You did tell her that she could stay in any of the rooms, didn't you?"

"I did. She was the one who asked about her old suite."

He exhaled, as some of the pent-up tension eased from his taut shoulders. That was a good sign, he hoped. He'd left her a note in her suite, as well as in two other rooms, but he was happy with her choice. Catherine went on. "She *was* upset when she arrived, not about anything in particular. I believe that returning was emotionally overwhelming."

"And you?" he prompted.

"Did what I do." Catherine's gray eyes dulled. "You know me—the *kind housekeeper.*"

Tony shook his head. "Stop it. She doesn't think of you that way. I believe she came here as much for you as she did me." Suddenly, that truth bothered Tony. He didn't want to share.

Catherine shrugged. "We spoke for a little while, she ate, and now she's resting. It was a long trip."

Tony inhaled deeply. "Ate? We're eating at the Bronsons."

"It was just a snack and she seemed… shaky."

"Shaky? Is that why she's resting? I want to see her."

"I can get her, but I suggest that you let her rest. Traveling can be tiring. You don't need to be to your dinner for almost two hours." Catherine's head cocked to the side. "You know, if you hadn't turned off the cameras, we'd know for sure if she were sleeping."

"I know. I also know that she hated those cameras. This is better." He turned on his computer and began to search the end of day stock-market analysis.

"She asked about the delivery." Catherine's statement caused the business at hand to disappear.

"Did you tell her?"

"No," she answered indignantly. "You said you didn't want her to know."

"I said that if you tell her, you're opening yourself up to her questions and suspicions. If you tell her, you might as well be willing to lay it all out. If you're not willing to do that—don't tell her." He lowered his tone. "At least *I'm* giving *you* the option."

Catherine looked away.

When she didn't look back, Tony asked, "What else happened? Is she all right?"

"Yes, of course. Why?"

"I get the feeling you're holding something back."

Her lips smiled. "I think you're looking for any excuse to get you upstairs to do what you want to do."

"I want her to be comfortable. If that means resting, then she can rest."

Catherine stood. "Very well, however, since you're not eating here this evening, I'll be leaving the estate in a short time. If she's not awake, you'll need to wake her."

"Where are you going?"

"Some things are none of your business."

He shrugged. "Where's Cindy?"

"An-thon-y," she said, each syllable enunciated. "Go to her suite. You'll do the right thing."

Catherine slipped from the office leaving Tony alone with his thoughts. All day long he'd anticipated this evening—coming home, not to an empty house, but to the place where Claire belonged. He reached into the drawer and found his new reminder below his old key ring; Tony pulled out the envelope. It wasn't special in any way; to the casual onlooker, or even the curious snoop, it was only an envelope, but it was so much more. When Tony's thoughts would begin to blur and red would slip inconspicuously into his vision, he'd remember this envelope.

Turning it in his hands, Tony heard Nathaniel's words from his dream. Although he'd only had the dream once, every second of it had replayed in his mind so many times that he'd sometimes forget that it hadn't really happened. Peering into the depths of the envelope, for the millionth time, Tony vowed to fill it. He wouldn't allow it to stay empty, not because Nathaniel had said he failed, but because he'd succeeded. Tony had fulfilled his obligation: the Nichols family had suffered. Now, he wanted to exceed Nathaniel's wishes just as he'd done financially. His grandfather had told him that he would survive. Tony had done more than survive: for a short time, he'd had *everything*.

A memory resurfaced, not of a nightmare, but a memory of one of Tony's last visits to Camp Gabriels, the prison where Nathaniel died. There were times when his grandfather would repeat the same thought over and over; however, on occasion he'd share a nugget of truth. That happened on the day in Tony's memory, yet Tony didn't realize the treasure until almost twenty-five years later:

Tony stood as Nathaniel ranted on and on, lost in a tirade about Tony's father, Sherman Nichols, and Jonathon Burke. Then without warning, Nathaniel turned his dark gaze on his grandson, and in his deep, menacing voice asked, "You know what?"

"No, sir," Anton replied.

"You can't lose everything until you have everything to lose. I had everything, and now look at me!"

It all made sense: after all of these years, Tony knew the truth. With Claire gone, his envelope was empty. In his dream, Nathaniel said that Tony received what he gave—and Tony finally conceded that his grandfather was right. Tony had given Claire a life with everything and then had taken it away—for the sake of the vendetta. In that process, he'd lost everything—everything he never realized he wanted. After she was gone, he still had the money, the estate, and the prestige, yet his life was as empty as the envelope in his hand. The vengeance had not only punished the people on their list, but it had punished him, taken away his *everything*.

It wasn't until Claire was out of prison that Tony began to see. He'd been blinded by her actions and hadn't realized how much he'd lost. Perhaps it was true and he was a selfish bastard, but seeing her beginning a new life, one without him, one with another man, cleared away the fog of Nathaniel's vendetta.

Tony couldn't make the past go away—if he could he would—however, he could spend forever showing Claire that he wanted her in his life, that without her, his world was empty. By allowing the vendetta to take away the only true happiness Tony had ever known, he'd failed his grandfather's legacy. The Rawls name may be gone, but never had Nathaniel wished for an empty envelope—that was how Tony had failed.

Tony wasn't sure how he would do it, or if it could be done, but he knew the woman asleep upstairs was his life, happiness, and future. In order to fill his void and honor his grandfather, he needed to make her see that, too. He needed to do more than that; he needed to control the one thing that could control him. Tony needed to control the *red*.

He had done it before, while Claire was in prison, and from high school until his acquisition of Claire. When Tony was at Blair Academy, before he turned off the red, he remembered life as highs and lows. After Nathaniel told him that fighting was unacceptable, he turned it off and everything was even. If a bump occurred, Tony eliminated it. If a company didn't perform, he sold it. If the bottom line was red, Tony cut the overhead. Everything was black and white—no red.

That all changed when he brought Claire into his life. Tony tried to believe she was nothing more than an acquisition, someone who could be eliminated, but that wasn't true. She filled his world with color. Oh, there was red—too much red—but there was also blue, yellow, and most vividly, green. She made him see the sky, trees, and lakes. With her, he saw the snow on the mountains and surf at the shore. Life was no longer a series of numbers and ledgers.

He didn't recognize any of that when they were together. He'd been too consumed with controlling her. It wasn't until after she was gone that he comprehended the truth.

To win her back, Tony knew he had to narrow his color spectrum. He wanted the highs, and after a year and a half of black and white, Tony even welcomed the lows. It was the red he needed to eliminate. The way he saw it, he'd built a billion-dollar industry from nothing; removing red from his world couldn't be that difficult. One factor that he needed to depend upon was Claire. *Could he ever truly trust her again?* After all, she'd been the one to leave him. *Would she once again follow his rules?* Perhaps together, they could remove the red.

Placing the envelope back in the drawer, Tony checked the time—almost 6:00 PM. They needed to be at Tim's in an hour and a half. Refocusing on his computer, Tony reviewed the end-of-day numbers. When he was done, he planned to shower, and if Claire weren't awake, he'd go to her suite—*her suite*—and wake her. His lips turned upward, liking the sound of calling it her suite. It didn't matter if the walls were painted a different color. It would always be her suite.

Tony reached for the knob of Claire's door. As he grasped it, he remembered her requirements: she wanted a door with a lock from the inside. Straightening his shoulders, he tried unsuccessfully to hide his smile. As his knuckles rapped the hard wood and he waited for a response, Tony recalled the only other time he'd ever knocked upon her door was the night of their wedding. After a moment, he knocked again. When she didn't answer, he slowly moved the lever, opened the door, and peered around the barrier. His breath caught in his lungs as he saw Claire; she was asleep in the king-sized bed. With all his might, Tony wanted to reconnect the electronic lock and keep Claire there forever.

Memories of them in that bed swirled through his consciousness as he moved closer. With each step, he said her name, "Claire." He didn't want to give her the wrong impression, although *that* impression was paramount in his mind. She was a vision of peacefulness. "Claire—Claire, you need to wake. We're supposed to be at Tim and Sue's in an hour." Approaching the bed, her serene expression transfixed him. Hoping not to startle her, he spoke louder, "Claire? Claire?" Partially out of necessity, but more out of desire, Tony touched her exposed shoulder. "Claire?"

She began to stir. His fingers purposely grazed the light blue satin bra strap. The allure of moving the covers and discovering the remainder of her attire was almost irresistible. Tony wondered if she could possibly be wearing matching light blue panties.

Suddenly, her eyes opened wide as she sat up and pulled the blankets around her body. "Tony! What are you doing in here? You promised!"

He chuckled at her modesty. "I promised a lock, but the door wasn't locked. I knocked multiple times. You must have been very tired."

The alarm that was evident only moments ago dissipated into her beautiful pools of emerald. Even her tone eased. "I think I was. I have that jittery, just-awakened feeling." Her long brown hair fell in waves around her beautiful face as she sighed and laid her head back upon the pillow. "What time is it?"

"Six-thirty, and we need to be at Tim and Sue's in an hour." As if his feet were blocks of concrete, he stood statuesque, transfixed by her presence.

"Well," she quipped, "if you're going to stand there, then go find me a robe so that I can get ready."

Slowly, willing his feet to move, Tony walked to her dressing room. Since she'd refused his credit card, he asked his personal shopper to supply a wardrobe for her to access in Iowa. Turning on the light, he saw a long pink robe. No doubt, that was what she had in mind; however, Tony knew there were other items of lingerie. If he found the right one, he might learn the answer to his burning blue-panties question.

When he emerged, he held up a transparent, black-silk negligee robe. It was a robe, he mused. When his eyes met hers, her eyebrows rose, lips pursed tight, and head shook from side to side. With a feigned pout, he reentered the dressing room and returned again with the long pink robe.

"That's better," she bantered. "Now, if you don't mind?"

Tony gallantly turned away, though every muscle in his body wanted to do a full three-sixty. "Don't you think this is a bit ridiculous?" he asked. "We were married."

"No, I don't." After a moment, she added, "You may turn around now."

When he did, she was the only thing he could see. Her hair was slightly tousled, her cheeks blushed, and her eyes sparkled with a glow that could mesmerize him for hours. It was all he could do to remember his mission. Blinking twice, he forced himself to remain on task. "I thought we could talk about tonight."

"Not now. I need to get ready. We can talk in the car. If you leave me alone, then I'll be ready in thirty minutes."

Tony silently laughed at her sense of empowerment. Mockingly, he bowed, blew her a kiss, and left the room. Once the door closed completely, he allowed the small rumble of his amusement to come to life.

Leaning against one of the grand doors, Tony waited. It had been almost thirty minutes since he'd left Claire's suite before he looked up to see her descending the main staircase. He remained still as he scanned her from head to toe. As much as he appreciated appearance and perfection, there was something about the recently-awakened Claire that he longed to see again. Once she reached the marble floor, he straightened and said, "You look amazing—as usual. Is that an outfit you brought or one from the closet?"

"One I brought. The closet seems silly. I'm leaving in three days."

"You refused to take a credit card, so I hired someone to shop for you." He shrugged. "You may decide to wear some of those clothes to our other public functions."

Claire came to a stop and looked up defiantly. "Tony, I'm not falling into that same trap. I don't want the media accusing me of *reconciling* with you for your money."

He hadn't thought of that. It wasn't what he was trying to do; nevertheless, he understood her trepidation. Attempting to reassure her, he said, "Tonight there won't be media, just friends."

Claire exhaled and her shoulders slumped.

"What's the matter?"

"Are you sure they want me there? I would rather face the media than *your friends,* considering what they think I did."

Tony grasped her hand. "I promise. I've spoken to everyone, most in person. I spoke to Mary Ann and Eli on the phone."

"And...?"

"And they *understand*. I was distraught, but we're reconciling."

Tony placed his arm around her waist as she closed her eyes and exhaled.

"It will be all right. This is supposed to make tomorrow and the wedding easier." As he led her outside, he asked, "You do want to be at the wedding, don't you?"

"I do," she said, as her eyes widened. Tony followed her gaze. He couldn't blame her reaction: she was seeing his newest car for the first time. It was a Lexus LFA. There was no question, that other than Claire, cars were his passion. This little two-seat super car with a V-40 valve V-10 was no exception. He opened the door and she lowered herself into the bucket seat. When he got in and grinned, Claire said, "This is a very nice car. Would you mind not going too fast?"

"It can do zero to sixty in three point six seconds."

"I believe you, but do you remember my reaction to the bacon the other day?"

He did and Catherine had said she was shaky. "Yes." He frowned. "Are you still not well?"

"I'm not back to myself."

"Maybe you should see a doctor."

"I have an appointment in a few weeks."

After they began the drive, Tony looked to his right. Claire had her head laid back and eyes closed. Sick or not, they had things they needed to sort through before they arrived at the Bronsons'. Turning down the radio, he said, "We need to discuss your behavior for tonight."

Claire opened her eyes and looked in his direction. "Tony, I wouldn't be here—of my own free will—if I didn't completely comprehend my behavior. Don't patronize me. I've done this dance before."

"Are you implying that when you were with my friends in the past, it was a performance?"

"No. I'm saying that there were times I wasn't happy with you, but no one knew."

Looking her way, he asked, "You aren't happy with me?"

Her petite hand reached over and covered his. "Tony, we're doing what you want; it's a performance. I can't say I don't want it to be real, but for now, it isn't. Let's not add unnecessary layers to this charade."

As he listened to her words, something gave him hope. "So there's a part of you—I'll settle for a small part—that wants what we're about to do to be real?"

She exhaled. "Yes, Tony, a small part of me wants *us* to be real."

Tony relaxed against the leather interior and enjoyed the bends and curves of the country roads. He would've loved to have pushed the gas pedal harder and watched the speedometer climb. It gave him an undeniable rush; however, for now, he'd take the adrenaline that came from the woman in the seat beside him. As they conversed about nothing, he contemplated his friends. Tony wanted the night to go well, for Claire. Of course, he'd laid himself on the line for this, too. Truthfully, he wasn't even sure how Sue would react when they arrived. Looking to his right, he wondered if Sue was as good at hiding her true emotions as Claire. When they neared Tim and Sue's home, he slowed the car and said, "Perhaps we should review the rules."

Once again, Claire closed her eyes, laid her head back, and exhaled. Her next sentence came with no emotion. "Maybe I could save us some time and summarize? Do as you say, no public failure, and don't divulge private information."

"Are you summarizing or mocking?"

"For the sake of argument, I'll call it summarizing." He didn't dare look her way; he could hear the sparks of fire crackling below the surface. Claire continued, "As I said earlier, I've done this before. Perhaps you've forgotten, but I'm perfectly capable of doing as you wish."

"No, Claire, I haven't forgotten your abilities. I just need confirmation that we're on the same page as we enter the Bronsons' home."

"Tell me the number, and I'll turn right to it."

With the car now stopped along the shoulder of the country road, Tony reached for Claire's chin and turned her glaring green eyes toward him. In the split second before he spoke, he remembered the envelope. Clenching his jaw, he searched desperately for his calmest tone. The end result slowed his words. "I believe I'm tiring of the sexy, bold, and cheeky."

"Then stop this charade."

He maintained his hold and reminded himself again. Exhaling, he asked, "May I please have reticent and genteel while in the presence of others?"

The green fire ebbed. With a faux Georgia accent, she responded, "Why, Mr. Rawlings, your wish is my command."

As she mocked him with her fluttering lashes, his heart raced, and the temperature inside the car rose exponentially, gluing Tony's hand to her chin. He couldn't let go and release that green stare if he tried. Unconsciously, he leaned toward her and commanded, "Kiss me."

He hadn't meant to say it with such need, but it was true. He needed a release, and lashing out wouldn't get him the results he desired. Thankfully, she didn't protest. Obediently, her eyes closed, lips parted, and their mouths united. Fire ignited as their hands sought what only the other possessed. If it weren't for the damn seatbelts, Tony would have forgotten that they were on the side of the road, only a mile from his vice president's home. When reality struck, he leaned back and confessed, "If we weren't expected at the Bronsons' any minute, I'd like to put more effort into exploring the *wish-and-command* possibilities."

To his surprise, Claire leaned her head against the seat and laughed. Seeing her genuine smile, the threat of red, the tension, and the nervous energy slipped away. It wasn't until she said, "I'm nervous to see all of them again," that he realized how truly difficult this was on her. He'd tried to pave the way, but he'd also been the one to set up the roadblocks.

One more time, he reached for her chin, but without the earlier tension. Tony wanted nothing more than to help. "There may be questions—personal questions. This isn't the press. They're people who know me—know us—and they're going to want to know what happened."

Claire nodded.

"I've given this scenario a lot of thought. We both know that we can't be one hundred percent truthful."

"Obviously," Claire murmured.

Tony cleared his throat. "Like I said, we need to be on the same page. I contacted you while you were in prison—"

"You did no such—"

His darkening gaze stopped her protest, as his baritone voice dropped an octave, slowing his words. "We *must* be together on this. No one's going to believe that this *just* happened. We have to let them think that it's been in the works for a while. Besides, that's what the press release said. We need to create a believable history."

Claire sucked in her cheeks, pursed her lips, and lowered her chin. Turning toward him, she said, "Fine, you're the master of deception, what's our *believable history*?"

"I contacted you at the prison—first by letter, and eventually, I began to visit." He waited for her rebuttal. When none came, he went on, "Initially, we were both upset—and *hurt*. After all, I believed you tried to kill me, and you believed I abandoned you."

Crossing her arms over her chest, she agreed. "All right, *abandoned* is appropriate."

He closed his eyes and took a deep breath before continuing, "Communication—we began talking. I realized that it was all a misunderstanding. Despite the evidence, you convinced me that you weren't responsible."

"Then who?"

"We may never know. There had been some deliveries and some new groundskeepers had been hired. Perhaps it was a business rival—we'll probably never know. The clues are long gone and the police concentrated on the wrong person."

With each comment, Claire's gaze mellowed.

Tony continued, "I personally went to Governor Bosley. He attended our wedding, and in the past, I'd done him some favors. He agreed to your petition for pardon. Since then..." Tony continued weaving a history that his friends would accept. Slowly, he saw Claire's stance relax and her gaze become more accepting. It seemed that Claire, too, wanted this evening to go well. *Was it because there was a small part of her that wanted it to be real, or was it because she was afraid of the consequences if she didn't?* Tony prayed it was the former.

Upon opening Claire's door, Tony looked into her nervous expression. "I'm not leading you into the den of lions," he whispered.

"No," she sighed. "You've already done that."

"This time I won't leave you," he promised. "I'll stay by your side, and you won't be alone."

Nodding, Claire grasped his extended hand. Their fingers intertwined as they approached the stately home. He leaned down. "I'd hoped seeing everyone here first would be easier than seeing them for the first time in a crowd."

"It probably will be; nevertheless, I think I'm going to be ill."

He pulled her to a stop and searched her face under the darkening sky. "Your color looks good. You look amazing. I promise," he said, squeezing her hand. "I'm right here." His grin broadened. "A man of my word."

Claire reached up and kissed his cheek, sending a wave of warmth through his entire body. In her voice he heard true gratitude. "Thank you." He didn't deserve it; Tony knew that. Nonetheless, it was wonderful to hear.

Before they pressed the doorbell, Tim opened the door. With Sue by his side, he politely offered a greeting, "Welcome to our home, Tony, Claire."

Tony glanced to Sue. She motioned toward their sitting room and said, "Please come in."

Everyone was there—all of Tony's closest friends. Six pairs of eyes stared as the room fell deadly silent, and Claire tightened her grip of his hand. Tony was about to speak when Courtney placed her wine glass on the table and walked toward them. It was as if she didn't see Tony, as her blue eyes glassed over with tears. Suddenly, Claire was engulfed in Courtney's embrace. He had no choice but to release her hand.

All of his work to prepare Claire was a waste of time. The two women were hugging, crying, and holding on to one another for dear life. Tony watched in horror, as one by one, the other women joined the hugfest until Claire was surrounded. Helplessly, he watched as all of the women disappeared into the kitchen. It wasn't until Tim slapped him on the shoulder and said, "It's a good thing," that Tony released the breath he didn't know he'd been holding.

The advantage to dating women whom you cared nothing about was the lack of drama. While Claire was gone, he never brought anyone around his friends; there was no need. Now that he had Claire back with the few people in the world whom he respected and valued, he knew beyond a shadow of a doubt, that he'd never figure out women. They were far too complicated.

The evening progressed exceptionally well. Most of the time when Tony looked to Claire, she was by his side, saying or doing the perfect thing. At one point, Tony realized that both Claire and Brent were missing. Remembering Brent's icy response from less than a week ago, Tony's heart beat quickened as he searched. Courtney saw his concern and joined him. Together, they found Brent and Claire in the kitchen simply discussing California. When Courtney asked Claire for her cell number, Tony filled with relief, seeing that his friends were truly supporting his decision.

It wasn't until Brent announced that he and Courtney needed to leave, that Tony asked to have a private talk amongst the four of them. Suddenly, Claire's performance faltered. She seemed anxious. *Why could she talk to them in the house, but feared being alone?* Tony wanted to reassure her that it was all right, that his friends were already helping her more than she knew.

As they thanked Tim and Sue for hosting the dinner, Sue asked, "Could you please wait just a minute?" Without waiting for an answer, she hurried away toward the stairs.

Puzzled, Tony looked down to Claire and heard Courtney say, "I think she's going to get Sean. He's upstairs with the nanny." Claire didn't verbally respond, but her eyes did. He'd seen that look before, questioning, asking. He shrugged and Claire turned to Courtney. "Can you stay for a few more minutes? I know you have a lot to do, and Tony wants to talk—"

"Oh, honey," Courtney replied, "I always have time for babies. Wait until you see him!"

While they waited for Sue to return with Sean, Tony remembered Sue's initial reaction and realized what a big step this was for her. Obviously, even without that knowledge, Claire recognized it. When Tony refocused, Courtney and Brent were talking about grandchildren. Moments later, Sue appeared with a pajama-clad Sean. The last time Tony had seen their son had been at his birthday party. Kids' parties weren't really Tony's thing, and he hadn't stayed long, but the kid was cute with blonde hair like his mom's. Tony met Sue's gaze and nodded approvingly, before she turned toward his ex-wife. "Claire, I wanted you to meet Sean. I'm sorry. This is past his bedtime, and the poor little guy is getting tired."

"Hello, little guy, it's nice to meet you." Claire's voice sounded high. Tony wondered why normal adults talk strangely around kids, when she asked, "He's what—about fifteen months?"

"Almost." Sue smiled. "He's so much fun, getting into everything and learning new words every day."

When Tim stepped forward, Sean put out his arms, and Tim swung him into his embrace. "Believe me," Tim added, "it makes you think about every word when little ears are listening."

Tony thought it seemed like a lot of undue stress. He'd spent enough time thinking about what to say with Claire. Her emotion-filled voice refocused his thoughts as she patted the kid's head. "Thank you. I think you might have some difficulty getting him back to sleep."

Once they were out by the cars, Tony squared his shoulders and addressed Claire, Brent, and Courtney. It was time for Claire to understand that he was taking her requests seriously, and he believed it would sound more sincere if she heard it from Brent. Tony began, "I'm doing my best to be honest with Claire, and I expect the same from her." He wished she didn't look so nervous. "That's why I thought we should get this out in the open."

Claire interjected, "Tony, I think the Simmonses need to—"

"This won't take long." Tony turned to Brent. "I've trusted Brent with many things through the years. That's why I wanted him to be the one to tell you about his progress regarding your brother-in-law."

"Yes," Brent said, expelling a breath. Tony knew they had a lot to do for the wedding and rehearsal, but this was important. Brent went on to explain that some new information had come to the attention of the New York State Bar Association, and John's case would soon be coming up for review. If all went well, the result would be the reinstatement of his license to practice law. As Brent spoke, Tony watched Claire's eyes glow and glisten.

She sprung up and clapped. "Oh, thank you! Thank you, Brent. Thank you, Tony. I won't say a word. When will you know if it will be up for review?"

Brent answered, "It'll take a few months, and I should be kept apprised of updates."

Tony offered his hand to Brent. "Thank you." He shook Brent's hand. "I apologize for delaying your departure, but I wanted Claire to hear it from you."

Courtney smiled enthusiastically. "That's all right; however, now we really need to go. I'm so glad this was good news." Reaching out for Claire's hand, she continued, "Now, you need some rest. Tony's right—you've had too many things thrown at you. Look how emotional you are."

Claire nodded. "We'll see you tomorrow night, and before then, I'll call you."

Tony grasped Claire's hand, and they walked back to the car. As he opened her door, he bent down and whispered, "A man of my word."

She smiled all the way to her emerald eyes and kissed his cheek. "Thank you, I really mean that."

Through the high beams of the Lexus' headlights, the country roads wound like a ribbon over hills and between open fields. Tony squeezed Claire's knee, bringing her back from wherever she had been. He'd been explaining the whole reinstatement process, yet she seemed a million miles away. Tony went on, "There are so many levels and so much bureaucracy that it takes longer than you would expect, but Brent thinks it can be resolved before the end of the year."

"That's a long time away. How long did it take to set him up?"

His neck stiffened. "I'd rather not talk about that."

"Why? I know you did it. You told Brent and Courtney you wanted to be honest. So, be honest."

He sat taller and momentarily refused to look her way. *Damn it, he was helping her brother-in-law—why did she need to bring this up? Fine, she wanted to know.* "From the time he turned down my job offer." He peered toward his passenger. There wasn't an outward sign or hint of emotion as Claire pressed her lips tight and watched the road before them. When she didn't respond, he asked, "You asked. Now you won't comment?"

"I don't know what to say. Do you want my bold and cheeky response or the reticent and genteel one?"

He gripped the steering wheel, fighting the urge to lower his right foot and drive the damn car the way it was designed to be driven. "This is why I haven't answered all of your questions. You may think you're ready for answers, but you're not. Bits and pieces may help you understand, but the blatant truth is too much."

His blood boiled as Claire sat silently during the rest of the ride, keeping her head turned toward the window. He wanted to be open, to be honest, but her reaction proved that it wasn't possible. *Would Claire ever be able to handle knowing the whole truth? Was he a fool for trying?* With each minute of silence, Tony felt Claire slip further and further away; he didn't know how to stop it. Her expression was one of indifference; he'd seen it before. The news about her brother-in-law was supposed to show her that he was trying. Instead, her resulting coolness beckoned his red. He berated himself for even attempting to make amends when their gap was obviously insurmountable.

When Tony pulled the car onto the brick circular drive in front of his house, Claire turned to him and placed her hand on top of his. Shocked by her soft touch, his dark gaze stared momentarily at the size difference of their hands as he tried to corral the red hue. Slowly, he moved his eyes to hers. The fire he expected was absent.

The soft emerald soothed as she said, "Thank you. Thank you for supporting me tonight with your friends. I was very nervous. It turned out much better than I could've possibly hoped... and thank you for helping John. I know you don't like him, and that you created his problems, but helping him now—it means a lot to me." She leaned in and lightly kissed his lips.

With one hand, Tony gripped the door handle; it was a means of keeping himself grounded. One minute, he was happily explaining the progress they'd made with John, the next, he was driving in silence belittling himself and Claire for trying to be open and honest, and now she'd kissed him and he wanted nothing more than to pry her from this car and take her on the damn driveway. The emotional roller coaster was too much. Tony had said he wanted fuck'n highs and lows. He just didn't want them all at once over the course of twenty minutes. "Claire, I'm trying to give you space, but I'm on the edge."

She leaned back and undid her seat belt. "I know you're trying, and I appreciate it."

She was halfway to the front door when he caught up and seized her arm. Stepping nearer, he whispered, "I'm very glad you're here."

Claire smiled and looked up at the house. "I'm surprised at how much I like being here. I was afraid the bad memories would overpower the good."

"Does that mean... the good overpower the bad?"

Claire shrugged. "I don't know. I wish I could say *yes*. You said you want honesty, and honestly, I don't know. They're both there. It's just that the familiarity of *here* is heartwarming."

He kissed the top of her head. "I need to go into the office tomorrow morning. I hope to be done and home by noon. The dessert celebration isn't until 8:00 PM. Would you like to go for a walk tomorrow?"

"A walk?" she asked.

He grinned at her change of tone. "Yes, Claire—to *your* lake?"

She smiled and nodded. "I-I'd like that very much."

He kissed the hand he'd secured. "Please allow me to escort you to your suite. I'll give you Courtney's number, and you may use the lock you requested. Actually," his eyes narrowed. "I suggest you do."

Boldly, she leaned into his chest. If only she knew how much he wanted to repeat the scene in Amber's condominium. Her face tipped upward as she purred, "You know, we never did this."

"This *what?*" He couldn't think straight.

"We never *dated*. I guess we did on two occasions, in Atlanta." Her smile didn't falter at the reference. "I like it."

Tony gently squeezed her hand, and they ascended the front steps. "We'd better get you behind a locked door, so I don't do anything to ruin this *date*." He emphasized the last word.

Claire smiled slyly. "Actually, according to a definition I recently heard, we need to be in public for this to be a date."

Bold and cheeky. Tony gave her hand another small squeeze.

Changes – June 2013
(Truth Chapters 44 & 46)

There is nothing more profound or of lasting consequence than the decision to have a child.
– Raymond Reddington, *The Blacklist*

T he visit to the lake was everything Tony hoped for and more. It wasn't that it hadn't occurred to him over the last year and a half to visit Claire's lake. It had. The thing was, he wasn't adept at finding his way through the wooded terrain. Tony could face a table of adversaries knowing that he would cut off their financial lifeline. He could study a stack of spreadsheets and instinctively know which companies could be saved and which ones should be closed… but walking through trees, climbing slopes, and ending at a pristine lakeshore was nowhere in his skill set.

Claire, on the other hand—Tony had total faith in her abilities. Once they reached the shore and she asked if he'd been there during her absence, his answer was heartfelt, "No, I'd be lost without you."

Can one statement be layered in sentiment? If so, it was. Tony would never have found the crystal clear lake with glistening waves without Claire. To be completely honest, he had no desire. Spending the afternoon sitting on the lakeshore, while deals and opportunities came and went at record speed, was not Anthony Rawlings' modus operandi. But sitting on a lake shore, enticing the *one woman* in the whole world, to recognize that skinny-dipping was exactly what they both needed—well, that was Tony Rawlings' MO, especially when it came to the woman named Claire (used-to-be Rawlings) Nichols.

Of course she didn't agree. *Why did he think there was a chance?* She was the same woman who pulled a sheet over her beautiful round breasts and projected modesty at every opportunity. She was the same woman who'd put him in his figurative place, more than once. Claire was the woman who spun his otherwise calm, predictable life out of control. Her refusal spurred his desire more than an acceptance ever would.

When they returned to the estate, Claire said she was tired, and before they went to the rehearsal dessert and wine celebration, she wanted to nap. Tony willingly agreed; after all, between traveling and nerves, she had every right to be tired. He mused that if she planned to fly to him every two weeks for their scheduled appearances, Claire needed to get used to the traveling. Maybe this would be the perfect stepping-stone to suggest she stay in Iowa. He'd emphasize that it was for her benefit, to make it less taxing.

They planned to eat dinner on the back patio before going to the celebration. In the past, it had been their practice that Tony would retrieve Claire from her suite for dinner and walk her to the dining room or patio; however, since they hadn't specifically said, Tony went to the patio and waited. With each passing minute, a voice from nowhere—one he tried to ignore—reminded him about his aversion to waiting. Each glance at his watch made the voice clamor louder about the consequences of tardiness. By most people's standards, Claire wasn't late; however, she most definitely wasn't on time. If Catherine hadn't reassured Tony that Claire was awake from her nap, he could assume that she was still asleep and go wake her as he'd done the day before.

When 7:00 PM came and went, Cindy asked, "Mr. Rawlings, would you like me to serve your meal?"

No. No, he wasn't eating alone. That was the point of having Claire on the estate. "Not yet, Cindy."

"Would you like me to check on Ms. Claire?"

Throwing his napkin on the table, he replied, "No, I'll go."

Each step toward her suite was a battle against the red. Claire wanted to be bold and cheeky, fine, but rules and expectations didn't change because she wanted to spout a daring retort. Tony made himself stop before opening her door. He inhaled and exhaled... and knocked. He waited, perhaps not long. When she didn't respond, he turned the handle. Scanning the suite, she was nowhere to be found. *Could she still be getting ready?* He called out her name and reached for the handle to the bathroom door. Suddenly, the cloud of displeasure that had grown in intensity dissipated into a storm of concern. Sitting on the edge of the whirlpool tub, wrapped in the pink robe, was *his Claire*, her complexion ashen, her face drenched in perspiration, and her body trembling. Tony fell to his knees as his mind went into overdrive. "What's the matter with you? Are you sick? I'll get you the best doctors..."

Instead of replying, Claire shook her head and bolted from the tub's edge. Tony was at a loss as he listened to Claire vomit within the confines of the small, attached room that contained the lavatory. *Did he go to her? Did he stay where he was? Did he call a doctor? Call Catherine?* While he debated, his mind searched for answers—that's what he did. Anthony Rawlings found answers. First, he needed to know what questions to ask. The first stop would be a doctor.

By the time Claire walked out of the small room, her petite frame had regained some semblance of normalcy. Tony stood silently, as Claire walked more steadily to the sink, rinsed her mouth, and then turned toward him and proclaimed, "Tony, I'm not sick."

He gently reached for her shoulders. "What do you mean? You're obviously ill. I'll call Brent. They'll understand."

"No, I want to go. I'll be better soon. It usually doesn't hit this hard in the afternoon. I think I'm just stressed."

"What doesn't hit...?" He studied Claire's green eyes. Along with her strength, color now returned to her once pale cheeks. The information was processing at record speed: her aversion to bacon at the restaurant, her ravenous hunger this afternoon, her frequent naps. Tony's tone unconsciously morphed from a concerned companion to a CEO in need of answers. "*What doesn't hit?*"

"The nausea."

Each word came slower and deeper than the last. "Brought. On. By. What?"

Tears cascaded down her cheeks as she replied, "I'm seven weeks pregnant, almost eight."

Pregnant? She was pregnant? Seven weeks? When was he in Palo Alto? How long ago was that afternoon in her condominium?

Before he could process, Claire went on, "Yes, Tony, *we* are going to have a baby."

Words weren't forming, only her words bounced through his brain. *We—a baby—mother—father.* This wasn't supposed to happen. She had that damn insert. Of course, that was years ago. He tried unsuccessfully to process. Finally, he asked, "How did this happen?"

The look she gave him momentarily stilled any further questions. "That's a great question, since I have no recollection of letting *you* back into *my* condominium, but nonetheless, the timing works perfectly."

He stared dumbfounded as he tried to make sense out of this new paradigm. "What are we going to do about..." he motioned toward her midsection, "...this?"

"I don't know what *we* are going to do. *I'm* going to have a baby, with or without you."

"But you're twenty-nine years old; I'm forty-eight!"

"Yes, and when we married, our age difference was the same."

"We never discussed children."

"It's a little late for discussion." The fire in her eyes was back and blazing bright. "Now, if you'll excuse me, I'll be downstairs in ten minutes for dinner, and we can continue *your charade*."

Tony shook his head. Shit! From the look on Claire's face, he'd totally screwed this up. Well, he had—literally and figuratively. Tony moved toward her and fought to sound understanding. "I'm sorry. You surprised me. Let me think about this for a while."

"Fine, Tony, you *think* all you want. Your thoughts and decisions don't matter. I'm having this baby."

"Of course you are. I never suggested otherwise." As the walls of the bathroom began to close in, he kissed her cheek, and explained, "I'll be downstairs on the patio," and backed away.

Once in the hallway, Tony stopped and inhaled the air-conditioned air. It took a minute or two, but slowly his lungs began to re-inflate. The walk from her suite to the patio was a blur. The next thing Tony knew, he was sitting on the patio, sipping iced water, and contemplating bourbon. Actually, he had some nice cognac in his office.

As the dust from Claire's bombshell began to settle, Tony searched the debris. *A baby. Him a father. Claire a mother. He didn't have a clue how to be a father. Did she know how to be a mother? How do you learn that? Experience? Books? The Internet? Could he do it? What about his age? Shit—the kid would be eighteen and he'd be sixty-six!*

Each thought and question came with the memory of Claire's expression as she shared their secret: the tears rolling down her cheeks, the need in her emerald eyes. Her expression wasn't exactly as he'd remembered it from years ago when she so desperately sought his approval. The look, moments ago, asked for something much simpler: it requested understanding, and in typical Anthony Rawlings fashion, he'd been an ass. Then again, she could've found a better way to tell him than making him believe that she was dying of some unknown disease.

Tony had forgotten how worried he was about her only minutes ago. At that time, he was ready to fly her to the edges of the earth if that was where she'd find the best medical care, and now, now he knew that she wasn't dying. No, she's having a baby. *That was better—right?*

When Claire stepped onto the patio, Tony attentively stood and pulled out her chair. She radiated beauty. Outwardly, it appeared as though their little conversation upstairs had never occurred. He assessed her complexion as he sat and thought how their day at the shore had done her skin tone some good: her cheeks had a nice rosy glow. Still scanning, the neckline of her dress and her blossoming cleavage distracted his thoughts. Without a doubt, her breasts appeared larger. *Did pregnancy do that?* Hell, he needed to do research. Tony hated not having answers.

With all sincerity, he asked, "How are you feeling?"

Genteel and reticent, she responded, "I'm feeling better. Thank you for asking."

After Cindy brought them their meals, Tony asked, "Have you had many bouts like what just happened?"

Her emerald eyes peered at him from beneath thick lashes. "I do like this dress. It's one from the closet. Thank you for having it purchased."

Each of Tony's attempts to discuss the pregnancy was met with a dutiful response; however, she wasn't providing answers, simply conversation. He received her message loud and clear: she was upset and he'd screwed up. It was a message meant solely for him: no one else would have known—not his staff as they brought their meal and not their friends at the dessert celebration. Claire performed perfectly, staying dutifully by his side. To everyone, they appeared the happy couple trying for reconciliation. He did see a genuine smile when he asked the waiter for two glasses of nonalcoholic champagne. It was the most disgusting bubbly grape juice that Tony had ever tasted. If pregnant women were supposed to drink shit like that—well, no wonder they felt ill.

Throughout dinner and the celebration, Tony tried to think of a way to apologize, to help her understand that his initial reaction was not because he didn't want her to have the baby. It was shock. His mind went back to another apology years ago.

Claire hadn't wanted to go with him. Never, since she'd first been brought to the estate, had he seen her react as vehemently and violently as she did that afternoon. All Tony had wanted to do was to get her away from the estate. It had been almost two months since she'd gone anywhere. Nevertheless, when he led her past the front doors and she saw the car waiting, Claire lost it. Right there on his front steps, she broke down in a fit of hysteria. Tony had never seen anything like it. For over a month she'd been calm and accommodating—too calm. That afternoon, all of her emotions bubbled over. She spewed hateful things as she fell to the ground, refusing to budge. He recalled the daggers in her no longer calm green eyes as she told him that she hated him.

It had been Catherine who'd whispered and explained to let her go. In all the time since her accident, she'd not broken down. Catherine explained that it was part of the healing process.

That day Tony knew Claire needed more than a release. She needed— no, she deserved—to hear his honest apology.

The circumstances were totally different, but as they left the dessert celebration, Claire needed the same things from Tony as she had that cold afternoon. Driving through the night, he peered to his right, trying to assess if Claire noticed that they weren't headed home. His glance confirmed what he'd seen all evening: the perfect companion. Even when they detoured down a dirt road, Claire appeared unaware. Tony stopped the car and allowed the headlights to shine into the meadow. It was *their* meadow, the place where he'd apologized for her *accident*, for losing control, and the place where he'd asked for her forgiveness. That day had brought the spark back to Claire's dead eyes.

Tony had pushed away the memories of the month following Claire's accident. Though she obeyed, or more accurately, acquiesced to everything, she was a walking shell. Tony refused to allow this baby or his reaction to take her back to that place. He didn't want the *perfect companion*. Tony wanted Claire—her fire, her brazen spunk, and even her bold retorts. If she needed to yell at him, so be it. If she needed his apology, he'd give it.

When she didn't speak, he asked, "Do you know where we are?"

Claire looked from side to side. "No, I don't."

He got out of the car and walked to her door. After opening it, he extended his hand and asked, "Will you please walk with me a moment?"

Her glance diverted to the floorboard. "I don't think my shoes were meant for—"

"I don't give a damn about the shoes." His polite invitation gave way to the emotions he'd kept suppressed all evening.

Claire nonchalantly shrugged and accepted his outstretched hand. Her facade was once again secure as she replied, "Of course, Mr. Rawlings, I'd be delighted."

They took a few steps before Claire stumbled and fell into his arms. He wanted to hold her forever, in the moonlight, under the stars, enjoying the perfect June evening. While he prayed that she'd understand his intentions, she straightened herself and stood on her own.

"Have you figured out where we are?" he asked.

"I really don't know."

"This is where I brought you the day I apologized for your accident."

Claire's back straightened, and her chin rose indignantly.

He added, "I meant every word that day."

"Tony, I don't want to talk about—"

"I've done some things in my life that I'm not proud of. I never in all of my life considered having a child." He had her full attention and continued, "I can run businesses, make deals, and multitask better than most." His volume increased. "Nothing frightens me. I can take on an entire board of directors and know that tomorrow they'll all be jobless. I have eliminated adversaries and obstacles." He silently pleaded with her. "This is totally new territory."

Her facade melted. "I know and it scares me, too."

Was he scared? He was. The memories of this meadow and his last apology brought back other memories, times that he'd seen fear in her eyes. "Do I?" He needed to know. *Did he scare her? Could they overcome the past and raise a child? Did she even want to?* Waiting, he held his breath.

Finally, she replied, "I'm afraid of what you're capable of doing. You made a point of showing me your control over my friends' futures." She reached for his hand. "But of you *personally*? Not anymore. There was a time, but I've changed and you've changed. No, I'm not."

There was hope in her answer, real hope. While Tony reeled with this new reality of his world spinning out of control, he reached for that small flicker. Though more than he deserved, it was there. "I don't want you and this baby living in California."

"I know, but, Tony, I can't go back to the past."

"To here?"

"No, I love *here*. I won't go back to your supreme control over my every move. I can't and I won't allow that kind of life for our child."

"*Our* child," he repeated, as he gently touched her midsection. Those words would unite them forever. He wouldn't allow her to be thousands of miles away—not with *their* child.

Claire nodded with a new gleam to her moonlit eyes. "I went to the doctor on Wednesday. She did an ultrasound. I saw the image of our baby and his heart beating. The sound of his heart reminded me of my lake— here. From that moment on, everything felt right."

"You keep saying *him*?" His cheeks rose. *A boy? Could Claire know this soon?*

She mused, "I have no idea of the baby's gender. *Him* sounds better than *it*, don't you think?"

"You know," he continued, trying to be honest, "you're very good at pretending. I knew it before, but tonight you were perfect at every turn. I felt your anger, yet you appeared perfect. How do I really know how you feel?"

"How do I know how *you* feel? Or that you won't do something to me like you did before, with the attempted murder?"

He closed his eyes and lowered his lips to the top of her head. "I guess we need to trust one another."

"Can we do that?" Claire asked.

"I don't know," he answered honestly.

He pondered her question as he took her hand and helped her back to the car. *Could they? Could they trust?* This wasn't the time to remind Claire that she'd been the one to leave him, the one to fail the test and sever that trust.

On the ride home, Tony asked questions and Claire answered. No one else knew about the pregnancy. She'd wanted to see Tony and decide what to do, which from the moment she saw the ultrasound, Claire knew that *not having* the baby wasn't an option. She told him about the sickness, what she'd thought was food poisoning, and the bacon. He asked when she suspected. Had she known when he was in California?

"Sunday, less than a week ago, was when I first started questioning. I did a home pregnancy test, and on Wednesday I went to the doctor."

Today was Friday. It had all happened so recently. In less than a week, both of their worlds spun into a new orbit. The little life inside of her would change them forever. When they entered the estate, Claire said good-night to Tony at the bottom of the stairs. Holding tightly to her hand, he replied, "I'd like to join you, just to talk."

"Not tonight." She smiled sweetly. "I've got a lot to think about."

He didn't argue; he, too, had much to ponder.

After he watched her disappear up the stairs and down the corridor, Tony went to his office to check his messages. With everything that happened, he hadn't checked his phone since before dinner. Peering at the screen, he touched a missed text message from Phillip Roach. The words were a punch to his gut, pushing the air from his lungs:

"MS. NICHOLS' APARTMENT WAS BROKEN INTO EARLIER TODAY. NO ONE WAS HOME. IT APPEARS ONLY HER BEDROOM WAS RANSACKED. I'LL SEND MORE INFORMATION AS SOON AS I CAN."

Twelve

It's a new game, with new rules – June 2013
(Truth – Chapter 47)

The reality of the other person lies not in what he reveals to you, but what he cannot reveal to you. Therefore, if you would understand him, listen not to what he says, but rather to what he does not say.
– Kahlil Gibran

Tony woke early with his new reality running laps through his brain. Claire was pregnant—with his child. How it happened, or even why, was no longer worth his consideration. Where to go from here was what he needed to decide. He'd wanted to convince Claire that being in his life was where she needed to be. This baby changed the game: he or she was forcing moves that neither Claire nor Tony had imagined making this soon.

Tony wasn't sure how to convince Claire, but he'd been dead serious when he said that he didn't want her and the baby living in California. When it was just Claire, he was willing to wait and let her come to that realization; however, that was no longer the case. The baby may be residing within Claire, but it was half his. In Tony's opinion, that gave him the edge he needed in his negotiation.

As the morning progressed, though he didn't want to wake her, he desperately wanted to be near her. Between his workout, shower, and reviewing a few proposals, he'd already accomplished more than most people do in a day. However, if he had his way, his morning would have been spent showing his ex-wife just how much he wanted her around. From someplace deep, a place where he'd suppressed the memories of them, Tony recalled mornings spent watching her sleep and times when his desires would not allow him to let her sleep. He also remembered mornings he'd slipped from their bed with nothing more than a brief kiss to her hair. Suddenly, he regretted those days—days that his work seemed more important than her.

Time was a stubborn bastard. No matter how much money or influence Anthony Rawlings possessed, he couldn't change time or turn it back. What he could do was promise that the future would be different. He glanced inside of his desk drawer. For the first time since his dream, the envelope made him smile. For the first time, Tony had hope, genuine hope—that his envelope would not remain empty. He'd never considered filling it with more than Claire, but now—now there was also a child. Tony wasn't sure why God thought he deserved this opportunity. He wasn't questioning; instead he wanted to prove—to Nathaniel, to a higher being, to Claire and to his child that he would succeed.

Failure had never been an option and this was no exception. The difference that tugged at his heart was the knowledge that he would never succeed on his own.

Alone, he'd accomplished great things throughout his life. This was different. The realization created an unfamiliar sense of vulnerability. To not fail, to succeed, Tony needed Claire. He needed her help and her guidance. He'd never be able to parent without her. Hell, he wouldn't have a clue. To make this work, it would take both of them. It was no longer a matter of him having the answers to her requests and questions—this was a whole different world. Suddenly, he had questions and she had answers. The realization left him uneasy.

Tony decided to concentrate on the present. For the time being—if only the next two days—Tony would enjoy having Claire with him. He would work to show her that Iowa, more specifically their estate, was where she belonged. At a little before 7:00 AM, he sent her a text:

"IF YOU ARE FEELING UP TO BREAKFAST, MEET ME ON THE PATIO AT 8:00 AM."

After he hit *SEND*, Tony suddenly worried. He'd been thinking the fresh air would be good for her, but what if she was ill? She'd told him about the morning sickness. He didn't want her to be concerned about rushing down to breakfast, if she wasn't feeling up to it. Apparently, time wasn't the only thing he couldn't take back—he couldn't retrieve a text once it was sent, either. He called the kitchen and informed them of his plans, and that Ms. Claire *may* be joining him.

As soon as Tony saw Claire through the French doors, he remembered her new aversion to coffee, moved his cup away, and greeted her, "Good morning. I wasn't sure you would wake for my text."

"Good morning." Her smile made his cheeks rise. "I did."

Before he could say another word—tell her how amazing she looked or how he wanted to keep her captive forever—Cindy was by her side, offering her coffee or tea and discussing food. Damn, he needed less attentive staff. As she spoke, he assessed her complexion. To him she was beautiful. When they were finally alone, he asked, "How are you feeling this morning?"

"I'm feeling well, which is surprising, considering how early this is in California."

"I think you're getting used to being in Iowa. It probably isn't a great idea to keep changing time zones. Maybe you should stay here."

Smirking, she replied, "I don't think that would resolve any of my current issues."

"Oh, but you're mistaken. It would be ever so helpful." Tony reached for the bowl of fresh fruit. "Would you like some fruit?"

After Claire spooned some fresh melon and grapes into her bowl, she asked, "Why did you summon me here so early?"

He reached for her hand. "Claire, why do you think everything has double meaning?"

She swallowed her fruit. With her beautiful emerald eyes glowing, she answered, "Because I know you."

He laughed. "Better than most."

"What's your plan?"

"I wanted to discuss the day. I plan to work from home this morning and was hoping we could spend time together before the wedding."

"I told Sue that I might be available to meet her and Sean this morning in Iowa City. I think I'd like that."

The playful banter came to a screeching halt. She wanted to leave the estate, to drive away. The last time... Tony didn't want to go there in his mind. He didn't want to remember the last time—the *only* time—Claire had driven off of the estate. Finding an acceptable concession, he replied, "Eric can drive you."

"I was thinking that perhaps you have a car—one that isn't worth half a million—that you'd let me borrow for a quick drive into town?"

His thoughts battled with one another as their new reality fought with their old. Tony had always prided himself on his ability to maintain a poker face during stressful negotiations. However, when he looked at his ex-wife, the gleam in her eyes and smug smile on her face, Tony knew that she was reading his every thought. She truly knew him like no other. With a smirk, he asked, "Are you enjoying yourself?"

Claire grinned. "Immensely, thanks for asking."

"The last time you drove away—"

"This time I'm talking to you about it," she interrupted. "I want to meet Sue for coffee. I'll return and then you and I will go to the wedding together."

"I thought coffee made you ill?"

Claire shrugged. "Coffee is an expression for getting together. I can guarantee that I will *not* be having coffee."

"Getting together? About what?" Just days ago, Sue didn't want Claire near her child. Now they were going to meet for coffee? It didn't make sense.

Claire's shoulders straightened and she leaned across the table. Tony's gaze struggled to find her fiery eyes instead of concentrating on the way her robe gaped open, giving him a great view of her cleavage. Her hushed but determined tone refocused his view as well as his thoughts. "This is what I don't want."

"Concern, Claire, that's what I have. After all, someone broke into your condominium last night. Don't you think you should be concerned?"

After Claire thanked Cindy for her food, she returned her attention to Tony. "How do you know about that?"

"So you aren't surprised?"

"No. I spoke to others about it last night, and I suppose I'm not surprised you know."

"Others?"

"Yes, Tony—friends. Harry called. I spoke to him and then to Amber. They're both well, *thank you for asking*."

All right, so he'd never given them any thought. *Why would he?* Roach had said it happened when Amber wasn't home. That still didn't explain her indifference: this was serious. "Why aren't you more upset?"

"I was initially, but now I think you're responsible."

It was his turn to respond with indignation. "Claire, why would *I* have someone break into *your* condo?"

"I don't know, but whoever it was took my laptop. The only secret information on there is about you." Claire continued to eat.

Tony sat his cup of coffee on the table. "Me?"

"Yes, I've been trying to reconstruct the information from the box I received. I've spent a lot of time looking up information about your grandfather and father. It's on my laptop." She spoke as though she'd just told him that she had recipes on her hard drive, not secrets he'd worked diligently to keep buried.

"I have nothing to do with this break-in," Tony said. "I do, however, think you should consider staying here. It is significantly safer."

"Well, Tony, I'm being honest with you. That laptop contains information regarding Nathaniel and Samuel Rawls. If you aren't the person responsible for its disappearance, then perhaps you'd like to learn who has it."

"I'll do my best. This is getting out of hand."

"Well, back to my original question: do you have a car I can take into town for coffee with Sue? I need to call her."

First, her damn detective work and now her brazen pursuit of a subject he didn't want to broach. Tony leaned forward. "Claire, are you asking? I'm having difficulty with your wording."

"Are we in the presence of others?" She dramatically turned from her right to her left and lowered her tone. "No, I'm not asking permission to go into town, only permission to use one of your cars. I would hate to be accused of stealing."

He pressed his lips together. "Claire, that's ridiculous, I'd never accuse you of stealing—"

"No, just attempted murder," she interrupted. "I'd rather avoid repeating *that* history."

The muscles in his neck tightened. "Claire..."

She didn't miss a beat. "Tony, it happened. I told you that I'm not going back. I'm not going to a time and place of unapproachable subjects or closed conversations. If you want this charade to continue, and if it has a snowball's chance in hell of being something more, you'll be open and honest."

Closing his eyes, he took a deep breath. "Please, by all means, take whichever car you'd like. If you plan on driving yourself, I recommend you avoid the limousine and the Lexus LFA." He watched as she slowly shook her head. "Not because of their price, I don't give a damn about that; however, they require a little more behind-the-wheel experience."

"Thank you, I hardly want to drive a limousine by myself or your Batmobile—a simple car will do."

"Batmobile?" His brows arched. Claire giggled and the tension eased from his shoulders. Giving her everything she rightfully deserved and desired wouldn't be easy. It would be a continued battle, but somehow they'd stopped this conversation from becoming a total disaster.

"That was what I thought it looked like when I first saw it."

"Hmmm," he mused. "If my memory serves me right, that would make you Catwoman, and if you're willing to try on the suit," he said slyly, raising his brow, "then I'll wear a cape?"

Claire shook her head. "I will take that as a *yes,* on borrowing a car?"

Tony shrugged. "Should I call my personal shopper for some pointed ears?"

Her expression turned quizzical. "Only if Batman wore pointed ears."

His laugh reverberated over the expanse of their back yard.

During Tony's unpleasant conversation with Mr. George, he glanced at the clock. The wedding wasn't until 5:30 PM and it wasn't even noon. Nevertheless, he had no idea when Claire would return. After he'd told Catherine where she'd gone, Catherine recommended sending Eric to watch her and be sure of her return. Tony refused. Obviously, Claire would recognize Eric and know who sent him. No. Tony decided he would do what they'd promised: he would trust in her return.

Mr. George's broken phrases came through Tony's phone. "I'm sorry." "She was supposed to let me know." "I've tried."

Tony was done with the conversation. "As you know, my original directive was two days ago. I wanted an answer yesterday. Your incompetence is…" Tony's speech stalled. A knock and simultaneous opening of his office door caused him to turn. He expected to see Catherine and glared at the interruption. That quickly changed to shock, when he saw that Claire was the one who'd entered. There was a time when she was not allowed to enter his office without his permission. Obviously, Claire was now playing by her own rules. He stifled the chuckle that threatened Mr. George's verbal lashing. Unable to contain the grin, Tony kept his gaze fixed on his ex-wife and continued his tirade. "It seems as though another pressing matter has come to my attention. We will postpone this conversation. Mr. George, I expect to hear from you Monday morning. Do *not* disappoint me." Tony disconnected the line.

Claire smiled as he walked around his desk. With each step, he assessed the woman before him. Having her return—as she'd said she would—propelled his senses to an unexpected high.

"That should be your tagline." Claire said as he stopped mere inches away.

"Oh, but you are so right. I don't like being disappointed."

"I remember that about you." She hesitated. He said a silent prayer that Claire would lean forward—press toward him—and he'd feel her warmth against his chest. Maintaining their distance, Claire continued, "Your car has been returned in one piece, scarcely a scratch."

The tips of his lips twitched, and his eyebrow cocked. "A scratch?"

Claire's grin broadened. "Wasn't that your concern, that I might scratch it?"

Tony took the initiative and closed the gap. *Was it her erratic heartbeat that he felt or his own?* "I don't recall being concerned with a scratch. The whole damn car can be replaced. I believe my concern was with your safe return." His willpower was suddenly spent. Wanting Claire closer, he wrapped his arm around the small of her back and pulled her against him as he cupped her chin, maintaining his gaze of her sparkling emerald eyes.

Her words slowed with breathy expectation. "I have returned."

"You, my dear, are continually teaching me new things."

"What, pray tell, have *I* taught *you*?"

His lips tenderly brushed hers. "I believe I mentioned before that I liked the black panties. The other night, the light blue satin bra strap monopolized my thoughts. Every time I looked at you, I wondered if it was part of a matching set." Claire nodded, their noses brushing one another's with the movement. "And just now, I realized how much more satisfying it is to have you bring yourself home, freely, willingly, than to know you have been driven—perhaps reluctantly."

"It seems..." Claire giggled. "...you *can* teach an old dog new tricks."

His hearty laugh rumbled from his chest.

She went on, "And as I recall, you've taught me quite a few things, too."

"I had been thinking about the pool, but I'm up for review if you're willing?" By Claire's expression, she knew he was speaking literally. No other woman in the world could take him from angst on the phone to the edge of ecstasy in such a short time. *Would she allow it?*

Her hands reached up to his hair as her eyes opened wide. He pulled her closer, pressing his hips to hers and flattening her growing breasts. They fit together perfectly. When their lips connected, the room around them disappeared. Tony no longer cared about Mr. George or Sophia. Rawlings Industries could crash and his estate could burn. Tony didn't care. What he wanted was in his arms, after returning completely on her own. He needed more. When she parted her lips, his tongue plunged deeper, tasting her sweetness and feeling her warmth.

He bent down, touching his nose to hers and asked, "Are you sure?"

"Yes. I'm sure."

Tony didn't ask again as he bent slightly and scooped Claire into his arms. He carried her away from the office, past the grand staircase, and down the corridor to his room. With each step, he fantasized about the woman in his arms. Once they arrived, he laid Claire on his bed and slowly, reverently, began to remove her clothes. With each item, their eyes met. The sultry gaze he saw was one that he hoped he was mirroring. Today, she wore pink underwear, matching the color of her top. He slowly removed the lace bra, freeing her beautiful breasts. There was no doubt they were growing, and by the way her nipples hardened and her back arched, they were ultrasensitive to his touch. As he suckled the pink nubs and she called out his name, Tony's slacks grew uncomfortably tight. The small bow below her bellybutton again reminded him of a present—never had anything been wrapped so beautifully or presented so perfectly.

He wanted to reconnect in a way like never before. He longed to feel her hugging him, surrounding him, and responding to him, but before they made love, he needed to be confident that she was with him willingly. As he was about to ask again, Claire called out, removing all doubt and breaking all barriers. "Oh, please, Tony, I need you."

Midday turned to early afternoon as they reached new heights and took their reunification to the next level. With his sheet covering them and the sun streaming through the uncovered window, Claire nestled her head on his shoulder and asked, "Do you think we could have lunch at the pool and enjoy some of this day outside?"

He turned to her with a grin. *Could her preoccupation with food also include an appetite for sex?* Both seemed somewhat insatiable, not that he was complaining. With a sultry tone, he replied, "I'd like to stay here forever, but I like the idea of getting you more sun."

Her lips found his neck and began to roam, and between suckles, she said, "At this second, I wouldn't argue with staying here." A low growl rumbled from his throat as she continued, "But I'm hungry, and that sky looks beautiful."

He rolled her onto her back. As her long, brown hair fanned the pillow, he studied her glowing pink cheeks and swollen red lips. "Not as beautiful as you look this moment." He nuzzled her collar bone and moved south.

"Mr. Rawlings, I believe we were discussing lunch?"

It amused him how she continually worked food into the conversation. With a sigh, he stopped his descent, allowing her to sit up. It was then she stammered, "T-Tony, h-how long have you had that there?"

He followed her astonished gaze. It was her wedding portrait. He hadn't even considered its presence when he brought her to his room. Sheepishly, he replied, "Ever since you left."

"But why?"

Tony took her hands and cupped them in his own. "You said no more closed conversations. I'm not closing it, but understand, I can't answer you—*I don't know*. Despite being angry with you, I do know that I've spent the last year and a half staring at you every night before I went to sleep." Before she could respond, Tony gently kissed her lips and added, "For now, will you please let that be enough of an answer?"

With tears glistening in her stunning eyes, Claire nodded.

Thirteen

I hoped you'd consider yourself home – June 2013
(Truth – Chapters 48 & 49)

Where we love is home—home that our feet may leave, but not our hearts.
– Oliver Wendell Holmes

Tony was pleased that Courtney had facilitated the get-together at Sue and Tim's house. It truly helped to ease Claire's anxiety at being with everyone. The atmosphere at the wedding and reception was festive and friendly. It seemed as though all of the discomfort of Thursday night was a distant memory. From the ceremony, where Claire held tightly to his hand, to the reception where they moved fluidly as one across the dance floor, Tony enjoyed every minute.

Tony had promised Courtney increased security and delivered. No one advertently singled Tony and Claire out of the crowd, yet from time to time from the corner of his eye, Tony saw a cell phone or two pointed their direction. He didn't mind—the way he saw it, maybe Baldwin would see the pictures and realize that what he and Claire were experiencing wasn't purely for show. Even Claire admitted as much while they danced.

As the guests began to thin out, Tony suggested they head back to the estate. Although she looked disappointed to leave their friends, Claire didn't argue. She truly had the reticent and genteel in the presence of others down pat. Tony hoped that they'd all be together again soon. The day—no, the entire weekend—had exceeded his expectations. The only flaw that ate away at him was the break-in at Claire's condominium.

During the reception, Tony had received an email:

To: Anthony Rawlings
From: Phillip Roach
Subject: Ms. Nichols
Date: June 8, 2013

I've confirmed with security at Ms. Nichols' condominium: her unit was indeed breached. It wasn't until the perpetrator was leaving her unit that security devices indicated a violation. Until Ms. Nichols can confirm that the only item taken was her laptop, it is safe to assume, since her room was the only one disturbed, she was the intended target.

According to the records of my indicators, the front door to her condo was opened Friday, June 7, at 20:15. The violation was noted when the door once again opened at 20:27. Security cameras did not show a clear picture of the person in question. It appears to be a man who's bald or balding. I will increase my surveillance and report any suspicious activity.

Please confirm the time and place of Ms. Nichols' arrival. I know her reservations have been changed. I will look for the new times and places.

Thank you.

Tony didn't mention it during the festivities, but once they were alone in the car, he wanted to know more about the contents of her computer. "Have you spoken to anyone from Palo Alto lately?"

"I haven't even looked at my phone since we left for the wedding. Why? Has something else happened?"

"Not to my knowledge; however, my source tells me that the intruder to your unit was not interrupted. His only intention was to access *your* room and take your laptop."

Tony watched from his peripheral vision as Claire contemplated his words. Finally, she asked, "Why would anyone want *my* laptop?"

"What was on it?"

"I don't know... my bank accounts, my travel itinerary..."

Tony was immediately glad he'd cancelled her flight. He didn't want this intruder knowing Claire's plans. He refocused as she continued. "...information about your past, and a rough draft from Meredith about her boo—articles."

He gripped the steering wheel trying to temper his tone. "I thought this stupid Meredith Banks thing was over?"

"It is," she replied. "With the money you gave me to give her, she'll keep it quiet, unless, as you and I agreed, something happens to me or someone I care about."

He tried to process the contents. "What do you have regarding my past?"

Fidgeting against the leather seat, she answered, "Seriously, I've spent so much time on this; it's hard to condense it into an elevator pitch."

"Give it a try," his tone dripped with sarcasm. "I'm sure you can do it."

Claire inhaled. "Fine. I confirmed Nathaniel and Sharron Rawls had a son named Samuel. He married a woman named Amanda; they had a son named Anton, born February 12, 1965—the same day as you. That, plus a picture in Newsweek showing your grandfather's home confirmed to me that you were indeed Anton."

"Well, you know that's true. Why are you continuing this research?"

"I really don't want to discuss this... please?"

"Despite your suspicions, I had nothing to do with the break-in. I need to know what the perpetrator now knows."

"My computer is password-protected. No one besides me can access it."

He didn't speak, but looked at her, questioning her secure laptop. He assumed it was password protected with PASSWORD123 or her birth date—some fail-safe, impenetrable barrier.

Eventually, she said, "Obviously you disagree. If someone is able to access my information, they'd see documents and reports from your parents' death."

No longer was peripheral vision enough; Tony turned to stare incredulously at his ex-wife. "What possible business of *yours* is my parents' death?"

"I suppose that before, it was morbid curiosity. I wanted to know if you were truly capable of hurting your own parents. Now, however..." She hesitated and sat straighter, defiantly. "...now, it is very much my business. I need to know about *my* child's family history."

He exhaled, releasing some of the stress upon the leather wheel. "I suppose that's true." He paused. "I didn't harm my parents."

Claire reached out and covered Tony's hand, a simple touch that reassured him more than words. "I know that now. I've known for a while. It wasn't you—it was the woman in a blue Honda."

His newfound calm disappeared. Before he could process, Claire continued. "Whoever that woman is, you've been protecting her for years."

"Protecting her?"

"Yes, whoever she is, you've kept her secret secure."

Tony struggled with Claire's knowledge. *How could she have learned about Catherine's car?* That information, as well as eyewitness accounts, had been disposed of years ago. *Could he now tell her the truth?* After all, Catherine had opened his secret world when she mailed that damn box. Should he return the favor? First and foremost, he needed to get her laptop back and discover who took it. "So all of this is on your laptop?"

Claire nodded. "Yes."

He contemplated her return flight. No doubt she'd be upset that he'd cancelled her flight; perhaps he could make her think it was her idea. "I want you to seriously reconsider your return to California. The estate is much safer and more secure than a condominium that has already been broken into."

Her petite hand once again made contact. Reaching for his knee, she explained, "I've had a wonderful time. Please don't ruin it. Let's just take all of this one day at a time? I'd like to think about tonight now and tomorrow later."

Tony didn't argue. It wouldn't matter; she no longer had a seat on the commercial flight. When they reached the estate, Tony opened Claire's door and took her hand. She'd said she wanted to concentrate on tonight. So did he. Even without the airline ticket, Tony doubted he'd be able to convince her to stay an extra night, week, or month—that left tonight. Gazing into her emerald eyes, he touched his lips to the top of the hand resting within his. Silently, they walked hand in hand into the house. At the base of the grand staircase, Tony whispered, "I suppose this is good-night?"

She stretched her toes allowing her lips to linger on his. When she pulled away, she suckled his neck, just above his perfectly starched collar. Tony's grasp of her small waist tightened as he pulled her hips toward his and a low groan escaped his clenched teeth. "That's up to you," Claire purred. "I don't plan on using that lock."

With their fingers entwined, they made their way toward her suite. He wanted what was beyond that door, what they'd done in that room hundreds of times. However, if he didn't tell her about the ticket, was that lying? He began to confess, "There's more for us to discuss—"

Claire's finger reached out and covered his mouth. He pressed his lips together and watched as desire and determination swirled before him, creating a beautiful, blazing emerald fire. It wasn't sparked by anger, but yearning. He'd seen it before and knew it was being reciprocated in his gaze. Slowly, below her touch, the tips of his lips moved upward. She whispered, "Tonight is about us, no charade, nonperformance. If you want something different, go downstairs."

She wanted control; he'd allow some. They wouldn't discuss her return flight, her computer, or his history. Instead, they'd continue their reunification within the walls of their shared history. It was a room that contained memories—both good and bad—of domination and consent, and of lust and love.

Love? Tony couldn't believe it was real, yet it was. He'd never wanted love. *Why would he?* He wasn't even sure it existed, until her—the woman once again willingly beneath him. Their roles were redefined: Tony no longer desired domination, and Claire wasn't submitting. She was an active, willing participant, capable of accommodating his needs as well as voicing her own. Her beautiful eyes saw into his soul, and her petite body dominated his thoughts. Despite all of his mistakes and manipulation, Tony was once again where he longed to be.

He knew it wouldn't be easy. Each moment was an internal battle. Instinctively, he wanted to control Claire and limit her access to his past and his heart; however, Tony knew it was too late. She'd already managed to unearth emotions he never knew existed, and now they had a child coming. Despite his power slipping through his fingers, when Claire opened her eyes and Tony saw the shimmering emerald irises glow and her lips form a smile—he no longer cared. Within the copper walls and satin drapes of Claire's suite, it was only the two of them—and that was all they needed.

The next morning when Tony woke, he didn't slip from bed as he'd done in the past. He lingered, enjoying the warmth of Claire's body against his side, the sweet smell of perfume that whiffed from her hair, and the soft tickle of her breaths across his chest. Everything within him wanted to wake her and repeat last night's activities; however, the entire weekend had gone too well. He didn't want to push her any further than she was willing to go. With their relationship still undefined, Tony forced himself from her bed.

Once within his office, it didn't take long for the knock and opening of the door. Catherine entered silently, not waiting for an invitation. "Tell me, how was the wedding? You haven't said much of anything since she arrived."

Tony ran his hand through his hair. He didn't want to share any of the weekend with anyone except Claire. Exhaling, he opted to pacify. "The wedding was nice. What more do you want?"

"I don't know, perhaps how she was received? How she did? I've seen pictures from the wedding on the Internet. Did you know they were being taken?"

He shrugged. "I saw some people snapping pictures, and I don't care. It's time people see her with me and not him."

Catherine sat, perched forward on the edge of the chair. "Anton-thony, are you positive this is what you want? I mean, she was unsure at first. What if she leaves and doesn't come back?"

Tony shook his head. "She won't. She left to go out with Sue and came back."

"So, you trust her to leave today and return?"

He exhaled. "I think I've answered that."

Catherine lowered her gray gaze. Peering upward she proclaimed, "I'm proud of you."

His brow arched. "Why?"

"I wasn't sure you'd be able to forgive her after everything she did, but once again, you've proved me wrong."

"It's more complicated than you know—and I want it to work."

She patted his hand. "I can tell you do. Of course it's complicated—she's a Nichols."

Tony glared. "We agreed that was done."

"Yes, of course, it was. It is," she corrected. "That doesn't change her last name. Certainly that'll always be in the back of your mind. Is that why it's complicated?"

"Believe it or not, it isn't and it won't be. If I have my way, her last name will be *Rawlings* again one day, hopefully sooner rather than later."

"Don't get me wrong, I'm happy to see you happy, but you know as well as I that she can never share your real name. Besides, aren't you rushing things?"

"She can and she did. Rawls is gone. I've resigned myself to that and you need to also. My name is Rawlings and she'll have that name again."

"You seem very sure of yourself. So why is it so complicated?"

Tony debated his answer. "Do you remember me telling you that Claire had been doing some detective work?"

Catherine nodded.

"Well, she knows about the blue Honda."

Catherine gasped, "That's impossible—how?"

"I don't know, but she knows that there was a woman."

"And...?" she probed.

"If she knows your identity, she hasn't shared."

Catherine ran her hands up and down her thighs rubbing the smooth fabric of her slacks. "How is that even possible?"

"You started it with your delivery. I'm not going to tell her, but if she learns, you only have yourself to blame."

"B-but that's not true. I didn't send any information to lead her in that direction. It was all meant as a way for her to understand *you*." Catherine stared pleadingly. "And it's worked. Look how well it's worked."

"I'm not going to debate your motive or even the outcome. You know as well as I that it could have gone much differently. Claire isn't the problem; it's that her laptop has been stolen and is in the hands of some burglar who now has access to our family history."

Catherine paced the length of his desk. "What are you going to do?"

"Anything I can," his baritone voice hardened. "I will get that damn laptop back and find out who stole it and why."

"Do you think Claire knows?"

He leaned forward. "Catherine, she knows that my parents were killed. She said she believed me that I wasn't responsible, that it was a woman in a blue Honda. If anything, she sounded more sympathetic than judgmental."

Catherine's shoulders straightened as she hummed through tightly pursed lips.

This was why Tony didn't want to have this discussion. Whenever his parents were mentioned, even after all of these years, Catherine's stance hardened. "It is time to let it go," he reminded her.

"You're telling me that Claire is on the verge of learning information that could land us both in prison, and I should feel good about it?"

"I'm telling you that I won't tell her. It's a secret we've kept this long, and I believe if she ever does learn the truth, she's trustworthy."

"I hope you're right. Please find that laptop."

Tony nodded. "I have people working on it. Now, if you don't mind." He gestured toward the door.

"It's good to see you happy. I hope she doesn't disappoint you—again."

As Catherine left the office and closed the door, Tony contemplated her comment. He didn't want to be disappointed; however, more than that, he didn't want to disappoint. It wasn't only Claire, but also their child. He wanted to believe that if he continued to keep his word, show Claire how important she was, and how much they belonged together, then they could avoid disappointing one another.

There was a time, long ago, when they'd had a different mutual agreement. He'd promised to not hurt her again, if she promised to follow his rules. In many ways it was the same; however, the rules were different and so was the pain. After experiencing her accident and the aftermath, Tony truly didn't want it to happen again. Now that the threat was no longer physical, perhaps the new fear was greater. Never, even when they were married, had he wanted to allow her access to the real man behind Anthony Rawlings. Tony didn't know if it was the child or her newfound strength, but regardless of the reason, he wanted to share. That desire incited a fear deep within him as he'd never known. *Was this what it was like to truly love someone? Did it mean more than a promise of obedience and togetherness? Did it also mean allowing yourself to be vulnerable?*

Later in the morning, while reviewing emails, the door to Tony's office burst open. There was no knock, no request, just a very determined Claire as displeasure emanated from her very being, setting the mood of the room before she ever uttered a word. "Tony, what the hell have you done?"

"What are you talking about?"

"After I got dressed, I checked my emails. One is a confirmation of my airline reservation *cancellation*." She stood defiantly before him. "I did *not* cancel my reservation. I called the airline, and they informed me my seat has been sold. They have no open seats for my original flight or any others until tomorrow. I told you I was going back to California today. You promised me!"

Despite her obvious angst, her boldness intrigued him. He tried to conceal his amusement as he replied in a soothingly calm voice, "I promised you a return ticket. I'm a man of my word; you have a ticket."

"A voided ticket—semantics!" Her volume rose with each phrase. "I want to be on that flight!"

"Claire, listen to reason." He gestured toward the chairs. "Have a seat."

"No." Her arms crossed defiantly across her heaving breasts.

The muscles in his neck tightened as his eyebrows rose. "Very well, stand if you prefer. How are you feeling today?"

Claire glared. "You're not changing the subject. I'm going home."

"I hoped you'd consider yourself *home*."

Claire exhaled, paced the length of the desk and back, and then collapsed into one of the chairs she'd just refused. "Tony, why do you have to push and push? I truly have had a wonderful weekend, and I've surprisingly enjoyed being on your estate, but I have a life. I have plans. Amber is leaving for a conference, and I want to see her before she leaves. John and Emily will be in Palo Alto Monday. They're spending four days looking for housing. I need to be there."

"Amber is leaving?" he asked with obvious concern. "You'll be alone?"

"I won't be with anyone in public, if that's what you're asking."

"That goes without saying. I'm asking you if you will be alone?" His volume rose. "Christ, Claire! Your condominium was broken into. It isn't safe!"

"You're trying to scare me into staying. I'm not falling for it. My building has top-notch security, Harry is utilizing more SiJo resources, and then there are always your people watching me. I lead a damn parade!"

"Your laptop was stolen."

"Stuff happens. It isn't a cause to stop living."

He tried to reason. "We have plans beginning Friday in Chicago. *In your condition*, you shouldn't be flying all over the country." He exhaled and added, "In a commercial plane. Do you know how many people get ill after breathing that recycled air?" Tony had recently read an article on the homepage of his browser about increased illnesses on airplanes and figured it was worth a try.

"You're really stretching here. Tell me how I'm getting back to California—*today?*"

He sighed. "I want to take you back upstairs and lock that door," he glared and emphasized, "from the *outside*."

Expecting Claire to retreat, as she would have done years ago, Tony watched, astonished, as Claire stood and walked *toward* him. Her closed lips formed a soft smile as she peered deep into his eyes. With her petite hands framing his cheeks, she bent toward him until their noses touched, and brushed her lips to his. "Tony, I believe you. I know that's what you want. I drove to town yesterday, and I came back." She kissed him again. "I will go to California today, and I'll be back in Chicago—on Friday. Remember what we said the other night?" She didn't wait for his answer. "We said we needed to *trust* each other."

With his face still in her hands, he closed his eyes and nodded.

She continued in her soft and steady voice. "I trust you not to lock my suite from the outside. You need to trust me to return."

Tony reached out and encircled her waist. His touch found its way beneath her blouse and caressed the soft skin in the small of her back. The contact soothed him as he tugged her onto his lap. She reached out and circled his neck. In a gentler tone, he said, "You don't need to believe me. I know I need to earn that right, but I *did not* have anything to do with the break-in. It wasn't a plan to scare you into staying here. I'm concerned."

He kissed her lips and moved his hand to her stomach. "And not just for you."

Claire lowered her face to his shoulder. "Thank you. From the moment I saw the little blue plus, I've been concerned too. You have to know, I'll do anything necessary to keep myself and our baby safe. I just need to be in California, especially this week. I have a lot going on."

"What if I told you that you shouldn't have a lot going on? You deserve to rest and allow others to do for you. If Catherine knew about the baby, then you'd never lift another finger."

She lifted her head; her eyes glistened as they met his. "I have something to show you."

He raised his brow. "Oh?"

Ignoring his suggestive tone, Claire removed a piece of paper from her pocket. With trembling fingers, he took the grainy picture from her grasp. "Is this what I think it is?"

Claire nodded, barely able to contain her emotion. "Yes, it's our little one's first picture."

Tony looked from the picture to Claire and back to the picture. Grinning, he said, "I want her to have your eyes."

Claire smiled. "I know you are used to getting your way, but sex and eye color are non-negotiable."

"I don't know... sex sounds great, and I love your eyes. Would you like to negotiate?"

Claire's cheeks blushed as she shook her head. "How am I getting... back to California?"

"The same way you're getting to Chicago—in a private plane. I know you refused it before, but it's a safer mode of transportation, and there's no public record of your itinerary."

She exhaled. "Thank you."

"Since you don't have a gate to reach at a designated time, I'd like you to stay here until we can share an early dinner."

She kissed his cheek. "I think that can be arranged."

Claire hadn't been gone from his office for long when Tony knew his work could wait. He wanted to spend as much of the day with her as he could before she left. He'd been contemplating a question he wanted to ask, and after the picture she'd just shown him, Tony knew what he wanted to do.

He made his way to her suite; however, before he knocked, his back straightened as Catherine's voice came into range. Tony didn't need Catherine fishing for information. *Didn't she realize that it would fuel Claire's curiosity more than it would squelch it?* As he opened the door, both ladies turned in his direction. "Oh, am I interrupting?" he asked, feigning surprise as a fleeting glare went Catherine's way.

Claire walked to Tony and took his hand. "No, but since you're here...?"

He looked at her, questioning. "Yes?"

"I think I'd like to share something with Catherine, but not without you."

Their news. A soft smile came to his lips. "Catherine, I suggest you sit."

Although she looked at him suspiciously, Catherine silently made her way to the sofa and sat as Claire handed her the ultrasound picture. It took a moment to register, but finally her gray eyes widened and she proclaimed, "You're pregnant?"

Claire beamed and nodded.

It was then that Catherine looked toward Tony, who stood with Claire's hand in his and his chest proudly puffed. Catherine continued with both shock and amazement in her voice, "The two of you?" She sprang from the sofa and embraced Claire. "Oh my, a Rawls-Nichols baby. I can't believe it."

Tony glared at Catherine over Claire's shoulder while simultaneously fighting the red. Not now, he told himself. Not in front of Claire, but when they were alone, he and Catherine would have words. Tony didn't know how to make it any more clear—this was a *Rawlings* baby!

Fourteen

Heaven to Hell – June 2013
(Truth – Chapters 49, 51, & 52)

Life moves very fast. It rushes from heaven to hell in a matter of seconds.
– Paulo Coelho

W hile they waited for dinner, Tony and Claire relaxed in the pool. Everything was perfect, from the warm June sunshine to the blue Iowa sky. Tony recalled Claire once calling their pool her slice of heaven, and he hoped she still felt that way as he asked his very important question. The last time he'd asked her to marry him, it was elaborately planned, but this was different. The first time he'd told her that he knew what it was like to have her gone during her *accident*. Now, he truly knew what it was like to have her gone, and he wanted her beside him, now and forever. It wasn't about a name or letting the world know she was his. It was about his envelope, about his family, about keeping them safe and making them happy. With all of his heart, Tony believed it was about *love*. He'd called it that before, but this was different than what they'd shared in the past. Maybe, just maybe, this was what love really was.

Swimming the length of the pool, Tony surfaced at Claire's feet. Her giggles as he pretended to pull her into the water rang over the grounds, filling him like no business deal ever could. Then, just when she thought she was safe, he scooped her into his arms and into the water. It was after she feigned fighting that she finally submitted to floating within his embrace. Though her eyes were closed, Tony watched her sun-kissed cheeks and nose, and fought the urge to kiss her pink lips. He observed as the water ebbed and flowed over her firm stomach, and her dark hair floated in a halo around her face. *How long would it be until it was obvious to the world that she was pregnant?* Tony truly knew nothing about the subject and vowed to learn more before they met again in Chicago.

Although their plans were to take place in only five days, it seemed like an eternity. Summoning his courage, as she lifted her head from the water, he said, "I want to show you something."

"I'm curious," she asked with a seductive smile, "is it something I've seen before?"

He grinned, returning her sparkling gaze. "Yes, but not what you're thinking."

Tony led her up the steps, out of the pool, and over to one of the umbrella tables. Sitting knee to knee, he reached into the pocket of his bathing suit and pulled out Claire's engagement ring. As soon as he opened his palm and the sunlight reflected off the brilliant diamond, she gasped and searched his face. "Tony, how did you...?"

"I bought them back," he timidly answered, trying to gauge her reaction for the right words.

"I'm sorry. I needed money—"

He interrupted, "If I give them back, will you promise not to sell them?"

"Why would you give them back?"

"Do I need to get on one knee?" he asked with a hopeful grin. "I suppose I didn't do that the first time."

Suddenly, Claire stood and backed away. She moved so fast that Tony feared she would trip and fall. Finally, with her eyes still large, she said, "No, I'm not ready for anything like that."

He looked back at the ring in his hand and asked, "No, never—or no, not yet."

Kneeling before him, Claire appeased him, "Tony, slow down. I told you that I like the dating thing... we never did that. Please don't push too hard. In the last week, we've survived a major game changer. I think we need to proceed with caution."

He reached for her left hand and slipped the diamond ring onto her fourth finger. Of course it fit: it was hers. With a mischievous smile, Tony explained, "I just wanted to make sure it still fit."

Removing the platinum engagement ring, Claire placed it back in his hand and closed his fingers around it. "I appreciate the offer. Don't make me give you a definite answer. If you do, you won't be happy. Let's be content with what we have—for now."

Reluctantly, he accepted the ring and her touch. Instead of replying, he took her hand and kissed each finger, one by one. Kisses became suckles as he tenderly caressed her with his lips and tongue. Slowly, he moved up her arm until he was at that spot between her neck and collarbone, the one that produced goose bumps. Between kisses, he confessed, "I've made some bad decisions... and done some things in my life that I regret... but without a doubt... what I regret the most... is divorcing you." He searched her emerald eyes for any sign of hope. "If you tell me there's hope, that one day you'll be Mrs. Rawlings again—I'll wait." As his lips roamed her moist body, Claire's eyes closed, and moans replaced words. It wasn't the answer he wanted, but it was the response he loved. "May I get you out of this wet suit, *Ms. Nichols*?" he emphasized her name.

She heatedly answered, "Yes... and Mr. Rawlings... there's always hope."

Though times had changed, they both knew the staff wouldn't intrude. It wasn't until later, when both of them were again covered by bathing suits and Claire napped while Tony reapplied her sunscreen, that anyone came to the deck to announce their impending meal.

Tony reminded himself that it was the right thing to do, as he kissed Claire good-bye, saw her disappear into a car, and watched Eric drive away towards Rawlings Industries' private airport. Although he wanted to accompany her, Tony feared that once he was at the airport, he'd want to fly with her. Then, once in California, he wouldn't want to leave without her.

Only five days.

It was his new mantra, until it was four, then three…

Trying to concentrate on work and catch up with Roach and Andrews on all things private detective, Tony heard his phone buzz and checked the text message. It was from Claire:

"THANK YOU FOR A LOVELY WEEKEND. I'M SO THANKFUL I WAS ABLE TO ATTEND THE WEDDING."

Tony responded:

"I HOPE THAT WAS NOT THE ONLY PART OF THE WEEK-END YOU ENJOYED?"

Seconds later, Claire replied:

"I BELIEVE THERE WERE OTHER PARTS TOO. BUT SINCE YOUR PLANE IS MOVING, I NEED TO TURN OFF MY PHONE—CAN'T ELABORATE."

Grinning, he sent one more message, hoping to catch her before her phone was off:

"OH, BUT HOW I WOULD LOVE FOR YOU TO ELABORATE!"

He waited. When she didn't respond, Tony knew that Claire was en route to California.

Five more days!

Simultaneously, Tony carried on another text conversation with Phillip Roach. Interestingly, it was occurring between where he was and where Claire would soon be—Palo Alto:

Anthony Rawlings (AR):

"WHAT NEW INFORMATION DO YOU HAVE RE: BREAK-IN?"

Phillip Roach (PR):

"BUILDING SECURITY TO SEND ME ENLARGED IMAGE OF PERP—WILL FORWARD AS SOON AS I RECEIVE. NOT CLEAR ENOUGH TO BE USED WITH RECOGNITION SOFTWARE."

(AR):

"SEND VIA E-MAIL, EASIER TO ENLARGE ON MY END."

(AR):

"MS. NICHOLS WILL ARRIVE PALO ALTO AFTER 6:00 PM, PST. KEEP HER IN YOUR VIEW UNTIL SAFELY RETURNED TO HER CONDO. ARE YOUR SENSORS IN PLACE?"

(PR):

"YES, SIR. MS. MCCOY JUST EXITED UNIT."

(AR):

"SHE IS GOING OUT OF TOWN."

(PR):

"HER FLIGHT PLAN IS FOR LOS ANGLES WITH RETURN FLIGHT THURSDAY." Phil obviously wanted to show that he knew what was happening.

(AR):

"KEEP ME CONSTANTLY APPRISED."

(PR):

"YES, SIR."

Sitting behind his large mahogany desk, Tony tried in vain to read the documents on his computer. The words entered his mind and disappeared before he digested their meaning. His gaze fluttered between the ultrasound picture Claire had left and the clock in the corner of his monitor. Finally, his cell phone sounded and vibrated upon the smooth, glossy surface. Hastily, he swiped the screen—1 Text Message Claire:

"JUST LANDED. THANK YOU AGAIN FOR EVERYTHING. I SLEPT THE ENTIRE FLIGHT... VERY COMFORTABLE WITHOUT ALL THAT RECYCLED AIR!"

He smiled at her cheekiness. Maybe the recycled air was a stretch, but he'd undoubtedly preferred to have her in Iowa as opposed to California. Nevertheless, they'd made progress this weekend. They both knew it. His phone sounded and vibrated again—1 Text Message Phillip Roach:

"MS. NICHOLS' PLANE JUST LANDED. MR. BALDWIN WAITING AND LUGGAGE BEING PUT INTO HIS CAR. I WILL FOLLOW."

The muscles in Tony's neck tightened. *Does picking her up at the airport constitute a date?* Tony tried to tell himself it didn't. *Besides, would he rather have her in a taxi with some stranger?* They'd spent four days together, made love on three different occasions, and had a baby on the way. While reasoning words went through his thoughts, the clenched jaws and tightened shoulders revealed the jealousy coursing through his veins.

Tony replied to Phillip Roach:

"KEEP HER IN SIGHT. LET ME KNOW IF THERE ARE ANY STOPS ON THE WAY TO THE CONDO. WHERE IS THAT PIC-TURE?"

Text message number two, to Claire:

"OUR AGREEMENT FORBIDS PUBLIC EXPOSURE WITH ANYONE ELSE! I THOUGHT I'D MADE THAT CLEAR! WE HAVE AN UNDERSTANDING!"

Exclamation marks were so overused in text messages—Tony hesitated. Once sent, he wouldn't be able to retrieve it. He repeatedly hit the backspace and typed once again:

"I'M GLAD THE AIR WAS TO YOUR LIKING. REMEMBER OUR AGREEMENT. CALL WHEN YOU'RE SETTLED."

The restraint was difficult, but he knew he wasn't going to win her back without effort. Although the damn press would have a field day if they saw her with Baldwin, Tony reminded himself to do what he'd told her to do—*trust*.

Exhaling, he tried. It wasn't easy, especially since he'd never done it before.

The sound and vibration announced another incoming text message. This one was from Phillip Roach:

"THE PICTURE WAS SENT TO YOUR EMAIL. LET ME KNOW IF YOU DON'T HAVE IT."

Shit, Tony had been trying to read the acquisition documents and forgot to check his email. He switched screens. There was the email from Roach with an attachment. Opening the attachment, Tony looked at the grainy photo. The poor quality was undoubtedly due too many enlarging attempts. Tony pushed his leather chair away from the screen, and tried to focus and refine the image before him. It was a man with little to no hair. *Was he older and balding or younger with his head shaved?* Looking closer, Tony guessed he was older. Normally, Tony was excellent with names and faces, and he saw a hint of familiarity. Perhaps it had been a long time since he'd seen him, or maybe the man had been on television or in the news? Regardless, the twinge of recognition bothered Tony. *Why would someone he recognized steal Claire's laptop?*

339

Two more text messages came through his cell phone. The first one, from Claire:

"I DO. I WILL LATER."

Tony exhaled. It took every fiber of self-restraint to not get on another plane and bring her home.

Second message, from Phillip Roach:

"DID YOU GET THE EMAIL? I CAN RESEND."

Tony replied:

"I DID. KEEP CONSTANT SURVEILLANCE. I DON'T LIKE THIS."

About ten minutes later, Roach texted again:

"MS NICHOLS ARRIVED AT CONDO. NO STOPS ON WAY."

Tony breathed a sigh of relief. She could follow his rules. *Five more days...*

Tony's cell phone rang. The screen read PHILLIP ROACH. Panic bubbled below the surface as he answered. "Hello, Rawlings h—"

Roach's words came fast, sounding as if he were yelling and running at the same time. "I just read my sensors. She's in her unit *and* it was opened twenty minutes ago."

"What the hell do you mean it was opened twenty minutes ago? I thought Amber was gone? Roach? Roach! Answer me, God-damn-it!"

Instead of answering, Tony heard Roach speaking with someone on the other end. "Has anyone been to unit 4A recently?" Roach repeated himself louder. "The unit that was broken into last week—has anyone been up there?"

Tony's world, which only hours ago had been a slice of heaven, plunged into the depths of hell. Not only was his worst nightmare coming true, but from thousands of miles away he was powerless to stop it. Tony continued to scream into the phone, "Get to her. Someone get to her now!"

From his earpiece he heard voices: "Yes, there was a delivery. The man had the appropriate documents."

"Is this the man?"

"I don't know. He had documents. Yeah, maybe... he was bald."

"Call 911 and get me up there right away!"

Tony heard everything, yet could do nothing. *How long would it take to get up four flights?* He disconnected from Roach and scrolled through his contacts, finding Harrison Baldwin. Tony hit *CALL*.

After three rings, the call went to voice mail. Tony disconnected and called again. This time Baldwin answered. Tony didn't wait for pleasantries. "Mr. Baldwin, this is Anthony Rawlings. Go to Claire's unit immediately. You have to listen to me. Someone's in there and she's not safe."

When Baldwin didn't respond, Tony continued, his voice louder by the second as he screamed in desperation. "Damn it! I know you can hear me! I know you just drove her home! Go to her—before it's too late!"

"Is this some kind of joke? How would you know—"

"Please! Please, Mr. Baldwin, there's no time to lose." Tony believed his chest would explode as he pleaded with this man thousands of miles away. Tony never should have let Claire go, not now, now that he knew about the baby. If anything happened...

Baldwin had responded and Tony heard commotion. It was the most helpless he'd felt in his entire life. *Did he hear Claire? Was there a scream?*

Catherine came rushing in. "What's happening? Why are you yelling—"

Tony silenced her with his eyes as he continued to listen in horror. The echoing of an explosion came through the phone. *What was it? Was it a gunshot?* Tony couldn't ask. The phone went dead.

Tears threatened Tony's eyes as he looked at Catherine and said, "Oh my God, I don't know." He called Eric and told him to get him to the airport. "Yes, I know my jet isn't back from California. I don't give a damn— I'm flying to Palo Alto immediately." Before he finished with Eric, Roach's call came through.

Trepidatiously, Tony answered. "Roach, tell me she isn't dead."

"Sir, she's not dead. The perpetrator is."

Tony exhaled as the cyclone of impotence gave way to relief; however, it was short-lived and rage prevailed. "How in the hell did you let this happen? Tell me what's going on there!"

Tony listened as Roach replayed the scene. A man, the same man from the picture, was in Claire's unit. At this moment, neither his identity nor intentions were known; however, he'd accosted Ms. Nichols, who was currently being treated by paramedics. She was unconscious and it appeared as though they were taking her to the Stanford Medical Center. The assailant was shot by the building security guard and died on site. Roach promised to learn more.

"I want answers and I want them yesterday."

I dreamt about you – June 2013
(Truth Chapter 52 & 53)

You have to dream before your dreams can come true.
– Abdul Kalam

The entire way to the airport, Tony barked orders. He called Brent and told him to hire someone new: Roach was finished. After his epic fail, Tony didn't intend to employ him another hour, much less a day. Tony needed people he could depend upon—Phillip Roach was obviously not one of them. Tony wanted information about this assailant: was he working alone? What did he want? Tony also called Baldwin. Though the conversation was short, Harrison confirmed Claire's location as the Stanford Medical Center and assured Tony that she had a solid support system, including Emily and John, who were on their way.

Tony called the Palo Alto police and the emergency room at the hospital. By the time his company plane left Iowa, he was no closer to learning anything. Repeatedly, he was informed that he had no legal right to Ms. Nichols' private information. Tony wanted to scream, "Fine! But what about my child—I have the right to know if my child is all right." The only thing stopping him, keeping him from proclaiming his impending parenthood, was the fear of their answer. *How badly had this man hurt her? Would she survive? Had their baby?*

When he landed, Brent sent him the contact information on a new investigator, Clay Winters, ex-secret service. Tony immediately contacted him and explained the situation. He emphasized that regardless of his legal rights, he wanted answers and he wanted Claire protected. Clay went to work, while Tony found a small visitor's lounge a floor away from Claire's room and set up a home base.

One of Claire's attending nurses agreed to enlighten Tony when Claire regained consciousness. Tony asked about Claire's condition, her prognosis—anything! The nurse wouldn't give any more answers. Apparently, a *Do Not Disclose* order had been put into place. No information regarding Claire Nichols was to be leaked by staff or the hospital without a hefty fine and promised legal action. The nurse agreed to accept Tony's money, but refused to risk her job or the hospital's reputation with anything further.

Answers slowly trickled in regarding the incident. When Tony read that the assailant's name was Patrick Chester, all of the air left his lungs. He knew the man was familiar; however, it'd been over twenty-five years since he'd last seen him. According to the information, Chester had planned to kidnap Claire and ransom her to Tony. It didn't make sense. *How did Chester know about his connection to Claire? How did he know that the same man who'd been paying him for all of these years was Anthony Rawlings?*

As hour after hour passed, Tony's impotence wore on him. He was so close, yet so far. He didn't want to think about Claire's *accident* or compare the circumstances; however, the similarities screamed for acknowledgement. Almost three years earlier, she'd been in a similar situation and so had he. Tony remembered Dr. Leonard asking him to leave the room. His exact words echoed in his mind: *Mr. Rawlings, she is not related to you. We must allow her some privacy.* Those words continued to haunt him. Once again, he wasn't related —yes, that was his doing, and he regretted it more than anything in his life, but it was still the truth.

The question that tumbled through his mind, resurfacing at the most inopportune times was *did she lose the baby?* When she told him that she was pregnant, Tony didn't know what to say or do. When he took her to the meadow and explained, it wasn't truly to say he *wanted* a child, only that he was *unsure*—Claire had used the word *scared*. Truthfully, in the meadow he was unsure; now, he was frightened. Tony didn't only fear the loss of the child; he told himself repeatedly they would survive as a couple, and if Claire wanted children—fine, they'd try again. What he feared, as hours turned to another day, were his memories of after Claire's accident and before her breakdown on the front porch. Those weeks preoccupied his thoughts.

As soon as Tony returned from work, he met Catherine in his office for an update on Claire's condition. Unfortunately, after over two weeks of consciousness, her activities were virtually the same from day to day. She'd eaten two meals, although Catherine mentioned that she'd eaten very little of those two meals. After bathing and dressing, she napped. After lunch and reading, she napped. Catherine assured him that she was now awake and waiting for his arrival.

Tony approached the door to her suite with a combination of anticipation and dread. If only he'd find her talking and flitting around the suite as she used to; instead, he feared he'd find what he'd found the day before, and the one before that. Slowly, Tony opened the door and spotted Claire on the sofa. She was reading, or pretending to read. Silently, he watched as her eyes drifted toward the fireplace and stared. The reflection of the flames was the only spark of life he'd witnessed since she woke.

Securing a smile, he opened the door further and announced his presence. "Good evening, Claire," he said, as lightheartedly as he could manage.

When she turned, her dead gaze met his and her lips obediently move upward. "Good evening, Tony. Is it that late already?"

Kissing her cheek, he assessed the woman before him. She was dressed impeccably with her hair and makeup flawless. "You look lovely tonight. Obviously, you knew it was time for dinner."

Lifting the blanket that covered her legs, Claire gazed at her attire. With no emotion, she replied, "Oh, yes, that's right. Now, I remember."

Offering his hand, he asked, "Won't you join me? You're too beautiful to keep in this suite. Besides, you must be tired of these four walls. Let's go to the dining room."

The stillness of the flat green gave way to an instant of panic before settling again into nothingness. "Tony, I'd rather stay here, if that's all right with you. The dining room is so far away."

He didn't argue that night or even the next few. It wasn't until almost November before he convinced her to leave the suite. Then, slowly, he made more progress. First, it was the dining room, then the sunporch, eventually they made it outside. Even the fresh air didn't bring back the sparkling emerald he craved. Tony tried gifts. It didn't seem to matter if it was an inexpensive scarf, a newly released book that she'd been anticipating, or jewels valued in the thousands of dollars—though her lips smiled, her eyes remained dead.

That was why he'd talked to Courtney about a visit with her and Brent. Tony had hoped that taking her anywhere would help. He never expected that it would be the practice drive that would bring her back to life.

What if when Claire woke and if their baby was gone—what if her eyes were once again dead? With each hour, Tony promised he'd move heaven and earth to assure the spark of life in her eyes. If it meant he had to walk the gauntlet of her family and friends, he'd do it. Whatever she wanted, he would do.

His phone rang. "Anthony Rawlings," he answered.

"Sir, she's awake." Tony's heart leapt. "The doctor is with her now." The line went dead. Seconds later a text came through from Clay:

"THE DOCTOR LEFT MS. NICHOLS' ROOM. SHE IS AWAKE. HER FAMILY AND FRIENDS ARE HERE."

Tony didn't know if they would all be in her room or not—it didn't matter, he was going in. As he approached he saw his ex-in-laws by her door. John was the first to see him. The combination of hatred and shock in John's gaze fueled Tony's determined steps. Tony wasn't stopping until he was in Claire's room. He couldn't. He had to see her—see her eyes—and know that she was all right. He needed to be near her, to take her hand and promise more children.

"*You* are *not* welcome here," John proclaimed, as he stepped in front of the door. "I can't believe you would have the nerve to show your face after all you've done."

Tony saw Clay sitting inconspicuously in a nearby waiting area and shook his head in his direction. He would handle this on his own. Ignoring the daggered stares of his ex-sister-in-law, Tony stopped within a few feet of John. "I want to see her."

"I don't care what *you* want. I don't even know how you learned that she's awake, but you're not going near her."

Emily backed her husband. "She doesn't want to see you."

Making no aggressive movements, Tony ignored Emily and continued with John. "I suggest we ask Claire."

"I'll call the police," Emily said, as a crowd began to gather. Tony recognized Amber from Simon's funeral, but he didn't know or care about the identity of the man by her side. Baldwin was missing from their group.

John interrupted with a tone of superiority, "I'm sure *Mr. Rawlings* doesn't want it to come to that. After all, we'd hate for him to go to jail—unnecessarily. Leave now, before—"

Claire's door opened, silencing the growing crowd as Baldwin emerged from within. Tony's chin lifted indignantly, knowing that Baldwin had been where he wanted to be.

Harrison Baldwin spoke, "John, stop! Claire wants to see Mr. Rawlings."

Emily gasped before she said, "I haven't even seen her yet. She's my sister."

"*Claire* wants to see *him,* now," Baldwin repeated.

Tony shifted his gaze from John Vandersol to Harrison Baldwin, and replied, "Thank you, Mr. Baldwin." He then offered Harrison his hand, and the two men shook as John and Emily turned away. Tony hoped that he and Claire would be granted privacy, but Baldwin followed him into her room. Clenching his jaw, Tony summoned his courage as he assessed his ex-wife. He'd prepared himself for the worse. She was bruised and battered, one eye in particular was darkened; however, that wasn't what he saw—he saw the emerald glow as a tear trickled down her cheek. When Tony's gaze met Claire's, the rest of the world disappeared. Before him he saw the spark he'd feared was gone.

Relief opened the floodgate to rage. Red seeped from the corners of the room as Tony imagined someone doing this to her. Breaking his trance and the deafening silence, Claire spoke. Her words were a reminder that Baldwin was still present. "Please give us a moment alone, Harry. I promise I'll be fine."

Tony turned to the young man, summoned his public persona, and said, "Mr. Baldwin, I will only stay as long as Claire allows."

After a moment of staring at Tony, Baldwin stepped toward Claire and squeezed her hand. Tony tried to ignore their familiar interaction, as Baldwin said, "I'm right on the other side of that door."

"Thank you," she replied. "For everything."

After a prolonged stare at Claire, and then again at Tony, Baldwin silently opened the door, allowing the protests of Claire's family to infiltrate the room. Her family's words barely registered over Tony's anger, as the memories of her *accident* intermingled with the new source of his red. Claire's voice came like a lifeline, pulling him from the downward spiral. "I'm so glad you're here."

He took her hand, noticing her moist cheeks, and said, "The last time I saw you like this..."

"I'm all right."

Tony refocused his anger, his threat sounding more like a growl. "If that son-of-a-bitch weren't dead, I'd kill him myself."

"Tony, *we* are both okay."

His eyes opened wide; the hours of tension and worry fled from his muscles, leaving him momentarily stunned. "I haven't been able to get any specific information. I just assumed—"

Claire interrupted, "The doctor was just here. She said *our* baby is fine."

Her words overwhelmed him, causing his vision to blur. It was too much; their baby was all right. His baby—her baby. Tony didn't realize how much he truly wanted this child until that moment. He paced near the end of her bed, allowing his thoughts to settle. Finally, he spoke, "Claire, just like your accident, this is my fault, too." She shook her head, but he continued, "I don't know how Chester found you or knew of our connection. I don't even know how he knew me. I knew him when I was Anton." He moved closer and started to reach for her chin, but stopped, afraid that if he touched her, he'd hurt her. "And now look at what he's done."

Claire reached for his hand and lifted it to her face, completing the contact he sought. "Thank you for coming. I feel so much better having you here."

As her face inclined to his touch, Tony's forehead fell to her chest, and he sighed with relief. "I knew my presence wouldn't be welcome. I've been waiting on another floor for word of your waking."

She smiled. "Yes, I heard your welcoming committee."

He looked into her eyes, and his voice hardened with each phrase. "When you're well enough to travel, you're coming home where you'll be safe, and where Catherine can take care of you."

Claire's eyes narrowed. "That didn't sound like a question."

He returned her glare. "It shouldn't. I would hate to mislead you; it wasn't."

Claire exhaled. "Chester is dead—no more danger."

Tony leaned closer. "Are you seriously going to argue about this, covered in bruises, and carrying my baby?"

Defiantly, she raised her chin and kissed his pursed lips. "Not right now," she mused. "Let me get some rest and get a little stronger. Then I will."

"Good." He kissed her again. "I look forward to it." Squeezing her hand, he continued, "We don't know if Patrick Chester was working alone. Until we find out and locate your laptop, this isn't negotiable."

Claire sighed. "I need some sleep for this headache to go away, and then I'll respond with the appropriate cheekiness for you."

Tony grinned. "Even looking like you do, I think you're sexy as hell." He gently kissed her forehead. "Do you think now is a good time to tell your entourage our news?"

Claire looked down. "No, they know." Tony's eyebrows went up as Claire continued, "The doctor told Harry before I woke. He told everyone else."

Red once again threatened. "Why would the doctor tell *him*?"

"She assumed he was the father."

Tony tried to process. "And does *he* assume that as well?"

Shyly, she replied, "Yes."

If she'd slapped him, he couldn't have stood faster. Suddenly, Tony's envelope ripped open and the relief he'd just experienced evaporated. *"You got what you gave."* Tony searched for the source of Nathaniel's voice as he paced around the hospital room. *"You got what you gave."* He could hear the words as plain as day. The divorce was his doing—not hers. He had a chance for happiness staring at him from behind a bruised face.

Would he let this news steal it away and leave him again with nothing? When Tony turned back to Claire, her eyes were closed and her head rested against the pillow. She'd said she had a headache. He knew he should let her rest, but first Tony needed confirmation. "You're sure that *I'm* the father?"

Emerald green filled his vision, as she replied without hesitation. "Yes, you were at the condominium two weeks before Harry and I—well, at the ultrasound, the doctor said the heartbeat isn't detectable until six weeks. If he were the father, I would've barely been five weeks along—at that time, I was seven." She reached out to him and after only a moment of hesitation, Tony stepped forward and took her hand. Claire went on, "Tony, I didn't know we were together until you confirmed it at the gala. I remembered it, but I'd convinced myself it was a dream."

He sighed and resumed his seat on her bedside. "You were very tired, but you were talking. You mentioned something about a dream. I may be guilty of taking advantage of a tired woman, but nothing else."

"How did you get back in the condo? I remember closing and locking the door."

"You closed it, but you didn't lock it, or it didn't lock. I came back to say something, and I heard something fall. It sounded like it broke. I listened, but I didn't hear anything else, so I decided to check on you. The door opened." He confessed, "I didn't knock. When I walked in you were asleep on the couch, so I carried you to your bedroom. I can say *with honorable intentions*, but that wouldn't be entirely true. Claire, I asked you multiple times. You *never* said *no*."

She sighed. "I remember wanting you. I'd spent half the night dreaming about you until I gave up and stayed awake. That's why I was so tired."

The red dissipated as green prevailed. "You dreamt about me?"

"Yes, it was after our dinner. I hadn't seen you since... the jail in Iowa."

He softly kissed her lips and asked again, "You dreamt about me?"

Claire smirked. "Yes, you egotistical narcissist. I did."

"I've dreamt about you, too. I think it may have something to do with seeing your beautiful face above my fireplace every night before I fall asleep."

The door opened, and a nurse entered. "I'm sorry, sir, Ms. Nichols needs her rest. I'm closing her door to visitors for a while."

Tony stood with Claire's hand still in his. "What about...?" he asked.

"I'll tell them. I was about to tell Harry when you showed up."

Tony turned to the nurse. "How long is *a while?*"

She looked to Claire. Claire's answer told Tony everything he wanted to know. Nothing else mattered. "*I want* Mr. Rawlings here whenever possible."

Brightness filled his world with a brilliance he'd never known. With Claire's entire family a few feet away, she said that she wanted *him*. It wasn't like before—it wasn't his mandate. No, this was *her* choice, and without warning, she'd laid it on the line. The deep lines of worry and stress momentarily left Tony's eyes, as soft chocolate saw only Claire. No longer was the world a threat to their relationship. It surrounded them, but they were safe and secure within a bubble of *their* choices and decisions. The nurse's voice returned Tony to the present as she answered, "Let her sleep through the night."

Tony nodded. "I can do that." He smiled as he bent down and kissed Claire. "I'll be back in the morning."

"Good. I think you look like you could use some sleep, too." Her emerald eyes glistened through her bruised face.

Turning toward the door, Tony saw the five sets of glaring eyes watching their good-bye. Her family remained silent as he politely passed their human wall. With Claire's words ringing in his ears, he smugly walked the gauntlet. Despite their objections, Claire *wanted* him. Therefore, he would be there, and when she was better, she would be in Iowa. Until they found that laptop, they weren't taking any chances.

Late Wednesday afternoon, Claire's doctor released her from the hospital and gave her a referral in Iowa City. Tony had planned on driving her directly to the airport and getting her to the safety of his estate; however, Claire refused. She didn't refuse the impending trip. It was that she wanted to gather some of her things before they left. Tony promised to have everything sent, but she wanted to do it herself.

As they entered Amber's quiet condominium, Tony remembered emptying Claire's apartment in Atlanta. He suddenly understood why this was important to her. She hadn't had the chance to do it then, or even after she was arrested. Again, that had been Tony. Although she didn't mention the other two moves, Tony suspected that her lack of control in the past, helped facilitate the need she now possessed. Nevertheless, neither one of them was prepared for the sight of her bedroom. Drawers emptied and contents strewn across the floor. Clothes and shoes pulled from her closet; even the bed was disheveled. When they entered, Claire stood paralyzed, looking at the debris. Tony considered again offering to hire someone to clean and pack, but the look in her eyes told him that it was something she needed to do. Biting back his offer, Tony hugged her reassuringly and asked if he could help. Together they righted the wrong that Chester had done. In the grand scheme, it wasn't much, yet as the room began to take shape, Claire's determination returned.

As they were finishing her room, building security called to confirm that she was home to receive a delivery. After the flowers at the hospital came addressed to *Claire Nichols Rawls* with the strange note that read:

I've learned that ***you*** *are well… But now,*
there's another body to add to the count…

They should have been on guard. Tony should've received the delivery; instead, it was Claire. This time it was also flowers, and the card was again addressed to *Claire Nichols Rawls*. When Claire called out for Tony and he read the name on the envelope, he emphatically ordered the deliveryman to take them away.

As upsetting as the name was to both of them, what deflated Tony's lungs and returned red to his vision were the contents of the envelope—nothing, it was empty. Though he tried to hide his anguish and assure himself that it wasn't the fulfillment of his dream, he couldn't contain the emotion from his own voice. "I'll find out who's doing this, I promise."

After a moment, Claire stood straighter and nodded. Although he admired her strength, watching her hold back tears was almost too much. When she started to walk past him toward her room, Tony seized her arm and stopped her movement. Indignantly, Claire looked up at him. His voice echoed against the long hallway and wooden floors. "You are *not* staying here another night." Despite him sounding to the contrary, Tony was exercising all the self-restraint he possibly could. Claire's bruise-covered face, pained expression, and the empty envelope had him on the edge of sanity. Obviously, the person with the laptop was warning them that he wasn't done. Tony's proclamation wasn't debatable.

Thankfully, Claire understood. "I know. I want to finish packing."

AUTHOR'S NOTE

This POV was originally written as a gift to my amazing readers in the Goodreads Group: The Consequences Series Group Reads, Therapy, and Hugs. I wrote it as a thank you when that group reached 1000 members. At last check, that amazing group has surpassed 4000 members!

There is no doubt. I have the greatest readers in the world!

The version you're about to read has been tweaked and edited for Behind His Eyes Truth.

Thank you for joining me on this dark and insightful journey.

~Aleatha.

Say you are mine – June 2013
(Truth Chapter 54)

Love is about giving freedom and power,
not about gaining control or possession.
– Jeffrey Fry

Tony steered the rental car through the now familiar streets of Palo Alto. Glancing toward the passenger's seat, he couldn't help but grin. Somewhere between the last stoplight and now, Claire had fallen fast asleep. With all she'd been through in the last few days and, of course, her condition, she had every right to be exhausted. Tony understood. Lately, exhaustion had become his norm. He hadn't had a good night's sleep since he was with Claire in Iowa. He definitely hadn't had one in the last few days. Truthfully, he didn't anticipate having one for a while. There were just too many unanswered questions and too much uncertainty. Focusing on the road before him, Tony contemplated the recent events.

It seemed like a lifetime ago, but in actuality it had only been six days since Claire had come to Iowa, not just Iowa, but to the estate. Reaching to his right, Tony gently brushed her hair away from her sleeping face. Through the dimly lit interior, Claire's features came into focus and his smile quickly faded. Though difficult to see by the dashboard light, the swelling near her eye was no longer red. Now, it was blue. He knew from experience it would change to purple, green, and then yellow before it faded away. Tony wished with all his might that he didn't know that information, that he hadn't seen her face this way before, and that neither one of them had those memories.

Refocusing on the road, Tony pushed the thoughts of her *accident* away. This wasn't the time. They had too many other issues at the moment. The most pressing was getting Claire back to Iowa. Tony chastised himself. If he'd only kept her there in the first place. If he'd never paid off Chester. If he could start his whole damn life over. None of that was possible. Besides, when did Anthony Rawlings have regrets? He reminded himself: regrets don't solve problems—actions do.

By God, Tony was taking action! Tomorrow Claire was going with him to Iowa, and he would move heaven and earth to find out who'd sent the flowers with the name *Rawls*. Thankfully, Claire had agreed. This wasn't like the first time. They both knew the estate was the safest place; however, if she woke in the morning with a changed mind... Tony wasn't against forceful persuasion. Her safety was not debatable.

Hearing Claire groan, he turned, seeing her shift in the seat and wince. Slowing the car for a red light, Tony reached over and pushed the button to fully recline her chair. He watched as she settled against the soft leather and her expression relaxed.

The car behind him honked, alerting Tony that the light had changed. Pushing the gas pedal, he thought about how it wasn't only the *light* that had changed: his whole life, her whole life had too. They were going to have a baby! He'd experienced many life-altering events, but none of them had hit him like that news. Everything in his life was planned. Well, everything up until Claire and that ultrasound picture. After she left for California, he'd stared at it for hours. It didn't look like anything really, mostly fuzz, but it was a part of him. *How could someone he'd never met, who didn't have a name, and whom he couldn't even visualize, have captured his heart so completely?*

Then with Roach's call, Tony's life stood still. Phillip Roach hadn't kept Claire safe. It wasn't as if Tony expected miracles from the man, but how difficult was it to keep a psychopath away from Claire?

As Tony pulled the car into the hotel's garage, he remembered his relief when he entered her hospital room and saw Claire sitting up and awake. Yes, she was bruised and battered; however, he didn't see the red and blue colors. No, all he saw was green—the most beautiful, sparkling green eyes in the world.

Walking around to Claire's side of the car, Tony thought *God help the person who tries to stop me from keeping them safe.* As he opened her door, he bent down and kissed her cheek. Instantaneously, he was once again peering into seas of emerald. Despite the week from hell, a smile came to his lips and he said, "I'd gladly carry you to my suite, but I'm afraid we'd attract more attention than either of us wants."

"I'm pretty sure I can walk." Claire gripped Tony's hand as she stepped from the car. Although she tried to pretend it didn't exist, pain radiated behind her gaze as her jaw clenched and body tensed with the effort of standing. Before he could speak, she continued, "I could do this alone, but I'm so thankful I don't have to." Unexpectedly, she tilted her face toward his and gave him a fleeting kiss. "Thank you."

He contemplated telling her how none of this would've happened if she'd just stayed in Iowa. The words were right there, wanting to come out; instead, he tenderly wrapped his arm around her shoulder and pulled her into his embrace. Nearing his lips to her ear, he whispered, "Thank you for letting me."

She didn't respond verbally; the squeezing of his hand as she molded against his side was enough. Tony scanned each corner of the quiet garage as they walked toward the elevator. Until they recovered Claire's laptop, there was no guarantee of safety. Tony was certain that Chester's accomplice was the one sending the flowers. They'd accessed Claire's information on her computer and now this person was setting them up. The question was what did he want? Was it money to keep the past buried? Would he try to finish what Chester started? Tony didn't know, and that uncertainty was hell.

When the elevator doors opened to an empty lift, Tony let out his breath. Every face and every person was suspect. Tony refused to trust anyone until he had Claire home. Silence prevailed until they entered the presidential suite and Tony scanned the empty living room. Dark sky filled the large windows with lights from below. The view reminded him of the late hour. "Perhaps we should order some food?" he asked.

"I just want a shower and some sleep," Claire replied, as she walked toward the bedroom.

Tony secured the locks on the suite door and watched Claire disappear into the bedroom. Although he'd love to help her with that shower, an overwhelming sense of relief caused him to stagger forward. It was the first time since Roach's call that Tony had felt a semblance of control. Whether it was the helplessness of the thousands of miles of distance, the inability to visit her hospital room and know her condition, or the dead ends regarding the sender of the threatening flowers, the sense of impotence was stifling. For days and nights, every muscle and fiber of his being had been wound tight. No wonder he hadn't been able to sleep.

Entering the bedroom, Tony heard the shower running and saw the light stream from the bathroom across the darkened carpet. Nearing the slightly ajar door, he fought the urge to open it wider when his shoes encountered something on the floor. It was Claire's jeans—no, not just her jeans. On the floor near the bed were *all* of Claire's clothes, lying in a pile, left behind, as if she'd evaporated into thin air. His heart clenched at the thought; he wouldn't lose her again.

The warm steam infiltrated the coolness of the air-conditioned room as he reached for her jeans. Nestled within the denim was a pair of lace panties. It wasn't a conscious decision, more a reflex; nonetheless, without thinking, Tony fingered the small bow and inhaled her scent.

The relief, which moments earlier had filled his tired body, vanished, and memories of the last terrible week came crashing down, buckling his knees, and forcing him to sit on the edge of the king-sized bed. His mind swirled with questions: *What if Chester had succeeded? What if Claire had died?* Roach was supposed to keep her safe! Tony swore he'd never entrust that job to anyone else, ever again. *Why hadn't Claire listened?* He told her he wanted her with him in Iowa—only there could he ensure her safety. Relentlessly gripping the lace, his mind relived the phone calls: first with Roach and then with Baldwin.

Baldwin. Harrison Baldwin. *Harry.*

Tony looked down at the twisted lace in his hands and threw it to the ground with a sigh. If he'd held it any longer, he probably would have torn the panties to shreds. Pacing about the dark room, he listened to the repetitive beat of the water from the nearby shower as the floral scent of shampoo penetrated the air around him. If he went into the bathroom now he'd most definitely scare Claire away. Hell, the rage rushing through his veins frightened him; he couldn't let her see it.

The cause of this bubbling fury wasn't only Chester. It wasn't just the threat of someone else, some accomplice. Those were beyond Claire's control. After all, Chester went after Claire because of him. Just like the *accident*, the attack was his fault. They would find this accomplice, and in the meantime, Claire would be safe in Iowa.

What accelerated Tony's heartbeat and dyed the room a sickening shade of crimson *was* in Claire's control. It had been. Tony acknowledged that she didn't ask to be Chester's target; however, she had willingly accepted Harrison Baldwin's advances.

The sound of silence overtook the room. Claire had turned off the shower. The sudden stillness pulled Tony from his internal tirade. Somewhere within his senses he acknowledged that his anger toward her wasn't fair. After all, *he* divorced *her*. Nevertheless, as he stood silently in the dark bedroom waiting for the bathroom door to open, his mind filled with thoughts of her with *him*. His back straightened and muscles tensed as he prepared for the confrontation. If she entered the room now, it was meant to happen.

Claire didn't emerge. The sound of water running in the sink came to his ears. Closing his eyes, images of her with Baldwin ran loops through his mind. Tony knew what it was like to be with Claire. In these new images, he replaced himself with Baldwin. The temperature of the room continued to rise.

How could she?

The realization hit him. *What was he thinking? Was he seriously going to confront Claire in her condition?* Not only was she healing from an assault, she was pregnant with his child. *His* child! Their child!

Abruptly, he turned toward the hall, exited the bedroom, and closed the door. In his heart of hearts, Tony knew the confrontation should never occur. It would not end well. If he wanted Claire in Iowa—willingly—he'd have to accept the past and move on. That was much more difficult to do than say. His whole life had been about the past. *What had that given him?* Nothing. An empty envelope. Now they had hope of a future—if he didn't ruin it.

The cool air of the living room peeled back the layers of the red. Peering about the room, Tony's gaze settled upon the wet bar. By his standards, it wasn't impressive; nonetheless, it was present. He scanned the bottles and poured a small bottle of Maker's Mark into a tumbler. After swallowing the contents in one gulp, he called room service for more.

How much did he drink? Tony wasn't sure. *How much time had passed?* He didn't know that either. He did know that he'd made himself a bed on the sofa, and sooner or later he'd willingly lie down or unwillingly pass out. Either way, he was prepared. Food would've been a good idea, but somewhere between thoughts of Chester and those of Baldwin, Tony's appetite disappeared.

At one point he went back into the bedroom and found Claire sound asleep. She looked so peaceful. Her swollen cheek didn't detract from her beauty. He couldn't—no, wouldn't—wake her. *What would he say if he did?* Tony was pretty sure he'd used all his forgiveness credits. He didn't want to risk saying or doing anything that would push her away forever.

With sleep creeping closer, the sound of footsteps shattered the stillness of the suite. Closing his eyes, Tony clenched his jaw and exhaled. *Why did she have to wake? Didn't Claire know the precarious situation she was about to enter? Didn't she understand how dangerous he could be?*

Her voice echoed through the quiet suite, momentarily stilling his internal monologue. "Tony? Are you all right?"

Praying that she was a figment of his imagination, maybe one of his daydreams, he stared toward the voice. Perhaps if he tried, he could make her image disappear. After all, she always disappeared in his dreams just before he reached her. If she weren't real, Claire could sleep contently and never know the depths of his anguish. He scanned her frame. In their rush to leave her condominium, they hadn't brought any of her packed things; she was wearing one of his t-shirts. It swallowed her petite body and hung to her knees, yet he could still see her curves and her nipples as they reacted to the cool air. Damn, he'd never again look at one of his shirts the same.

"No," he finally answered.

"What's this?" She motioned toward the sofa. "Why aren't you in bed with me?"

All sense of inhibition disappeared with the last few fingers of bourbon. Claire was the one who started this conversation; she'd better be prepared to finish it. Throwing caution to the wind, Tony answered honestly, "I don't trust myself."

"I trust you—"

Interrupting, he explained, "I went in there and kissed you. You were sound asleep." Her warm smile melted the ice that over the past few hours had begun to build within his chest. He went on, "I watched you, saw your expression and your bruises." Her smile disappeared. With his impaired thinking he tried to remember what he'd just said. Oh, the bruises. Grasping her dangling hand, Tony scolded, "Stop that."

"What?"

"You're beautiful!"

She pulled her hand away. "I've seen me. *Beautiful* isn't a word I'd use."

Closing his eyes, Tony leaned back and rubbed his face. This wasn't going the way he wanted. Blinking his eyes, he focused on Claire. She wasn't a figment of his imagination; he'd just touched her hand. She was real and the bruises were real. Seeing them was like that damn knife again. It was being plunged deep into his heart. If only he'd made her stay in Iowa. This was entirely his fault. Like the ripping of a Band-Aid from his skin, Tony decided he needed to see the extent of her injuries. It would be better to just twist the damn knife and get it over with. "Take off my t-shirt."

"Excuse me?"

Although indignation rippled from her tone, Tony's focus was on her injuries. He stood and repeated, "Take off my shirt."

"Tony, I didn't bring any night clothes... I didn't think you'd—"

He should've heard her impending concern, but he didn't. "I don't give a damn about the shirt. I want to see you."

"See *me*?"

"I can see your face and your legs. I want to see what that bastard did to you."

The touch of her hands blurred his objective. She sounded so strong. "I'm fine, but I want you to come to bed—with me."

Tony tried to make her understand. "I planned to call for dinner; instead, I found the bar. It's been a rather stressful few days." When she moved toward him, he grasped her shoulders. "I should never have let you return to California." Shaking his head, he released her, and stepped backward. No, he needed to do this, needed to see. Straightening his stance, he commanded, "I believe I've said this more than once. Take off the damn t-shirt."

Claire reached for the hem and lifted the white shirt over her head. It was worse than he'd imagined. Her side was a purplish blue, and it extended from below her breast to her pelvic bone. She was wearing the panties he'd found with her clothes. Of course, she didn't carry an extra pair in her purse. As his eyes scanned her form, it finally registered. This wasn't about him. It wasn't about seeing what Chester had done. It was about Claire. At this moment she was trembling. *Was it the air conditioning or was it—?*

Perhaps it was the alcohol, but Tony suddenly felt ill. It was him! She was trembling because of him. He fell to his knees and gently clutched Claire's hips. Beyond the bruises was the woman he'd hurt too many times. Beyond the bruises was his child. Wanting to make the trembling stop, he kissed her stomach and inhaled her clean warm scent. Tenderly, he brushed his lips over her wounds as his hands tightly held to her firm behind. While he continued to caress her skin, she reached for his head and wove her fingers through his hair. Beyond the sounds of their breathing, he heard her pleading voice, "Please, Tony, please, can we go to bed?"

He didn't stop—he couldn't. He couldn't take away her pain, but he could try to make it better. Her grip of his hair tightened just before her knees buckled and she knelt before him. As he fought to focus, the vision before him filled with emerald green. The knife no longer twisted. Hell, the world no longer turned. Tony could die as long as the last thing he saw was her eyes.

"You're mine." He hadn't planned on staking his claim, but once the words were out, he didn't try to retract them.

"Tony, bed... please?"

"I'm trying so hard. You have no idea of the restraint I'm enlisting." His thoughts went back to Baldwin. *Had the two of them ever been like this?* He clenched his teeth, closed his eyes, and fought to keep the red at bay. "Yet all I can think about are his hands on you."

"Tony, I'm fine. I'm all right. I'm with you."

"But you weren't. You were with *him.*"

"He just wanted your money—"

Pulling her closer, his voice hardened, and he bathed her cheeks in warm, whiskey-scented breath. "I'm not talking about Chester!"

There, he'd said it. The truth was out. Without doubt, he was a selfish bastard, and the idea of Claire being with anyone else filled him with palpable anguish. Before Tony could look away, Claire's hands framed his face.

Her voice was a melody, contrasting the tirade in his head. "I wasn't with you. We weren't together."

The sound that came from his throat was unintentional. Truthfully, he'd tried to remain silent, yet Claire's words didn't make sense. They'd *always* been together.

She continued, "But now..." Her lips touched his. "Now, I want to be. Please, Tony."

Thoughts weren't forming with any kind of reasoning. The only thing Tony knew, with one hundred percent certainty, was that he wanted her. He wanted her more than he wanted air. If she wanted that too, all walls were down. *Could she handle it? Could she handle him—the real him?* It was now or never. No more pretenses, no holding back. This would be the real him, raw and uncensored. Claire would either run for her life or be his for eternity. It was too late to turn back.

As Tony's fingers seized her loose, damp hair, his mind told him to be gentle; however, gentle fell off of Tony's radar many shots ago. He couldn't turn down his desire if he wanted, and at this moment, he didn't want to. Pulling her head back, he exposed her slender neck. With little concern for his ferocity, his lips attacked the soft skin as a shocked moan escaped her lips. *She'd asked for this, but was she ready?* He needed to know. "Are you sure?"

He didn't pause or wait for her answer; instead, with one hand still entangled in her long, dark hair and the other pulling her closer, he continued to claim the woman before him.

Finally, her words rose above the internal mayhem. "I am."

All indecision was gone. The world was no longer red, yet it wasn't clear. Tony wasn't thinking anything through... everything was visceral and primal. Claire belonged to him.

Yes, she could be her own woman. It was true: Tony liked her independent spirit. However, in the grand scheme, that was irrelevant. All that mattered was that she was his—wholly and completely. As Tony gave in to his desires, he knew one of two things would occur. When the night was done, Claire would either be his like never before, or she'd leave him behind and life would cease to exist. Stopping now wasn't an option. Continuing his unrelenting claim, he held her tighter pulling her against his chest. Their hearts beat together as he wildly repossessed everything before him. His words come out like a growl, "You are mine."

When he released her hair, Claire's lips touched his neck and her hands caressed his shoulders. He couldn't contain the rumble from the back of his throat as he tried to think, tried to reason. Claire wasn't fighting—she was responding. Hell, she wasn't just responding. She was seducing him. *Did she truly know what he was offering?*

It was love and it was forever.

Tony loved Claire more than he could articulate; however, they both knew, his *love* wasn't all wine and roses. He was damaged. Chalk it up to a screwed-up childhood, blame it on tragedies—the cause was irrelevant. Tony was a sick son-of-a-bitch who had certain requirements. Claire needed to decide if she was willing to submit to his requirements and follow his rules. This was her last out, the last chance. If she didn't run now, he would never let her go.

Tugging once again on her hair, she gasped as he tipped her head until their eyes met. The gaze before him was stunning. In those eyes, he'd seen fear and love. Tonight, he saw passion, a heat that threatened any remnants of restraint he might still possess.

Laying it all on the table, he demanded, "Say it!"

Behind the passion and fire, her confusion surfaced. Tony explained, "Say you're mine and nobody else's."

Claire's confusion melted into green pools of desire. Her voice resonated above the sound of their breathing and the frantic beating of their hearts. "Yes, Tony, *you* are mine and nobody else's."

He stared. *What did she just say? You* are mine and nobody else's.

Tony tried to focus. It wasn't what he wanted; it wasn't what he expected, yet it was perfect. Claire was more than he deserved and a hell of a lot stronger than he'd ever known. No other woman could or would accept him. No one ever had. Not that he'd tried. The realization struck him with a tremendous force. Claire Nichols not only knew what she was getting herself into, but she wanted it. She wanted *him*.

Claire's acceptance fueled Tony's new strength and sobered his thoughts. His words began as a whisper and rose in volume. "Yes... mighty fine and sexy as hell." Claiming her lips, he added, "And mine!"

He stood, seized Claire's wrist, and pulled her up toward the bedroom. If they were taking this re-acquisition to the next level, they weren't doing it on a hotel room floor. They were doing it right. He laid her upon the bed, pausing only for a moment to take in her nearly naked form. The bruises no longer registered. Within seconds, his shirt was gone and his body covered hers. The weight of his chest flattened her breasts, as he relished the warmth of her soft skin. She wasn't protesting and he was beyond the ability to stop. Securing her hands above her head, he forcibly seized her mouth as their tongues united.

Once her breathing became labored, he moved to the end of the bed, began at her ankles and worked his way toward her injuries. As his lips inched upward, her scent beckoned his approach. Maybe he wasn't the only one to be here, but he sure as hell would do his best to make her forget anyone else. The lace panties didn't stand a chance as the delicate fabric ripped under his determined grip. Looking up, he suddenly worried that she'd be upset; instead of anger, Tony saw yearning and desire. Instantaneously, his cheeks rose and he flashed a devilish grin. They both seemed to understand that he had a mission and there would be casualties—the panties were the first to go.

Tony was exactly where he wanted to be. It was familiar territory and he knew all the secret passages. He knew what Claire liked and what made her feel good. He knew that when his teeth nipped her hard nipples, she would arch her back and pull him tightly to her breast. He knew when her nails clenched his shoulders and words became difficult for her to articulate, she was only moments away from the throes of ecstasy. He also knew that as the night progressed, she'd be willing to take this renewal beyond the confines of the king-sized bed. Against the wall, across the desk or in the shower were all acceptable alternatives.

Although Tony would've liked to accept full credit for the heights they achieved, Claire was not an innocent bystander. Her confidence and independence were not limited to verbal retorts. Her boldness both surprised and satiated him. At one point, Tony questioned who was claiming whom. Remembering her words, *Tony, you are mine and nobody else's,* he acquiesced; he'd met his match.

Perhaps he'd helped to create the woman before him. At one time he'd wanted nothing more than to subdue, control, and dominate her. *How could he have been so wrong?* While she was gone, his life was empty. Yes, there were things and money—none of that mattered. None of it held a candle to the way her words touched him, or the sensation of her tongue on his neck, her lips upon his skin, or her hands caressing...

She wasn't only an amazing lover, but an amazingly strong woman who'd found a voice and was willing to speak to him like no other. Yet she would also allow him *reticent* and *genteel* in the presence of others. It was more than he'd ever imagined, more than he deserved.

When they finally submitted to sleep, no need was left unfulfilled. As his head settled against the soft pillow and Claire nestled against his chest, Tony wrapped his arm around her shoulder and allowed his body to relax. For now, she was safe and they were together. When her breathing slowed and her warm, sexy body melted into the crook of his arm, Tony inhaled her amazing aroma and closed his eyes.

For the first time in nearly a week, Anthony Rawlings fell into a deep sleep.

Seventeen

We said we would trust – Late Summer 2013
(Truth – Chapters 55 thru 58)

*Sometimes the strongest among us are the ones who smile through silent
pain, cry behind closed doors, and fight battles nobody knows about.*
– Unknown Author

The first mailing to arrive at the estate addressed to *Claire Nichols
Rawls* was a card, congratulating them on their impending
parenthood. The card wasn't signed, the address was typed, and the
return address was Cedar Rapids—too close for comfort. Tony's security
team intercepted the card based on the unfamiliar name. Other than the
name, there was no obvious threat; nevertheless, Tony met with his security team and household staff. Everyone was to be on the lookout for anything suspicious, and any such item was to be brought directly to him.
Claire was not to be burdened.

It wasn't a matter of hiding the truth from Claire; the way Tony saw
it, he was protecting her—just as he'd promised to do. After the deliveries
in California, Tony wanted Claire to feel safe. Though her laptop had not
been found, he and Catherine had done everything possible to facilitate her
sense of security, including maintaining Clay as Claire's full-time bodyguard.

Though Claire tried to act strong, the attack bothered her more than she wanted to admit. She'd even fooled Tony, until one night in late June when he realized she wasn't in bed. He scanned the large room and noticed the drapes amiss. Slipping quietly onto the private patio, Tony found Claire wrapped in the pink robe. Despite the warm summer night, she was hugging her midsection, shivering uncontrollably, and staring out into the sky. When he silently approached from behind, she jumped at his touch.

"O-oh, Tony, I didn't hear you." Her dampened cheeks revealed her hidden tears.

"What is it? Are you all right? Is the baby—"

She leaned into his embrace and nodded. "We're fine." The shuddering of her shoulders told another story. "I didn't mean to wake you. I'll be better soon."

Cupping her chin, he pulled her gaze upward. "What do you mean you'll be better soon? What's happening?" When she didn't answer, he asked, "Has this happened before?"

Nodding, she replied, "I-I see him... it's like he's right here... I feel like I can't breathe... sometimes it's like..." Her words faded behind her sobs muffled by the cotton of his shirt.

For the longest time, Tony held her tightly under the starry Iowa sky, as she trembled against his chest. Eventually, her cries lessened and the quaking subsided. "Can we go back to bed?" he asked.

Claire nodded.

Once they were settled, she confessed to recurring nightmares. Tony couldn't imagine. He'd only had his dream that seemed too real once, and she'd been battling these almost nightly. Hugging her, Tony asked, "Do you feel safe right now, here with me?"

Claire nodded against his chest. "I do. Now I do."

He pleaded, "Then let me help you, please. Don't try to fight him alone. I told you before that I wanted to kill the bastard myself. Please, Claire, let me help you do that. We'll kill that memory together. He took too much from you and could have taken much more, from both of us. Together, we won't let him take any more—not even your sleep. Please let me protect you."

Her tears once again dampened his t-shirt. "I love you," she whispered.

He kissed her hair. "I love you, too." They fell asleep.

Though the nightmares continued, with time their frequency and intensity began to wane, and Claire's sense of comfort around the estate continued to grow. She began acclimating herself in ways she'd never done when she lived there before. One of her favorite pastimes seemed to be gardening. They had multiple gardens, and Tony often found her outside in the sun, tending to the small plants. It wasn't that he wanted her to work, yet the pleasure she derived from the activity was obvious. He wondered why she hadn't done that when they were married. With her hands and knees covered in dirt, and a glow of perspiration, her smile brightened his world. Tony loved how when he'd get home from work, she'd drag him from flowerbed to flowerbed, explaining the different plants and telling him about their sun and moisture requirements. Although the flowers had always been present, without Claire he hadn't noticed them.

One Saturday afternoon while he was working from home, through his office window Tony saw Claire at the pool. Suddenly, his work paled in importance. He slipped to their room, donned his bathing suit, and joined her in the cool, clear water. Each act, whether gardening or swimming, reinforced Claire's increased level of comfort. With her hand in his, he noticed the dark evidence of her recent activity under her fingernails and teased, "I think you need a manicure after all of this manual labor."

Giggling, Claire pulled her hand away. "I wasn't planning on having anyone look that closely. Besides, I haven't had a chance to shower yet."

"Now that sounds intriguing!" He watched as his innuendo turned her expression sultry.

Since Claire's rejection of his initial proposal, Tony avoided asking directly if she'd marry him. She'd said that if he did, he wouldn't like her answer; therefore, he'd ease the subject into conversation. Though she'd continued to deflect his persistence—and he fully expected her to do it again—Tony wanted Claire to know that he wouldn't give up. The warm Saturday afternoon and relaxed setting seemed as good of a time as any. With a mischievous grin, he said, "In the meantime, I know a way to divert people's attention from your nails."

While holding his shoulders with her legs wrapped around his torso, Claire glanced toward her left hand. His heart clenched and time stood still at the realization that she hadn't immediately refuted his comment. Tony watched as her gaze lingered and her lips turned sweetly upward. With the reflection of the sun and water, her emerald eyes sparkled as Claire kissed him and replied, "Well, that shower I'm about to take... perhaps, if you can figure out a way to bring the ring in there, I'd slip it on. I mean—" she mused, "I wouldn't want it to go down the drain."

Grasping her growing waist, Tony gently pushed her away. He wanted—no needed—to see her clearly. "Are you finally saying yes, that you'll be Mrs. Rawlings again?"

If it were possible, her smile grew. Nodding, she lowered her lips to his neck, instigated a growl he couldn't control, and finally replied, "I'm willing to go from dating to engaged. Can we not rush the married part?"

As Tony took in his fiancée, Catherine's words of warning tugged at his potential happiness. He didn't want to be disappointed—he also didn't want to disappoint. Tony needed to make sure his rules were clear. "There is one condition."

"Yes?" she asked tentatively.

"I don't want to have to track this ring down again. Do not sell it, give it away, or leave it any place but on your beautiful finger." It was one of those undebatable statements.

Through a veil of thick lashes, she smiled and whispered, "I promise." They sealed the deal with a lingering kiss that took them from the pool to their suite.

Before entering the shower, Tony slipped the diamond on Claire's finger. "I thought it might be better if you weren't all slippery," he said.

Claire stared at the ring for the longest time. When she looked up, she replied, "I loved this ring once, but I need to be honest. I think I love it more today."

He pulled her close. "I know that I love you more today. You, my dear, have taught me what love truly is—and what it is not."

Claire snickered, "Whoever would've thought that Anthony Rawlings would be open to new lessons?"

"Oh, I'm open, but," his tone turned stern, "I meant what I said. I don't want that ring to ever be anywhere but on your finger. Are we clear?"

Claire lifted herself on her tipped toes and kissed his cheek. "Yes, we're crystal clear." As she stepped into the shower and steam filled the bathroom, Claire tilted her head toward the spraying water and teased, "Now, Mr. Rawlings, come here. Let's learn a few new things together."

By the time the first package arrived, Tony and Claire were officially engaged, and she hadn't experienced a nightmare in over a week. Tony refused to let the mailing threaten her newfound security. He wouldn't allow anyone or anything to risk renewing that terror. Without fully explaining the threat, Tony reassured her that he didn't care where she went or what she did as long as she wasn't alone. It didn't matter if it was an outing to the store, lunch with a friend, or a weekend to visit her sister, Tony's one requirement, one undebatable rule, was that either he or Clay be by her side.

For obvious reasons, Clay accompanied Claire during the weekend trip to Emily and John's. Claire wanted to inform them in person of their engagement. When Claire returned, she didn't say much about their visit; however, when Tony asked if she was planning another, she told him that for the time being she was restricting her travels to trips with him. Though he didn't like seeing her disappointed, Tony was glad that she didn't want to travel without him. He wanted to do everything within his power to create a stress-free environment where Claire felt not only safe but loved. Over the course of time he, Catherine, and the security team succeeded. Until the rattle.

Other packages had been intercepted prior to reaching the estate, but the rattle made it inside their home. Luckily, Clay saw it and called Tony before Claire noticed it. Tony immediately rushed home and called Catherine, Clay, and Eric to his office. Before berating the security detail, Tony needed to know exactly what had happened. As he listened to their information and voiced his opinion, Claire silently slipped into the room.

Tony didn't want her to know about *any* of the mailings—especially this one. The engraved message of: *Baby Nichols-Rawls / R.I.P.* could definitely be considered a threat. Therefore, when his eyes met hers, he silently pleaded, then demanded that she leave his office. Following his gaze, everyone turned to her, yet instead of leaving, she asked, "You're all very loud. Is this about me?"

"Claire," Tony said, summoning a calmer tone than the one he'd been using. "Please don't worry about this. I'm taking care of it."

As she stepped toward him, Tony looked to Catherine. "Catherine, if you could please help Ms. Claire? She may need some assistance."

Though Claire obviously understood what he wasn't saying, she pressed on. "Clay, what *others* have you intercepted?"

"Ma'am, nothing that concerns you."

"I don't believe you."

Catherine tried to assist. "Claire, let's get you something to drink. It's very hot outside."

Defiantly, Claire proclaimed, "I'm not leaving."

Tony fought the red that wanted to stream towards his fiancée. *Didn't she understand that this wasn't the time for bold and cheeky?* "Claire," he warned.

Surprisingly, wearing her swimsuit, cover-up, and flip-flops, Claire walked toward Tony, to his side of the desk, ignored him, and addressed their staff. "Catherine, Eric, and Clay, could you please excuse us for a minute. Mr. Rawlings and I need to speak privately. I would assume he's not done with you, so please stay close. This won't take long."

He'd never heard her take that tone with anyone. It wasn't demeaning as much as it was authoritative. Despite her attire, Claire was asserting herself in the position Tony wanted her to assume—lady of the house. Everyone in the room turned to him for confirmation. The tension was palpable. Finally, through clenched teeth, he agreed. "Do not go far. I'm *not* done. Clay, make some calls. After Ms. Claire and I have finished, I want answers."

Of course, Tony saw Catherine's glare as they all hurried from the room. He didn't have the time or energy to worry about her wounded ego. The way he saw it, it was her fault for not confiding fully in Claire.

"What's happening?" Claire's question brought Tony back to present.

"How did you hear? You were at the pool."

"How could I not hear? Everyone in a three-mile radius could hear you. Tell me, what's so important to bring you home early from work? The sooner I know, the sooner you can continue your *meeting*."

"Damn it, Claire! I don't want you worrying." He paced to the window and back. "Besides, who in their right mind would come in here while I'm teetering on the edge of sanity? Did you see how fast they all left?"

Claire smiled as she placed her hands on the lapels of his dark suit. "No one. Just ask my family, I'm definitely not in my *right* mind, and if I'm correct, the only thing that can get you this worked up is something about me." She turned and picked up the package addressed to *Claire Nichols Rawls*. "So I don't get to open my own mail anymore?"

"Seriously, some asshole found you here, knows our address, and you want to complain about opening mail?"

She turned and faced him. With her spine straight and chin up, her voice stayed calm. "No, it scares the hell out of me, but anyone can learn this address; it's public record. The stupid press has told anyone who wants to listen that I'm living here." She lifted the box. "What was in it? And how many packages or letters have come that I don't know about?"

"It was a silver baby rattle—engraved."

"Where is it?"

"Clay bagged it. He's having it processed for fingerprints. Hopefully, the asshole touched it."

"Engraved... what did it say?"

Tony seized her shoulders and pulled her close. "Claire, let me handle this. Show me you have faith in me."

Her face tilted upward. "I wouldn't be here if I didn't." She kissed him. "What did it say?"

"Baby Nichols-Rawls."

"That isn't so bad, considering the way it was addressed. Why didn't you want me to know about it?"

He directed her to his large leather chair behind the desk. It was his throne of control—in his office, his estate, his world. Tony wanted Claire to know that he welcomed her sharing that power, but with the responsibility came the burden. One that he feared would require her to sit. Claire obediently bent her knees, and he said, "That wasn't all. Under the name it read *R.I.P.*"

Her eyes misted in shock, and her hand protectively covered her midsection. "Oh my God, Tony..."

Kneeling before her, he tempered his tone. "I told you once before, too much information isn't good for you. Will you please learn to trust me and enjoy the bliss I'm trying so hard to provide?"

"B-but... that has to be considered a threat. Can't you take it to the police?"

"We are, but what will they do that we aren't already doing?"

Embracing her shoulders, her body trembled as tears coated his jacket. When a semblance of calm prevailed, she said, "I'm going to lie down. Will you please come to our room when you're done with the others? Or are you going back to work?"

"No," he reassured. "I'm staying here. I'll be there as soon as we're done."

When the others returned, Tony learned that the package had inadvertently been brought inside with the rest of the mail. The police had been informed and additional cameras and sensors were going up all around the estate. The difficulty was the size of the property. Tony worried about Claire's walks to her lake. He didn't want to take that freedom away from her, but he didn't want her hiking alone.

Tony had a trip planned to Europe in early September. He had meetings that he needed to attend to in person, as well as his semiannual obligation to move and reinvest Nathaniel's money. Repeatedly, he asked Claire to join him, and repeatedly, she said no. Claire explained that she felt safer on the estate and didn't want to be overseas. If there had been any way to avoid the trip, Tony would have done it.

The morning he left, Tony tried one last time to convince her to accompany him. Though she was sleeping in their bed, in the suite that used to be his that they now shared, he kissed her gently and her eyes fluttered as her sleepy voice questioned, "You woke me up before you left?"

"You told me to."

Her eyes opened, revealing a bewildered expression.

"Why are you looking at me that way? You said you wanted me to wake you."

"I know." She sat up, their gaze unbroken. "I'm just not used to you listening to me, or doing what I say."

He pressed closer, feeling the sensation of her breasts against his chest. "Well, we could go back to—"

Claire shook her head as she once again embraced his neck. "No, I like this better."

His devilish grin made his brown eyes shimmer. "Well, last night you didn't seem to mind a few directions, or should I say, suggestions?"

Her cheeks reddened as she buried her face in his shoulder and muffled her confession. "Yeah, well, I like that, too."

Taking her chin in his gentle grasp, Tony searched her eyes. He could get lost in the depths of the green—emerald green, so deep and rich. "I was hoping I could change your mind about joining me on this trip."

Their noses nearly touched as her lids fluttered and expression softened. "When do you need to leave?"

It wasn't the response he wanted; he wanted her to say she'd come to Europe with him. "The plane's ready. Eric's waiting in the car."

Claire's expression beckoned, her fingers found the buttons of his shirt, and her words came between butterfly kisses to his neck, "I don't think" "Eric would mind" "waiting a little longer" "Besides" "you're going to be gone" "for almost two weeks." As Claire's fingers moved toward his belt and her lips touched his newly exposed chest, Tony's travel plans seemed suddenly insignificant. For the next forty minutes they were lost within one another. Tony couldn't help caressing and kissing her midsection and their unborn child as he moved up and down her sensual body. Her soft skin and amazing scent dominated his thoughts. As often happened when they made love, the worries or concerns outside of their bubble momentarily disappeared.

When he finally redressed and started to leave, Claire's aura pulled him back for one last kiss. "I love you and I'll be back as soon as I can. I wish you were coming."

Her eyelids fought an unseen weight. "Travel safely. I love you, too."

As he tucked the covers around her soft body, he asked, "Are you going back to sleep?"

She nodded. "Yes, I think after that strenuous morning workout, I need a nap."

Grinning, he kissed the top of her head and watched as her smile faded, her eyes closed, and she appeared blissfully serene. It was then Tony remembered the security. He didn't want her to think things were different because he wasn't home. Utilizing his CEO tone, he added, "Claire."

Her eyes immediately opened. Although she didn't speak, she obviously recognized his change in tenor. Perched on the edge of the bed, Tony reminded her, "If you leave the estate—"

She stilled his words with the touch of her hand. The large diamond on her fourth finger glistened, as she responded appropriately, "I promise, I'll take Clay."

"This isn't debatable."

"Tony, I'm not debating. I'm trying to sleep."

He kissed her lips. "I'll call when I touch down in London."

She nodded. "Be safe. I think Eric's waiting."

Three days later, Tony received word of an attempted break-in at the estate. Thankfully, Clay had thwarted the attempt. Unfortunately, the perpetrator had not been caught. It seemed obvious that Chester's accomplice was becoming bolder with his threats. More than anything, Tony wanted to get back to Iowa.

To that end, he rescheduled a few of his meetings and contemplated waiting for another time to visit Switzerland. The money could wait. It hadn't been discovered in over twenty-five years. One extra six-month period of accumulation wouldn't make that big of a difference. He had two more days before he could leave, when he received the call from Clay explaining that someone had tried to run him and Claire off the road. Tony didn't give a damn about any more of the meetings—he headed home.

Twice before he took off, Tony tried to reach Claire. The first time, Catherine answered. He was shocked to hear her voice on Claire's private phone, but it made sense when Catherine explained that Claire was shaken by the incident and was sleeping. The second time he tried, his call went straight to voice mail. As soon as his plane landed in Iowa, he tried to reach her again. This time, it continued to ring. Even the voice mail wouldn't activate. Next, Tony tried Catherine. She answered right away.

"Catherine, can you go to Claire? I've been trying to reach her, but she isn't answering."

"I would, Anthony. However, she isn't home."

He exhaled. "All right, maybe she forgot her phone. I'll call Clay."

"He's here. She left yesterday after her nap and we haven't seen her since."

His world imploded. "What do you mean she left yesterday and hasn't come back? How could she leave without Clay?"

"She said she was tired of the constant surveillance and needed a break."

"When? Why haven't you called me or the police?"

Catherine tried to justify her reasoning. "Yesterday evening... I assumed she'd be back. It wasn't until this morning we realized she hadn't returned. You were in the air; I couldn't reach you. I haven't called the police. What was I supposed to say? A twenty-nine-year-old woman drove away, on her own, and now I can't reach her? Once Clay learned she'd disappeared, he followed the GPS, and your car was located outside Des Moines... Anton, I'm so sorry. I truly thought she would return after she got her break. I was doing what you said to do—trust. You know how the hormones are making her emotional. I'm very worried."

"Eric! Hit the damn gas! I need to be home!" Tony's mind scrambled as he spoke to Catherine through the phone. "Des Moines? Jane Allyson is there. I'll contact her."

"Claire left her phone and iPad here. I can tell you, she's missed many calls from people, especially her sister."

"Shit, someone will need to contact Emily." The jet lag was nothing compared to the chaos occurring in his mind. "What if Chester's accomplice has her? We need to get the police involved. Have I received any ransom requests?"

"No, nothing here."

"So a car tries to run Clay off the road, and later that same day, Claire decides to leave. Doesn't anyone else think that this is suspicious?" His question was rhetorical; he'd disconnected their call.

Three days passed. The police came and went. Tony made phone calls and offered rewards. Every nut job came out of the woodwork, yet no one could find Claire. For endless hours, he stared at the monitors in his office. The large screen was subdivided into many smaller screens. At the top was a live feed from outside his office door. He didn't want *any* intruders. Below were multiple smaller screens changing constantly with various locations on the estate. The bulk of the screen held two videos. He controlled the speed and sound of each one. On the left, he saw Claire in his garages, rushing to the key cabinet and removing the key to a Mercedes-Benz. In the lower right corner the date read: 01/17/12. On the right was the video of Claire walking casually to the key cabinet that no longer held a lock. He watched as she removed the keys to a BMW and calmly walked toward the car. The date in the lower right corner read: 09/04/13. Repeatedly, he paused and scrutinized the scenes. With all his might, he tried to read Claire's facial expressions.

In 2012, he saw fear as Claire looked around nervously. On the video recorded only days earlier, Tony wondered what he saw. No, he knew what he saw: she was wearing her mask of steely determination. What he didn't know was what emotion was hidden beneath it.

When the police saw the 2013 video, they theorized that Claire left of her own free will. *If* that were true, wouldn't she have taken more belongings? Wouldn't she have taken more money? She had access. She had credit cards and an ATM card, yet they were all found in an Illinois hotel.

Being nearly 2:00 AM, Tony was alone in his office. The various screens displaying the estate were devoid of people. Everyone was fast asleep. Even the crickets outside his open windows knew to leave him in silence, yet with no one to hear, he spoke the question he'd been wrestling with for days, "Why, Claire? Why?" In one gulp, he downed the amber liquid from the crystal tumbler. Though the rich Glen Garioch whiskey went down smoothly, it didn't ease the ache in his head or the pain in his chest.

Maintaining his facade for the last few days had successfully drained his strength. Tony needed sleep, but how could he sleep in *their* bed? He couldn't even stand to enter *their* room or see the unfinished nursery. It was the *not knowing* that hurt the most. If he knew she were safe... If he knew she did this of her own free will... but he didn't know. Last time—in 2012—he knew, and without a doubt, the pain he'd put her through back then added to his current torment.

How could Claire evaporate into thin air?

The BMW she'd driven was thoroughly searched by Iowa's top CSI. Only her fingerprints, Clay's, Eric's, and Tony's were discovered... no unknown clues.

For the first time in his life, Tony had dared to believe in happily-ever-after. It was a risk. At a young age he'd learned that it was unattainable; therefore, he'd never even tried... until Claire. Somehow, for a few short months, his *everything* was at his fingertips. The wealth, homes, and appearance of stability and sanity all meant nothing when he saw the pictures of Claire with Harry. Tony couldn't be at that damn gala and know she was there with *him*. Hell, Tony hadn't even known about their baby. He just knew, for the first time in his life, Anthony Rawlings was willing to risk public scrutiny to have what he wanted most. What mattered to him above anything else—the contents of his envelope. The problem was making *her* realize it.

Tony reached into his drawer and removed the envelope. It no longer brought the smile to his lips as it once had. Now, it was a blatant reminder of all he'd lost. Tossing it back into the drawer, he turned off the screens, and lay upon the soft leather sofa. His mind went back to 2011. On this very couch... on this luxurious carpet... on his desk. He smiled. There was hardly a place where they hadn't been together. Damn, they'd been great. Despite the happy memories, the knife in his heart twisted. The things he'd done to her, the emptiness he'd given her—the regret was almost paralyzing.

Then somehow in this totally screwed-up world, when all was said and done, she'd taken him back. The happiness faded as doubts infiltrated his mind. *If Claire left of her own free will, had any of the past four months been real? She'd accepted his ring. He told her every day how much he loved her. Had it all been a charade? Did she have her own agenda of revenge for his past sins?* Tony didn't want to think it was possible.

The pounding in his head brought moisture to his eyes. His words were barely audible. That was all right; they weren't intended for anyone except the woman who wasn't there. "I'm so sorry... for everything. Why? Why did you leave me?" As the tears coated his cheeks, he told himself, *Anthony Rawlings doesn't cry. He doesn't apologize, and he doesn't cry...*

Reunited – October 2013
(Convicted – Chapter 14)

Perhaps there were stars falling, volcanoes erupting, or epic winds blow-ing. Truthfully, at that moment, the entire world could've been lost and neither one would have known.
– Aleatha Romig, *CONVICTED*

The small plane circled the island, losing altitude with each pass, until it finally came to a rest upon the calm, crystal-blue waters of the lagoon. From the air, Tony had seen the main home sprawled on a hill above the beach, as well as multiple other dwellings partially hid-den by vegetation. From the lagoon, Tony looked up and saw a large patio. All he could make out were people whom he didn't recognize. The propel-lers slowed as the engine died. Following Roach's lead, Tony removed the sound-muffling ear phones.

"Are you ready?" Roach asked.

Tony had better be ready; he'd eluded the FBI and traveled halfway around the world for this. He prayed it was worth it, that Claire would, at the very least, hear him out. After all, the last time they'd spoken, he'd allowed his own disbelief and hurt to distort the meaning of her words. She'd tried to clarify, and he'd stayed true to form and been an ass. Tony hadn't even considered what she'd been through during the past month, and when she tried to explain, he hung up on her. Steeling his shoulders, Tony replied, "I am. Do you think she's up at the house?"

"I'm sure she heard the plane," Roach replied. "I'd expect her to come down to greet us."

"Us?"

"Well, there're two of us. She doesn't know you're coming, but no one except me knows her location. I'd assume she's expecting me."

Tony nodded, as Phil stepped from the now beached plane. The hot, humid breeze filled the cabin, while white sand and palm trees brought back memories of his and Claire's honeymoon. He wondered if Claire ever thought about that—if she thought about him. Taking a deep breath of salty air, Tony exited the plane. His shoes sunk with each step as sand covered the leather loafers. Looking up toward the greenery and flowers, Tony's world stopped.

Standing beneath a canopy of vegetation was his dream, his life, and the contents of his envelope. She was a vision in pink. Claire's neck straightened as her shoulders went back. Her emerald gaze met his. It was their connection, a means of communication that no one else could ever have understood. Without a word, he called to her, told her he loved her, and begged for forgiveness. *Was Roach speaking? Was there even anyone on the earth besides the two of them?* Lost in her penetrating stare, Tony didn't know or care.

He continued forward until her beautiful body was against his. Their baby had grown, making its presence known as he pulled Claire toward him. Tony had planned to explain, to apologize, to discuss, yet words didn't form as he captured her neck and brought his mouth to hers, claiming what was his. She didn't protest, as a matter of fact, she didn't say a word. No, the sounds coming from Claire were the moans of pleasure and desire that he'd feared were forever gone. They were the sounds he heard in his dreams—but this wasn't a dream, it was real. Peering once again into her shimmering eyes, he intertwined his fingers in her hair, and repositioned her head. Seconds before he returned his lips to hers, she whispered, "I'm sorry."

Their tongues united and her radiating warmth pulled him closer. Breaking their seal, for only a second, Tony replied, "No, I'm sorry."

The relief of her embrace and the parting of her lips, allowed him full access to what was his, overwhelming him, bursting their bubble and exposing them to the world. The ocean breeze returned, stinging his eyes, causing moisture to pool. He blinked it away before Claire could see, because… Anthony Rawlings didn't apologize and he didn't cry… that's the truth.

THE END

GLOSSARY OF CONSEQUENCE SERIES CHARACTERS BOOKS #1, #2,

– Primary Characters –

- **Anthony (Tony) Rawlings**: *billionaire, entrepreneur, founder of Rawlings Industries*
- Anton Rawls *(birth name): son of Samuel, grandson of Nathaniel (birth name)*
- **Claire Nichols (Rawlings)**: *meteorologist, bartender, woman whose life changed forever, wife and ex-wife of Anthony Rawlings*
- Alaises: *Lauren Michaels, Isabelle Alexander, C. Marie Rawls*

- Catherine Marie London (Rawls): *housekeeper, friend of Anthony Rawlings, 2ⁿᵈ wife of Nathaniel Rawls, Anton Rawls' step-grandmother*
- Derek Burke: *husband of Sophia Rossi, great-grandnephew of Jonathon Burke*

- Harrison Baldwin: *half-brother of Amber McCoy, president of security at Si-Jo Gaming*
- Sophia Rossi Burke: *adopted daughter of Carlo and Silvia Rossi, wife of Derek Burke, biological daughter of Marie London, and owner of an art studio in Provincetown, MA*

– Secondary Characters –

- Amber McCoy: *Simon Johnson's fiancée, CEO of Si-Jo Gaming*
- Brent Simmons: *Rawlings Attorney, Tony's best friend*
- Courtney Simmons: *Brent Simmons' wife*
- Eric Hensley: *Tony's driver and assistant*
- Emily (Nichols) Vandersol: *Claire's older sister*
- John Vandersol: *Emily's husband, Claire's brother-in-law, attorney*
- Nathaniel Rawls: *grandfather of Anton Rawls, father of Samuel Rawls, owner-founder of Rawls Corporation*
- Phillip Roach: *private investigator hired by Anthony Rawlings*

– Tertiary Characters –

- Abbey: *nurse*
- Allison Burke: *daughter of Jonathon Burke*
- Amanda Rawls: *Samuel Rawls' wife, Anton's mother*
- Anne Robinson: *Vanity Fair reporter*
- Bev Miller: *designer, wife of Tom Miller*
- Bonnie: *wife of Chance*

- Brad Clark: *wedding consultant*
- Caleb Simmons: *son of Brent and Courtney Simmons*
- Cameron Andrews: *private investigator hired by Anthony Rawlings*
- Carlo Rossi: *married to Silvia Rossi, adoptive father of Sophia Rossi Burke*
- Carlos: *house staff at the Rawlings' estate*
- Cassie: *Sophia's assistant at her art studio on the Cape*
- Chance: *associate of Elijah Summer*
- Charles: *housekeeper, Anthony's Chicago apartment*
- Cindy: *maid at the Rawlings estate, adopted daughter of Allison Burke and her husband*
- Clay Winters: *bodyguard hired by Anthony Rawlings*
- Connie: *Nathaniel Rawls' secretary*
- Danielle (Danni): *personal assistant to Derek Burke*
- David Field: *Rawlings negotiator*
- Elijah (Eli) Summer: *entertainment entrepreneur, friend of Tony's*
- Elizabeth Nichols: *wife of Sherman Nichols, Claire and Emily's grandmother*
- Agent Ferguson: *FBI agent*
- Francis: *groundskeeper in paradise, married to Madeline*
- Mr. George: *curator of an art studio in Palo Alto, California*
- Agent Hart: *FBI agent*
- Hillary Cunningham: *wife of Roger Cunningham*
- Jan: *housekeeper, Anthony's New York apartment*
- Jane Allyson: *court-appointed counsel*
- Jared Clawson: *CFO Rawls Corporation*

- Mr. and Mrs. Johnson: *Simon Johnson's parents*
- Jonas Smithers: *Anthony Rawlings' first business partner in Company Smithers Rawlings (CSR)*
- Jonathon Burke: *securities officer whose testimony helped to incriminate Nathanial Rawls*
- Jordon Nichols: *father of Claire and Emily Nichols, married to Shirley, son of Sherman*
- Julia: *Caleb Simmons' wife*
- Kayla: *nurse*
- Keaton: *love interest of Amber McCoy*
- Kelli: *secretary, Rawlings Industries, New York office*
- Kirstin: *Marcus Evergreen's secretary*
- Dr. Leonard: *physician*
- Liz Matherly: *personal assistant to Amber McCoy*
- Dr. Logan: *physician*
- Madeline: *housekeeper in paradise, married to Francis*
- Marcus: *driver for SiJo Gaming*
- Marcus Evergreen: *Iowa City Prosecutor*
- Mary Ann Combs: *longtime companion of Elijah Summer, Tony's friend*
- Meredith Banks Russel: *reporter, sorority sister of Claire Nichols*
- Sergeant Miles: *police officer, St. Louis*
- Monica Thompson: *wedding planner*
- Naiade: *housekeeper in Fiji*
- Chief Newburg: *chief of police, Iowa City Police Department*
- Patricia: *personal assistant to Anthony Rawlings, Corporate Rawlings Industries*

- Patrick Chester: *neighbor of Samuel and Amanda Rawls*
- Paul Task: *court-appointed counsel*
- Quinn: *personal assistant of Jane Allyson, Esquire*
- Judge Reynolds: *court judge, Iowa City*
- Richard Bosley: *governor of Iowa*
- Richard Bosley II: *son of Richard Bosley, banker in Michigan*
- Roger Cunningham: *president of Shedis-tics*
- Ryan Bosley: *son of Richard II and Sarah Bosley*
- Samuel Rawls: *son of Nathaniel and Sharron Rawls, husband of Amanda Rawls, father of Anton Rawls*
- Sarah Bosley: *wife of Richard Bosley II*
- Sharon Michaels: *attorney for Rawlings Industries*
- Sharron Rawls: *wife of Nathaniel Rawls*
- Shaun Stivert: *photographer for Vanity Fair*
- Sheldon Preston: *governor of Iowa*
- Shelly: *Anthony Rawlings' publicist*
- Sherman Nichols: *grandfather of Claire Nichols, FBI Agent who helped to incriminate Nathaniel Rawls. FBI alias: Cole Mathews*
- Shirley Nichols: *wife of Jordon Nichols, mother of Claire and Emily*
- Silvia Rossi: *married to Carlo Rossi, adopted mother of Sophia Rossi Burke*
- Simon Johnson: *first love and classmate of Claire Nichols, gaming entrepreneur*
- Dr. Sizemore: *obstetrician and gynecologist*
- Sue Bronson: *Tim Bronson's wife*
- Terri: *nurse*

- Tim Bronson: *vice president, Corporate Rawlings Industries*
- Tom Miller: *Rawlings attorney, friend of Tony's*

THE CONSEQUENCES
SERIES TIMELINE

-1921-

Nathaniel Rawls – born

-1943-

Nathaniel Rawls – home from WWII
Nathaniel Rawls marries Sharron Parkinson
Nathaniel begins working for BNG Textiles

-1944-

Samuel Rawls – born to Nathaniel and Sharron

-1953-

BNG Textiles becomes Rawls Textiles

-1956-

Rawls Textiles becomes Rawls Corporation

-1962-

Catherine Marie London – born

-1963-

Samuel Rawls marries Amanda

-1965-

February 12

Anton Rawls – born to Samuel and Amanda

-1975-

Rawls Corporation goes public

-1980-

July 19

Sophia Rossi (London) – born/adopted by Carlo and Silvia Rossi

August 31

Emily Nichols – born to Jordon and Shirley Nichols

-1983-

Sharron Rawls exhibits symptoms of Alzheimer's disease
Marie London starts to work for Sharron Rawls
Anton Rawls graduates from Blair Academy High School

October 17
Claire Nichols – born to Jordon and Shirley Nichols

-1985-

Nathaniel Rawls begins affair with Marie London
Marie London loses baby
Sharron Rawls dies

-1986-

Rawls Corporation falls

-1987-

Anton Rawls graduates from NYU
Nathaniel Rawls found guilty of multiple counts of insider trading, misappropriation of funds, price fixing, and securities fraud

-1988-

Nathaniel Rawls marries Catherine Marie London
Anton Rawls graduates with Master's degree

-1989-

Nathaniel Rawls – dies
Samuel and Amanda Rawls – die

-1990-

Anton Rawls changes his name to Anthony Rawlings
Anthony Rawlings begins CSR-Company Smithers Rawlings with Jonas Smithers

-1994-

Anthony Rawlings buys out Jonas Smithers and CSR becomes Rawlings Industries

-1996-

Rawlings Industries begins to diversify

-1997-

Sherman Nichols – died

-2002-

Claire Nichols – graduates high school
Claire Nichols – attends Valparaiso University

-2003-

Simon Johnson begins internship at Shedis-tics in California

-2004-

Jordon and Shirley Nichols – die

-2005-

Emily Nichols – marries John Vandersol

-2007-

Claire Nichols – graduates from Valparaiso, degree in meteorology
Claire Nichols – moves from Indiana to New York for internship

-2008-

Claire Nichols – moves to Atlanta, Georgia, for job at WKPZ
Simon Johnson begins Si-Jo Gaming Corporation

-2009-

WKPZ – purchased by large corporation resulting in lay-offs

-2010-

March

Anthony Rawlings – enters the Red Wing in Atlanta, Georgia
Anthony Rawlings – takes Claire Nichols on a date
Claire Nichols – wakes at Anthony's estate

May

Claire Nichols – liberties begin to increase
Anthony Rawlings – takes Claire Nichols to symphony and introduces "Tony"

September

Meredith Banks' article appears – Claire Nichols' accident

December 18

Anthony Rawlings – marries Claire Nichols

-2011-

April

Vanity Fair article appears

September

Anthony and Claire Rawlings attend a symposium in Chicago where Claire sees Simon Johnson, her college boyfriend

November

Simon Johnson – dies in airplane accident

-2012-

January

Claire Rawlings drives away from the Rawlings estate
Anthony Rawlings – poisoned
Claire Rawlings – arrested for attempted murder

March

Anthony Rawlings divorces Claire Nichols

April

Claire Nichols pleads no contest to attempted murder charges

October

Claire Nichols receives box of information while in prison

-2013-

March

Petition for pardon is filed with Governor Bosley on behalf of Claire Nichols
Petition for pardon is granted; Claire Nichols is released from prison and moves to Palo Alto, California
Tony learns of Claire's release, hires Phillip Roach, and contacts Claire

April

Claire and Courtney vacation in Texas

THE CONSEQUENCES SERIES TIMELINE

Tony travels to California. He and Claire have dinner and reconnect

May

Claire meets with Meredith Banks in San Diego
Claire and Harry connect
Claire and Harry visit Patrick Chester
Claire attends the National Center for Learning Disabilities annual gala where Tony is the keynote speaker
Claire takes a home pregnancy test

June

Caleb Simmons weds his fiancée Julia. Tony asks Claire to accompany him to the wedding
Claire is attacked by Patrick Chester
Claire moves back to Iowa

July

First mailing arrives to Iowa addressed to *Claire Nichols Rawls*

September

Tony leaves for a ten-day business trip to Europe
Claire leaves Iowa

October

Claire moves to paradise
Phil Roach takes Tony to paradise

A complete Consequences series timeline (spanning all 8 years of the epic journey) is available at the end of *Beyond the Consequences*.

WHAT TO DO NOW...

LEND IT: Did you enjoy BEHIND HIS EYES COMPANION BOX SET? Do you have a friend who'd enjoy BEHIND HIS EYES COMPANION BOX SET? BEHIND HIS EYES COMPANION BOX SET may be lent one time. Sharing is caring!

RECOMMEND IT: Do you have more than one friend who'd enjoy BEHIND HIS EYES COMPANION BOX SET? Tell them about it! Call, text, post, tweet...your recommendation is the nicest gift you can give to an author!

REVIEW IT: Tell the world. Please go to the retailer where you purchased this, as well as Goodreads, and write a review. Please share your thoughts about BEHIND HIS EYES COMPANION BOX SET on:

- Amazon, *BEHIND HIS EYES COMPANION BOX SET*, Customer Reviews
- Barnes & Noble, *BEHIND HIS EYES COMPANION BOX SET* Customer Reviews
- iBooks, *BEHIND HIS EYES COMPANION BOX SET* Customer Reviews
- Goodreads.com/Aleatha Romig

ACKNOWLEDGEMENTS

Thank you to everyone who has made my story real! Thank you for your support and devotion. I'm constantly awed by your dedication to Tony and Claire. If it weren't for your questions and messages, I would never have continued with these reading companions.

Thank you for encouraging me to experience the other side of the Consequences!

NOW THAT you've been Aleatha'd
you will want MORE Books by
New York Times bestselling author
Aleatha Romig:

INFIDELITY SERIES:

BETRAYAL
Book #1
(October 2015)

CUNNING
Book #2
(January 2016)

DECEPTION
Book #3
(May 2016)

ENTRAPMENT
Book #4
(September 2016)

FIDELITY
Book #5
(January 2017)

THE LIGHT SERIES:

INTO THE LIGHT
(June 2016)

AWAY FROM THE DARK
(October 2016)

THE CONSEQUENCES SERIES:

CONSEQUENCES
(Book #1)
Released August 2011

TRUTH
(Book #2)
Released October 2012

CONVICTED
(Book #3)
Released October 2013

REVEALED
(Book #4)
Previously titled: Behind His Eyes Convicted: The Missing Years
Re-released June 2014

BEYOND THE CONSEQUENCES
(Book #5)
Released January 2015

COMPANION READS:

BEHIND HIS EYES—CONSEQUENCES
(Book #1.5)
Released January 2014

BEHIND HIS EYES—TRUTH
(Book #2.5)
Released March 2014

TALES FROM THE DARK SIDE SERIES:

INSIDIOUS
(All books in this series are standalone erotic thrillers)
Released October 2014

DUPLICITY
(Completely unrelated to book #1)
Release TBA

ABOUT THE AUTHOR

Aleatha Romig is a New York Times and USA Today bestselling author who lives in Indiana. She grew up in Mishawaka, graduated from Indiana University, and is currently living south of Indianapolis. Aleatha has raised three children with her high school sweetheart and husband of nearly thirty years. Before she became a full-time author, she worked days as a dental hygienist and spent her nights writing. Now, when she's not imagining mind-blowing twists and turns, she likes to spend her time with her family and friends. Her other pastimes include reading and creating heroes/anti-heroes who haunt your dreams!

Aleatha released her first novel, CONSEQUENCES, in August of 2011. CONSEQUENCES became a bestselling series with five novels and two companions released from 2011 through 2015. The compelling and epic story of Anthony and Claire Rawlings has graced more than half a million e-readers. Aleatha released the first of her series TALES FROM THE DARK SIDE, INSIDIOUS, in the fall of 2014. These stand-alone thrillers continue Aleatha's twisted style with an increase in heat. In the fall of 2015, Aleatha moved headfirst into the world of dark romantic suspense with the release of BETRAYAL, the first of her five-novel INFIDELITY series (This series is not about cheating). Aleatha has entered the traditional world of publishing with Thomas and Mercer with her LIGHT series. The first of that series, INTO THE LIGHT, was published in 2016. AWAY

FROM THE DARK concluded this duet and was published in October of 2016

Aleatha is a "Published Author's Network" member of the Romance Writers of America and represented by Danielle Egan-Miller of Browne & Miller Literary Associates.

STAY CONNECTED
WITH ALEATHA

Do you love Aleatha's writing? Do you want to know the latest about Infidelity? Consequences? Tales From the Dark Side? and Aleatha's new series coming in 2016 from Thomas and Mercer?
Do you like EXCLUSIVE content (never released scenes, never released excerpts, and more)? Would you like the monthly chance to win prizes (signed books and gift cards)? Then sign up today for Aleatha's monthly newsletter and stay informed on all thing Aleatha Romig.

Sign up for Aleatha's NEWSLETTER
(https://goo.gl/U4tJcw):
(recipients receive exclusive material and offers)

You can also find Aleatha @

Check out her blog: http://aleatharomig.com/aleatha

Facebook: http://www.Facebook.com/AleathaRomig

Twitter: https://twitter.com/AleathaRomig

Goodreads:
http://www.goodreads.com/author/show/5131072.Aleatha_Romig

Instagram: http://instagram.com/aleatharomig

Email Aleatha: aleatharomig@gmail.com

You may also listen Aleatha Romig books on Audible:
http://goo.gl/Qnmlmm